ALL THE THINGS
YOU ARE

ALL THE THINGS YOU ARE

Declan Hughes

This first world edition published 2014
in Great Britain and the USA by
SEVERN HOUSE PUBLISHERS LTD of
19 Cedar Road, Sutton, Surrey, England, SM2 5DA.

British Library Cataloguing in Publication Data

Hughes, Declan, 1963–
  All the things you are.
  1. Suspense fiction.
  I. Title
  823.9'2-dc23

ISBN-13: 978-0-7278-8371-1 (cased)
ISBN-13: 978-1-84751-506-3 (trade paper)

All Severn House titles are printed on acid-free paper.

Severn House Publishers support the Forest Stewardship Council™ [FSC™],
the leading international forest certification organisation. All our titles that
are printed on FSC certified paper carry the FSC logo.

Typeset by Palimpsest Book Production Ltd.,
Falkirk, Stirlingshire, Scotland.
Printed and bound in Great Britain by
TJ International, Padstow, Cornwall.

To Patricia Lucey

Acknowledgements

I am grateful to a number of people who helped me in a variety of ways while I was writing this book. In Madison, Patricia Lucey, Michael Lucey and Tom Colby. In Chicago, Theresa Schwegel and Kevin Lambert. In Dublin and London, Sheila Crowley, John Connolly, Diarmuid O'Hegarty, Alan Glynn and Jessica O'Leary. At home, Kathy, Isobel and Heather.

Out of Nowhere

Sunday, October 23

Danny Brogan burned his future wife's family to death when he was eleven years old. Whether by accident or design, he's not entirely sure, or at least that's what he's always told himself. It was probably no great surprise that as a result he should develop a morbid fear of fire, nor that this fear should stay with him throughout his life. Fear is a man's best friend, or so the song goes, and Danny carried his fear of fire, just as he carried his fear of the friends that were with him that night, until it sometimes looked like the twin burdens might overwhelm him.

No one really knew what he had done except his friends Dave and Gene and Ralph, and even they differed on the details, and while they had all promised never to tell, there was always the fear that they might. Not at first, not in the immediate aftermath, the whole city in shock, the church services and processions of mourning, the burial of the dead, the tiny white coffins. Not in the following weeks and months, the surviving child placed in foster care and then with adoptive parents miles away, the burnt-out house demolished and rebuilt until you'd never know there'd been a fire there at all. Not in the years after that, as junior high gave way to the high-school riot of sports and studies and hormones, Brains, Emotions and Muscles vying daily for supremacy, like in the old comic book advertisement. No one ever said a word. It was as if it had never happened, as if their *childhoods* had never happened, as if memory was no longer necessary. The future was the only game in town: the next exam, the next football game, the next pretty girl. Who cared what happened when they were kids?

It was only later, when they had kids themselves, that things changed. You relive your own childhood when you have children, Danny came to understand. Danny's elder daughter, Barbara, was the same age now as Danny had been when the fire took place. And once the kids had started coming, that was when the memories began, that was when the questions started, that was when the past became present. And for Danny, that was when the fear took renewed, *redoubled* hold. That the guys had all drifted apart was perhaps inevitable. After all, how many eleven-year-olds remain friends for the rest of their lives? But it increasingly seemed (even if it was never spoken of) as if the fire at the Bradberry place was the only thing they had left in common.

But Danny Brogan refused to let his fears overwhelm him. He met his fear of fire head on, spouting and sputtering from the gas burners in the kitchen of the bar and grill he owned and ran. And when the season was right and his family clamored for barbecue, Danny met his fear there also, even though the reek of burning charcoal and seared meat sometimes infused his brain with visions and sense memories all the more insidious for being imaginary (for Danny was out cold before the Bradberry fire took hold and had little real recollection of it). They didn't cook out nearly as often as other families, Danny's excuse being that it was too much like bringing his work home with him. But the family barbecue can't be avoided altogether.

And here it is, the last of the season, on a clear and bright October day, the leaves turning, the air still mild but with a bite, a cold admonitory finger warning of frost, and more, to come. Halloween's just a week away now. The lanterns have been lit and the pumpkins carved. In the windows hang curtains of black net, watermarked with spiders and skulls and witches in flight. And everyone's here, in the rolling backyard, vampires, werewolves, spooks and ghouls, and their kids, and their dogs. Everyone's here. The turn of the year. The harsh Wisconsin winter looming, but for now, the air still mild, just, as fall's cold blaze flickers along the apple trees heavy with fruit at the foot of the garden and out across the wall and spreads like, yes, like wild fire through the forests of the neighboring Arboretum.

As the afternoon wears on, and the beers take hold (cocktails for Danny and his noisier friends, brandy Old Fashioneds, the local favorite), as the flames twist and turn, wrestling with the shimmering light, as the charcoal smoke stains the haze inky black, reality seems momentarily suspended. Talk gets heated, wild and reckless, painted cheeks flush and masked eyes glitter, and fleetingly, anything seems possible: someone else's wife, someone else's life! All are called to the masquerade! Louder music, wilder women, stronger wine!

And speaking of wilder women, there goes Karen Cassidy, Danny's indispensable chief bartender, teetering about on six-inch heels, part of a customized Catwoman costume that sees her blonde hair lacquered and coiffed into two pointy kitty ears, the heels-and-ears combination hauling her five feet in height perilously close to six. Day-to-day, Karen (apart from dressing like a finalist in a Dolly Parton lookalike contest) is dependably level-headed and smart, not to mention hard as nails, but once she's had a drink, or in this case, five brandy Old Fashioneds and half a bottle of chardonnay, well, there she goes! Danny once had to shut himself in the janitor's closet at a staff party because Karen wouldn't take no for an answer (she never remembers anything the following day, and woe betide anyone who challenges her).

Karen demands that eleven-year-old Barbara put 'Highway to Hell' by AC/DC on the sound system at full volume, that it be turned up to eleven, and that everyone dance to it out on the deck, no stop-outs or dissenters. Having had her eye for a good hour or more on one of Claire's theater friends, Simon, who is dapper and handsome and charming and dressed in a (big clue this) sailor suit, there she goes, big time, her Catwoman tail shaking, her arms around his neck, his face snug in her cleavage, and there they go together, stumbling off the deck and toppling into the herb garden, and there they lie, thrashing among bushes and low trees, bruised in thyme and sage and bay. 'That's what I call a *bouquet garni*,' Simon's boyfriend, Todd, says.

It's then that Danny sees it. Flames have erupted suddenly from the barbecue, hot fat crackles and spits, and Danny has turned away from the commotion, away from the house. As he rakes the embers and banks down the fire, it's then that Danny sees – through the smoke, through the apple trees, through the wrought-iron bars of the old garden gate that leads to the Arboretum

– the unmistakeable figure of Death. The Angel of Death in his black cowl, faceless and strange, scythe in one hand, the other raised in greeting, or rebuke, and then lowered to try the handle of the gate. For a split second, through the smoke, through the trees, Danny thinks it *is* Death, come to claim him. Then he sees the letter *P* scrawled on Death's chest – *P* for Pestilence, *P* for Plague – and he realizes it must be one of his old friends: Dave Ricks, or Gene Peterson, or Ralph Cowley. The Four Horsemen, that's what they were, or at least, that's what they became, the Halloween they were eleven years old, the Halloween that changed everything. The Four Horsemen of the Apocalypse.

It's then that Danny leaves the party and walks down past the apple trees to the gate, to his old friend, unseen, he thinks, by everyone. He's only gone a couple of steps when he stops and turns back to the fire. Through the haze he sees his wife, Claire, wiping tears of laughter from her eyes as Simon struggles vainly to free himself from Karen's horizontal attentions, and Barbara, pulling cartoon faces to indicate her embarrassment and disbelief, but unable quite to hide her excitement, and eight-year-old Irene, who is making her own fun, rolling around on the lawn with Mr Smith, the Brogans' springer spaniel. He sees his family. This is what is at stake, he thinks, this is what he could not bear to lose, and he stows the eight-inch Sabatier knife he used to carve the meat deep in the pocket of his butcher's apron. He turns and walks down through the drifting smoke, through the falling light, beneath the aching branches of the apple trees to the old gate, unobserved, or so he thinks, and out into the Arboretum to meet the Angel of Death, who knows everything Danny wishes he could forget.

PART ONE
The Night Before

Claire

I'll Be Seeing You

Sunday, October 30

Walking through Madison Airport always makes Claire feel like she has stepped back in time. It's partly the compact scale of the terminal building and partly the absence of crowds, but mostly it's the muzak: delirious, string-drenched arrangements of melancholy old standards that seep into her brain and make her mysteriously nostalgic for the time before she was born: 'Laura' and 'Autumn Leaves' and now 'I'll Be Seeing You.' *In all the old familiar places*, she thinks, the lyrics second nature to her. Outside, she almost expects to see the old familiar places as they had been in the early sixties: cars with tail fins and women wearing swing skirts and men in trilbies and those narrow-lapeled FBI suits. Meanwhile, her perfect sitcom family awaits, just like in *The Dick Van Dyke Show* or *I Love Lucy*. Hey honey, I'm home!

She feels this way each time, and each time it almost makes her laugh. Almost, but not quite, because deep down she knows the suburban life she is living with her husband and children and dog is not too different from what she supposes it must have been like for her parents. Sure, she has a job teaching drama a dozen or so hours a week, but that's not what she *does*. Day to day, Danny goes out to work and Claire ferries the girls to school and to soccer practice, to opthalmologist and orthodontist, to swim meet and sleepover; she buys the groceries and cooks the meals; she makes sure the carpets are clean and the linen is fresh and there are flowers in the hall and a fire in the grate. Or at least, that the heating is on. Like the wife in the Mary Chapin Carpenter song, she drives all day. When she was in sixth grade she remembers scoffing in homeroom when her friends were sharing their plans for the future and Pattie Greer said she wanted to be a housewife.

No way was Claire Taylor ever going to settle for that. Now Pattie Greer is Patricia Price of Butler Price and Stone, and Claire Taylor is Claire Taylor, homemaker. She has kept her name, but in pretty much every other respect, has she settled?

Well, maybe, but, you know, what*ever*, she thinks, almost *says*; she certainly rolls her eyes, and actually manages an audible laugh, which she quickly stifles, as she is standing alone by the baggage carousel and doesn't want to look like a crazy lady. Or does she? Maybe she doesn't care what she looks like today. (Which is probably just as well, since the accumulator hangover she is running after a week of late nights and tequila shooters and other stuff she doesn't even want to think about has brought her skin out in blotches and crimped her hair to an attractive straw-like consistency.)

A week ago, flying out to Chicago, she cared. A week ago, the muzak was just another nail in her mid-life coffin, 'All The Things You Are' at check-in an ironic requiem for the life she had once planned for herself: a life on the stage, a life in the theater, a life devoted to creativity and self-expression (she had used exactly those words in the painfully earnest journal she kept at university). All The Things She's Not.

She had given that life a shot. In her twenties, she auditioned for every theater company in Chicago, graduating from walk-ons to one- and two-line speaking parts to small but significant character roles. Then she formed her own company with Paul Casey, her director boyfriend, so she could play the leads she wasn't being offered. She even directed some of the plays herself, working for peanuts, waiting tables and tending bar when she wasn't handing out flyers and designing posters. She had worked at it. And not without success. One year, their company was tipped to be the next Steppenwolf. Not, admittedly, in the *Tribune* or the *Sun-Times* was this brave opinion ventured, but in the kind of entertainment free-sheet drinkers use as a supplementary beer mat or bar towel. Still, it was said. And they always got good reviews in the press, or at least, if not always, they got reviewed as if they were just as good as anyone else. If not quite as good as Steppenwolf.

Yes, she had worked at it. Tugging her bag towards the exit doors and out to a waiting line of taxis, she allows herself a rueful smile that maybe aims for justified pride and lands on woulda-shoulda-coulda. 'Oh, you must wear your rue with a difference,' she murmurs to herself, not that she ever played Ophelia. Too old now, and when you get older, rue is rue and regret is regret, and it doesn't make a damn bit of difference how you wear it. You've just got to fight every day to make sure it doesn't end up wearing *you*.

She had worked at it. It hadn't worked out. Or maybe she hadn't tried hard enough, hadn't given it her best shot. Maybe she didn't have a best shot to give. No, that wasn't true. Easier sometimes if it had been, if she simply hadn't been good enough. But she had the talent, everyone agreed, if not quite the luck. She had been beaten to the punch so many times for the bigger parts – down to the last two for Laura in *The Glass Menagerie* at the Goodman and Viola in *Twelfth Night* at the Shakespeare, and two callbacks for Mary in *Juno and the Paycock* at Steppenwolf itself. There was a cartoon in the *New Yorker* where an actor hangs up the phone and says to his friends, 'My agent says it's down to two – me and the guy they're going to give it to.' Paul Casey got it framed and gave it to her as a birthday present. Halfway through the second bottle of wine, she stopped seeing the funny side and broke it over his head and they ended up in the emergency room. That had been a big night. The relationship – and the company – didn't last much longer.

Oh yes, she had worked at it all right. She just hadn't stuck with it. The theater was like a marriage, and you had to honor it in good times and in bad, for better or worse, in sickness and health all the dada-da-da. There were so many fine actors who'd only started to get the breaks in their thirties, even their forties. So many in Chicago, and more than a few of them took the time to tell her they'd noticed her and admired her work, made a point of encouraging her to keep her nerve. To stick with it.

But she was tired of coming second best, tired of blaming it all on luck. She was tired of dive bars and damp apartments and nothing on the horizon but hope. She was tired of smiling tightly as her friends with careers in law or medicine or finance began to settle down and have children and buy property when she still found making the rent a monthly roller coaster. The limit came when the boy-wonder director of a new *Uncle Vanya* told her

they'd be looking to cast Sonya a little younger for this production. She was a week past twenty-eight. That night, she called
Danny Brogan and cried down the phone. And Danny said, 'You
know I'm here. I've been waiting. Come home.'

Home meaning Madison, Wisconsin. Madtown itself: 'Sixty
square miles surrounded by reality.' They had met at UW, the
University of Wisconsin, on their first day as undergraduates.
Got drunk their second night. Going together within the week.
They were the kind of couple who held hands in lectures, the
kind of couple that united a class of freshmen, hitherto strangers,
in the sweet complicity of eye-rolling revulsion. They even
inspired a headline in the fledgling *Onion* newspaper, and gamely
posed for a photograph, playing up the lovestruck sap factor:
*Death Penalty to be Reintroduced for Icky Undergraduate
Romances: Area Man says, 'I'll flick the switch myself.'* They
bonded over a love of thirties and forties retro. They drank cocktails and listened to swing and bebop and dressed in thrift-store
duds and generally carried on like they were starring in their
own black-and-white movie, which they kind of were. They both
acted in the University Theater, Danny for the fun of it, Claire
with increasing dedication, and together, memorably, in their
penultimate year, as the lovers in Congreve's restoration comedy
The Way of the World, given a screwball comedy/Art Deco treat-
ment (Claire's idea).

That was the show that changed everything. Word spread about
a brilliant production of a rarely staged play, and about Claire, and
People From Chicago came down to see it, people from Steppenwolf
and the Goodman and Second City, and they gave Claire their
cards and their numbers and told her she had a future on the stage,
and any lingering doubts Claire may have had about her talent or
her path were set aside. Danny got a few cards and numbers as
well, but if he used them at all, it was only to fire up another joint.
And that was the way things would go. In their graduation year,
Claire worked and dreamed of the life to come, acting and directing
and visiting Chicago at weekends, inhabiting the world of the
theater as if she were already a part of it, while Danny took a
sidetrack into an all-male world of beer and brats and bongs, of
Badgers games and all-night Playstation marathons.

Had he already been preparing himself for the bust-up? She

had tried to talk to him about the future, but he refused to engage. It wasn't that she didn't love him, but she didn't want to get married at twenty-one, and she didn't want to stay in Madison, and she didn't want him in Chicago while she was trying to make a go of things. Had he known all along that she was pulling away? Was dwindling into a stoner and a slacker simply a way of protecting himself? After all, his future was mapped out: his father was already a sick man, and Brogan's Bar was Danny's to manage whenever he was ready, or when his dad dropped dead, whichever came first. Sometimes he had spoken of other plans, but only half-heartedly: deep down, she knew that's what he was going to do and so did he. He was older than her by eight years, and had learned the ropes at Brogan's before he went to UW, and he would run it when he left: it was just the way things were. When the time came, they made love one last time, and she cried, and so did he, and he saw her off at the bus stop by the Union. On the bus to Chicago, she felt like a weight had been lifted off her shoulders, and then guilty for feeling that way, and finally relieved at the lightness – the lightness, even in fear, when the past is past and the future all there is.

They're passing through downtown now, heading west, the houses and storefronts festooned with Halloween pumpkins and lanterns, witches and ghosts and ghouls. Stopped at the lights on Gorham at State, she sees students queuing in the brightly lit Jamba Juice on the corner, and more ambling along the street. Used to be, in her early thirties, Claire liked living in a college town, liked the sense of energy. She looked young for her age then, even after the kids, still got carded in bars. She maybe identified with the students, as if passing for one meant somehow she was going to beat the clock. Now she was in her fortieth year, and felt the opposite: their presence was a sting and a reproach, a constant reminder that she was headed in one direction only, and that a lot of the things she'd hoped for in life – all that creativity and self-expression, to take one small example – simply hadn't happened, and almost certainly weren't going to, and all she was doing now was running out of time.

She looks at the students. Almost everyone is wearing at least one plaid item, mostly red plaid, the boys shirts and coats, the girls scarves and skirts. Is plaid just always in fashion these days?

Or is it a Mid-West thing, a Madison thing? The red is a Wisconsin thing, of course, a sports thing, for the Badgers. Everyone wore plaid twenty years ago as well, although rarely did they wear skirts that short. Claire did though, when she tired of retro chic: a tiny red tartan kilt, punk-rock style, with torn black hose and motorcycle boots. Claire wants to wear a skirt that short now. She still has the legs. Women her age wear them. But they look wrong. They look, not quite desperate, but kind of angry, defying you to criticize them, to tell them they're not twenty-two any more, when it's obvious they aren't. They look nuts. Good luck to them. But she can't do it. She can't do it, but she can't rest easy about not permitting herself to do it. Looking at these girls heading up State Street, she knows she should be thinking of Barbara and Irene, and how in no time at all they will be at university, that this will be them in a mere few years. She knows that's where her focus should be, that you have children to cushion the blow of aging in so many different ways. She knows how she should feel. But she doesn't feel that way. She looks at the girl with the long legs and the red plaid mini-skirt and thinks, *that's still me*, and knows it isn't, and wants to scream. As the cab crosses State, the college kids stroll on up the street, the illuminated Capitol dome seeming to hover above them, splashes of red shimmering in the falling darkness, like the flashes she gets behind her eyes when sleep won't come.

Barbara and Irene, Barbara and Irene, Barbara and Irene. They'll be waiting for her – not quite the way they waited when they were six and four, say, but still. She hasn't even spoken to them for a week, nor to Danny; they agreed, no phone contact. Or at least, she agreed with herself, and he agreed to agree with her. He had her hotel number in case of emergencies, a Kimpton in the Loop, the something or other, Allegro? She wants to call the girls now, but her cell ran out of juice on the Tuesday and she didn't bring her charger. She goes into the Macy's bag she has their stuff in, dresses and tops and accessories, some J. Crew, some A & F, vampire costumes she got in a Halloween store, too much, really, but it's been a week and she wants to spoil them. Checking now to see if it's all there, her hand closes on a card and she pulls it out, thinking it's a receipt and wanting to put it in her bag in case anything needs to be returned.

It's not a receipt.

On the envelope is her name, Claire Taylor.

In Paul Casey's handwriting.

Paul Casey, her ex.

Whom she had not intended to meet, had not contacted, but who showed up on the first night in the Old Town Ale House with all the old crowd. Just like she kind of knew he would.

What she didn't know was that he'd be divorced. No kids. And a little quieter, a little more somber, as if life had dealt him a setback or two. A little silver through that dark hair, a few lines creasing the pale milky skin, a couple shadows in those vivid blue eyes. Haunted, that's how he had always looked, or so she remembered, like an English romantic poet who would die young; haunted even more so now, with a melancholy that finally seemed earned.

She can feel the heat in her face now. What if Danny had found the card? Or one of the girls? What would she have said? She hadn't planned to mention even seeing Paul to Danny. She was trying to avoid mentioning it to herself.

When had Paul put that in there? In the bar, after Macy's?

Or later, in the . . . or later?

She can't look at it now. She stuffs it inside her purse and tries to bring her breathing back inside the range appropriate to a wife heading home to her family. The calm, steady, deliberate breathing of a woman who has settled, and is happy with her choices. A week ago, the way she saw it, no question: she had settled. Whether she was happy or not, she didn't want to say. Maybe it would have been futile to ask.

She doesn't see it that way any more. The way she sees it now, she's been given, not an actual second chance, but maybe the glimpse of one. Is she going to take it? She doesn't know. She doesn't know what she's going to do. She doesn't know what to think. But she thinks she knows what she feels. It's been a long time since she felt it. That stirring in her stomach, the flutter in her heart, the sudden bursts of laughter and exhalations of breath and random idiotic announcements, at what? At nothing? Not nothing, no. At a feeling. What she feels is suspiciously like happiness. The kind of happiness she didn't think she'd ever feel again.

A Cottage for Sale

The cab driver has long gray hair in a plait and silver sleeper rings in both ears, a classic Willy Street sixties survivor, or casualty, take your pick. He's already asked for extra directions, as if Madison is some sprawling metropolis and not a city of under a quarter million people, and he's made his ritual little dig about the upscale West Side, as if it's all Beverly Hills and Rodeo Drive over here and not the American Mid-West 101. Although Claire doesn't exactly live in the 101 tract, but on a sparsely inhabited tree-lined road in the heart of the UW Arboretum. The car pulls up outside the black iron gates of the old house. Claire doesn't have her remote with her, so she gets out of the cab to open them by hand. The driver gets out too.

'There's a chain around it,' he says.

The approach light clicks on. She's never seen the heavy link chain before. A haunted house game the girls were playing, maybe. There's no padlock, and it's easily removed. She can see the lights of the house up the drive. The night air is crisp and refreshing after a day of hotels and flights and taxis, and the walk will do her good. She pays the driver and he gets her bag out of the trunk, then looks up and down the narrow, deserted road, the inky darkness almost glossy, like paint, a fragment of moon glowing dull, as if behind a veil.

'You sure about this?' he says.

'Sure about what? You think I don't know where I live?' Claire points up the drive. 'Look, the house lights are on.'

'I didn't know there were houses out here.'

'Just little old us.'

The driver shrugs and smiles.

'Well, you know where you're going. No need to worry.'

'That's right,' Claire says, smiling herself, suddenly glad to be safe home. And as she walks up the drive towards the welcoming

lights of her hundred-year-old Queen Anne house, her fairytale
house with its turrets and towers, she shakes her head a couple
of times and actually says 'No!' out loud, followed by 'Nothing!'
and 'No problem!' and 'Fine, thank you!' – not at the prospect
before her but to banish what has just been, whatever it was,
whatever Paul put in that damn card. It's like she slipped and
fell in the street and found her feet immediately and is marching
on undaunted, daring anyone to question or commiserate, trying
hard not to stumble again. Whatever happened in Chicago, stays
in Chicago. That's the official version now. Happiness? Jesus.
She's not a teenager any more. So she feels guilty. That's her
problem; don't make it Danny's, let alone the girls'. She's nothing
to feel guilty about anyway, not really. Not *really*. No problem,
no problem!

The first glimmer she has is Mr Smith doesn't bark when
she turns her key. Normally, he brings the house down at the
merest hint of a visitor, not angrily but with excitement. He should
have started when he heard her footfall on the porch, or when
she started talking to herself. But there isn't a sound, not a scratch
of his paws.

'Hey, honey, I'm home!' she says, with sitcom brightness,
as she pushes the door open. If she had known that nothing
would ever be the same again from this moment on, maybe she
would have chosen her words with less irony. But change so
often comes without warning, like the secret policeman's dawn
knock, and we rarely have our faces fixed or our stories straight
to greet it.

The extent of what has happened is not so apparent in the hall,
apart from the marks on the wallpaper where all the paintings
have been removed, and the fact that the long red Ikea table that
ran along one wall is gone. It's when she leaves her bag down
and moves into the living room – she remembers later feeling
as if she was on castors, so involuntarily, so inexorably was she
drawn in search of what's no longer there. No battered old brown
leather three-piece suite that they know is past its best but can't
bear to get rid of for sentimental reasons. No TV, no books, no
bookshelves, no rugs on the floor, no art on the walls. Through
to the dining room, and it's as bare: the heavy-legged mahogany
Chippendale table and matching chairs Danny insisted on keeping

from his grandfather's time are gone, as is everything else. Up the stairs, and yes, there it is, whatever it is, gone: the beds, the closets emptied, the girls' toys and books and games, the rugs, the linen, gone, all gone, the *lampshades.*

She's standing on the landing, empty rooms on either side of her, exposed gables above, the arched entrance to the tower ahead. She's never seen the house like this. When they moved in, Danny's sister Donna had been living here; before that, it was the family home, back through Danny's grandfather. Sure, they – *she* – redecorated, stripped walls and polished floorboards and flung out dumpster loads of trash, but one room at a time. How hard she had fought to make their mark on it all, replacing heavy drapes with blinds, bulky old Victorian furniture with contemporary pieces, little by little working to open it up and modernize, to lay the ancestral ghosts and make it theirs, make it *hers.* Now it's bare throughout, as if she has never lived here at all, as if no one has. In Chicago a day, mere *hours* ago, she found herself daring to wonder what it might be like to break free of what held her. Now it feels as if she made a wish, and it's come true, and all she wants is what she has lost.

In the bathroom, the empty bathroom, she sits at the edge of the tub, breathing deeply, Jesus, Jesus, Jesus Christ, over and over again. Claire is a lapsed Catholic, which means she isn't really religious, or hasn't been for some time, but Jesus Christ Almighty, what the fuck is going on? She leans a hand on the mirrored door of a cabinet mounted above the bath, and it snaps open, and Claire almost cries with relief to see it full of stuff, *their* stuff, tins and tubs of talcum powder and Vaseline and calamine lotion and athlete's foot spray – proof, precious proof, that she hasn't been sucked into some parallel universe. And then, when she sees the Sponge Bob Band-Aids and the Colgate Smiles toothpaste and the Sure Girl deodorant Barbara suddenly, urgently needed about six months ago when her body started to change, Claire does cry. Where is Danny? Where has he taken her girls? Why is the house cleaned out?

Minutes pass; she doesn't know how many. She wipes her eyes, mascara and eyeshadow mackerel staining the backs of her hands. She's shivering. She needs to call someone: Danny, her friend Dee, the cops. She goes back into her bedroom. No phone.

No phone downstairs in the hall either. They took the phones. Who would take the phones? *They took the phones.* That's a line from something. Don't think like that, not everything is a line from something. Back upstairs, she opens the study at the base of the tower. Her cell-phone charger should be in the desk drawer. Should be, and would be, if there was still a desk there, Jesus. She casts around the bare room, the floorboards dusted with dead bugs and plaster crumbs where cables were ripped from the wall, the walls seamed with bookcase shadows, the spiral staircase ascending to the upper level.

Finally her eye lands on something, on the mantelpiece and above it, two actual objects, watch closely now. The first thing is a picture, a photograph, of her and Danny in thirties evening clothes in *The Way of the World*. They played the leads, Mirabell and Millamant, and the photo was taken during their love scene, when, having agreed to marry, they make promises to and demands of each other for the future. The second thing is a porcelain statuette of two lovers in old-fashioned costume in some kind of pastoral setting, maybe a shepherd and shepherdess, they've never been sure, Danny got it made to resemble the one in *The Palm Beach Story*, one of their favorite movies. How it worked in the film was Claudette Colbert, who is looking to snare a rich husband, tells Joel McCrea, the husband whom she still loves but who can't seem to make enough money to keep her, that as long as the ornament stands intact on the mantelpiece, he'll have nothing to reproach her with. She won't have strayed. Everything will be as it was.

Claire slides down the wall and comes to rest on the dusty boards by a phone socket. They took the phones. *Glengarry, Glen Ross*, that's what it's from – shut *up* Claire. Can't she for once feel a thing directly, without reference to anything else, especially not a quotation from a play? 'Shakespeare is full of quotations.' Shut up shut up shut up. She needs to think, needs to *do* something . . . but she just sits there on the floor in the tower and stares at the porcelain lovers, and slowly, steadily, starts to feel calmer. Whatever has happened – and evidently it involves a removals firm packing up the entire contents of their home and taking them away, and her husband and daughters disappearing – Danny is letting her know it's all right. There's nothing to worry about. He's always been able to make her feel like this. She knows that's part of why she married him: because a life based on chance and uncertainty had spooked her, she craved security, and she felt safe in Danny's arms. *Danny is letting her know it's all right.* But why in such a cryptic way? There must be something else, some kind of message. Her laptop. She remembers him saying, 'Take your laptop, restaurant reservations, flights, the *weather*,' but she didn't want to. 'I can do it all on my phone,' she said. And then deliberately left her charger behind. She wanted to be out of reach. She wanted – didn't she – to be in situations where her husband simply couldn't get in touch. Now her phone is dead and her laptop is gone and she can't get in touch with her husband.

She lets her eyes follow the wood and steel spiral staircase up to where it disappears through the trapdoor. Up above is her nook, her refuge, her sanctuary, fast at the top of the tower. A room of her own. It's where she keeps all her treasures: old photos, letters from boyfriends past, theater programmes. She doesn't feel ready to climb up now and find them all gone.

She goes downstairs and out through the kitchen and crosses the yard to the garage, not even sure what she is looking for any more but in a hurry to find it. But the garage, at least, is untouched: tools still on the wall, screws and bolts in their airtight plastic containers, hose pipe and electrical cable in coils. More to the point, both cars, her bashed-up Chrysler Pacifica and Danny's old Karmann Ghia, are there. She has the keys to both, and pops each trunk just in case, nightmare images flashing through her mind, but no one has been stowed there. Nothing but spare wheels and Mr Smith's smelly old rugs. Did Mr Smith go with? Who else would take him? How did Danny travel anyway? On the plus side, there's a phone charger in the glove box of the Chrysler. That's at least one of the things she's looking for. She turns the engine on and sits in and plugs the lead in the cigarette lighter socket and waits for her phone to fire up sufficiently for her to use it to call her husband and ever so politely ask him what the fuck is going on.

Maybe he followed me to Chicago, Claire thinks, flushing in fast-acting hangover panic, heat sparking on her scalp, a sharp ache of anxiety creasing her belly. If he went through her computer . . . had she said anything in an email to Dee? No, she wouldn't be that stupid, or indiscreet. Besides, she hadn't had any plans in that direction, or at least none that she had admitted, even to herself, let alone to other people. On the other hand . . . Dee. God, Dee and her dirty mind. Dee checks out every guy they see when they're out together, flirts compulsively with the waiter, the bartender, the cab driver for God's sake. Had Dee speculated on what Claire might get up to in Chicago? Had she put it in an email? She could well have; it's got so Claire screens out most of what Dee says; it's all talk anyway. At least, she thinks it is. Still. Maybe Danny was uneasy after being out of touch, or simply decided he wanted to surprise her, do something romantic and spontaneous, just like she complains he never does any more, and parked the girls for a sleepover with his sister, Donna, and arrived at the Allegro and . . . no, no, *no*. He had left the signs deliberately, the photo and the statuette of the lovers, to reassure her. Hadn't he?

Her phone should have enough juice now. She pops the switch and waits and up flashes the screensaver photo of the girls among the apple trees, taken two years back but still her favorite. When they're grown and have kids of their own, this is still the image she'll keep in her mind's eye. These are her girls. Stop, stop, the tears are welling again. Keep moving, Claire, that's the trick, don't sit still. She grabs the phone and steps out and slams the car door and locks the garage and heads down through the backyard towards the trees. The sensor light doesn't come on. Maybe it's broken. There's a faint spill from the half moon now, the veil blown aside. She's wearing flat white rhinestone studded sandals, the grass damp between her toes. The wet grass, beneath the apple trees.

Her phone chimes out its message alert. *Do not ask for whom the bell tolls.* Three voice mails, two from drama students who can't make it to class this week and one from Dee checking to see if she's home yet and demanding chapter and verse on what she got up to. Seven text messages, four from students, two from teachers at the school, one from Dee. Nothing from Danny. Nothing from the girls, even – they sometimes leave messages when she's away for longer than they expected. What has Danny done? She thinks of those newspaper reports where some guy is going bankrupt, or finds his wife is cheating, and kills the entire family. That's crazy talk – Danny would never raise a hand against her, or the girls. But isn't that the profile those guys have too? The quiet, ordered family man who suddenly explodes? She calls his cell, but it goes straight to message.

'Danny, I'm home. Where are you?'

She swallows, more a gulp than a swallow. Finding she can't continue to speak, she ends the call. *Where are you?*

She feels a mounting panic now, her breath coming in short gasps. Her feet are wetter than they should be, as if she's stepped in muddy ground, or apples that have started to rot. She moves her feet, and one of her sandals comes loose, and her bare foot plunges into something marshy, sticky even, not apples, not grass. Twigs there, maybe, twigs and straw, and something thicker, like resin, like sap. She looks down, using the face of her phone for light. First she sees red, on her foot, on the ground, not flashes behind her eyes, red stains, and not on the ground; she's standing on fur, on flesh; she's standing on the torn-apart carcass of a dog, a springer spaniel, *her* springer spaniel, her beautiful Mr Smith. His body has been gutted, eviscerated, spatchcocked, his poor head half severed but still attached, still intact. *Make it not be, make it not be, make it not be*, she prays, the prayer that is never answered. Claire falls to her knees and holds the dog's heavy head in her hands, his wide snout, his beautiful, beseeching eyes staring into nothing. She opens her mouth to howl, to scream, but nothing comes except a high-pitched keening sound, and then the tears, a child's brimming, boiling tears, tears overflowing until she can barely breathe, wracking sobs that convulse her until she can cry no more, and then a whimpering sound not unlike the sound Mr Smith used to make when he wanted a treat, or a walk, or to nestle in her arms. She brings her wet face down to Mr Smith's head, still warm, her fingers chucking his chin, her lips, her nose, deep in his hair, just as she had every single day of his life, and breathes in his precious musky scent for as long as she can bear.

Where Are You?

Claire is five miles on the road to Cambridge before she even knows she's in motion. A quick call to Donna first, but the phone goes straight to voicemail. Seconds later Claire's in the car; minutes after, she's on the Beltline, the lakes to either side like dark glass, like black mirrors, opaque, implacable. It feels a bit like a row with a boyfriend, back in her drinking days, when rage would overtake her and she'd up-end a bar table and be halfway down the street, her body doing the thinking for her overloaded brain. Look at her now, frightened, shaking, blinking back tears, blazing down the 12-18 trying to get ninety out of the Pacifica without the old heap collapsing in steel ribbons all over the highway.

Barbara and Irene, Barbara and Irene, Barbara and Irene. As soon as she saw poor Mr Smith's body, any solace she found in the signs she thought Danny had left was swept away. Something bad has happened. Please let it not have happened to the girls. If they're not at Donna's, then God knows where they are. Neither Danny nor Claire have any other family in the area, and Donna is their only steady babysitter. Claire can't think of anywhere else Danny might have stowed the girls before taking off. Unless he's taken them with him. Either choice works better than the alternative: that they've been taken against their will.

Not for the first time, Claire's hand hovers over her cell, ready to call 911. Not for the first time, she tries to talk herself down. Danny ran out with the girls, knowing the bad guy or guys – meaning whoever killed Mr Smith – were on their way. That's as much as Claire can cling to for the time being. Never mind that the entire house had been stripped of furniture and belongings, suggesting a certain amount of forward planning. Never mind the question of why bad guys could possibly be after her husband, a suburban bar and grill owner with no criminal record or major gambling or drug addictions. The girls were with their father, and he would never let anything bad happen to them. Don't think about their coming to harm.

Forget about bad guys. Kids probably killed Mr Smith, some kind of horrible Halloween prank. Vicious kids; spoilt, decadent rich kids, high on drugs, too impatient for Freakfest tomorrow night, goading each other into cruelty and wickedness. Just kids.

Approaching the house, she tries Donna's number again, with the same result as before. She parks the Pacifica outside the big wrought-iron gates and hits the buzzer once, twice, three times. The house is not visible from here, and there's no sign of light in the garden. Maybe they're all on the lake side. Maybe they've all gone to bed. She buzzes a fourth, fifth time, and leans on it. Nothing.

Maybe Donna's away. If so, Claire doesn't have a clue where she might be. She doesn't really know very much about her sister-in-law, and doesn't want to know any more than she knows. There was a time when they might have made friends. Claire can see that, despite her sharp tongue and fearsome temper, Donna is funny and smart and a good aunt to the girls – strict but fair, like an old-style teacher, in fact, which is what she would probably have been in another age, an age before drugs and biker gangs and serial monogamy. When Claire and Danny married, she could have done with a strict-but-fair presence to help her settle, an older sister who could have given her familial advice and whose know-it-all bossiness she would have enjoyed resenting. But Donna was either indifferent or actively unpleasant, more like Danny's ex-wife than his sister. It's not impossible to dislike someone at first and later become her friend – she flashes on the title of Barbara's first Beacon Street Girls book: *Worst Enemies/Best Friends* – and Claire certainly feels she gave it a good shot with Donna, above and beyond. But there's a point you reach with someone where you realize that even if you wanted to forgive her, you're no longer capable. The nerve endings are trashed, the synapses have been burned away, the affection cannot be restored. It's good that the girls have an aunt, have any family at all beyond her and Danny, and it's clear that Donna is trustworthy and responsible. And that's the end of it.

No one home, Claire says aloud into the crisp night air. She shivers, releases the buzzer and sits back in the car. She tries Danny's cell again, redials half a dozen times, hangs up without leaving a message. There's no one else to call. There's nowhere else to go except home. But nobody's home, at home. *Where are you?*

'So which is it, sweetheart: you want to call the cops, you don't want to call the cops, or you're not sure either way? Because a decision always brings relief. Unless, of course, it doesn't. Tell you what: while you're deliberating, have another drink.'

Dee is here, at least. When Claire got back, she hoped the whole thing might have been, if not quite a dream, at least a mistake; there'd be a removals truck in the drive, Danny and the kids in the house and an explanation for everything. But everything was just as mysterious and empty as it had been, and that's when she cracked and called Dee, her best friend, who joins her now on the couch because Claire is not so much crying again as leaking a little, and instead of giving her a shoulder, goes for the upward-palms-cupping-the-elbows, gently-rocking, come-on-now, grief-coach approach.

The couch is upstairs in the tower. At first Claire figured the removals guys didn't take it because it would have had to come out the window by winch, since that's the way it came in, the spiral staircase barely wide enough for one person not being nearly wide enough for a couch. But then she saw that everything else was here as well: her theater posters and photos and mementoes, all her plays and bound playscripts, everything from Chicago, and before. All the things she used to be.

Once she had called Dee, she'd made her way out to the apple trees and hunkered down by Mr Smith's body for a spell. What kind of savages would do something like this? She felt she should bury him, but if the cops were summoned, they'd need to see what had been done to the poor dog. She settled for getting one of his old blankets from the car trunk and covering him with it where he lay.

Fearing she was going to lose it again, she made herself walk the yard, breathing the cold night air, trying to recover her nerve, her focus, her clarity. She established a route, her sandals crunching on the frosty grass. She found that if she got close

enough to the rear of the house, the sensor light finally came on
and flooded the yard. She walked in a broad oval between Mr
Smith's body and the house and then down towards the gate that
leads out to the Arboretum. That's about as far as she could get
before the light cut out. Each time she completed the route, she
felt a little more self-posessed, a little less panicked. The ground
was bumpy underfoot – she had wanted a wild country garden,
not a manicured suburban lawn – and she thought of Katharine
Hepburn in *Bringing Up Baby* when she loses a heel, chanting
'I was born on the side of a hill.' She didn't feel much like
chanting though, not when she remembered that the dog who
played George in *Bringing Up Baby* also played Mr Smith in
The Awful Truth, which is where they got the idea for the name.
Danny had wanted to call him Asta, the role he took in *The Thin
Man*, but Claire had won out. She didn't feel like chanting, but
she wasn't going to curl up and die. So when she finally saw the
wolf's head stuck on the bough of an old apple tree, she was not
only able to process the sight without screaming, she also realized almost instantly that it was no wolf's head but a werewolf
mask. The sensor light cut out, but she approached the tree and
examined the mask by the light of her phone. It was a full face
job with fake fur and vulcanized rubber teeth bared in a grimace.
The mask came away from the tree easily – it had just been
wedged between two branches – and something fell from it as
she tugged it free. Claire bent down and picked up a postcard
which bore the simple legend: *Trick or Treat!*

She had guessed correctly – Mr Smith's horrible death was
someone's sick idea of a Halloween prank. One mystery solved,
at least. She made her way inside, fully resolved now to call the
cops. But when she found herself back in the house, she noticed
just how much of Mr Smith's blood there was on her feet and
legs and hands, and when she reached the bathroom she saw she
had blood on her face. She grabbed body wash and shampoo
from her suitcase and took a long shower. Beneath the torrent
of hot water, the tears came again, not just for her dog, but for
her pathetic, deluded self. One minute she had been headstrong
and reckless, giddy with notions of escaping the nest, high on a
vision of freedom spied through the distorting lens of a vacation
flirtation; the next she had been reduced to a whimpering animal

pining for her master, a panicked child praying: *Let this be a sign; let that be a sign.* Anger bubbled up next, this time directed at her husband. Never mind hints and signs, what kind of bastard would abandon his wife like this without a concrete message? If he couldn't phone, could he not have, what, left a note in back of the photo frame in the study (she checked, no dice) or under the mat, or in one of the goddamn cars?

What had she done? Nothing. Nothing *really*; nothing in Chicago, nothing to merit *this*, surely she had done nothing else? She tormented herself with the idea that this must be her fault, but could find nothing beyond the mild feelings of discontent and disaffection and, frankly, boredom that must visit fifteen-year-old marriages the world over. A big fat dose of Is That All There Is? Cause for concern, you bet, but for this? Insufficient grounds.

She had no towels in her case and was reduced to drying herself with a t-shirt. At least she had clean underwear, and socks, and a top and jeans that had only been worn once. She pulled her boots on, zipped up her scuffed old suede jacket (the reassuring feeling, like the protective arm of an old friend) and gave the house one last go-round. That's when she climbed the spiral staircase from the office to discover her nook still intact. And that's when Dee arrived.

They say a best friend is one who'll drop everything, no matter when, and come to your aid. The only person Claire knows she could ask to do that is Dee St Clair. And here they are, Claire wiping her tears away, Dee doing that thing with her face (she's known for her faces) where she warns you she's going to say something serious by setting her mouth and going all scowly with her eyes, which always makes Claire laugh, even now.

'Crying, laughing, mother of God, if it was the fifties, I'd get to slap you for being hysterical.'

'If it was the fifties, I'd probably take it.'

'You'd probably like it. Here, drink some more whiskey.'

'I don't even like whiskey.'

Claire drinks some anyway – Woodford Reserve, bourbon Danny got as a gift that mysteriously found its way up here. For which relief much thanks: there's nothing else in the house, and she needs a drink.

'Atta girl,' Dee says. 'Now. Let me try and recap on our situation here. Your husband has cleared the house of possessions, furniture and fittings and split the scene *with* kids in tow but *without* letting his wife know where he's going, or why he's going, or even *that* he's going. Now, it's unlikely that Danny's done this of his own free and rational will. Either he's been coerced, or he's lost his reason: either way, the girls are in danger. How am I doing so far?'

'He could well have a good reason.'

'And what might that be?'

'I don't know, obviously.'

'Another woman? Money troubles?'

'Hey! Back off, Nancy Drew, and let me think.'

'I'm sorry. Between the helpful friend and the bossy bitch, it's a fine line.'

Claire takes a sip of whiskey, grimaces and looks at Dee, who is midway through her third without any apparent ill effect. Dee with her sallow skin and black eyes and corkscrew curls, raven feathers skeined with silver now, Dee with her velvet and leather and lace, her bangles and beads and hoop earrings, Dee working her Californian gypsy rock chick thing. Dee landed in Madison because the guy she met and married in LA when she was nineteen ran an antiques business here. Before he was killed in a traffic accident a couple of years later, he set her up in her own hair and beauty salon on Dayton.

They met when Dee cut Claire's hair the Christmas of her second year at university. They've been friends ever since. Maybe it's on account of Claire having no family outside Dan and the kids (even her adoptive parents are dead, and she has no step-siblings) that Dee gets bumped up the ranks and accorded family status. And Dee has no family either, just a flaky mom who shows up beween husbands for sympathy and understanding which she doesn't deserve, but invariably gets. They are effectively sisters and, as with sisters, love can quickly turn to hate, usually within the time it takes to empty a glass.

The brashness, the outspoken, loudest-girl-in-the-class quality that Claire loves about Dee (because Claire may have worked in the theater, but in manner she is anything but theatrical) can in an instant appear crass or gauche. The constant stream of sexual innuendo and inquisitiveness runs sour and desperate. And even though Dee does seem to have sex on her mind at all times, there's something, not quite prissy or repressed, but, for all the flirting with wine waiters and bell hops, a tangibly non-sexual, almost other-worldly vibe about her. Maybe it's the sacred and profane Californian divide – in the mountains, the quest for the spiritual, the lure of every new pseudo-religion and cult; in the valleys, the all-night debauch of movies and pornography – hence the ability to be naive and cynical, idealistic and venal, pure and lecherous. Claire can imagine her in school, the bossier girl in the group who knew what dirty words meant first, found her mom's boyfriend's porn, was brash and forward with boys and actually turned out to be a bit prudish and was the last to lose it. Turned out, beneath it all, she was a bit frightened and uncertain.

But that could be Claire applying an actor's technique to real life: confidence is always a front for some kind of insecurity or neurosis; the talkative person is blustering to cover some up some guilty secret; the sexy girl will be a lousy lay. It could as easily be the other way round: that Dee's sassy-girl-with-a-dirty-mouth act is just that: a routine, a burlesque got up to pass the time, or to conceal the real her, or even – and Claire can totally identify with this – to stand in for a person-ality she's not sure she possesses. Claire felt that way about acting – sure she liked to show off, to be the center of attention, but she also needed for sustained periods of time to pretend to be someone else. It was so much easier than pretending to be yourself.

'All right, sweetheart,' Dee says, in her talking-the-suicide-down-from-the-ledge voice. 'Look at it another way. Can you think of any reason he might have done this? According to your account of it, married life has not been the most exciting for the last stretch, but storming out after a row and crashing in a hotel for a couple nights usually works for most people.'

'No. I can't think of any reason he might have done this.'

'No little *amour* you might have confessed to him?'

'Shut up!'

'Money worries?'

'The business is booming, far as I can tell. There was no real hit from the recession, not in Brogan's. And Danny owns the freehold. And there's no mortgage on the house. So, you know, there's no major overheads, there's a limit to how exposed we could be.'

'No investments that went wrong?'

Deep breath, Claire.

'Well . . . since you mention it . . . we had some money . . . the girls' college fund, basically . . . with Jonathan Glatt.'

Blame it on my Youth

When Dee hears Jonathan Glatt's name, she does her Edvard Munch *The Scream* face, and Claire feels like doing it right back. Jonathan Glatt was indicted last year for wire fraud and money laundering and is currently being held without bail at the Federal Prison Camp in Oxford, WI. What he did was what Bernie Madoff did, using one client's investment to pay off another, except Glatt only needed twenty million for his expenses, and his clients were mainly middle-class families with college funds who were tempted by his ability to get a substantially higher return on their money.

Danny met him through an old school friend of his, Gene Peterson. Claire and Danny then had dinner with Glatt and his then-wife, and they were everything she expected a financial advisor and his wife to be: earnest and faintly humorless, discreetly but expensively dressed, full of small talk about golfing breaks and ski lodges and a discussion about retirement plans Claire thought would never end. Claire felt they deserved the extras for that evening alone. And the thing about it was, it never really felt like greed, because it was a friend of a friend, and being in the right place at the right time, but of course greed is almost certainly what it was.

When they began to read in the newspapers that Glatt's marriage had broken down and he was to be seen around Milwaukee in

the company of a cosmetically enhanced stripper and 'adult entertainment performer', the ex-girlfriend of a Green Bay Packers
linebacker, they felt this was not a reassuring sign. When he
was arrested in a house near the UW Milwaukee campus in
possession of a bag of hydroponic marijuana and three grams of
cocaine, in the company of three partially dressed UW undergraduates, the writing was on the wall. Within twenty-four hours,
the bulk of Glatt's clients had demanded their money; within
forty-eight, his attorney had summoned them to a meeting at the
Pfister Hotel on Wisconsin Avenue, where he read a short statement from his client to the effect that he had been borrowing
from Peter to pay Paul – or at least, to pay Paul a higher return
than the market would allow – and now Peter's money was all
gone. And so was Paul's. And none of the other apostles were
doing too good either.

'Oh. My. God. And . . . does that not mean you guys are in
trouble?'

Claire shrugs and shakes her head, almost embarrassed to
admit it.

'Not really. I mean, yes, OK, we're broke, we have pretty
much no savings. We've got to start again in terms of the college
fund. But we can, I guess. We have income. We're not under
pressure otherwise, financially, I mean. Or any other way. At
least, that's what I thought.'

'Are you thinking again?'

'*No.* Danny let me know . . . I know it sounds stupid, but . . .
there's a picture and an ornament downstairs . . .'

And Claire takes her through it, Mirabell and Millamant and
The Way of the World, the ornament of the lovers from *The Palm
Beach Story* and how it's a sign that all is well, the laptop packed
away on which there may be an email. As she explains it, each
piece of reasoning sounds even more lame than the last. Dee
nods her way through it all as if she's agreeing, then tips her
head from side to side to weigh it up.

'So why is there no message on your phone?'

'I don't know.'

'Why not leave a note under the ornament, or up here?'

'He was in a rush?'

'If he had time to leave the ornament and hang the picture,

he had time to write a note, even a scribbled "Don't worry, love Dan" on the back of an envelope.'

'I don't know. In case someone found it?'

'Someone else? Who? Whoever killed the dog?'

'No. No, the dog was a sick Halloween prank.'

Claire shows Dee the werewolf mask, which seems to freak Dee, and the postcard, which seems to freak her even more. The picture on the postcard, which Claire hadn't registered until now, is a blurry painting of what looks like two faces staring out of a window, glowing red flames all around them. Let's hope that's not supposed to be a clue.

'Kids, on drugs,' Claire says. 'It probably had nothing to do with everything else.'

'But you can't be sure.'

'I can't be sure about anything. But that's what my guess is. That's what I would tell the cops. Except I don't want to call them.'

'Because . . .'

'Because I've always trusted Danny. And he's never let me down. And he has to have had a good reason for what he's done. And if he's in trouble, I don't want to make more for him.'

'Do you think there's someone pursuing him? And that's why he had to get out so fast?'

'There could be. I don't know why, but . . . there could be.'

'Is there a Halloween connection? Trick or Treat, this says.'

'I told you, it's probably kids.'

'Say it isn't. Say it's all connected.'

Claire flashes on their Halloween party of a week ago, the last time she saw Danny. The guy in the Death cowl who appeared at the Arboretum gate, Danny pocketing a chef's knife before going down to see him. She can't tell Dee about that, not yet.

'I don't know. Ask me something else.'

'Why take your laptop, which presumably was up here, but nothing else?'

'I don't know. Wait. No, it wasn't up here, it was in the kitchen, I used it to check if there were any delays at the airport before the flight. I left it on the kitchen table. So he didn't come up here; he just, I don't know, left things as they were.'

'All right. What about your email, you can get it on your phone, right? Have you not checked it yet?'

Claire shakes her head. 'I don't have my phone set up to get email.'

Dee looks at her with eyebrows raised, as if she'd said she didn't have a cell phone, or that she didn't believe in the Internet. Dee upgrades her laptop as soon as a new model appears. She has waited in line for an iPod, iPhone, an iPad. Dee has over seven hundred friends on Facebook, yet there were only seven people at her fortieth birthday dinner, five of them her employees. Dee has signed Claire up for Facebook too, and recruited friends on her behalf, but Claire has no interest in visiting the site, considers it some kind of bizarre high-school regression mechanism, even though everyone she knows seems to be on it, all the moms at school, the women in her book club, the theater people. And what about that woman in England who said she was going to commit suicide, and all her twelve hundred or so friends did was sneer and laugh at the prospect, not one of them tried to stop her. And she went through with it. Brave New World. Without Claire in it.

She's not a complete luddite. She does use email (but email is so last century, Dee says) and obviously if she wants to book a flight, or buy a book – although she'd still much rather go to a store like Mystery to Me or Avol – but she doesn't want to view the sex tape of some celebrity she's never heard of, or make contact with someone she didn't even like when she was at school and who fate intended she never meet again, and quite right too. So why does Claire always feel the need to justify herself and her own lack of interest in technology? Because, of course, at this stage of the twenty-first century, Claire, the tech-refusenik, who doesn't want to be connected to everyone all the time, is emphatically the odd one out. There used to be a time when being the odd one out was cool. Not any more.

'I . . . never really saw the need,' Claire continues. 'I mean, it's not as if I'm in business or anything. No one is sending me an email so vital I have to answer it when I'm in line at Target or somewhere. It's always only an hour or two until I'm home.'

Dee makes her patience-of-a-(medieval)-saint face and extends her palm without a word. Claire places her cell phone in it.

'I think I have all your details, except your password. Mind if I go ahead?'

'Please.'

Claire stands and walks to the window, unable to bear the seizure of pleasure that animates Dee's features as she gets to grips with the iPhone Claire only has because Dee insisted she upgrade from the battered old Nokia she actually liked, and understood how to operate.

'I think my password is—'

'Barbara1,' Dee trills. 'I tried Barbara, and then added the numeral; it's the obvious choice if you want a mix of letters and numbers but need to make it easy to remember. Nine out of ten moms pick the eldest child.'

Claire knows she shouldn't really feel as irritated as she does. Dee is only trying to help, actually *is* helping. She has constructed a website for Claire as well, listing all of her stage triumphs, with photographs and a résumé that starts off bright and busy and then tails off into idleness. The most recent entries were a couple of days as a special extra on *CSI: Miami* and *Law and Order*, engineered by an old friend working in television to help her get back in the swing after Barbara was born and she was freaking out about the life sentence that is motherhood. But she didn't get back in the swing. She didn't like the obsession with her looks she had contracted, the panic over aging, the absence, however fleeting, from her baby. Maybe if the parts had been substantial, had been actual *parts*. But 'Four dollars, please' and 'Take the back stairs and it's on your left' didn't mean more to her because she was saying them on TV than they would if it had been real life. She knew she was supposed to look at them as somewhere between a refresher course and a new beginning. But for her, they served as the opposite. And then she got pregnant with Irene and that was the end of that. The last entry in her online résumé is:

Acting Teacher, Madison School of Dramatic Art, 2004–Present.

It's not just that she doesn't use her website: she avoids it.

She looks out across the backyard to the oak prairies of the Arboretum. There's just enough light in the sky now to make out the leafy outlines of the trees, just enough days shy of the first big wind of fall for the leaves still to cling. She has lost herself for hours on end at this window, staring out at the heavy old oaks, listening for the lapping sound of the waters of Lake

Wingra. She didn't question that this was where they should live when Danny suggested it, even though he didn't seem particularly keen; she grew up close to woods and a lake herself. But often over the years she has felt it might have been better for him if they had found somewhere with no trace of his family or his past; somewhere to start afresh. Better for them both.

'Here you are, babe, forty-eight new messages,' Dee says, passing the phone to Claire.

She scrolls quickly through them. None is from Danny. She shakes her head.

Dee does her scrunched-up you-may-not-like-what-I'm-going-to-say-but-I'll-say-it-anyway face.

'The other thing to consider, maybe, sweetheart, is that Danny got some notion about what you were up to in Chicago, and went there – and forgive me if I'm, like, *fishing*, but you know I'm dying to know – found out something he wasn't supposed to, and went off the deep end and has gone on the lam like a spurned and betrayed Lothario. Care to comment? Paul Casey? Miss Taylor?'

And Claire, looking at the white filigree of dog hair that coats the floor and feeling her spirits flag, begins faintly to nod her head, thinking of Chicago, yes, Chicago a week ago, that reunion of middle-aged people who were once going to be somebody and only succeeded, if at all, in becoming themselves. It might have looked, if you didn't know for sure, like something *did* happen between her and Paul Casey, and she's not one hundred percent sure something didn't, although it doesn't matter a damn now.

But she's also thinking of Chicago fifteen years ago, when she and Paul got around, and did things they don't do any more, and met a lot of people she ordinarily wouldn't have met, including a) one of Danny's oldest friends, and b) the only people she's ever met in her life who could have done what somebody did to Mr Smith, or ordered it done, could have, and would have, without a second thought. And now Claire wonders for the first time if what has happened may in fact be her fault.

Ill Wind

Claire is usually good, perhaps too good, at locating the detached place inside her head, the one that supplies her with apt wisecracks and quotations from books, plays and films, usually at inappropriate moments, just to make reality that bit easier to bear. But the simultaneous arrival, at seven a.m. on Monday morning, of two deputies from the Dane County Sheriff's office, there to serve her a reminder notice (a *reminder* notice) that the property she is standing in must be vacated within the next thirty-one days, as per the terms of the court-ordered foreclosure against the house three months previously, so as to enable free and vacant possession for its auction one calendar month from now, and two detectives from the Madison Police Department, there for reasons they have yet to disclose, stretches her to the limit. Some vague formulation about a sitcom written by David Lynch scuttles across the shore of her brain, but she's pretty sure it's second-hand.

She's standing, literally shaking (she can see she's shaking because the notice to quit in her hand is flapping in the air) in the doorway of the house as the deputies depart and the detectives move in. Claire knows they are detectives because they show her their badges, and because she knows they are detectives. Who else would come this early in the morning, dressed in suits that don't entirely fit them, the man's gray and shiny at the seams, sagging and loose at the shoulders, the woman's navy and new, bulging between the two buttons of the two-button coat?

The woman, who is in her thirties and not really overweight, eight pounds tops (maybe the suit was a stretch to begin with) looks at the paper in Claire's hand and raises her eyebrows in, not quite sympathy, that would be unprofessional, but what-are-you-gonna-do empathy, or so it seems to Claire, and bats it towards her partner, who is brown-eyed and fleshy faced and has eighties hair in a side parting, and does not look like he is in the empathy business this morning.

'Ms Taylor?' he says.

'Mrs Brogan. Ms Taylor, yes.'

'Detective Fowler, of the Madison Police Department. This is Detective Fox. We'd like you to come take a look at something in your backyard.'

Mr Smith. Oh My God, Mr Smith. Claire had finally fallen into a blessed, bourbon-induced sleep somewhere around four, four-thirty. Since she awoke a couple of hours later, fully clothed, to the sound of the doorbell, she has simply been reacting – to the sheriff's deputies, to the cops – all the while having forgotten most, if not quite all, of what happened last night:

The emptied house;

The vanished family; and

Mr Smith.

(And what happened to Dee? Wasn't Dee here? Where did she go? Home, let's hope, so she doesn't a) get caught up in this; and b) witness Claire's further humiliation.)

Jesus Christ, the court-ordered foreclosure *three months ago*? Her house is about to be seized within the month and auctioned off to the highest bidder, because it isn't her house any more. And now cops are here, like at the beginning of some TV show, leading her to the scene of the crime, and she has to figure out what to say about her dead dog. Claire is aware, as she follows the detectives past the deck and down towards the apple trees in the backyard, that they are looking at her strangely, as if she is not sufficiently surprised or upset by their arrival. But she knows what they're going to find, and in any case, what is the appropriate way to behave when you're confronted with the kind of news she has had? She has been more or less gaping for the twelve or so hours she has been home, gaping and bailing and gasping for breath and waiting for the camera crew to appear out of the bushes and say 'Surprise! It's all a big hoax! Here's your husband!'

So she can kill him with her bare hands.

It's not that the death of her dog is the least of it, but she does wonder if, across the United States, whenever a pet is found dead, two detectives are dispatched to the scene as a general rule, or is it just a Mid-West thing? Since she has no direct experience of the

police to date, she can't say, but it does strike her as unlikely. And
how do they know anyway? The thought sequence, again on loan
from a TV cop show: helicopter surveillance (at night); infra-red
photography (she's not sure what this is, but has a notion it's what
you need to use); cops identify and secure crime scene. And sure
enough, she can see two officers in uniform unspooling yellow tape
and a police vehicle disgorging a photographer and some kind of
forensic specialist in a white paper suit. For a dead dog? It briefly
reminds her of a TV detective show the girls used to watch, but
instead of humans, everyone was an elephant or a hippo or a chimp,
and the dog wouldn't have been dead, it would just have had a sore
paw. But the girls would never watch such a show now, considering
themselves far too old for such childish nonsense, and neither, probably, would anyone else, unless it winked over the shoulders of the
children with allegedly humorous allusions to sex and drugs and
political scandals. She tears up suddenly, vivid with the sense of
passing time and lost innocence, of infants growing old and cynical,
of the sad inevitability of decay and death, an entire bolt of somber,
Four-Last-Things thought and feeling unfolding and falling through
her mind in a lurid cascade. As they pass beneath the gold- and rust-
and red-leaved apple trees, her feet crunching on fallen fruit, shivering
now in the sharp October air, she braces herself for the sight of Mr
Smith in full light, ashamed that she didn't bury the body, or do
more than strew a blanket over it, ashamed that she failed to treat
him with the respect she feels was his due. But how could she have
buried the family dog without the girls, without Danny?

'It's Mr Smith I feel sorry for.' That was what Danny used to
say whenever some domestic crisis hit, and Mr Smith, merrily
oblivious, couldn't understand why no one was playing with him.
And of course Mr Smith, in his merry, giddy oblivion, was the
great disspeller of domestic crisis, the repository, as the girls grew
older and complicated and *human*, the locus of sheer happiness
in their house, the only one when domestic crisis hit that you
could play with, that you *wanted* to. Claire is shaking now, her
eyes so blurred with tears that she is upon the scene before
she can discern that what is lying there is not remotely what she
expected. Her first thought is: maybe it was a dream after all!
Because Mr Smith's body is nowhere to be seen. Instead, there
is the body of a man, his hair and clothes stained with mulch

and dead leaves and clay, his clothes torn, dark smears of what might be blood around the four or five wounds to his stomach and chest. The body of a dead man, not a dead dog. It was like a sneeze, she says later, as involuntary as a sneeze, the sound she makes, the *laugh* she laughs, as if some sorcerer had waved his wand or cast his spell and reality had been overthrown, and there, before the fascinated, appalled eyes of the detectives, stands a woman *laughing* at the sight of a corpse in her own backyard and, indeed, resisting a powerful urge to clap her hands.

'Ms Taylor?' Detective Fowler says, and there's a tone to it, a 'pull yourself together woman, for God's sake' undercurrent she almost appreciates, as if it is clear she's being hysterical and in truth deserves a slap.

'I'm sorry,' she says. 'It's just . . .'

'Just what?' says Detective Fox abruptly.

But Claire can't really say what it's just.

It's just that someone has gotten rid of the body of her slaughtered dog and replaced it with the body of a man she thinks she recognizes, a man she suspects she saw a week ago at the barbecue, disguised as the Angel of Death, standing at her garden gate, waving his hand (or shaking his fist) at her husband.

It's just that her husband armed himself with a knife before he approached this man, and then they disappeared out into the Arboretum together.

It's just that she never asked Danny what had happened (she was in a hurry after the party to get to the airport for her Chicago flight, or at least that's what she told herself) even though she could see he was shaken by whatever *had* happened.

It's just that she didn't see this man's face then, but she recognizes him now. She knows that he's one of Danny's oldest friends; she knows his name.

It's just that she's pretty sure her husband didn't know she knew him. Or that she had met him. Or that she had as good as slept with him.

'Ms Taylor, have you ever seen this man before? Do you know who he is?'

Claire reckons she has to say something, and better, when the cops are involved, that it be true.

'Yes. His name is Gene Peterson.'

Last Night When We Were Young

F owler and Fox. That's what they went by. It always sounded like an old English firm to Nora, makers of saddles, or boots, or marmalade. Fowler and Fox, by Royal Appointment. And by rights it should have been Fox and Fowler, given she does all the work. All right, that isn't entirely true. Just all the legwork, what most people would call the policework. And the fact that it suits her means she isn't resentful, much. It's just, when they catch a case, when they arrive at a crime scene, when the whole deal is breaking, is *real*, it has gotten so she can actually sense these waves of apathy, of indifference emanating from her partner, indifference and, worse, actual hostility toward the business in hand. It isn't laziness – sit Detective Ken Fowler at a desk and he'd pull a twelve-hour shift – and it isn't because he's eight months away from his twenty (although that hasn't exactly helped matters). He's always been like this.

He simply doesn't like being out and about. In someone else's house, on a call, on patrol, it doesn't matter: if Ken can't be in his own home, he likes to be in the station house. It's something deep in his wiring. He is the most domesticated man she has ever met. Even when his marriage was in trouble on account of his wife running about town drinking and screwing around, he still wouldn't stay out for more than a second drink. 'I've got to get home,' he would say, and he would go on saying it for as long as she kept making a fool of him, and after she left him, and when it was more than clear even to him that she was not coming back. 'I've got to get home,' Ken would murmur, and slope off into the night, flicking his hair back from his forehead in that eighties way he had, too much a creature of habit to imagine what his life might be like if he were to contemplate changing it.

So she knows that he will suggest to Claire Taylor that she

come down to the station to talk to them there as a matter of course, not because he has weighed up the pros and cons, or thinks she might respond positively to the stimulating environment of an interview room, or has considered whether, because she's probably never even been arrested before, she might in response get intimidated and anxious and freak out and lawyer up on them, but simply because he wants to get back to his zone.

It's not that he's a bad detective. Each of the squad, or at least each of them in the West District, which is all she knows about, has at least one major flaw, something the others have to put up with and work around. With Nora, it's an impatience, a pride in not suffering fools, a harrying, chivying impulse and a caustic tone of voice that can turn a simple cross questioning of a witness – never mind a suspect – into a hectoring confrontation. To guard against which, she has to watch herself like a hawk: no hangovers, no sleepless nights, rigid impulse control. Easy.

With Ken, it's the urge to bring everyone downtown, no matter how counter-productive it'll turn out to be: kids, old people, informants who don't want to be outed, rich people who alternately despise and think they own the cops. It doesn't matter to Ken: come on over to my place. The shame of it is, he is twice the interrogator Nora is: subtle, empathetic, able to manipulate and steer a conversation without anyone being aware of it, even him, or so it sometimes seems. In that interview room, Ken can seem like some kind of intuitive artist, an actor improvising a scene, seamless, flawless, just pulling it out of the ether, etching it on the wind. Provided, of couse, he hasn't queered the pitch by insisting on jumping the gun, Nora thinks, smiling at how the cliché overload would make Ken wince. Between them, they make one good cop: the Pantomime Detective, Don Burns, their sergeant, calls them, occasionally with the capper that it's just too bad they're each the ass end.

So it's second nature to Nora this morning to pay as much attention to Ken as to Claire Taylor, and just when it looks like he's going to succumb to the temptation to invite Claire down the station, Nora clears her throat and catches his eye. Sometimes, stubborn, ingenuous, he can affect not to understand what she means; this morning, he takes the point clear enough, as well he might, given the thorough-going complexity, not to say epic weirdness of the situation. For a start, when Claire Taylor initially saw the body, an exhumed corpse lying in her own backyard, her reactions were, firstly, to yell with laughter, like she was . . . *relieved*, it looked like, almost triumphant. Then, having identified the body, she burst out crying. And then, when the tears banked down, this:

Claire: 'Where's Mr Smith?'

Nora: 'I beg your pardon?'

Claire: 'Mr Smith! Mr Smith!

Nora: 'I don't understand, Ms Taylor. Mr Smith?'

Claire: 'Yes, Mr Smith. Last night, this guy wasn't here.'

Nora: 'By "this guy", you mean the body you have identified as being that of Gene Peterson?'

Claire: 'Yes, yes, Gene, Gene Peterson. He wasn't here. Mr Smith was here. Mr *Smith. (Sobs.)* Oh God. Oh my God. Sorry, I'm sorry. I stepped on him, you see. Mr Smith's body, last night, in the dark. I got blood on my shoes. Mr Smith's blood. The poor little *guy.* And so . . . so someone must have taken his body away and put this body here . . . why would anyone have done that? Jesus Christ, this is so fucked up.'

Ken: 'Ms Taylor. Is Mr Smith . . . a dog?'

Claire: 'Of course he's a dog. What did you think I was talking about?'

This is when Ken looks like he's beginning to flail a little, and his fringe falls in his eyes, and Nora clears her throat and suggests to Claire that maybe they could go in the house and talk, her manner as gentle and solicitous as she can manage. And Claire says OK, but they'll have to sit on the floor, as all the furniture has been cleared out. Like she said, weird.

As it turns out, there is some furniture remaining, a couch and a couple of chairs and an oak desk in a kind of den up a spiral metal staircase, and that's where they're sitting now. Kind of a student crash pad, Nora thinks, with plenty of actual student memorabilia, posters and photographs and so on, but more, or less, than that: a messy, uncertain, semi-formed feeling, the couch and chairs not really matching the carpet or the wallpaper or each other, dolls and soft toys and postcards and concert tickets and theater programmes scattered about, as if the room belonged to an actual university student and not the extremely well-kept late-thirties-looking woman sitting across from her.

Ken arrives back with some takeout coffee from Michael's Frozen Custard on Monroe, since there's nothing left in the kitchen to make coffee with or in, or drink it from, and once they've had some, and tasted some pastries, Nora makes eye contact with him. He flicks his fringe and gives her the raised-eyebrow invitation: 'Whenever you're ready.'

Nora takes it with a barely perceptible nod, but is in no hurry to get started, or rather, is biding her time until she figures out what to start with. She looks at Claire Taylor, who is sitting perfectly still on the couch, long legs tucked beneath her, fingers steepled above her empty coffee cup, head tilted back, eyes staring at the ceiling. For someone who has been through what Claire has just told them she's gone through, she's looking pretty together: long auburn hair sleek and straight and shining, skin clear and creamy, blue eyes startling in their intensity. Claire has the look, Nora thinks, the tall and slender with long straight hair look Nora once thought she maybe might contract as a teen. Then she realized, somewhere around fifteen, when other girls had grown into it and she was still five-three, and, not exactly squat, quite shapely actually, but with hair that had kinks and waves an iron couldn't satisfactorily remove, and always only a pound or two away from fat, that she was never going to morph into tall and slender with long straight hair. And twenty years later, when the look is triumphantly back in style, it kills her just a little that she still minds quite so much. Nora nods her head briskly, her face creasing into a characteristic smile, as if a little embarrassed by her narcissistic reverie (but then she is always a little embarrassed by something) and clicks the top of her pen a couple of times.

'So, Ms Taylor . . . maybe we should start with the dead body. You say his name is Gene Peterson. Could you tell us, what was your relationship to the deceased?'

Claire lays her cup on the sofa beside her and looks directly at Nora, her blue eyes cold, her expression haughty. 'I didn't have a "relationship" with Eugene Peterson,' she says, with some heat.

Nora doesn't exactly lean forward, but it's all she can do to keep still: the most innocuous question in the book meets with a XXL-sized tell, which she doesn't want to flag by greeting it with one of her own.

'All I mean by a relationship is, how did you know him?'

'He was an old friend of my husband's. They were at school together.'

'And you've seen him over the years? Your husband kept up with him?'

'Not really, no.'

'Then how do you know who he is, Ms Taylor? How were you able to identify him so confidently?'

Color rushes into Claire's face, and she looks away.

'I understand your reluctance to speak, Ms Taylor . . . *Claire*. I know you want to think the best of your husband, and of course you want what's best for your children. But you've got to understand that these two wishes may not be compatible. The facts as we know them are, without your knowledge or consent, your husband has left, with your kids, having let the bank – I took the trouble to talk to the Sheriff's deputies before they left – having let the bank initiate foreclosure proceedings, right from underneath you, so to speak. On top of that, we've got the body of a dead man, who you claim was one of your husband's oldest friends, in the backyard. Now, at the very least, you have been lied to, Ms Taylor. At the very least. And I know you want what's best for your children, and I can certainly tell you that I – that is to say, Detective Fowler and I, on behalf of the Madison Police Department – want to find your children safe and sound. That's our number-one priority. And I can assure you, in cases like these, where the husband has absconded with the children – well, let's just say time is a significant factor. Urgency is what's needed now. You understand me? So maybe the first thing you should do is tell me about this man, Gene Peterson.'

Claire blinks and nods and begins to speak.

'I met Danny at UW, and we were together for three years, and then we broke up and I went to Chicago and lived there about eight years. And then I came back and married Danny and we had our babies and we've been together ever since, twelve years? And when I was in Chicago, there were men, a couple serious, a couple not. And one of the nots was Gene Peterson.

He . . . I'd never met him before, but he knew who I was – I was working as an actor back then, and he came to see a show, and stuck around after, and introduced himself, said he'd heard about me from Danny. And . . . he was nice, at first, and I was broke, and he took me out to dinner, and he was only in town for the night, and . . . well, in the end, nothing really happened, it . . . we didn't hit it off. And that was that until Sunday a week ago.'

'What do you mean, that was that?'

'I mean, Danny never wanted chapter and verse on who I dated when we were apart. So I never told him. I mean, he knew about a couple guys, the serious ones, but I wasn't going to say, "Oh, you know that friend of yours from way back?" As far as I was aware, he never knew. Until Sunday a week ago, we had a barbecue here, a lot of friends, last day in the outdoors before winter, a big party. Suddenly, there's a guy appears at the back-yard gate. Gene Peterson.'

'Did you recognize him?'

'No, he was . . . he was wearing a mask.'

'A mask?'

'A cowl, actually. You know, the Angel of Death. It was a Halloween party. Early, because I was on my way to Chicago.'

'So you didn't see his face?'

'No.'

'All right. Tell me what happened.'

'Danny went down to see him. He vanished outside and . . . and that was that.'

'There you go again. That was what?'

'Well, I was on a plane that night to Chicago, it was a big party, a lot of drinks had been taken, I was more concerned with making my flight than, who was that guy? And you know, the gate gives on to the Arboretum, it's public access there, it could have been anyone.'

'Did you ask?'

Claire shakes her head.

'I was somewhere between don't forget to do the lunch boxes and feed the dog and passport-ticket-money, I just forgot about it. If I even registered it as anything.'

'But you don't think it was just anyone?'

'I saw . . . I saw Danny look at the guy as if *he* recognized him. Cowl or no cowl. And now we see, here's Gene Peterson, he's dead. So I guess we make the assumption. Or at least, I do.'

'Ms Taylor, is your husband the jealous type?'

'There's nothing to be jealous of! And no, he's not the jealous type. He's not the violent type. I don't believe he did it, or could have done it. For God's sake, the idea he would do that to Mr Smith!'

'You're taking it for granted that the same person who killed Gene Peterson killed your dog.'

'Well. At first, I maybe thought it was some kind of horrible Halloween prank. But that was before a man was killed. And that's another thing, Gene Peterson's body wasn't here last night, so whoever put it there must have done it in the early hours of the morning.'

'You're sure you didn't just miss the body?'

'There was a moon – not full, and it was cloudy. But OK, say I did miss the body, say the body was out there. Mr Smith's body was what I stepped in. He was there, for certain. And now he's not there any more. So at the very least someone must have moved the dog's body.'

Claire says this without a flicker. Nora nods her assent.

'Now there's absolutely no way Danny is going to kill a man and leave his body in our yard, or bury the body but leave the eviscerated carcass of the dog he loved, then come back the following night when he knows I'm home and secretly dig up the man's body while burying or otherwise removing Mr Smith. Does that make any sense, Detective Fox?'

Nora nods again, as if conceding the point, which on the face of it does make considerable sense. The problem is, nothing else about this case does.

'What about you, Claire? You say you made it back from Chicago last night. Presumably you have proof of that.'

'I have a plane ticket. I was on the flight. I stayed at the Allegro Hotel in Chicago. I can show you receipts, I have them somewhere.'

'Detective Fowler will want to see all of your documentation, along with names and numbers of the people you spent time with in the city.'

'You don't think I killed him? That I could do anything like this?'

Claire's voice is suddenly shrill with indignation.

'What we're trying to do is eliminate all the possibilities, Claire,' Nora says, turning to her partner.

'Time of death, Ken?'

'The medical examiner was only getting started. But indications are, the body is comfortably post-rigor, so we're talking thirty-six to forty-eight hours at least. Abdominal swelling is still relatively minor, which would indicate no more than four days on the other side.'

'So, Claire, provided you were where you say you were, that pretty much rules you out. Now, at the risk of repeating ourselves here, your husband's vanished with your children and all your possessions, he knew your house had been foreclosed against, he hasn't told you where he's gone or why. Not a note, not a message. That's right, isn't it?'

Claire nods, unable or unwilling to meet Nora's eye now. She is fidgeting with a coil of her long auburn hair, teasing it between her fingers, then moving to a silver sleeper, twisting it around in the lobe, then back to the hair. For such a poised, controlled lady, Nora reckons this is Claire's idea of a freak-out. *Let's see if we can stir the pot.*

'*That* doesn't make any sense to *me*,' Nora snaps. 'So what are you telling me here?'

Nora looks up and catches sight of Ken Fowler, briefly: he nods and flashes a wry smile. She acknowledges it, while shrugging it off; she's still feeling her way; too early to come to any judgements or conclusions.

'I'm telling you the truth,' Claire says. 'Isn't that the easiest thing? Because I would like you to help me.'

And when Claire looks at Nora Fox, they are both surprised to find that Claire has tears in her eyes.

'All right then,' Nora says. 'Tell me about the money, Ms Taylor. Your husband must have been under huge financial pressure.'

'I knew nothing about it,' Claire says.

'About the foreclosure? Well, that's clear from your reaction. But modern marriage being what it is, you must have known something of the family finances that led up to it? It can't simply have come out of the blue. Unless . . . did your husband like to gamble?'

'We had savings invested with Jonathan Glatt,' Claire says, lobbing this nugget toward Detective Fowler.

'How much?' Fowler says immediately, his tone poised unsteadily between professional and inquisitive.

'A low five-figure sum,' Claire says tightly, the good daughter putting a brave face on it, not about to tell the neighbors the family's business.

'And that didn't put you under financial pressure?' Detective Fox says, her tone skeptical but humane, and Claire shakes her head.

'It was the girls' college fund, a lot of money. But we have no mortgage on the house. Or at least, that's what I understood. And Brogan's . . .'

'Brogan's is an institution in this town,' Nora says, deciding they've probably got enough. She is pretty sure Claire has had no idea what has been going on, money-wise.

'I'm sorry. I know it sounds like something from the Olden Days, but Danny takes care of the money side.'

Rich bitches, Nora thinks by reflex, *skinny rich bitches don't know they're born*. On the other hand, likeliest scenario is, the husband's gone off the deep end and the kids are in danger. If they're not dead already. And all the money is long gone. Have to feel sorry for her. Nora stands up.

'As I say, Ms Taylor, it's the kids we're most concerned about.'

Nora nods to Ken, who clears his throat.

'In order for us to get moving on a search for your children, we need you to come downtown with us and file a missing person's report, Ms Taylor. That way, we can notify our Dane County colleagues, state police and the federal authorities, and make the best start in trying to track them down. If necessary, issue an Amber Alert.'

Nora Fox is waiting for Claire to respond when Officer Colby appears in the doorway with a large plastic evidence bag. She walks across to him, and he holds the bag out for her to examine; inside, there is a large knife, its blade stained black and red.

'Murder weapon?' she says.

'Looks like.'

'Sabatier. That's a pricey knife.'

'European?'

'Sounds like. Open it up so we can all have a look.'

Colby is wearing protective white paper gloves. He opens the bag and lifts out a knife and holds it out. Claire Taylor makes a sound in her chest, somewhere between a sigh and a gasp. And begins to shake.

'Your husband like to cook, Claire?' Detective Fox says. 'Sure he does: Brogan's Bar and Grill, known for its meat. And you had a barbecue here a week ago, he would have cooked at that for sure – barbecue is a man's job. So we'd like to know if you think there's any chance this might be his knife?'

Ralph's Book

Whanat happened was the Bradberrys were a family had a whole bunch of stories told about them, stories Danny Brogan had heard even before he got to Jefferson Junior High and was put sitting next to Jackie. Nowadays, people would describe their domestic situation as chaotic, and you'd hope they'd be the subject of assorted child protection investigations and have caseworkers on their backs all the time, although given the stories you read almost every day about this murderer and that abuser with precisely the same kind of background, you might be hoping in vain, but in any case, thirty years ago, they seemed to fly under the radar, maybe because they once had money, or the remnants of it. The father was a doctor, and used to be a good one, long as you caught him before lunchtime, but he had been struck off for malpractice (people said he'd misjudged a prescription and killed a man), and the mother was lace-curtain Irish from Chicago, Lincoln Park, with notions about how much she had sacrificed for the man she referred to as a country physician. Maybe she had, although when Danny saw her, whatever looks she might have thought she had were long gone. Maybe it was the drink, because it wasn't just him, she drank too. A family can just about survive one drunk parent, as Danny well knew; much harder to get past two, especially when the mother seemed to be drinking to spite the father, and all the kids got caught in the crossfire.

Anyway, there was a Bradberry in every class, and everyone knew they were trouble. One of the elder Bradberrys had been in juvie in Racine for some kind of assault, Danny heard it was rape, back when you were eight and rape was a word like sex or breasts, and you knew it was wrong but it was kind of exciting too, because you didn't have a clue what it really meant. All the Bradberrys were kind of unkempt, bordering on smelly, and underfed, and they used to fall asleep in class, and they never had the right textbooks or permission slips or milk money, and the brothers were quick to start fights and the sisters wore the year before last's tattered clothes and ratty hair styles, and were whispered about by the other girls, and like their brothers, they were quick to bully and to fight.

After his first day, when Danny was put up the front of the class sitting next to Jackie Bradberry, instead of down the back beside Dave Ricks, Danny and Dave forever, and behind Gene Peterson and Ralph Cowley, which is where he had sat all the way through elementary school, Danny came home and complained to his mom about how Jackie Bradberry was kind of dumb, and his fingernails were filthy and he couldn't do multiplication, and his mom just said it was a shame, what had happened to that Bradberry family, and there but for the grace of God, and Danny should make an extra special attempt to be nice to little Jackie, for her sake, and Danny saw how sad his mom looked and thought of laying awake at night listening to his dad yelling at her and he resolved to be Jackie Bradberry's friend.

The only thing was, he wasn't really cut out to be Jackie Bradberry's friend. For a start, Jackie had his own buddies, a couple of dim kids called Jason and Chad who laughed at his jokes and did what he told them, which was mostly to persecute the soft boys who couldn't or wouldn't fight back. And Jackie didn't play sports, or watch sports, and he didn't read books, not even comic books (he had dyslexia or something) and he didn't listen to music, and the only movies he had seen were horror flicks like *The Omen* and *The Exorcist* and *The Evil Dead* that Danny wasn't old enough to watch. And the guys, Dave and Ralph and Gene, well, they didn't give a damn about Jackie Bradberry, and none of their moms had said a word to them about maybe trying to be kind to him, and after a week of grunts and shrugs from Jackie, who didn't seem interested in Danny either, Danny decided enough was enough and went back to ignoring Jackie as best he could, given he was sitting beside him, and then Gene's mom, who was on the school's board of management, had a word with the assistant principal and suddenly Danny was back sitting beside Dave, and Jackie was back with one of his cronies, and their class teacher Mrs Johnson's experiment in social integration – which was what it had been, Danny discovered later – came to an end. And when Danny took his place by Dave, Dave leant into Danny and whispered in his ear a sketch he'd learned by heart from Monty Python, which Danny and Dave loved and used to recite at each other. And Danny laughed and laughed, at the silliness of the sketch, and the voices Dave used, and with relief that he was back among his own people. And when he looked around the class, still laughing, he saw that Jackie Bradberry was looking at him, staring at him with a mean look in his eyes. A half-hour later, the first note arrived.

Laugh at me an you are dead.

Danny simply ignored it, didn't even connect it with Jackie. The second note came an hour later.

You are dead meat. Killer.

This time it did register. Danny remembered Jackie insisting Jason and Chad call him 'Killer' and getting pissed at them because they kept forgetting to. Danny glanced across the class at Jackie, as if to say, 'What's this about?' Jackie's cronies looked astonished and outraged, as if Danny was some kind of telepath to have worked out who had sent the note in the first place. Jackie stared back at him, red-rimmed eyes dull, mouth slack, and shook a finger in the air. The third note was to the point:

Death ground. back of the Cemetary after school. come alone.

There used to be a patch of scrub ground hidden by pine trees between Forest Hill Cemetery and the adjacent golf course where older kids went to settle scores. The stories attached to it were legion: that kids who got killed in fights had to be buried there; that Hell's Angels used it as a site for their initiation ceremonies; that the ghosts of the Union dead from Camp Randall and their Confederate prisoners arose from their graves and did battle every night. Danny and his buddies had long speculated over which of them would be first to be called out to the death ground, a junior-high rite of passage they were all simultaneously dreading and dying to get out of the way.

Now Danny was the first chosen, but it wasn't the way he had imagined it. He thought it would be, this big bully would challenge him, and he'd accept, and then all his buddies and all the bully's gang would assemble at the death ground and the last man standing would be the victor, and it would be Danny, and the next day, the whole school would know. Instead, Jackie Bradberry had called him out alone, and when he had done it, when he had shaken his finger at him as if he was defiant and angry, well, Danny could see that he wasn't really, that there was something in his eyes that looked a lot like fear.

Danny hadn't shown Dave or any of the other guys the notes Jackie sent, had been almost embarrassed by them, as if it was all happening the wrong way and he was somehow implicated in that. After school, he told Dave he had to pick up a book in the library and to go on without him, and then he cycled straight to the death ground, coming in off Speedway Road, swarming over the wall at the golf-course end and dropping down among the pines.

Jackie Bradberry was waiting, alone, no sign of Jason or Chad, and Danny looked at Jackie, at how slight he was, at how his bike was an old hand-me-down caked in rust, at how the dull glow in Jackie's eyes was less violent than reproachful, peevish, even, as if Danny had hurt his feelings in some way. This isn't a proper fight, Danny thought, where it's you against a bully or a creep. This is like at home, after Dad has stopped yelling and is sleeping and Mom is sitting in the living room with the blinds drawn even though it's daytime, and no one is allowed to speak, and you don't know what you've done but somehow it's not just their fault, it's your fault too. But how is this Danny's fault?

'What's up, Jackie? Or would you prefer if I called you Killer?'

Jackie flinched, and his freckled face reddened. Almost all the Bradberrys had red hair and pale blue eyes (except for the elder brother who'd been in juvie in Racine, who was dark and who people said was a bastard, in both senses of the word), but Jackie had the worst of it, hair that looked like it had faded in the sun and tiny, watery eyes, and when his face flushed, he looked like a little pig, the runt of the litter, and Danny suddenly realized he wasn't afraid, not remotely, remembered Jackie was the Bradberry his brothers picked on, Eric and Brian, even his sisters used to slap him across the back of the head, Jackie Bradberry who stopped playing sports because he'd always get picked last. Danny Brogan could take Jackie Bradberry with one hand tied behind his back.

'Killer,' Danny said, and laughed, fed up with having to feel guilty for his father making his mother so sad. He had done what she asked, he had tried to be Jackie's friend. It hadn't worked out. He wasn't to blame.

'What's up? What's up, "Killer"?' Danny said, taunting now, not bothering to hide his contempt.

'What's up? I called you out, that's what's up,' Jackie said, his voice creaking, its pitch uncertain.

'Why? I didn't do anything. I don't want to fight you.'

'Oh, what, are you chicken? You afraid to fight me, is that it?'

'Nah, I just . . . I just don't see the point. I mean, a fight should be for a reason, and I didn't do anything to you, did I?'

'I saw you,' Jackie said, and he contorts his face into a snarl so cartoonish it makes Danny laugh, involuntarily.

'That's right, laugh. That's what you were doing with your buddies, weren't you, laughing at me?'

'Why would I laugh at you, Jackie? Sorry, Killer. Why would I bother? I mean, you've got your friends, I've got mine. What's the big deal?'

Jackie flinched again, like Danny sort of knew he would, like a dog that's been hit too often, all you've got to do is raise your hand; Jackie'd been told he was dumb so many times he smarted at the hint of it. He flashed back to their second day, when Danny was trying to make the effort with Jackie, for his mom's sake. Some kid had brought in his father's Purple Heart from the Korean War for Show and Tell and it had gone missing, and Mrs Johnson started this whole big investigation where she asked everyone in the class if they had taken it, and then she was going to search everyone's bag, and she said she had ways of finding out who had taken it so the guilty person had better just own up now, and Danny leaned into Jackie and said, 'Who does she think she is, Sherlock Holmes?' And Jackie had looked at him blankly, and said, 'Who is Sherlock Holmes?' And even if he hadn't read any Sherlock Holmes stories, 'cause he couldn't really read properly, he should have heard of Sherlock Holmes from the old movies, which were always on TV, or when Daffy Duck played Dorlock Holmes, and without meaning to, just by reflex, Danny made a face, the kind of face he would have made with Dave or Ralph, a face that said, 'what's the matter, are you dumb or something?' And Jackie's face just fell, like he'd been asked that question for real a hundred times a day every day of his life. He flinched and he flushed and he turned away, humiliated, belittled, back in his box. *Who is Sherlock Holmes?*

Jackie was trying to say something, to explain, to justify himself, but he couldn't get past the sneer on Danny's face, past the barrage of words: *what's the big deal, why would I laugh at you, why would I fight you, why would I give a damn about someone like you?* So he gave up trying, and hurled himself at Danny, like a maddened girl, Danny told the guys later, like your sister when you got her worked up good and mad till she can't be teased any more and loses it. The guys had cracked up at that, he remembers them laughing, for real this time, all laughing at Jackie Bradberry, gathered on their bikes outside Mallatt's on Kingsley Way later that evening drinking sodas, Dave and Ralph and Gene, laughing at Jackie Bradberry who fought like a girl, who Danny tried to go easy on, but even though Jackie couldn't fight his way out of a paper bag, he kept on coming until Danny bloodied his nose and blackened his right eye and doubled him up with a punch to the solar plexus that made him bring up his lunch. Danny left him there, hawking his guts up in the dirt. He hadn't felt like laughing at him then. But later, with all the guys, he told the story, and they laughed and he laughed.

It was the last time he would laugh at Jackie Bradberry.

The next day, Brian and Eric Bradberry were waiting for him when he was cycling along Vilas Park Drive to school. He sometimes wonders, maybe if he had just kept cycling . . . what? He would never have started the fire, and Brian and Eric, not to mention Jackie, and all the other Bradberrys, would still be alive? That was lame reasoning. You couldn't run away forever. They were going to get him sometime. May as well be now. He pulled into the side of the road and followed them, wheeling his bike. They had their dog with them, a 57-varieties mutt called Killer. Jesus, Danny thought as he followed them in among the trees of Vilas Park, Jackie wanted Jason and Chad to call him after his brothers' fucking *dog*?

The worst of it wasn't the beating, although Eric and Brian didn't leave anything out: not content with bloodying his nose and blackening both eyes and making him throw up, Eric and Brian, who were thirteen and fourteen, used their boots. They kicked him in the balls, and in the head, and in the ass, right up the ass, which hurt in the worst fucking way, like a needle or something, and they kicked his shins and his back. They kicked the shit out of him, and Killer danced around, barking with excitement. And when he thought they were finished, when he begged them for mercy, when he wept, they stopped, panting.

'Now you see, you little bitch,' Eric said.

'Squally little brat.'

'You touch our brother again, you get that ten times over, you hear?'

'Yes,' Danny whimpered.

'You squeal on us, you get it twenty times.'

'You hear?'

'Yes.'

'You swear?'

'I swear.'

'What do you swear?'

'I swear I won't touch Jackie again. I swear I won't tell.'

'Little bitch. Look at the little bitch, weeping for his mommy.'

Danny was kneeling, heaving, crying, trying not to cry, eyes closed. The dog had stopped barking. He wondered if they had gone. He was afraid to open his eyes and check. But then he found out that they hadn't gone. The dog had stopped barking to take a crap, and Eric and Brian found a couple of sticks and skewered the fresh dog shit and dumped it on Danny's hair, rubbing it in with the sticks, through his hair, down his neck, around his cheeks, up his nose, down the front of his sweatshirt. It took him weeks before he didn't think he smelled *of* dog shit; months before he didn't think he could smell dog shit.

'Smelly little bitch.'

'Bitch stinks of shit, doesn't she?'

And that wasn't the worst of it.

The worst was what followed.

Every day, Jackie Bradberry passed a note along the class to him, written for him by Jason or Chad, mostly Jason, because Chad was even dumber than Jackie.

you are dead. killer

and

death ground after school dont be Late KILLER

and

See what a fare fight is like, bitch boy

Once, Danny put his hand up immediately after one of the notes had arrived, to answer a question, except he couldn't help notice the stricken expression on Jackie's face, as if he thought he was going to rat him out. Jackie was still scared, and Danny still almost felt sorry for him. *Who is Sherlock Holmes?*

But whether he was scared or not, it amounted to the same thing: Jackie could do what he liked now, and Danny couldn't lay a finger on him.

At first, Danny just tried to avoid him, slipping out of school before he got a chance to catch him, taking the long way home and into school, keeping constant watch on where he might be at any time. But you couldn't run away for ever. He met him one afternoon at the death ground. Jackie's note had said:

death ground call you out and bring two of yore fag freinds for back up

Dave and Gene came with him.

Jackie was there with Jason and Chad, who looked petrified, and with good cause, as Eric and Brian had said nothing about protecting either of them, and before Jackie could raise a hand, Gene Peterson was on top of the pair of them and actually knocked their heads together, twice, and they took off over the wall like they had jet engines up their asses. Jackie started squealing about his brothers, and Gene, who was a head taller than anyone else in the class, and the guy they'd all have liked to be – not the smartest, or the coolest, but the most manly; the one whose approval you looked for; the guy you tried to make laugh and wanted to impress – Gene looked at Jackie Bradberry and said, 'Go ahead, Jackie, you can do what you like now, on account of your brothers.'

And Jackie walked up to Danny and hit him hard in the stomach, and in the ribs, and hit him a few times in the face, splitting his lip, and then swung at him with a left hook that knocked him down. When Jackie tried to follow through with his feet when Danny was on the ground, Gene Peterson came in and bundled him out of it.

'My brothers said . . .'

'"My brothers said." You little sissy boy,' Gene said. 'You should be ashamed of yourself. What do you think you've got here, target practice? "My brothers said." Fuck off. Now!'

And Gene lifted a right hand the size of a shovel, and waved it at Jackie, and Jackie took off. But he walked slowly, and resentfully, reluctantly, stopping at the wall.

'I'm gonna tell Eric and Brian about this.'

'That figures,' Gene said. 'A snitch, a little rat as well as a sissy. Go tell your brothers.'

Jackie told Eric and Brian, and two days later, they caught Gene Peterson in Wingra Park and broke his arm with a tire iron. Gene said he caught them each a couple of good shots, and maybe he had, but everyone knew it didn't make any difference. That was it as far as the resistance to the Bradberrys went. From then on, it was note after note, threat after threat, all from Jackie to Danny. Danny went back to the death ground twice more on his own, didn't even tell the guys, because Jackie didn't want him to, or because he feared they wouldn't come and back him up even if he asked them, for fear of what Jackie's brothers might do, and let Jackie Bradberry kick the shit out of him each time, and stopped feeling sorry for him pretty smartly. And then he tried to deal with it in other ways. First, he'd play sick at home, and get off school that way. But the doctor would be called, not all the time, but often enough. So then, what Danny did was, when he'd get the note, he'd start to shake, and he'd feel the heat in his brow, and he'd actually start to cry, and when Mrs Johnson noticed him, or some kid brought it to her attention, Danny'd say he had a terrible pain in his stomach, some kind of cramp, or spasm, and sometimes he'd get to see the nurse, and sometimes he'd just get sent home, and every one of these times, he'd see the stricken, scared face of Jackie Bradberry.

And everyone else's face was kind of weird, because everyone else in the class knew what was happening, but it wasn't happening to *them*, so they didn't really give a shit, and besides, Danny was eleven, and look at him, every other day, there he was, crying. Jesus. What a fucking crybaby.

And that's when Danny decided that there was only one solution: Jackie Bradberry was going to have to die.

Extract from
Trick or Treat
Unpublished manuscript by Ralph Cowley

Danny

A Couple of Swells

While Jeff Torrance does the driving, Danny Brogan wonders if it was the house that had been the root of the problem. The original sin, the worm in the apple. Danny's grandfather, Old Dan Brogan, had made a lot of money selling land to the University of Wisconsin back in the 1930s, when they were originally establishing the Arboretum, now over 1,250 acres of forestry and horticulture tended to resemble the original wilderness as it would have been before white men arrived in Wisconsin. Pre-settlement Wisconsin. A vision, a dream of Eden. Old Dan kept back a plot of land on which his own house stood, running between the track that would become Arboretum Avenue and Lake Wingra, and enclosed the grounds in a dry-stone wall with high iron gates to front and rear, and retreated inside and drank himself to death while his wife raised Danny's father, Dan Junior. The house came down through Dan Junior, who in due course pulled much the same kind of exit as his father, to Danny, who bought his sister Donna out and moved in when he and Claire married. It was the only dwelling for a couple of miles. The university had initially tried hard to persuade Old Dan Brogan to relocate but he was reclusive and ornery and had come out to the unsettled West Side to get away from people in the first place and refused to move. And however each successive Brogan male differed from his father, they resembled each other in this, at least: the Brogan house was a part of the woods, and there it would stay.

But Danny knew that if it hadn't been for the daily charge of Brogan's Bar and Grill, he would have gone mad out there himself and plugged steadily into the same arrangement as his father and grandfather before him. Maybe he was starting to go that way anyway. Maybe the house was haunted with failure and self-pity, and worse. Maybe that's what had caused Claire to pine for her

old life. Not that he would know. One of the things he and Claire
shared, along with an unfashionable dislike and distrust – disdain,
even – of technology, was an equally unfashionable discomfort
with full and frank conversation. It wasn't that they wanted to
keep secrets from one another, more that neither felt their
marriage vows entitled them to be told anything the other didn't
feel like telling.

So Danny had never asked Claire about her relationships in
Chicago, and she had never asked what he had got up to while she
was away. They had both agreed: the problems in a marriage come
when there's no mystery, no distance, no *otherness* to the loved
one. Familiarity breeds, if not necessarily contempt then certainly
a level of disrespect. Their reticence with each other would help
keep things alive. And their diligence in this respect was rewarded:
the problems in their marriage, when they duly came, had the
distinction of not being the ones they had guarded against.

They had headed north on I-39 for about fifty miles last night
and stayed in a bed and breakfast place that didn't quite call
itself an 'Inne' but may as well have; there were pieces of lace
over every available seat back and the antique furniture looked
like it was going to buckle if you breathed on it. They rose before
dawn and left without waiting for breakfast, partly because they
wanted to be at Oxford Federal Correctional Institution by eight
a.m., but mainly because the proprietors of the Inne that didn't
call itself an Inne, Larry and Jennifer Pyke, a man and woman
of uncertain age and appearance, appeared starved of human
society. It had taken Jeff and Danny three-quarters of an hour to
get away from the Pykes the previous evening, such was their
determination to share details of their past lives in Chicago and
New York, where they may or may not have achieved great things
in The Theater. Danny found it almost impossible to focus on
what they were saying, so fascinated had he become by the look
of the couple: Larry thin, almost shrunken, but still vigorous,
with a vermilion ascot, a quilted smoking jacket, gray pants,
patent leather shoes, a plume of dyed black hair and what looked
very much to Danny like eye shadow; Jennifer an overly made-
up, golden-haired ex-beauty, like a late-period Gabor sister, or
Ginger Rogers in her talk-show phase, coquettish and predatory
and grotesquely overweight in black and gold Chinese robes and

tiny little red high-heeled Dorothy slippers. Jeff was in no great rush to abandon the conversation, admittedly, which ranged across subjects as various as Ronald Coleman, the Dolly Sisters, the films of Mitchell Leisen and Hollywood actresses who portrayed nuns as opposed to those who *became* nuns, and would have happily sat up drinking tea with them into the night, thereby slaking his taste for the bizarre and relish of the absurd, not to mention his general preference for the company of old people.

Danny looks across the table at Jeff now. He is so much more reliable than he lets on; even Danny forgets it now and then. It's like a front he keeps up to fend off the world: the stoner, the slacker, the wastrel. They have found a Denny's for breakfast, the best they could do, and are on their third refill of coffee. It may be Monday morning but it's Columbus Day, so they had the place to themselves at six; it's filling up a little as it approaches seven-thirty. Everyone who comes in, male, female or indeterminate, takes a good squint at Jeff, which is the way it's always been. He's looking good as ever as he approaches fifty: his blond hair has not yet faded to gray, and he still wears it just long enough on the curve between youthful and delusional, pushed back from his chiseled, lean, tan face; he has always favored a hippyish, Native American look, with random beads and braids and strips of leather and even, in his hair, a couple of ribbons. At six-four, in Levis, black western shirt and cowboy boots, Jeff looks very well indeed, and you don't need to take Danny's word for it: if Jeff spends a night in Brogan's and goes home alone, it's because he's tired, and Danny usually has to commiserate with more than one disappointed customer wondering how she played her cards wrong.

Given the fact that Jeff has never held down a job it's maybe surprising that he should have kept in such shape. He has lived at home with his mom, a wealthy widow who adores her son and always thought it completely unnecessary for Jeff to go out and work when he didn't have to. In his twenties, Jeff thought this an excellent plan, since having a job would interfere with his other pursuits, namely smoking pot and staying up all night watching videos and playing computer games and reading three- and six- and nine-volume science-fiction sagas.

For a few years, after Claire left for Chicago, Danny hooked up with Jeff and they lived in a kind of dedicated drift, steadily adding stronger drugs and alcohol into the equation and dallying the while with the kind of women who were sufficiently under-motivated themselves to believe that such a plan was indeed excellent. The Torrance estate was happy to bankroll it all, as long as Jeff agreed to eat dinner with his mother every other night and to simulate a desire to 'be creative' in some non-specific artistic or literary way without going to the trouble of producing any actual work.

Then Danny's father died and Danny stepped up to manage Brogan's, which meant an end to aimlessness, for him, at least. He stopped taking drugs, even stopped smoking weed, which neither he nor Jeff considered the same thing at all. Jeff saw no need to follow suit, and continued on his merry, aimless way. There was never any shortage of aimless wastrels in Madison to accompany him, each with their own, invariably spurious, 'creative' alibi. Jeff's was writing, not that he did anything so vulgar as actually write.

This was the life Jeff led: the drinking and the smoking, the reading and eating dinner and listening to music with his mom, the sleeping with other men's wives and girlfriends (because single women, dazed with awe by the scale of Jeff's lack of ambition, always gave up on him as a potential partner-for-life, but often returned for respite, sometimes for years afterwards). And of course, the letting Danny know he would always be there if and when Danny needed him, because the reason Jeff ended up doing a three-year stretch in Fox Lake and not dead is because Danny helped him out, and someone else is dead and not Jeff. Danny didn't need to know what Jeff had done; the fact that he needed his help was enough. It was money Danny helped him with, mostly, money Jeff didn't want to ask his mother for, and Danny had always had enough money, although of course he doesn't any more.

Jeff looks him in the eye now, and despite the strain Danny's under – he slept heavily for about three hours and then lay awake from four a.m., fretting, and planning and, truth be told, crying, just a little, kettle-boiling-over kind of tears that quickly subside and get mopped up – he can feel himself about to lose it, and Jeff grins and says, quietly, ventriloquizing the fluted, fruity voices of their hosts, half Hollywood-Raj, half white-shoe country-club, 'We of the theater, you see,' and Danny cracks up. Jeff could always make him laugh at the best of times, simply by catching his eye, and he's an excellent mimic.

'Isn't that *extra-ordi*nary? You came from Cambridge, and here you are in *Oxford*!' Jeff arches a lazy eyebrow in tribute to the baroque eccentricities of their hosts at the not-Inne. 'You are among us here in Oxford, but you are lately of *Cambridge*! Do not think us strange: we are of the Theater, you see, the Theater.'

Jeff is an old hand at showbiz impersonations, adept at capturing the preposterous bullshit actors spout on chat shows, and Danny has always been a sucker for it. He has wondered in the past if some of his laughter has its roots in anger – anger towards Claire and what he sometimes feels are her illusions about her illustrious past, her talent, her wasted potential. She can still, watching a movie, be moved to tears of what Danny knows is not empathy with the character but envy at the actress, and it's always an actress, always of Claire's age, and a quiet couple of days will follow, and while Danny sympathizes, and never says anything, sometimes he just wants to shout, 'It was never that great to begin with, and it's over for good now. Do you think you're the only one whose dreams haven't worked out?'

He never does, and he's glad, because this is not how he really feels – or at least, not unless he's got half a bottle of Jack inside him, and if a man acted on all the things he feels when he's drunk on whiskey, he'd be dead or in jail. And because it would be unkind, and make him less of a man. And what dreams, exactly, did he have, aside from marrying the woman of his dreams?

'Rosalind and dear Audrey, *portrayed* nuns, but June Haver, having been a Dolly Sister, actually *became* a nun. Or at least, a novice. Before finally finding lifelong happiness with Fred McMurray.'

Danny's laughter is helpless, back-of-the-class stuff, like a mind-altering drug. If he can't get this release by letting himself cry full-on, maybe laughter is the way to go. If only Jeff had been around in junior high, Danny thinks. In fact, Dave Ricks was very like Jeff: easily as funny, as fine a mimic, with as acute a relish for the absurd. All he and Dave seemed to do was laugh together in, absolutely, the back of the class. Until that Halloween, when the laughter dried up for a time. When it came back, it was never quite the same. But Danny is sure Jeff would have known how to defuse the Bradberry situation. Even at the time, in the midst of his panic and his fear, Danny remembers thinking it was just dumb that it got so out of hand, and his friends were no help, apart from Gene Peterson, of course, but Gene had always been a stand-up guy.

Or at least, Danny had always thought so, until the past suddenly erupted out of a family barbecue, relentless and unalterable, ready as ever to destroy him. But Danny Brogan is not going to let himself be destroyed. Danny Brogan is going to fight back. And the first round in the fight is visiting Jonathan Glatt in jail.

The Boulevard of Broken Dreams

The Federal Prison Camp in Oxford is around the corner from the Correctional Institution, near the junction of county roads A and E. Danny presents his driving license, along with the visitor authorization form he had applied for two weeks back and finally received in the mail on Friday. He processes through a metal detector and sets it off. An officer pats him down with meaty hands, and his coins, watch and sunglasses are removed and stowed. He takes off his belt and is admitted to the visiting room.

An ex-con who drank in Brogan's once told Danny prison smells like when you have shit on your shoe, but before you figure out that's where it's coming from: there's a terrible, deathly smell, but you don't know what it is – *and it's like that all the time.* And that's what the visiting room smells like: sweat and stale air and body odor and pungent cleaning product and tobacco smoke and cheap air freshener. And shit. The chairs in the room are mostly too small, little child-size plastic chairs that are hard to squeeze into and out of. They don't appear to help the smell either, because once you sit, your knees ride up and your face comes closer to your feet, so even if you don't actually have shit on your shoe, you think you do. Like a demoralized priest who has heard one confession too many, Danny had forgotten what the ex-con told him across the sanctity of the bar counter; now, as he furtively checks the soles of his shoes and finds them clean, that's when he remembers.

There are about twenty-five people waiting, adults and children, seated around tables. Some of the adults even have adult-sized chairs. Danny stands and his chair comes with him, making him feel like a trainee clown. He unsnaps himself and tries another chair, but it's no better. He flashes on a visit he and Claire made once to a prospective, legendarily select kinder-garden for the girls, where they were seated in the same kind of chairs while the 'director' of the center, a humorless woman in a brocade coat and floral Birkenstocks and red-framed spectacles, talked at them about child-centered learning and whole-ness and wellness and the vital need for full parental participation and Danny suppressed the urge to ask, if they were going to shell out so much money, why they had to participate fully as well, only for Claire to announce, when the meeting was through, that her career, such as it was (and at the time, it didn't even amount to teaching) couldn't justify her parking the kids in a creche, even one so dedicated to child-centered wellness. He remembers the moment because of the chairs, but also because it was emblematic of one aspect of their marriage: behavior on Claire's part of which Danny disapproves (wishing to place the children in a creche when she has no job to go to) but tacitly appears to condone; and then a policy change where she comes around to his position, without his having argued his case. And so he feels triumph (that he will get his own way) and pride (that Claire and he are of one mind on so much) and a certain shame at his own passivity – what kind of man will not from time to time openly disagree with his own wife? The kind of man he is, it seems; the kind of man who would rather sit in a child's chair than walk around the room until he has found one to fit an adult. The kind of man who, rather than ask his wife if she's been unfaithful to him, rather than tell her the extent to which their life is falling apart, will vanish with her children so he can try and put a stop to it.

When the prisoners enter, all dressed in spruce-green work shirts and pants, Danny stands, wriggling once more out of his chair. A blond-haired, pasty-faced prison guard weighing maybe three hundred pounds approaches, his breathing audible before he speaks.

'Mr Brogan?'

Danny nods.

'Outside, sir.'

Danny follows the guard out, wondering what has gone wrong. Has he knowingly made a false declaration on his visitor application form? Maybe the cash in his wallet has been found to be counterfeit. That would be theater people for you. But now, here they are outside on a wooden patio stretching the length of the visiting room. There are four picnic tables fixed to the floor, and Jonathan Glatt in prison greens is seated at one of them.

'Said he wanted the air. Said you wouldn't mind,' the guard says.

'I don't.'

'Too cold out here for everyone else,' the guard says in a peevish tone, sounding as if it was too cold out here for him.

Danny can see the camp's perimeter fence, and Jeff's Mustang in the parking lot, and beyond the highway, a mix of trees stretching toward the horizon, some almost bare of leaves, some evergreen and glistening in the burning fall sunshine. He was going to have to tell Jeff something – not the truth, or at least, not the whole truth, but a more accurate version of the truth than he'd told his sister. In the meantime . . . in the meantime, it *is* cold out here, but at least it doesn't smell of shit.

'I won't be long,' Danny says to the guard, placatory as ever. Danny the pleaser. He sits down at the table opposite Jonathan Glatt, while the guard lingers on the steps at the rear entrance to the facility. Glatt, whose tan has faded since the last time Danny saw him, but who still looks like a guy with a winter tan, twenty pounds heavier with close cropped silver hair and silver-rimmed glasses, looks at his visitor through milky-blue eyes with no recognition whatsoever, taps a bitten nail on the cover of a black Moleskine notebook and begins to speak.

'Mr Brogan,' he says, nodding his head philosophically. 'I

may not remember every face, but . . . Danny Brogan, two hundred and fifty-seven grand . . . what can I say?' Glatt's accent is Chicago, Danny doesn't know which part, but it certainly sounds a lot more dis dat dese and dose than it did the last time they met, when he had the perky little Meg Ryan of a wife. Before Danny has a chance to say, 'Sorry would be nice, you dick,' Glatt starts up again.

'Sorry, of course, I can say sorry, and I *do* say that, but do you want to know something? And I appreciate you may not want to hear this, and objectively, hey, of course I regret, which is a mealy-mouthed word, I am *sorry* your money is gone. "Is gone", mealy-mouthed again. I am sorry I "stole" it. Except, thing is, since I had no *intention* of stealing money from anyone, I find it hard, not to say impossible, to "own up", to bear what you might think is an appropriate burden of guilt, because without *intention* . . . you see what I'm saying? I didn't break into anyone's house, am I wrong? And sure, it happened, and it's down to me: I had your money, and now it's gone, and who else is here? But it's, what will we say, like that kids' party game, musical chairs? Where they take away a chair each time and the children are caught standing while the music's playing? And then they're out of the game? That's how it happened, this whole financial melt-down: out of fear that the music's gonna stop and there'll be no chairs left. So someone panics, because of some fucking thing some guy says in a newspaper, or, or, the chairman of the Fed, or some mouth almighty in fucking *Frankfurt*, someone comes crying, he wants his money back, he tells someone *else*, then all of a sudden everybody wants his money so he can take it home put it under the fucking mattress. Now, forgive me, but if this is how everyone is going to behave, well, is that my fault? Because you cannot run a bank, an investment scheme, you cannot run a financial system, if everyone wants to keep their money under the fucking bed because they're scared for No Good Reason. And you, my friend, you got burned, I'm sorry, and technically, yes, I'm responsible, but I'm gonna tell you, it's like that guy wrote many years ago – The Madness of Crowds is what's to blame.'

Danny hadn't intended to lash out, judging it a waste of breath: get the information he needs and move on. But the human spirit, while it may be indomitable, is also only human.

'Are you kidding me? What a self-deluding asshole you are. They catch you cold in the street, you're out of your mind on *drugs*, you're partying with teenage *girls*, you've bought your stripper girlfriend a *condo* . . .'

Glatt nods and does the philosophical shrug again, an 'all the same to me' look in his eyes.

'No contest. Am I going to deny I turned into four-fifths of an asshole there? Lead us not into temptation, you know what I mean? They didn't make that prayer up for no reason. And I'm going to spend the rest of my life likely as not incarcerated, and my wife and daughters are never going to speak to me again. And as I am a man, let me be a man, and live with what I have done as a man. But what I want to say to you (because you might find it a help) is this: Jonathan Glatt was not a fantasy. Jonathan Glatt was not Bernie Madoff, my friend. The funds my investors placed in my trust were in turn invested, widely and wisely. Just, a) when returns weren't as eye-catching, or as brisk, as you wanted (I don't mean you personally, I mean The Public At Large), we proceeded to b) bolster the yields with a little help from the new accounts. Which is strictly speaking not permitted. But hey, it's what everybody wants, am I wrong? These days, everyone wants to think he's the smart guy with the edge on everyone else. Everyone has an entitlement complex. Everyone wants more than he deserves, believes he deserves more than he does. No one wants to wait in line. And as long as new clients kept arriving, and the old clients were happy with their dividends, as long as we kept all the chairs in the game, nobody lost. As long as we didn't stop the music, everyone was dancing. You wanna know something, Mr Brogan? And I concede, I took my eye off the ball there, what with the drugs, and the girls, and so forth, Jonathan Glatt is human, all too human, and he only has himself to blame, but, and I believe this: if everyone had kept their heads, and not called their money in, hey, we'd all be dancing still.'

Danny can't take any more: his head slumps and he holds his hands up above it, palms out, imploring Glatt to halt.

'This is not why I'm here in any case,' Danny says. 'I mean, not that I don't think you're a delusional fuck who will never get what he deserves, which is probably, I don't know, death by public burning or some such, maybe that medieval thing where they disembowel you but you're still alive—'

'Hung, drawn and quartered. I saw that on the History Channel. Or was it BBC World? First they—'

'Shut the fuck up and listen,' Danny says. 'I am not a member of your general public. I used to put my savings, when I had any, in the bank. You were recommended to me by an old school-friend of mine, name of Gene Peterson. An old friend I believed I could trust. Do you remember him? Gene Peterson? We met you for dinner.'

Glatt makes a thinking face, like a politician on TV pretending to consider a question, then he goes in his notebook.

'Gene Peterson, Gene Peterson. Yes. Gene Peterson. He brought a few investors my way, not just you.'

'All right. Well listen up, Mr Glatt. I'm not here to remonstrate with you or to ask you why you stole my money. I'm not even here to abuse you, although obviously the temptation is great. And I certainly don't want to hear your justifications and rationalisations, your, uh, "philosophy of life", such as it is. All I want you to answer, a couple questions about Gene Peterson. First, give me the names of the other investors he brought to you.'

'I don't think that would be . . .'

Glatt tails off, and makes a vague gesture with one hand.

Danny laughs.

'I'm sorry. What was that? Ethical? "I don't think that would be ethical", is that what you were reaching for there? You're a riot, do you know that, a laugh riot. You should take this act on the road. You're ready for prime time, yes you are. All right, let's do it this way: I say a name, and you say yes if I'm right, no if I'm wrong, how's that? That doesn't violate your "ethical code", does it?'

Glatt grimaces, rolls his eyes and shakes his head.

'Dave Ricks.'

Glatt nods.

'I know Ralph Cowley for sure.'

Glatt nods.

'That's the gang all there. And did they all lose out? Did you fuck them all over?'

Glatt goes in his notebook again.

'No. Matter of fact, each of them got out in time, and they were ahead when they did so.'

'How much? Given your twenty-five grand minimum?'

'Not like you. Less than forty K apiece, that kind of neighborhood.'

'And Gene?'

'Gene? Gene cashed out early too.'

'He *what*? He . . . so I was the sucker. Gene got me in, and I came in for a huge whack, and his reward was, he got out?'

'That's not exactly how I'd put it. But I can see that's how it appears.'

'How'd you know Gene?'

Glatt does the gesture with his hand again, a flourish in the air, redolent of complexity, the abstract, the uncertain. How does anyone know anything?

'I meet . . . I *used* to meet so many people,' he says. 'It could be anywhere. A dinner, a function, the gym. With Gene, our kids went to the same school in Chicago, in Oak Park, got to be friends, our wives, so on.'

'I thought you were based in Milwaukee.'

'Most of my business, my offices are . . . *were* in Milwaukee. My family lives in Chicago. My family . . .'

Glatt bows his head, shakes it, lifts it.

'You know they never visit, have never visited. My wife, maybe not a surprise. My *kids* . . . my daughters are fifteen and twelve. I haven't seen or heard from them in six months.'

Danny looks at Glatt, whose eyes have filled up, and thinks of all the families that he stole from, the families that he brought to ruin. He thinks of his own family, and tries to make it all Glatt's fault. But he knows it's not, knows that at least one of his old friends, his former friends, is to blame. Knows, too, that he is to blame himself. He thought he deserved extra. He thought he was entitled to something for nothing.

'So everyone has a sob story,' Glatt says. 'Gene . . . we played tennis. He's a guy, what, you were at school with him? I bet he was the captain of the team, whatever team, the guy you wanted to impress.'

Danny doesn't nod or agree, doesn't want to risk complicity with Glatt. (Although to be honest, how much worse could it get? There's nothing left for Glatt to steal.) But yes, that's exactly what Gene was like. Still is.

'Because all the time, people were asking me, how can I get in on this thing? Pushing themselves forward. Eager. Greedy. Breadheads. It used to disgust me. Human nature, it can be dismaying. Gene was different. First thing he asked was, could he bring other people in, people he thought deserved a shot in the arm. It was his condition for signing up. He got in himself, then, once everyone else was established, he got out. And he didn't lose a dime. In fact, he made a lot, quite a lot of money.'

Danny's heard enough. He stands, nodding at Glatt, unable for the moment to speak.

Glatt looks up. 'There was one other person,' he says, his finger scrolling down a page of the open notebook.

'Excuse me?' Danny says.

'There was one other guy Gene Peterson brought in. I never met him. But he got out ahead as well.'

One other guy. But there were no other guys. Just Dave and Danny, Ralph and Gene. No other guys who knew.

'And who was that?' Danny says.

'Looking for the name . . . here he is . . . in fact, not a he. Claire is not a guy's name, is it?'

'Claire? Claire who?' Danny says, his voice cracking.

'Claire . . . Bradberry, it says here,' Jonathan Glatt says. 'Claire Bradberry. Ring any bells?'

It All Depends on You

At least the kids are all right. That is the only thing keeping Danny even remotely sane as he and Jeff drive the I-90 to Chicago to check out Dave Ricks and Gene Peterson: the fact that Barbara and Irene are safely stowed with his sister Donna. Not that Donna had been especially pleased to see him last night. He had tried to get in and out without too much by way of explanation, but that was never going to work, not with Donna.

'Danny, the deal is if you want me to keep looking after your kids, you have to tell me what's going on,' she finally said.

Sunday night, same old, same old, Danny and Donna going at it head to head in the living room. He turned away to see them both reflected in Donna's picture window, stretching across one entire wall. Roll back thirty years and younger incarnations of themselves would have been taking the Sunday-night blues out on each other: what to watch on TV; who didn't help who with his homework (Donna never needed any help with hers); whose turn it was to walk the dog.

And there they were, at it again, not in the family home off Arboretum Avenue but in Donna's flat-roofed modernist house on the side of a hill overlooking Lake Ripley in Cambridge, Wisconsin. Danny had always wondered whether it was a Frank Lloyd Wright, or school of, if there was a school of. He had never wanted to ask Donna because if it was a Frank Lloyd Wright, she would be mad at him for being dumb, and if it wasn't, she would be mad because it wasn't. But that didn't seem like much of a consideration, since she was mad as hell at the best of times and for no reason at all. Still, Danny figured there was no point in provoking her, although throughout their lives, this had been a far from reliable plan: if Donna were a country, she would have been North Korea, hugely secretive and impossible to fathom, but liable at any time to drop a bomb on you or shoot at you from over the border, just to keep you on your toes.

She got the house as part of her settlement from the guy who was a Big Man in Computers, or Dot.Coms, or Finance, Brad, or maybe Thad; Danny only met him twice, once at the wedding, and then when he came into town on his own, got drunk at the bar in Brogan's, burst into tears and asked Danny if he thought Donna had ever actually liked anyone. Danny thought about it, although not for long, and then said no, not really. The marriage ended soon after.

Everything changed when Danny had kids. Suddenly there were two people Donna could definitely be said to like, not to mention love: Barbara and Irene. She started to show up at the house unannounced, which freaked Claire out, since Donna had never hidden her disdain for Claire, and never let pass an opportunity to mention some Chicago actor who coincidentally was Claire's age and was doing really well in New York or London or Hollywood, see, here she is on TMZ with Kate Winslet.

Eventually, Danny told her that if she wanted to see the girls, she had to either pretend to be polite to Claire or to just shut up around her, and Donna consented to a combination of these approaches, grunting helloes and goodbyes and thank yous through a fixed grin that looked like a four-year-old's felt-tip scrawl. Because she really did want to see the girls, and they really did want to see her. And she would take them at the drop of a hat for weekends and even on week nights, letting them sleep over and dropping them the twenty miles to school the next day, and for weeks at Easter and summer. And she was *nice* to them, in a kind of old-school strict-but-fair way, and made sure they read their Maud Hart Lovelace and Laura Ingalls Wilder before their Meg Cabot, and taught them to sew and to knit and to cook and lots of other stuff Claire and Danny couldn't or wouldn't have, or didn't have time to, using all the school-teacher skills she trained for but had never used, until 'When can we go stay with Aunt Donna?' became the most spoken phrase in the house. And since neither Danny nor Claire had any other living relatives, Donna's rudeness was allowed to dwindle into an endearing piece of family mythology, because where else were they going to get such reliable child care?

Danny looked back across the open-plan room and into the big kitchen, where Barbara and Irene sat around the table, their heads bent in concentration as they inked and colored and outlined some elaborate Manga-style comic they had created with Donna's assistance and encouragement, drawing each other's attention to this or that detail, laughing out loud at their work. He thought of how quickly, once they got over their disappointment at not seeing their mom, they had acquiesced in his suggestion that they stay with Aunt Donna an extra few days, an acceptance made easier by the DS games Danny had stopped off at Target to get and the new Halloween costumes he popped for at Mallatt's on Kingsley Way, vampire for Barbara, who's read all the Twilight and Vladimir Todd books, Kitty-Kat for Irene, who, well, likes kitty-kats.

Then he tracked back past Donna's glowering face to the window, the better to avoid replying to her question, clocking her reflection again. She was dressed in the Mid-West mufti she adopted after Brad or Thad split the scene: deck shoes and slacks and a plaid shirt over a turtle neck, her hair cut short and sprayed in place like a piece of hard candy, the Methodist minister's brisk, no-nonsense wife. Her sleeves were buttoned at the wrist and her turtle neck nudged her chin, because her arms and chest and, for all Danny knew, much of her lower body too, were a mosaic of lurid tattoos, a legacy of the five years she spent with that motorcycle guy in Oakland. Or maybe it was those motor- cycle guys. There was rehab after that, and possibly a short stay in a psychiatric unit. There were also gay phases, one as a dyed blonde (or it could have been a wig, Danny only saw photos) lipstick lesbian, one as a Goth (the piercings at least were easily removable). There was the buttoned-up secretary phase, which was when she met Brad, or Thad, who presumably found the fact that beneath her navy suit and high-collared blouse lay the body (art) of a hardcore rock chick a major turn-on. None of that evident last night, looking fully at home in her refuge in the piss-elegant bolt-hole of Cambridge, WI, with its twinky stores full of antiques and pottery and horrible paintings and over-priced chocolates. He wondered if she heard the clock ticking as loudly as before, if one morning it would be Donna who pulled yet another disappearing act.

Danny checked himself briefly in the glass. He was looking remarkably well, he thought, for someone going through what he'd been going through: collar and tie, three-piece dove-gray double-breasted, black Oxfords, he had even remembered to shave. Keeping up appearances: that was his legacy from his parents, just as Donna's rage was hers. Sometimes the self-assurance, the calm, the steadiness feel authentic; he knew Claire believed in them devoutly. But of course, they weren't. He occasionally thought that, of the two, he was the better actor. He'd never shared this thought, of course. He looked again at his mask of a face, and at his twin sister's: with their hair roughly the same length, they'd never resembled each other more. Danny may not have had an angel of death tattoo across his back, but he was equally skilled at keeping secrets.

'Is there someone out there?' Donna said suddenly, snapping off the lamp. The window crash-faded to black and Danny and his sister vanished, to be replaced by the sight of a red Ford Mustang on the gravel drive. The interior light was on, and a slender, middle-aged man with a blond pony-tail could be seen playing with a Nintendo DS console.

'Danny. Answer me. Christ, is that Jeff Torrance out there?'

'It is.'

'What is Jeff Torrance doing here? Why are you getting in a car with Jeff Torrance? Where is your car? Where is Claire? For the third time, what is going on?'

Donna had always had the ability to talk in a low voice but make herself perfectly audible, not to mention intimidating. Danny had had enough of intimidation, and felt he shouldn't have to put up with it from his own sister, however troubled their relationship.

'Was it the nagging that finally did for your marriage? I can see how it might have driven a man to the point of no return.'

'All right then, fuck off. Take the girls and put them in the . . . the car is filling up with smoke. Oh my God, the skank is smoking a joint. Jeff is smoking a joint.'

'Of course he is. That's what Jeff is for. It would be weird if he wasn't.'

'Those girls are not going in that car with Jeff driving.'

'Which is exactly what I'm saying to you.'

Danny almost laughed at the way this has come out. Donna didn't.

'Hey, dickhead, are you taking this seriously? You drive up here last week and ask me to mind your kids while you, what, "sort some stuff out", Claire isn't around and you need to "get your head straight on a couple things". Now you're back, you're telling me less, if that were possible, then last time, and you want me to keep them indefinitely, while you take off with Jeff Torrance to . . . where, Danny? Vegas, baby? If this is a midlife, good luck, but count me out. Where's your *wife*?'

Danny's eyes flashed quickly across to Barbara and Irene, but they couldn't hear, or weren't listening. He flicked his head towards the hall. Once Donna followed him out, he shut the glass door. There was a fountain and indoor foliage and a balcony above. Is that what they called an atrium? It felt more like a private healthcare facility than a home. He had to hand it to Donna, she had sure worked that ex-husband over good.

'Where's your wife, Danny? Have you left her, is that what this is?'

Danny shook his head.

'No. No, it's just . . . I'm in a bit of trouble, Donna.'

Donna looked at Danny with raised eyebrows, her pert mouth and pointed little nose flexing in what resembled contempt, but was actually what Danny recognized as Donna's own strained quality of concern.

'That's the first time in my hearing that you've ever admitted a weakness, little brother,' Donna said, making it sound not altogether like a sneer.

'You sure make a lot of those seventeen minutes, don't you?' Danny said.

They looked each other in the eye.

We haven't spoken this much in years, Danny thought. *Not since I told Dad to leave her alone, and when Dad said, 'Or what?' I showed him. I showed the bastard what.*

'You look like you could do with a drink,' Donna said.

'You have no idea. But I'm traveling with Jeff, so one of us needs to be sober.'

'You're right, I have no idea. But before we get to that, just tell me: what are you doing with that dope-addled buffoon?'

'I couldn't take either of my own vehicles, too easily identifiable. Jeff . . . well, simple as, I don't really know anyone else I can call out of the blue and say, "Hey, wanna take a trip?" and know the reply will be, "Sure," no questions asked, destination unknown. What else was he going to be doing anyway?'

'Waiting for his mom to die, so he can inherit the Torrance house.'

'Hoping his mom *doesn't* die, otherwise who's going to run the cleaners and the cook and the rest of the crew who keep the Torrance house going? Jeff's all right. Don't worry about Jeff.'

'Where's your wife?'

'Claire is . . . I guess she'll be home by now.'

'You guess. What, have you not spoken to her?'

'I've . . . left her a sign.'

Donna waited for her twin brother to explain; when he didn't, she snorted and her small brown eyes flared.

'You left her a *sign*? What is this, the Olden Days? The Streets of Laredo? Why didn't you call her on, you know, the telephone?'

'Donna, and I don't expect this to satisfy you, and I'm sorry, there's a lot I can't tell you, but someone is blackmailing me. Someone from my past.'

Donna laughed out loud, a mirthless, mocking affair.

'You? And your sinister past? Give me a break.'

Danny's face was set, his own small eyes glinting, as close as he came to confrontational.

'I know about the bikers and the rehab and the breakdown. Why don't you use that imagination of yours, which I know is still working overtime if the evidence of all those stories and comics you and the girls cook up together is anything to go by—'

'That's all their own work. And I did not have a breakdown.'

'Well, that's my point. There's loads of stuff I don't know about you, isn't there? We hardly know a thing about each other, haven't done for years, isn't that so? So just imagine what I might have got up to.'

'But all you've done is stick around. I mean, in town. You've run your daddy's bar, you got married, you had kids.'

'The End.'

'Pretty much.'

'Just imagine, Donna. Stuff that's happened to me that you know nothing about.'

'What "stuff"?'

'Stuff I'm not going to tell you about. Because if you don't know, you won't be able to tell anyone else.'

'I won't be able to tell anyone else – like who? Guys who break in to the house and try and torture me? The Agency? *Please.*'

'Someone is . . . on my trail. Which is why I can't call Claire, in case our phones are traced. And it's not just the blackmail. There's . . . some money I borrowed. And I got into trouble paying it back.'

'How much money?'

'A lot of money. I was able to pay it. And then suddenly, I needed more time. And as it turns out, maybe I ran out of time.'

'Danny, what are you saying, you borrowed against . . . what? The business?'

'No, the business is fine, the business is solid. You'll always get a drink and a steak at Brogan's.'

'The house?'

Danny turned away from his sister and stared through the glass door. He could see the tops of his daughters' heads in the warm orange light of the kitchen, their dark hair seeming to glow. When he turned back to speak, it felt to him as if he had borrowed another man's vocal chords. A man who had the strength he feared he lacked.

'Things look bad now, but I'm sure they're going to be OK. I know they're going to be.'

'What will I say to Claire, if she calls? *When* she calls?'

'Try and put her off as long as possible. Maybe send her a message. Don't tell her the kids are here.'

'Why can't I bring them back to her?'

'Because I don't want them in any danger.'

'What does that mean? Is she in danger?'

'I don't know. I don't think so. I hope not. But whatever happens, I want the kids kept safe. They're not safe with me, and they . . . *may* not be safe at the house. If you have to talk to her . . . tell her they're fine, they're with me, not to worry.'

'And the blackmail. Is that connected to the debt?'

'I don't know. Maybe. I can't really tell you any more.'

'Any more? You've barely told me anything in the first place.'

'Well. We all have our secrets.'

'Reasons.'

'Excuse me?'

'The line is "We all have our reasons". It's from a French film.'

'You sound like Claire. Everything's a quote from something. I like "we all have our secrets" better. Besides, it's what I mean.'

Donna looked at her brother closely.

'Do you ever visit their grave?' she said.

'Whose grave?'

'Our parents'.'

'Why would I want to do a thing like that?'

'I don't know. I suppose I always felt . . . it wasn't as bad for you. As it was for me.'

'I had it easy.'

'I don't mean that. Or, who knows, maybe I do. Also, I always thought you'd sell the house. Couldn't figure how you stuck living there.'

'You lived there. When Mom was still alive, and after.'

'That's true. Can't really figure that out either.'

'Lots of people had a tough time with their parents and shit. They seem to make a go of their lives, not let the past drag them down.'

Donna chewed her lip. 'That's true,' she said. 'But you know what the problem is? We can't be lots of people, can we? We can only be ourselves.'

'Most of the time, it's hard to manage even that.'

Danny saw Donna's eyes flicker. That was at least a smile, maybe even a laugh, in anyone else's terms. He looked at his watch. 'I've got to go. There are people . . . I need to track down.'

'Track down? What are you now, a detective? A bounty hunter?'

'No. You're right. I'm just a married guy. A bartender. A suburban dad. That's all. But I have to do this. I'm sorry I can't tell you anything more.'

'You're a secretive prick. You always have been. I just never thought you had anything worth being secretive about.'

'Just because I don't wear it on my sleeve. Or even beneath my sleeves.'

'Go say goodbye to the girls.'

Danny went in and sat with his daughters and told them he had to go.

Irene said, 'Is Mom going to be an actor now?'

Barbara said, 'Yeah right. I don't think so.'

Irene said, 'I miss Mom.'

Barbara said, 'Yeah, but we get to stay at Aunt Donna's for longer.'

Irene considered this, nodded, and returned to her coloring.

Danny hugged them both as hard and long as he could manage without freaking them out, and when each patted him on the shoulder to indicate that Dad should go away now, that's exactly what Dad did.

Ralph's Book

1976

What happened was it was Halloween, or the run up to Halloween, and most kids were on a longer leash than usual, running around at night, even on school nights. Danny was running with his buddies, Dave and Gene and Ralph. The Bradberrys lived over on Schofield, east of Lake Monona. They shouldn't have been at Jefferson in the first place, only for their father had gone there or something. The bullying didn't happen except when they were at school. Danny had a reprieve that summer, and then it all kicked in again in September. But at least he had the nights, and the guys were all saying they had to do something, they just couldn't let it continue the way it had been, and it was decided to stage some kind of Halloween prank over at the Bradberry place.

It was Dave Ricks, Danny thinks, who had the idea. Because the house was beside, or backed onto by, the Catholic church there, and so they could get over the wall or swarm in through the trees and they wouldn't have to go squat in someone else's yard, they could wait there and bide their time and watch for the right moment.

So they decided they would burn big skulls and spiders into the lawn with gasoline and set them ablaze, make a Halloween spectacular. The only thing was, they wanted to be around to see the fun. They wanted to see how absolutely shit-scared they could make, not just Jackie, and Eric and Brian, but all twelve Bradberrys, the whole family, or at least, apart from the two who'd left home. Fourteen, if you count the mom and pop.

They planned it every night, hanging out in the woods down below Nakoma: how they would each siphon the gas out of the

family car, maybe a soda bottle a day for a couple days beforehand, and hide them until Halloween; how they couldn't do it
too early, because it wouldn't be dark enough, and anyway, the
Bradberrys they wanted to scare wouldn't be home until midnight
or later because Jackie and his brothers were all let run wild.
How were they, at eleven years old, going to stay out until two
or three in the morning to put the fear of God into those fuckers
and their family?

Dave Ricks had the original idea, and Dave had the older sister
who made the idea possible. Dave's parents were going to be
away for some convention his father was attending, auto parts,
that was his line, and Dave's sister, who was seventeen, wanted
her boyfriend to stay over, and Dave said he wouldn't tell if the
guys could stay over too, so the sister faked a note from Dave's
mom for all the other moms, and since they were all eleven-year-
old guys, not girls, no one was too bent about the peril they
might get into to the extent of actually checking with Dave's
mom, on top of which, it was 1976 and parents were totally more
laid back about stranger-danger and shit and they all got their
overnight passes.

They found a sheltered area among the trees round the back
of the Catholic church and adjacent to the Bradberrys' backyard
and established themselves there. What had Danny felt that night?
Anger, or fear?

Anger, yes; fear, yes; but something more: the hatred that
comes from persistent, belittling humiliation. He had noticed that
Jackie Bradberry would occasionally forget about bullying him,
sometimes for days on end, Jackie happy enough with Jason and
Chad, tormenting younger kids for their milk money. Their eyes
would meet, and Jackie would half-acknowledge him, as if they
were friends, no, not friends, but contemporaries of equal worth
who had just followed different paths in life but respected each
other nonetheless. And then Jackie would arrive into school even
more disheveled than usual, clothes stained and stinking, hair
tousled and lank, homework undone, maybe even (at least twice,
if not more often) sporting a black eye, or a raw red ear. And
whatever had happened to Jackie, he would promptly pass it on
to Danny in the form of notes and menaces and verbal abuse,
and then of boots and fists. He understood that it wasn't entirely

Jackie's fault, that if Jackie hadn't had his brothers, or hadn't been part of that family, things probably would, or at least, could have been different. But they weren't different, and there was no one else to blame, and Danny hated Jackie Bradberry, so the only solution, because middle school, or junior high as they called it back then, would last until they were fourteen, another three long years of all this, it felt as if there would never be an end to it, Jesus, so the only solution was for Jackie Bradberry to die. But Danny Brogan had not gone out on that Halloween night of 1976 with the intention of making that happen.

There they lay all evening, the four of them, like hunters in a hide, a couple venturing out to trick or treat and bring the haul back to base, even though they considered themselves too old for that kind of kids' stuff: what the hell, they were gonna be hungry there. They dressed in Halloween costumes, ghosts and skeletons, but they'd customized them, with the help of Dave's sister, whose boyfriend played bass in a metal band, so they could be the Four Horsemen of the Apocalypse: Fire, Famine, Pestilence and Plague. All it meant was, they took basic costumes, three ghosts and a skeleton, and then they daubed the initial letters of the horsemen on the front, two Fs and two Ps. Danny was Fire, Dave was Famine, Ralph was Pestilence and Gene was Plague.

When it was Danny and Ralph's turn to venture out for Trick-or-Treat supplies, they had an encounter that would haunt them both for years after. They had collected two full bags of fruit and nuts mostly, the candy quotient not nearly as high as it would become. They were crossing the road by the Bradberry house when Jackie came out and turned right in front of the church and stopped and stared at them. Danny and Ralph were in their costumes; there was no way Jackie could have recognized them. Anyway, Jackie spotted them, and it was as if he could see through their masks, see into their hearts, his gaze was so intense. Jason and Chad had moved on, but Jackie just stood there, staring. There was a whoosh of fireworks in the air above, rockets or something, a trail of stars, and traffic oncoming, so they just had to keep walking. And when they were nearly on top of him, Jackie shook his head and started to grin. Maybe he was out of it on drugs or booze or something, and he started to grin, and

he pointed at them, his hand in the shape of a gun. 'You're dead!'
he said, and he laughed, and then ran on to catch Jason and Chad
up. What he used to say to Danny on every scrawled note. 'You're
dead!' And then he laughed. And that was the last time they ever
saw Jackie Bradberry.

They waited and waited, until the fireworks dimmed, and the
firecrackers died down, and they watched the house. First
the lights went out about twelve, twelve-thirty. They couldn't
see the front, couldn't see who was coming in, but they saw the
lights go on and off about one, and again about two thirty. By
which time they had already laid the ground work: they had
emptied the bottles of gasoline in the patterns of skulls and snakes
and giant spiders on the Bradberry's hardscrabble lawn. All they
needed to do was light the match.

The truth of it was, they never meant for it to happen like it
did. They made sure to keep the gas away from the house, ten
or twelve feet away. But there were a copule of factors that
played against them. First of all, Mrs Bradberry was paranoid,
not alone about burglars, but also about drafts, about night air,
the potentially damaging health consequences of it on the young
children she otherwise merrily neglected. And to protect against
this, she had vinyl windows with very tight seals and locks
installed, locks to which she kept all the keys (they were found
in the ashes of her nightstand). The vinyl frames of the windows
were petroleum based, and highly inflammable.

The second crucial element in accelerating the fire's progress
and preventing anyone in the house from getting out safely was,
Brian and Eric, the eldest of the Bradberry children, were distilling
applejack in their bedroom, and not alone had they containers
of the stuff under their beds, they had a propane-fueled stove
among their equipment, a canister of propane ready to blow. So
the only two Bradberrys who could have helped the others
to escape (because the parents, as usual, were in a drunken coma),
or who could have escaped themselves, played their part in
making sure the blaze was lightning-fast and unstoppable.

But the boys didn't know about the locks, or the vinyl, or the
applejack, or the propane. All they knew was, it was coming
up to three in the morning. Not a soul stirring. And it was all
down to Danny. The guys agreed, he was dealt the shit, he got

to be in charge of hurling it back. He took a firecracker and lit
it and tossed it into the yard and it set off one skull, one snake,
one spider, and whoosh, the whole yard was aflame, and Danny
standing in back of it, like the demon who conjured it up. And
then the other guys joined him, they couldn't resist, the four of
them dancing around like maleficent sprites, the lawn blazing
before them.

They were the Four Horsemen of the Apocalypse! They thought
it would be the greatest Halloween prank ever. They thought it
would go down in history. Two of the kids looked out their
window. Not Jackie or his brothers, the younger kids. They could
see their little faces. They looked frightened. The Four Horsemen
waved at them. They laughed at their fears. It was all in fun.
They thought it was all in fun.

And then the house caught fire. There was no wind that night,
but the house caught fire. Sometimes Danny liked to think it
was the propane stove, that the propane stove had, separately,
coincidentally, exploded, ignited by a lit cigarette, perhaps, or in
a case of spontaneous combustion, he had awoken from dreams
in which this had been proved to be the case and believed it for
precious minutes afterwards. But that was not what the police
and fire service investigations of the time found. What they found
was that the Bradberry house fire was caused, not by the blaze
on the lawn that had spread into the house, or by a propane
canister, but, according to the burn patterns and scorch marks,
by a missile flung above the kitchen door, a fire bottle, a Molotov
cocktail.

And Danny, it was agreed by them all, was the one who
threw it.

The only thing was he couldn't remember. Oh, he felt as if he
could, because it had been decided that this was what had happened,
had gone over and over it in his head so that it seemed as real
to him as a memory. But Danny had run into a tree and knocked
himself out, immediately after he had flung the bottle, coming
to moments later, apparently. So what Danny actually remembers
is the blaze, and then nothing, and then his head pounding as
they swarmed over the wall of the Catholic church and along the
streets to where they'd left their bikes and shot across to the West
Side, to Dave's house, to safety, still daring to hope and to pray

that it wasn't as bad as it turned out to be. And no one really talking very much about what had happened, just wondering why he had thrown the bottle, and Danny wondering too, and there being no actual reproach or recrimination, but the sense that what happened shouldn't have happened remained clear. And the next day, once the scale of the fire was made clear, the intensity, the *horror* of the fire, and then amid the aftermath, the funerals, the small white caskets, the outpouring of grief, genuine and feigned, the speeches from governors and congressmen and the senator from Wisconsin, the rituals and ceremonies and obsequies, amid it all, the boys never said a word, Danny and Dave and Gene and Ralph, they never spoke of it again. All Danny knew was he was responsible. He had done it. He never tried to wriggle out of it, to deny his guilt, except in dreams.

There was a time when he saw the frightened faces of those Bradberry kids at their locked bedroom window every night when he closed his eyes and when he woke before dawn, a time when he'd see them in the faces of his own daughters, waving out the car window as their mother drove them to school. When those night fears, those waking dreams, gradually fell away, he thought they had gone for good. But nothing that you do goes away; it's always out there, in the woods, in the trees, waiting to come back, to sit at your table, to tell the truth and shame the Devil and leave you without a moment's peace the rest of your life.

Extract from
Trick or Treat
Unpublished manuscript by Ralph Cowley

PART TWO
The Day After

I'm Gonna Live Till I Die

Charlie T has never been in an old-style gentleman's club, but he imagines it would look a lot like Mr Wilson's apartment on West Randolph Street: the wood panelling, the leather chairs and sofas, the dark wood tables and bookshelves filled with military history and biography, the paintings of army commanders and scenes of battle through the ages, the green lampshades. Of course, it would be a gentleman's club with a view: twelve floors up, the Chicago River running beneath, the *Sun-Times* offices to one side, the ornate Civic Opera House to the other, the buildings lending the scene dimension and scale, like a cityscape in a comic book. Chicago was the first place Charlie T came to in the States, and he's found everywhere else to be a disappointment: Manhattan was all right if you were outside it, approaching, on the ferry or in Brooklyn, but when you were right there in the city, the buildings may as well have been half the size: you couldn't see the skyline. Whereas here, or down at the Michigan Avenue Bridge, you could take it in all at once. It looked like America, so it did.

Charlie T arrived from Belfast in 1994, not long after the first IRA ceasefire. (His name is Charles Toland, but he decided to call himself Charlie T when he got here because he thought that sounded more American, although imagine what kind of clown he felt like when, a few days later, somebody called him Mr T?) He was twenty years old and had shot seven men in nine months without too many qualms, either in the run-up, or in the moment, or in the aftermath, very little in the way of second thoughts, and a few senior IRA volunteers in Belfast told him he should stick around, that the peace would never last and his services would be needed again. But he knew it was over: there was a disdainful thing coming from the IRA leaders, not just the ones who got on TV but the likes of his own OC, a kind of looking-down-the-nose

vibe at the likes of him and Gerry Daly, who had shot four and
was raging the ceasefire had come before he could catch Charlie
up (not that Charlie would have let him). *The day of the gun has
been and gone*, that type of thing. Plus, the loyalists were raising
their game, assisted by British intelligence, and a lot of IRA
volunteers were getting dropped in the streets; Charlie wasn't
three months in Chicago when he got word Gerry Daly had been
ambushed by the LVF. He'd never catch him up now.

No, Charlie had called it right. America, where you could be,
well, maybe not anyone you wanted to be, that was pie in the
sky, but where you could be somebody else. Charlie prefers it
at night, with the city lights glittering their promises and lies,
but he likes it well enough at any time, for instance, now, at
breakfast: coffee and bacon rolls, served by Mr Wilson himself,
who is immaculate as ever in navy chalk stripe three-piece suit,
white on pink contrast-collar dress shirt, tassel loafers. Admittedly,
Charlie would like it a lot better without the opera music playing
quietly on Mr Wilson's Bose Wave CD player. Charlie doesn't
know what it is, German, it sounds like. Maybe he looks in its
direction once too often because Mr Wilson looks up and says,
'Wagner – *Parsifal*' and smiles a like-it-or-lump-it smile and
continues with his breakfast, which is a mere cup of coffee,
Charlie couldn't figure it, the guy was forty-five pounds overweight, minimum, and yet he'd never seen a morsel of food pass
his lips. Wagner. *Parsifal*. Well, it could be worse. They could
be listening to it at night. Charlie T is not really an opera sort
of guy, and even if he were, he wouldn't be a Wagner type of
guy, like something you'd hear in a church except weirder, maybe
at a black mass, giving him the creeps so it is, especially in light
of what he had to do last night, and by the curl of a smile playing
around his mean little mouth he can see Mr Wilson knows it
right well.

'More coffee?' Mr Wilson says. 'And then we can talk.'

'More coffee, and change the music. Or turn it off,' Charlie
says. 'And then we can talk.'

Mr Wilson inclines his big blond head in a mock bow, and
smiles a thin smile, and tops up Charlie's coffee cup, and his
own, and picks up a little gray remote control and flicks the
music off.

'The decline of Western civilization,' Mr Wilson says, clicking his tongue and shaking his head.

'Thought your man Wagner was one of those Nazis there,' Charlie says.

'Given that he died in 1883, and the Nazis only came to power fifty years later, that would have been quite an achievement,' Mr Wilson says briskly, not wanting to have the conversation. 'Now, how did we get on last night?'

'Has your little pal in the Madison Police Department not told you yet?'

'How do you know I have a little pal in the Madison PD?'

'You have one everywhere else, why should Madison be any different? Do they ever do anything practical for you, like? Disappear evidence, warn when there's gonna be a warrant or an arrest, type of thing?'

Mr Wilson shakes his huge head emphatically, theatrically, as if Charlie is a slow study who can do better.

'Now that really would be dangerous. No, all you want is eyes and ears, someone you pay disproportionately well for inform-ation. No more, no less. That way, they don't really feel they're doing anything wrong. In fact, they feel a little guilty about getting paid so much for doing so little, so they really will do their best. So yes, I'm up to date with what you no doubt would call "developments", but I always insist on a report from the field, so to speak.'

'No "so to speak" about it, I was in a field so I was, digging up a dead man, and then burying a dead dog.'

'You buried the hound?' Mr Wilson says, a leer of derision rippling across his fleshy jowls. 'Above and beyond, Charlie, above and beyond.'

Charlie T sets his jaw, catches sight of his cheekbones in the plate-glass window. He read in a magazine belonging to his girlfriend recently about looking *over* your cheekbones as a way of improving your posture and, almost as a reflex response to Mr Wilson's lardy face, Charlie does so now, his gaze as intense as, in a hair-trigger instant, his feelings are.

'And God forgive the pair of us for leaving the poor creature the way we did,' Charlie says, and feels the wind in his sails as he sees Mr Wilson's dirty yellow snail-smear eyebrows rise above his porky wee eyes. 'It was a, a desecration, so it was, and I was proud to set it right. And that's what I want to say to you,' Charlie continues, the coffee refill doing the work a third drink would. 'The abuse of animals is not something I can condone or tolerate. In fact, my advice is tell the bad bastard behind all this he can go and shite. There's plenty more want a clean kill and are happy to pay for it; that's the kind of work you can sleep easy after, not this torture and, and stalking, aye, psychological terror, the only reason the poor wee guy was left out was to set your woman's wits astray. That's not right, Mr Wilson. And if that's how you want to run things, well, you'd better find someone of like mind. And so had I.'

Truth was, he hadn't been up to killing the dog at all; that had been Angelique, who persuaded him to bring her along. Angelique is the closest thing he has to a steady girlfriend, in the sense that a) he mostly crashes at her place and that's where his stuff is; b) she's not on drugs or a stripper or a sex worker, Charlie T's usual female companions (she's a geriatric nurse at Masonic in Lincoln Park); c) she's not an insane freak, although she is kind of flaky and drinks a lot and knows what he does for a living and doesn't care, in fact gets off on hearing about it, on top of which she's got a kink for S&M he doesn't always see the point of (she bites, and likes to be bitten back: why?); and d) he actually likes her. Mind you, he might have to revise (c) above in the light of what she was capable of doing to the poor wee spaniel. Still, she helped him out of a jam: he can't afford to turn down any work Mr Wilson brought him, not with the debts he owes. He bows his head now, caught between pride in his spirit and anxiety that he has said too much.

Mr Wilson's smile congeals on his face, where it will stay until he decides what to do with it. This is why he liked the little Irishman in the first place, because alongside a cold eye and a steady hand when it comes to a kill, he has a piss-and-vinegar spirit that Mr Wilson finds bracing to be around. And he's stable, or at least as stable as his chosen profession will allow, the harem of tramps he scampers about with being his sole apparent vice. But Mr Wilson is not going to respond to any ultimatums or threats Charlie makes, partly because he makes them so often they are almost entirely meaningless, but also because he doesn't want to betray a glimmer of the truth, which is simply that Charlie will not be permitted to walk away from his current employer under any circumstances. Even though each has enough on the other to guarantee Mutually Assured Destruction, and therefore in theory a cold-war degree of trust, the fact is Mr Wilson has no intention of letting Charlie outlive the business they do together.

Not that this was the business he began with, or the name, for that matter. Mr Wilson isn't Mr Wilson, and despite appearances, he has never been in the military, and he has tried his hand at a lot of things since he came out of juvie in Racine for that trumped-up rape charge (statutory rape, he'd only been fifteen himself so where was the justice in that?). Racine had confirmed a few things that, up to then, he had always been too drunk or stoned or otherwise distracted to understand about himself:

1. That he had little or no empathy for other people;
2. That sex was not a compelling impulse for him, except insofar as it could be used to get something;
3. That he had the ability to pass for upper-middle class and, back then, the physique to make that count for something;
4. That he could read and retain a good deal of information – history, literature, politics – and discuss it as if he knew what he was talking about, as if he were a cultivated, sophisticated man and not an ex-addict runaway without even a high-school diploma in his pocket.

When he got out, he stayed sober and worked in retail, in a succession of upscale old-style menswear stores, and became acquainted with a handful of wealthy, successful men who were willing to pay for his company after hours, both in bed and out. (He didn't particularly identify as gay, it was just that the only people who were willing to part with money for sex were men.) The threat of blackmail loomed heavy over these encounters, and Mr Wilson was careful never to appear as if he knew that, or had any intention of acting on it. So far so good, but limited, in its way. Then came the event which defined his life: his parents died unexpectedly, and there was a legacy to be split between him and his elder brother, John. Mr Wilson hadn't seen his brother since leaving home. When he met him at the funeral, the first thing John did was ask Mr Wilson if he could front him ten grand – there were street guys from Cicero on his tail over gambling debts. Not alone was John a degenerate gambler, he was an alcoholic just like their dear old dad had been, and mom too, for that matter. John had made no legal provision for the future, had no dependents and barely any ties.

It was clear to Mr Wilson that John was an entirely unsuitable person to be entrusted with the stewardship of so much money (although their parents had raised them in frugal neglect, they had left savings, investments and insurance policies amounting in value to close on nine hundred thousand dollars) and that it would be a better outcome by far if Mr Wilson were to be the sole beneficiary of the estate.

Mr Wilson was happy to commission the hit. His lack of empathy did not extend to an ability to push a button himself, another lesson learned at his Racine *alma mater*: identify what those who can protect you, and who can act on your behalf, *need*, and find a way of supplying it. And the business and political connections he had developed, even if they did know of such an operative, were likely to view inquiries of that nature as impertinent in the extreme. He could always have shopped John to his Cicero creditors, and probably would have, had he not got talking to an arrogant ex-IRA volunteer with pretty-boy looks and the gift of the gab and ice water flowing through his veins one night in the Dark Rosaleen pub. Mr Wilson's knowledge of military history extended to the war in Ireland, and Charlie T had been so impressed that he started to ignore the lit-up woman in the low-cut dress trying to attract his attention. One thing led to another, and Charlie's vanity demanded that he allude to, and eventually boast about, the part he had played in the IRA's glorious fight for Irish freedom. And Mr Wilson saw his opportunity.

He told Charlie T he was acting for a client (he always told Charlie T that), and that he would be paid twenty thousand dollars if he could do it and make it look like an outfit hit. Charlie T said nothing, so Mr Wilson asked him if there was anything he had in the way of needs or conditions. And Charlie T looked Mr Wilson in the eye.

'Three things,' he said. 'No children – I won't kill them, I won't hurt them, I won't have anything to do with them. I'll kill women, but no sexual assault, no torture, no cruelty. And I won't kill anyone one in front of a family member: no husbands shot in front of their wives and children, had a belly-full of that. I do a clean job, and I don't like mess. Right?'

'Do you want to know why you are to kill this man?'

'Twenty grand. That's why.'

'Really?' Mr Wilson said. 'It wouldn't help to know the guy had it coming?' (He had fabricated a story in which his brother was a serial child abuser, in case Charlie T had principles.)

Charlie T shook his head.

'I fight for a cause,' he said. 'Once, it was my country's freedom. Now, it's my own. All I need to know is that I'm getting paid.'

Mr Wilson couldn't help but be impressed. It was as cynical a statement of intent as he'd ever heard, but it was delivered with guts, passion and a kind of idealism Mr Wilson considered utterly American.

'Ten now, ten when the job is done,' Mr Wilson said.

Six days later, Mr Wilson took a call from a detective with the Cicero police department to tell him that the body of a man had been found in the street outside Hawthorne Race Course on the south side of town, and that the man had Mr Wilson's card in his pocket. Mr Wilson drove out to identify the body. As per the contract, he had been shot twice behind the left ear. And on the seventh day, Charlie T arrived to claim the balance of the money.

'Is your client happy?' Charlie T said.

'He is,' Mr Wilson said, wondering if Charlie T knew who John was, but somehow understanding that it didn't matter even if he did. And that was that, as far as Mr Wilson was concerned. He had enough money to buy the apartment on Randolph Street and to deck it out to his satisfaction. He had become who he had decided to be. But the menswear business wasn't enough any more. None of what had gone before could continue. He needed a change.

Then one night he was at dinner with Carl Brenner, who ran his own private security firm, Centurion, active in Iraq and Afghanistan, and who had become a friend. Carl ran weekend-long re-enactments of famous military engagements in a dedicated war-games room in his house on North Astor; Mr Wilson had helped to re-fight the battles of Waterloo, Crecy and Gettysburg in recent months.

With them were a couple of friends, one of whom had recently lost his daughter in a DUI incident. The driver had walked free, and the bereaved father was still reeling, visibly raw with grief and anger and set on revenge. Leaving the restaurant, Mr Wilson made a point of falling into step with the man, and tentatively suggested that something could be done about the situation, for a price. A deal was struck, and Charlie T was hired, and the business was concluded, the drunk driver losing control of his car and crashing into a wall, while drunk. Charlie T was artful, of that there was no doubt. Word filtered back to Carl Brenner, who was at first astonished, then intrigued, and then happy to act as a conduit for business of that kind which his firms couldn't touch. Soon they had a slow but steady stream of orders.

Mr Wilson tried to avoid any further work that smacked of organized crime because of the nature of the company they'd be keeping, although, as Charlie T said, they were the easiest, because you didn't have to stage them: two behind the ear was exactly the way you expected those guys to die. And they had handled three killings commissioned by a guy Carl introduced him to who reeked of spook, some murky government agency or other, Mr Wilson was pretty sure of it, and Carl didn't go to any great lengths to deny it.

The first thing he had done was increase the price: their going rate now was 100k a hit. That was way over the market odds, but it actually worked as an attraction to high-end clients who were used to getting what they paid for. It was clear what Charlie T got out of it: money, plus a way of using his God-given ability to kill without feeling a thing. But Mr Wilson wondered sometimes what on earth was happening to him. He found the entire experience absolutely exhilarating and all-absorbing. He grew obsessed with murder and violence, albeit at one remove: the timing, the planning, the methods. He liked to hear all about it. He didn't consider himself a cruel or a sadistic person, but he would like it if Charlie T was willing to employ a broader palate in his work: more frequent use of blades, for example, torture, mutilation, trophy saving and so on. It wasn't just that higher premiums could be charged for the employment of more inventive methods, there would simply be something more organically, more aesthetically pleasing about it. The work would be better if it was more various, that was how Mr Wilson had expressed it to Charlie T.

'Fine so, do it yourself,' Charlie had said.

Mr Wilson nods at Charlie now, neither agreeing nor disagreeing with the rights and wrongs of the evisceration of a dog. Personally, Mr Wilson doesn't like cruelty to animals, but their client has a lot of money and wants to spend it and was most insistent about the dog, and business has been quiet for a while.

'We can't terminate an operation in the middle, you know that. We've got to play this one through. And we could do with the money. At least, you could. I had to advance you a substantial loan last month, remember?'

Charlie T grimaces, nods, takes the point. Fucking Mr Wilson, maybe he should never have got himself involved in this, but there's no drawing back now. Mr Wilson passes four photographs across the table. The first is of a dark-haired man in a gray suit and a long-haired cowboy-looking dude getting into a red Ford Mustang.

'We should have coordinates for these guys shortly. They're on their way to Chicago. You'll know as soon as we know.'

Charlie T doesn't have to ask how Mr Wilson would know. Between police departments and highway patrols, Mr Wilson has a network of paid informers ever vigilant whenever information on a targetted vehicle is needed.

The next photo is of two kids, girls of about seven and nine, standing underneath apple trees in what looks like the Brogans' back garden. Before Charlie can say a word, Mr Wilson piles in.

'It's just for identification purposes, the picture of the kids. No harm is to come to them. It's the woman we're after.'

Charlie T looks then at a picture of a woman with tattoos, jet black hair and a few leather straps and bands placed at strategic angles in a biker bar, or a strip club, or both, and a second photograph of a blonde woman in heels and a sharply cut business suit.

'It's the same woman. Donna Brogan. She may not look like that any more. But the children probably do,' Mr Wilson says.

Mountain Greenery

Architecturally it's not the same kind of house, and there are no apple trees in her backyard, and Lake Wingra was further away than Lake Ripley is, but the essentials are the same: here they are, Donna and Barbara and Irene, having changed into their wetsuits and tramped their way down the hill through the stands of blue beech and sycamore and hung their towels on a hackberry tree. Here they are, squealing with the cold, and splashing to stave it off and, in Barbara's case, swimming fluently along the shore on a bright October morning with more than a touch of frost in the air, just like Donna used to do when she was their age. And the question she asks herself, not for the first time, is: why do we so often reassemble the elements of our childhoods in our adult lives, even when that childhood was not remotely happy? Why did she choose this house by a lake, isolated on a lonely road, surrounded by trees, as near as dammit a reincarnation of her family home off Arboretum Avenue, when Brad would have bought whatever kind of place, wherever she'd wanted?

Unfinished business. Not that she hasn't had enough therapy to last three lifetimes, but there is always more to be dealt with, isn't there? The past is always waiting for you. Maybe her childhood wasn't as bad as she thinks. Nothing actually happened. Technically. But maybe it would have, if Danny hadn't stood up for her. Her little brother, her hero, and how she can never thank him for it. Because they were all pretending it wasn't happening in the first place, her father staring at her, at her body, buying her clothes, asking her to sit beside him while they watched TV. He even brought his drinking back to a, she was going to say to a *normal* level, she likes that exotic word, but to a level where he didn't pass out unconscious on the couch, or stagger when he stood up. Little gifts, little jokes, little 'don't tell your mother this' secrets. At first, she loved it. Because it *was* normal, she thought. At last, after years of his being this menace in the house, either drunk and belligerent, slapping the shit out of Danny whenever he felt like it, rowing with Mother and making her weep (Jesus, the constant weeping) or hungover and seething with bitterness and disappointment, at them, at himself, at the Way Things Were, here he was at last, when she was fourteen, bit of a Late Developer, a Plain Jane who'd begun to blossom, here he was, snapping his fingers and stroking her cheek, like a Fun Dad on a TV sitcom, corny, sure, but she didn't care. She had longed for that, the attention, the sense at last that she was special. All she had got from their mom was, well, tenderness, sure, gentleness, but a sense of passivity, of sympathy almost, for her as a girl, but more for herself as a suffering mother, married to this broken-down heap of a man. And however true that was, it shouldn't be the daughter's job to commiserate with the mother.

He'd encourage her to dress up in the clothes he'd bought her, and then he'd take her out, to the movies, for ice cream, and the clothes were kind of grown-up, skirts and blouses like maybe a secretary might wear. She could see her mother looking on in dismay, but she never said anything, never *intervened*. Her dad took her to Brogan's, and that was the best, all the bar staff smiling and Daddy winking and everyone saying, 'Look at you! All grown up! A real little lady!'

And that's how she felt, like everyone was watching her, every song was about her. She felt special. But she wasn't all grown up. She wasn't a real little lady. And it wasn't normal. And just as she was starting to figure this out for herself, her little brother stepped in and, well, it wouldn't be stretching it to say, saved her life. Not that she saw it that way then, or for a long time afterwards: her rage was so unfocused, so scattershot that Danny had to take his unfair share, same as anyone else who came her way.

It was a weird time for him back then as well. Something had happened with Danny a couple of years before, around the time of the Bradberry fire. He'd been getting bullied, she thinks by one of the Bradberrys, she was in another class and anyway they didn't hang out together, God forbid, but there was a time at home when Daddy would tell Danny he had to stand up and be a man, no Brogan was raised to be a crybaby, and Danny would tell Daddy he didn't know what he was talking about, and Daddy would roar, actually roar like a bull, and hit Danny, knock him down. That happened more than once, and Mom intervened *then*, she heard it a few times but only saw it once, the old man attempting to hit Danny and Mother getting in between them and shielding her son and crying, 'No! No!' Pathetic and hilarious, it was like something from a silent movie. All Donna thought, really thought, was *She'll step in for him but not for me.*

Then the Bradberry fire happened and everything seemed to go numb for a while. It was like, after the deaths of the Bradberry children, all the kids in town had a sort of amnesty for six months or so, you could basically do what you liked and your folks would just shrug and let it go. Not that Donna had the confidence to do anything out of line except pout and sulk and feel sorry for herself. She looks at Barbara now, Donna and Irene on the shore, shivering into their towels, Barbara still in the water, her crawl a thing of beauty to behold, eleven and already a prey to adolescent mood swings, girls mature earlier these days, physically at any rate. Everything Donna suggests, Barbara's first reaction is '*No!*' She's a sweet kid at heart, and can always be talked around, but it sure feels like work. It's good, though, that she feels entitled to say it. A tribute to her mother, who Donna likes a lot more than she feels comfortably able to express, even if she is a precious princess pain in the ass. Who's done an amazing job with these two little girls.

So, what didn't actually happen was, after weeks of . . . *flirting*, Donna thinks it would be correct to call it, one night they are home alone together, Mother is out at the movies, Danny is over at a friend's house, Donna and Dad, just the two. She gets dressed up in a new dress he bought for her. She puts on make-up. He cooks her dinner, steak, salad, baked potato, the old Brogan's grillmeister magic, she hadn't seen *that* for a long time. He lights candles. He gives her a *beer*, her first. He talks to her about . . . well, she doesn't really remember what he talks to her about, only that he seems very sincere, and a little cross, and he keeps saying, 'I hope you understand,' and how one of the finest arts in the world is the art of keeping a secret. What she remembers is how it makes her feel: excited, and special, and scared, because she knows it isn't quite right. When he gives her a second beer, she says no, because she hasn't finished the first one, and anyway it's made her head feel all swirly, and he laughs and says that's the whole point of beer, to make you feel swirly, don't lose that swirly feeling, and he kisses her on the lips, a Daddy kiss, except he lingers just a little too long for Daddy, and when he moves his face away, Danny is standing in the doorway, headphones around his neck. Turns out he wasn't over at a friend's, he was in his room listening to Pink Floyd. Danny looks at her, and she sees him take in the dress, the make-up, the beer. She wants to explain, but she doesn't know how. She wants to apologize, but Danny has turned his attention away from her. Daddy is still smiling, the gracious host at whose table everyone is welcome. He offers Danny a beer, invites him to sit and join them. But Donna knows that isn't going to happen. Donna knows this is all over now. Danny walks up to his father – he's an inch taller, and filling out to be broader of chest, though he's not there yet – and he jabs his right index finger in the old man's face.

'You cut this shit out now, you hear me?'

And Daddy looks to her, his face a study in *amusement*, as if Donna and he are Park Avenue sophisticates who've been surprised by an uncouth emissary from the League of Decency. And Danny, whose eyes are glittering with anger, without moving the right hand, hits Daddy with a swinging left that nearly knocks him sideways, then hard in the belly with his right, and rounds it off with an uppercut to the face that lands him on his back. Danny follows through and stands over him and Daddy cringes and cowers, curled up in a ball, and Danny is going to say something but doesn't. He turns and looks at Donna, his face contorted with adrenaline.

'You should clean that make-up off your face,' he says. 'You look like a clown.'

Of course, instead of being grateful (because it ended right there) she was furious (because it ended right there). It took her a long while to unravel it all. She knew at some level her father had crossed the line, but he had never paid her such attention before – nobody had – and she felt bereft without it. And she blamed Danny. Truth be told, some part of her, some reptile self unsusceptible to reason or society, or sanity, still does.

Barbara is out now, and they're all toweled dry and huddled beneath the hackberry trees, leaves turned a rusty red but still clinging on, and they're drinking the steaming hot chocolate Donna brought in a flask and chattering happily about the TV show *Glee*, which Barbara adores as a harbinger of the unimaginably exotic teenage excitements the future will bring, and which Irene disdains on the grounds that the singers are all copy cats. At least, the girls are chattering and Donna is listening and wondering if that's why she adores being in their company quite so much, if it's a simple equation: her unhappy childhood for their happy ones. Maybe she should have had her own kids. Only there's no way, if she had, that they would have turned out as untroubled as this pair.

'What's that?' Irene says, the more observant of the two, looking up towards the house.

'What's what?' Barbara says, her mouth stained with chocolate.

'A rustling up near the house. Maybe it's a pussy cat.'

'I tawt I taw a putty cat. Maybe it's a *snake*.'

There's silence then.

'Maybe it was nothing,' Irene says quietly, uneasy at the notion there might be snakes anywhere nearby.

But Donna has heard it, or thinks she has, a rustle of leaves, or of wings, her nerves and senses doing double duty since Danny left, since the doorbell rang an hour later. It was Claire, of course, calling first and then driving over here, out of her mind with worry. Donna had wanted to let her in, but she felt she had to protect Danny, at least within an hour or so of his leaving. After that she was up five times, sleep broken by creaking floorboards or animal cries or wind through the trees, padding barefoot around the house, turning lights on and off, nothing to protect her but her trusty Glock 17, one of her souvenirs of eighteen months with the 'president' of the Milwaukee Outlaws Motorcycle Club (along with the tattoos, the gang rape, the 147 stitches and the nervous breakdown she told Danny she never had and the suicide attempts he doesn't even know about). She didn't need Danny to alert her to the potential dangers of living alone and in some isolation, even in a twinky little burgh like Cambridge, but Danny's crisis, whatever the hell it is, has ramped up the anxiety level more than somewhat.

'It's likely a racoon or an opossum,' Donna says, gathering the flask and the towels into her canvas tote and reaching for her glossy red clutch, where she keeps her essentials: make-up, house keys and gun.

'Come on, let's hit the shower, girls.'

Irene usually runs ahead, and Barbara lags behind, but this morning, Irene is in no hurry to run into a snake, so Donna is free to take the lead back up through the sycamore and blue beech, bright October sun coaxing wisps of steam from the soft forest scrub. Which is as she wants it. Just the same, she doesn't want to press so far in front that she loses them, or that they could be surprised from behind, so she stops every now and again and waits for them to catch up. As Donna waits for the second or third time, nothing stirring up at the house as far as she can tell, she clocks the red clutch in her hand, and flashes on how bizarre she must look, in the woods, in a wetsuit, with a glossy evening purse: all she needs is a pair of Laboutins and it could be some demented fashion shoot in a glossy magazine.

The girls catch up and she presses on, simultaneously thinking she's being ridiculous and yet all too acquainted with, and therefore prepared for, the worst. She doesn't know what kind of trouble Danny has got himself into. She's so used to assuming he walked the straight path, she the crooked, that she couldn't conceive of any trouble he *could* be in. He was right: she lacked imagination. Like the more partisan of her gay friends, she filed Danny and Claire under 'breeders' and neglected to give them rounded characters. And now they appear to have gone off the deep end, or at least Danny has. God knows what he was talking about, gambling debts, or maybe drugs, if that slacker Jeff Torrance had anything to do it. And implying that their house was under threat, Jesus. Blackmail from somebody in his past? No, Donna hasn't a clue. She can barely remember those halfwits he used to hang out with, Gene something, and Dave, and . . . Ralph . . . Jesus, was one of them actually called *Ralph*? What a bunch of whitebreads, jocks and demi-jocks, Donna thinks she might have had sex with one of them in the back of a car out

by the lake, but she can't be sure which one, or what kind of
sex, or whether it *was* with one of Danny's friends; she knows
she had plenty of sex in cars out by the lake, too much, in fact,
and most of it pretty disappointing in almost every way, thanks
all the same. But Danny really didn't register for her once she
put the whole thing with her dad behind her, or thought she had.
Sure, she was pretty much out of it a lot of the time from the
age of fifteen, grass and ludes and wine, but mostly she just
wasn't interested in him. Oh, she loved him and so on, but she
didn't really see him as anything more than her straight, boring
little brother. And now, after all this, he reveals a wild side?

There's another rustle, and branches sway in the backyard,
just above. Briskly now, to put some space between her and the
girls, Donna climbs the last few yards, hot in her wetsuit, trying
to keep her breathing hushed, and as she reaches the stacked
railway sleepers that do fence duty, two things happen at once,
sound and vision in a mixed-media spasm: her cell phone sings
out its shrill refrain, and she sees that the source of the rustling
is a *wolf*, a gray wolf prowling by the rear window of the house,
then turning and staring in the direction of the ringtone. Donna
goes rigid, meeting the animal's silver gaze, its breath furling its
great head in white steam. *It's* afraid of *you*, she thinks, because
she saw it in some documentary, along with *what the fuck is a
wolf doing this far south?*

The girls are approaching now, Barbara suddenly taking the
lead and ticking Irene off for dawdling, and Irene giving it look-
who's-talking right back to her sister, and the wolf's ears prick
up at the sound and it does a kind of shuffle, like it's stretching
out its limbs before attacking, perhaps. Donna fiddles with the
catch on her clutch, recalling that there has been at least one
wolf sighting annually in Dane County for some years now, not
that she really needs to reassure herself that this isn't a fucking
optical illusion as her hand closes around the Glock. No safety,
she'll shoot through the bag if she has to, and she'll hit it, she's
kept her eye in, target shooting at the Oakland Conservation Club
once a month.

Irene shouts, 'Aunt Donna, Aunt Donna!'

And the wolf skitters around on the frosty ground like a young
colt unsure of its hooves, and throws back its beautiful head and

appears to howl, soundlessly, a white plume of sputum sprayed above it like a mane, and then careens unsteadily around the side of the house and darts out in the direction of the highway.

'Aunt Donna!' Irene says. 'Tell Babs to stop being such a poo.'

'*Babs*,' Barbara says. '*Puh-lease.* Do *not* call me Babs. Anyway, she's the poo. What are you looking for in your bag, Aunt Donna?'

'My cell phone,' Donna says, truthfully, giggling a little in astonishment and nervous relief at the wolf, at its appearance and its departure.

'I'm getting a cell phone when I'm twelve. I could have had one last birthday, but Mom said either that or a laptop and I chose a laptop,' Barbara says.

'You're a lucky girl.'

'Mmmm,' says Barbara doubtfully. 'Megan and Susie have both. And Megan has an iPad also.'

'Megan is a snoot,' Irene says. 'But her brother Dougie is funny.'

'Dougie *is* funny. Why do you think Megan is a snoot?'

'She has a la-di-da accent.'

'She can't help that. Her mom is from England or Europe or somewhere.'

'So?'

'So she sounds like her mom.'

'Does her mom have a la-di-da accent too?'

'I don't think it's so la-di-da.'

'Law-dee-daw, law-dee-daw.'

'Shut up, Irene, you're being annoying.'

'Dougie doesn't have a law-dee-daw accent.'

'Shut up shut up shut up!'

'You're not allowed say shut up!'

And the girls walk on through the yard towards the house, bickering cheerfully, as if the wolf had never existed.

Donna has found her phone. The missed call is yet another from Claire. No voicemail. She should phone her, let her know the kids are OK. She doesn't want to mess with Danny's plan though, however half-assed it might prove to be. What did he say? That he'd 'left her a sign.' And that if she called, to tell her the kids were OK, that they were with Danny. She doesn't want to do that, doesn't want to tell an outright lie, doesn't actually want to talk to Claire at all. She's a good mother, that's clear from the girls, although actually it's a little dubious, in Donna's opinion, extrapolating from the children to the parents. What if your parents are idiots? Surely you have the chance to survive that, and to thrive, to become your own person, with no credit to the wretches who gave you life? Isn't that after all what this country is founded on, the belief that you can triumph over your own circumstances? Yeah right, and in so many cases, isn't that just the most unrealistic bullshit?

Donna unlocks the glass door and slides it back, and the girls head upstairs to the shower, tossing their wet swimming things on the floor as they go, their little voices chattering. So does that suddenly make Claire a bad mother? And Donna a cranky aunt? She's about to yell 'dump them in the laundry,' but she doesn't. Who cares? She assumes their parents yell at them every now and again. They'd have to. She won't. This is a house where they can come and never be yelled at, and that's how they'll remember it. As if the girls can somehow sense the wave of indulgence washing towards them, they stop at the top of the stairs and wave down at her. Sometimes, when she's with them and they're talking and laughing and goofing around, brewing up a head of noisy steam, they can seem older, seem close to grown. And then she spots them from afar, and they look so tiny again, so fragile, so vulnerable. She waves back, and finds she has to turn away. How did they get to be so beautiful?

All right, she has it. She goes to the Settings section of her iPhone, disables her Caller ID and composes the following:

You must be worried, but whatever you do, don't worry about the girls: they're fine.

She sends the text, thinking there's a fair chance that Claire will deduce it's her anyway, that this is a reply to her call, and that she'll be on the doorstep within the hour. And maybe, whatever Danny thinks he's doing, and despite the fact she'd like to keep the girls indefinitely, maybe that would be for the best.

Travellin' All Alone

When Claire makes up her mind to go, she can go pretty fast, and here she is already, back in Chicago less than twenty-four hours after she left, at the bar of the Twin Anchors restaurant on Sedgwick Street, waiting for Paul Casey to show up. He's late, which has always been his way, and not surprising, but much less endearing than it used to be, even last week. Last *week*. It's not simply that it feels like such a long time ago, it feels like it happened in an entirely parallel reality, an alternative Claire in an alternative life. And yes, that was the point, she realizes, that was the entire point of the exercise: to be the Claire she hadn't been, had failed to be, to try it on and see how it felt and . . . well, there wasn't much thought beyond that. Wasn't much reality to it at all. Even as she was walking up the drive of the house last night, before she discovered what had happened, it was click-clacking into her brain, in quickstep with her hangover: *it's very nice to go travelling, but it's so much nicer to come home.* Except when it isn't.

She orders a Diet Coke – she's tempted by the idea of a bracer, a Greyhound would be her preference, vodka and grapefruit juice, breakfast of those at their wits' end, but she doesn't think she has the stomach for it – and looks at the text message again.

You must be worried, but whatever you do, don't worry about the girls: they're fine.

It arrived just after the cops left. They had stayed another half-hour, asking her about the knife, which she said she didn't recognize, which was true insofar as it was kind of generic and she never used it, but they quickly found the matching set of knives in a block in the kitchen, and asked her again, and she just repeated what she had told them. They knew she wasn't telling them everything, and Detective Fox in particular began to lay a trip on her about the children and how Claire had to be sure, even for her own peace of mind, that she was doing absolutely everything; in cases like these, the merest minutes, that was the phrase she had used, *the merest minutes* could be vital. And then they wanted photographs, and she'd managed to find a shot of Gene Peterson she'd kept.

And then they left and, stricken with guilt, she phoned Donna again. The phone went to message and she hung up, but pretty sharply afterwards, she received this text message.

You must be worried, but whatever you do, don't worry about the girls: they're fine.

Was it from Donna? The message showed up as Blocked, and she had gotten texts from Donna before that had displayed her ID. She called her sister-in-law again two or three times, but the phone went to voicemail as before. Another mother would have called the cops. Maybe every other mother would have called the cops, showed them the message. Don't they have some way of figuring out the caller ID even if it is blocked? They go to the phone provider and get the subscriber details. Wouldn't any mother have done that for her children?

It might have been Donna. It might have just been a coincidence. It might have been Danny. It most likely was Danny, she thought, and that's why she wanted the cops out of the picture: because she wants to get to him first.

'Have you considered the possibility that your husband might himself be in danger? Or worse?' Detective Fox had said to her, as a parting shot. Of course she had, and if he was, it could well be because of what had happened in Chicago back in the day. It could well be her fault. But why would anyone who wanted to harm – or who had, God forbid, already harmed – the children have sent her that message? *Don't worry. The girls are fine.* Believe in it, and behave as if it is true. *Behave as if* – the actor's credo. Get to Chicago and figure it out.

After that, it was all pretty brisk: a shower, the last of her clean clothes, the bag she brought with her yesterday. The crime scene team were still all over the yard, photographing and forensicing and whatever else it is they do. She called Dee, and then a cab; when it arrived, and she went outside to meet it, Officer Colby, the uniformed cop who'd found the knife, was waiting at the gate.

'Ms Taylor. You mind telling me where you're going?'

'I'm going to visit my friend Dee.'

'And can I ask you the purpose of your trip?'

'The purpose of my trip? The purpose of my trip is food, and furniture, that type of thing. Clothes, for that matter. Shampoo. Soap. None of which I have here. That's the purpose of my trip.'

Claire gave Officer Colby Dee's address and got in the cab.

Dee lives downtown in a seventh-floor apartment on East Wilson that overlooks Lake Monona. Claire spent the cab ride trying to figure out how to block her own caller ID, having suddenly succumbed to another fit of the jitters over the girls. She decided that if she couldn't figure out a way to talk to Donna on the phone (and she feared Donna wouldn't take her calls, since apart from anything else, she didn't like her) she would have to drive out there again, not such a long trip but a ways out of her way. Finally, she located Show My Caller ID in the Phone section of Settings and turned it off. Standing on the sidewalk outside Dee's building, Claire called Donna – and this time, Donna picked up.

'Hello.'

'Donna, it's Claire, Claire Taylor. Did you by any chance just send me a text message?'

'Claire? No. No, I didn't . . .'

'Sorry. I guess I'm kind of freaking out here, I suppose. I don't know if he's told you, your brother's taken off, and foreclosure proceedings have been issued against the house?'

'*Foreclosure?*'

'Three months ago. I got a visit from the sheriff this morning, we have thirty-one days to quit. Or, I do. And he cleared out all our stuff. And there was a dead body there this morning, one of Danny's old friends from school. And Mr Smith . . . someone *killed* Mr Smith, Donna, cut his *throat* . . .'

Claire's voice broke now, and hot tears filled her eyes. Before she could say another word, Donna spoke.

'The girls are here, Claire. I looked after them last week, while you were away. Then Danny came by last night and asked me to keep them.'

'They're all right then? Oh, thank God.'

'They're fine. Do you want to talk to them?'

'Maybe in a minute. Let me get my act together, I'm a mess here. What did Danny say?'

'Very little. He's in some kind of danger, he's being black-mailed, or pursued, he has money worries. I don't know. He seemed to think it wasn't a good idea for you to know the girls were here, in case anyone is watching you. I asked him were you in danger, but he didn't think you were. I don't know, I mean the whole thing seems ridiculous—'

'And then there's a dead body, and a dead dog, and the cops swarming over the backyard of my house, a house that soon won't belong to me any more. Whatever it is, it's not ridiculous.'

Donna was silenced by this. All Claire could hear was the boom of traffic on East Wilson, and the beat of her heart as it subsided slowly from her mouth. Barbara and Irene, Barbara and Irene, Barbara and Irene. Did she ever really believe the worst?

'Tell me what you want to do, Claire. Come and see them, come and pick them up. Barbara's coming down the stairs, will I put her on?'

Dee was approaching now, Claire could see her in the distance, coming down Pinckney. She thought hard. Of course she wanted to talk to Barbara and Irene, to hear their voices, there was nothing she wanted more in fact than to go out there and spend the day with them. But that wasn't going to get her anywhere. And if they were happy with Donna – and they always were – then that was all she really needed to know. She needed to get moving. Some of this was down to Danny, no doubt, but some of it was down to her as well.

'Donna, I'd love to, but don't, it would just upset them, upset us all. Tell them I called, and I'm fine, and I love them.'

'Will do. I did . . . send you that text.'

'I know.'

'I'm sorry, I . . . thought I was being loyal to my little brother. I should have known it would spook you. I don't really know what's going on, Claire.'

'Neither do I. But I have to try and find out. I've got to get back to Chicago as soon as possible.'

'Good grief. You and Dan are the same. One day you're suburban mom and dad, the next you're Nick and Nora Charles.'

Only Asta is dead.

'Well. I can't do that with the girls to worry about,' Claire says.

'Don't worry about them, Claire. And good luck.'

Claire will always think of this moment, waiting for Dee to cross the street at Pinckney and East Wilson, this moment when, if she had spoken to the girls, Irene in particular, they would have worked on her so hard that she would have had no option but to travel to Cambridge to see them, and then no one else might have had to die.

And then Dee was upon her, having walked the five minutes from the salon on Dayton. They embraced, and took the elevator to Dee's apartment in silence. Inside, amid the Indian hangings and Persian rugs and Greek statuary, the musk of aromatic oil and scented candles on the air, in sight of the mist drifting above the lake, Claire drank chai tea and quickly told her friend everything that had happened since last night. When she was finished, instead of telling her what she had done wrong, or what Dee would have done in her place, or what an ass Danny was, Dee simply found her car keys and handed them to Claire, and held her close, and they took the trip back down to the parking lot beneath the building and Dee led them to her blue Toyota Corolla.

'Are you sure?' Claire said. 'The Volkswagen is older, I don't want to damage this and fuck up your insurance—'

'The Volkswagen is a rusty old heap. It's only fit for rural trails and trekking and hiking and so on.'

'But you never use rural trails. You're not the trekking and hiking type.'

'I know, I know, I got it when I was with that guy with the beard, the outdoor guy. But it turned out, I'm not an outdoor girl.'

'If only they made hiking boots with heels,' Claire said.

'Take the Toyota. Can't have you bowling around Chicago like some cheesehead on a day trip.'

When Dee said goodbye, she had her sad face on, for real, with tears in her eyes.

'I'm frightened for you, baby,' she said, and Claire had to work hard not to lose it there and then.

'I'll be fine. The kids are safe, that's the main thing.'

'That's right. Everything else, you can work out.'

'Or not,' Claire said.

'Danny's not a bad man,' Dee said, her face having morphed from sad to tragic, and Claire nearly laughed.

'Aren't you supposed to be reassuring me? I don't *think* he's a bad man.'

'I know. I'm sorry. I just don't know how he could have done what he's done. The *house*, oh my *God*.'

And Claire held Dee then, as if the misfortune had befallen her.

'I'll be all right. It's not all down to Danny. I have a plan.'

Dee nodded, tragic morphing into brave.

'So phew,' Claire said, 'that makes it all right then.'

And Dee smiled, and said, 'Look, Claire, if there's anything I can do, just say the word.'

Claire takes a pen and a notebook from her bag and scribbles on it.

'Well there is, actually . . . since I'm gonna be away, why don't you take Donna's number? In case there's anything with the kids. I mean, she can handle it, but God forbid she comes down with flu or something.'

'Sure. She's in Cambridge, right?'

'I'll put the address down too.'

'There's no need. Cambridge is the kind of place everyone knows everyone, I can just ask in a coffee shop,' Dee said. 'Or call in advance.'

'Well no, actually. Donna being Donna, she plumped for somewhere remote, by the lake.'

'We love our lakes,' Dee said.

'And she tends not to answer the phone.'

'Runs in the family,' Dee said, and they both laughed then, high laughter on the edge of tears, and hugged their last goodbyes.

'I'll be fine, don't worry,' Claire said as she got into the car.

'You sure, sweetheart?'

'Seriously, Dee – when you know your kids are all right, you can handle anything.'

But that's not what anyone would have thought if they'd seen her on the road. Did she cry continuously from Madison to Chicago? No, just for the first hour as the fantastic events of the past week coursed around her brain. Could Danny have murdered Gene Peterson? She saw him pocket the knife before he went down to greet him. Was he capable of such violence? Not to her knowledge. And certainly not because of some shambolic fling she and Peterson had many years before. But kill the man who had lost them so much money, who was about to lose them their house? Claire could stab Peterson herself. But then there was poor Mr Smith. And on the other side, the ornament on the mantelpiece, unbroken. Mirabell and Millamant, married. Round and round it went in her head, leaving her none the wiser.

The housing estates and motels flanking the I-90 fell away, and marsh and woodland, dotted by occasional farmhouses, took over. Somehow the sparse, dank beauty of the landscape seemed to act on Claire then, turning fear and panic into something more thoughtful and considered.

Because in a weird way, she had always been braced for this, or something like it, some disaster, some unforeseen but long awaited apocalypse. They argued over trivial stuff, she and Danny, but with the big things, they didn't really do confrontation; they tended to let it go. When 'don't go there' became the phrase of choice, back in the nineties, she remembers how they bonded in recognition of its rightness, both as a general principle and a description of their personal MO. Neither of them liked to go there, either with each other or, Claire often thought, with themselves. Maybe this was the reason the marriage always seemed so fragile, as if it was only ever one botched dinner date or missed sexual connection or argument over childcare away from the final break-up: they didn't really know each other, or themselves. And what was more, they didn't *want* to know.

How could she explain her unwillingness to find out who her birth mother and father were? It wasn't as if she even had to make much of an effort: on the day she left Rockford for UW Madison (having offered her the opportunity to find out regularly since she was twelve) the Taylors had given her an envelope containing the details of her origins. It's safe among all her personal stuff in the tower on Arboretum Avenue, waiting for her to inspect. One day. Of course, she could always have gone through the state adoption authorities that had handled her case, but she doubted she ever would. And in any case, that envelope had come with so much more, with flowers and leaves and herbs pressed within the pages of every play her green-fingered foster parents could find with a horticultural connection, be it ever so tenuous (invariably the title): *The Petrified Forest, The Autumn Garden,*

The Country Wife, The Field, The Cherry Orchard, Desire Under the Elms. They had come with her too, almost her last connection with the Taylors, who were killed in a car crash the summer before her final year. They had lived frugally, and died leaving Claire just enough to cover the rest of her fees, and the memory of their cheerful, gentle, unflaggingly positive encouragement, and their quiet, diligent, undemonstrative alcoholism. Claire wondered often if that was one of the unconscious attractions she and Danny had to each other, that they were both children of alcoholics – even if, in her case, it was nurture and not nature.

She didn't drink much any more, unless you count a lost week in Chicago. She didn't honestly know how much Danny drank any more; little or nothing at home, a couple of beers watching sports was all. At work was another matter. What happens in Brogan's stays in Brogan's. God, Brogan's. They had met there, on their first day at UW. Danny had sought refuge from the helter-skelter of university, and after all, it was his family firm. What was her excuse for skulking in a dark old Irish bar? She had found the going a bit frantic herself, and slipped downtown and found a volume of Dawn Powell stories in Avol's vast used bookstore on Gorham, the store itself almost every bit as exciting as university, and her eye was caught by the stained glass and brown wood paneling of Brogan's, the type of bar the actors in her beloved old black and white movies would have favored. (She had learned her love of those movies sitting with the Taylors each evening, the air sweet with the sugar-sour tang of booze as they firmly but gently self-medicated, so the lure of the bar was maybe no accident.)

And there, seated at the hushed, deserted afternoon bar, in a thrift-store gray 1940s double-breasted suit, reading *The Locusts Have No King* by, yes, Dawn Powell, and looking like an actor in a black-and-white movie himself, a dove-gray Fedora and a frosted martini at his elbow, there he sat, twenty-six to her nine-teen and, Claire thought, there and then, destined to be the absolute love of her life, the first *man* she had ever wanted, after the shambling, eager, clueless boys of Rockford.

She could see him eyeing her up as she approached the dark wood bar, enthralled by the beer taps and the mirrored wall of bottles, could see him clock *her* thrift-store forties look, her tailored

red jersey day dress, her low-heel pumps, her boxy black jacket, her black felt hat. Music was playing in the background, and she lilted along with it, tapping her feet to the samba-style rhythm.

'You like the music?' he said.

'Nelson Riddle. What's not to like?'

'I'm impressed. Not many people your . . . would even know who Nelson Riddle is.'

'Not many people my what?'

'I don't know. Your hat size. Do you know what it's called?'

'"Gold." From *Tone Poems of Color*. Is this the album?'

'It is.'

'Then "Black" by Victor Young is next.'

'I think that deserves a drink.'

'Not in this hat size.'

'Eighteen?'

'Plus one. Still a couple of years to go.'

'Well. It would have been fine in 'eighty-four, before Reagan stuck his dumb oar in. Let's see what we can do about turning back time here.'

With that, he got up and went outside. She heard him turning a Yale lock and running a bolt. He came back in and crossed to the bar and began mixing a shaker of martinis – Tanqueray, vermouth, cracked ice.

'We're closed for a half-hour. Is that all right with you?'

'It's fine. Except, if the cops call, it's your fault.'

'The cops won't call. They know we run a tight ship.'

'Where's the crew?'

'You're looking at them. Danny Brogan.'

'Claire Taylor.'

'I saw you on campus earlier. I like your get-up.'

'I like yours. You a senior?'

'No, I . . . had a late vocation. Freshman. I think we have classes together. Here you go.'

'Black' was playing now, preposterously romantic strings that, in concert with her first sip of ice-cold dry martini, made her swoon, or at least feel as if she was swooning.

'Good?'

'Very good.'

'Gin. With a little gin in it.'

'It's the kind of thing that might catch on.'

They talked about Dawn Powell, and Nelson Riddle, and Preston Sturges, and Danny told her he'd show her how to mix a martini, and Claire said she was a fast learner, and a half-hour later, after Claire had learned and shaken and poured, and Danny said he had to open the bar because the after-work crowd were on their way, Claire looked at him intently until he kissed her and, kissing him back, thought either she must be in love, or drunk. As it turned out, she was both.

The industrial estates and retail parks gave way to residential blocks as she reached the outskirts of the city, crying again, this time with a kind of sweet sadness. Where did that thing between them go? That charm, that easy desire, that lightness? From then on, Brogan's in the afternoon had been their sanctuary, their church, their sacred place. Now, and for many years, it was where Danny worked, and where he hid from her, where she was happy to let him hide. Don't go there, they said, holding a little back, and then a little more, until maybe each was keeping the best from each other. Don't go there. Until one day, like the autumn leaves you've been tracking that suddenly vanish, leaving bare silhouettes against the sky, one day you don't go anywhere. One day there's nowhere left to go.

The lunch crowd at the Twin Anchors is all a-clamor around her. She finishes the club soda and orders the Greyhound, wishing it was her second, that she could have her second drink first.

She thinks she knows what happened to her: having failed in the theater, she thought she could return to a life of domestic tranquillity and that that would be enough. And then she was too frightened to admit that it wasn't. (Where does the fear come from?)

But what had happened to Danny? What kind of gnawing sense of powerlessness, of disappointment, of fear, yes, fear, had led to him losing their house? What kind of trouble is he in, and how can she help get him out of it? She stares into her drink and thinks about Jonathan Glatt taking their money, how all Danny did was shrug his shoulders and say he could forget about early retirement, and she said well, he didn't play golf or sail so what was he gonna do with all that time, probably spend it in Brogan's anyway, so he might as well be on the business end of the bar, and they both laughed, still angry and upset but secretly relieved, or so she thought, that the unspeakable prospect of Danny's early retirement had been removed from view.

Now she sees, because that was only six months or so ago, that Jonathan Glatt's betrayal must have come as a total body blow to a man who was struggling to keep the house from being repossessed. Now she sees . . . but of course, that's just what she doesn't see, what she hasn't *seen*: her husband, a man who can keep so much from her, who can not only remortgage a house worth, what, they had it valued just for the hell of it the last time house prices took a hike, 450 grand two or three years ago, and now that house is a month away from being sold, what the fuck kind of money trouble had Danny got himself into and how the fuck had he not betrayed a single glimmer of it to his wife? The notion that she didn't notice a thing is a gall to her, a bitter reproach, she sees that at least, not just to her sense of herself as a wife, God knows what a hash she's made of *that* in various ways, but as what she has most prized herself to be in her heart of hearts, even after she failed at it: an actor, with all the arts of observation and sensitivity, the acute awareness of mood and feeling she has cherished in herself, falsely, if as it seems the man she has been closest to her entire life stands revealed to her as a complete mystery. Who is he? She doesn't really know.

Here comes Paul Casey now, talking of people she doesn't really know. She takes a hit on her drink and wonders once more if Danny had followed her to Chicago last week, or tracked her down while she was there. Had he seen her bring Paul Casey to her room? Had he seen her go to his apartment? Did he know for certain that she hadn't slept with her ex-boyfriend? Did she even know herself? Because she had probably done stuff that nudged up against what any reasonable person would consider the married line. Had she gone further? Paul said no, and she believed him. But she couldn't remember. And if Danny had tried to find her, for any number of legitimate reasons, and had caught the faintest whiff of what had happened, well, maybe that was what had sent him hurtling over the edge.

One for My Baby (And One More for the Road)

D anny is eating steak and French fries in a Ruby Tuesday's at the Clock Tower Square in Rockford, Illinois, or rather, he is nursing a Bloody Mary and chewing the occasional fry and thinking he should send his steak back because it is overcooked, but not wanting to cause a fuss, preferring to sit and sulk instead, about the steak, and other things.

Danny insisted on driving because he thought it would stop him thinking, not to mention freaking out, but neither the driving nor the comfort afforded by the knowledge that the girls were all right stopped him doing either of these things, or speeding, or shouting out random strings of obscenities, Tourette's style, about Glatt and his money and Gene Peterson, and his wife, Claire, and what she may or may not have got up to in Chicago with her ex-boyfriend and God alone knows what else.

When they crossed the state line into Illinois at 120 miles an hour, Jeff quietly but firmly told him they needed to take a break, and Danny, grateful despite his protests, because he knew Jeff wanted him to explain everything, and for all that Danny didn't want to explain (in the irrational hope that not putting it into words would somehow prevent it from being real), deep down he was of course desperate to tell all, to confess, as much for the relief of letting it out as for the urgent need to make sense of it and plan his next move. But he felt he was being crowded into it nonetheless, and by Jeff, whose role in Danny's life does not extend to bossing him around or making demands. Hence the sulking.

Jeff has finished his salad. He drinks his green tea and wipes his mouth with his napkin and looks at Danny with clear-eyed concern, and when Danny meets his eye and looks away quickly for about the ninth time since they sat down, Jeff speaks.

'Have you called Claire? Maybe it would be a good idea to let her know you're OK? And more to the point, that the kids are?'

'I can't call her.'

'Why not?'

'Because if I do, they can track my cell phone.'

'Who can?'

'Whoever's behind all this.'

'Where'd you hear that?'

'I saw it on TV. One of those cop shows?'

'What about a throwaway phone?'

'What's that?'

'You mustn't have watched that show to the end. A throwaway phone is where you buy a cell that's preloaded with credit. You don't need an account, so you can't be traced. And who's liable to be tracing you anyway, Danny? Cops? Bad guys?'

Danny shakes his head, unwilling to begin, unsure *where* to begin.

'What's going on? Is it something to do with the fire? The Bradberry fire?'

Danny's stomach lurches, like he's going to heave, and sweat seeps through his hair and down his brow. Instead of replying (because how the fuck does Jeff know about his part in the Bradberry fire?) he shakes his head and waves toward the window with the celery stick from his cocktail at the Clock Tower Square Resort, with its Best Western Hotel and Conference Center and its leisure facilities and so on.

'Places like this,' Danny says, knowing he sounds like a parody of an angry middle-aged man but unable to resist. 'Is it any wonder we're demoralized, as a nation, sitting in horrible chain restaurants like this in horrible parking lots like that, within earshot of the Interstate's roar, eating horrible food and gazing out at horrible red-brick buildings, and this is a *resort*? This is where we come to *enjoy* ourselves?'

Danny wants to add to this, or thinks he does, but he can feel his voice beginning to yelp, to creak, and in any case, the emotion roiling within him is too great and particular to be contained by a rant about the Best Western Hotel chain's lack of architectural distinction. Jeff pats Danny on the arm and catches the waiter's eye and asks for a second green tea and another Bloody Mary, and they sit in silence until the drinks come, and Jeff takes the tea and passes the cocktail to Danny and nods at him and smiles, as if everything is going to be OK.

'I'm the driver, no discussion. Drink.'

Danny takes a hit of the drink, which he augments with extra Tabasco before taking another and nodding to himself, the fiery burn of the vodka and spices granting him a blessed release from his burden and fostering briefly in him the unlikely notion that everything *is* going to be OK. Finally, it's time to talk. Not about the fire, not to begin with. Not about Claire. Claire Bradberry, Jesus, did Jonathan Glatt actually say that? Claire and her Facebook account, when she affects 'not to understand' technology. Claire sending sex messages via Facebook to her ex-boyfriend. Claire and Paul Casey in Chicago. Claire, the wife he knows all about and doesn't know at all. Not Claire, not yet. No, the money. Start with the money.

'I lost two hundred and fifty grand to Jonathan Glatt.'

Jeff's eyes widen.

'You said fifty. You told me fifty.'

'I told Claire fifty. I told everyone fifty. Sometimes I manage to convince myself it *was* only fifty.'

'And where did you . . . just have it sitting around?'

'Are you kidding me? Brogan's is a bar and grill, not a casino. No, I . . . I remortgaged the house.'

'For two fifty?'

'No, I had the fifty. So I could say, we lost that. But I borrowed an extra two hundred. Two hundred and five, actually. I . . . I don't know. I got greedy, I suppose. I could blame it all on Gene. I mean, he got me into it, and from what Glatt told me, he got out before the whole thing fell apart. Whether that means he knew what was coming and didn't warn me, I don't know. Or worse, he knew the whole thing was a fraud. But you know, no one made me borrow the extra funds. I . . . I felt like I deserved it.'

'And what does that mean? You couldn't keep up the payments? Is that why you cleared the house out, the bank foreclosed?'

The word is acrid in the air between them, like smoke from charcoal flames: *foreclosed*. Danny winces, then raises his eyebrows and nods.

'I don't get it,' Jeff says. 'Two hundred grand, depending on the term, that's what, twelve hundred a month? Brogan's is never empty, not even on Tuesday nights in February when no one in their right mind goes out, not even when the city is snowed in. What gives? How could you slip so far behind?'

'How do you know about the Bradberry fire?' Danny says, not so much dodging as deferring the question.

'What? Because you told me. Years ago. When you helped me stay out of jail, and out of the hands of those guys from Milwaukee, and I was grateful, and told you how unlikely it was that I'd be able to pay you back, and how ashamed I felt, I guess you wanted to make me feel like everyone had, I don't know, a secret shame, something they weren't proud of.'

'And . . . because I'm afraid I don't remember . . .'

'We were very, very drunk. And then stoned. It's just, that makes no difference to me. I remember everything.'

'Well then. What exactly did I tell you? What do you know?'

Danny's voice is louder now, alcohol removing his inhibitions. Some people at the adjoining tables look over, and he stares at them until they look away again. He sees Jeff watching him, as if he is a volatile compound that's going to bubble over at any moment, and gives him a smile that's intended to be reassuring, although he doesn't really see how it can be. Slow down, drop your voice, don't over-enunciate, keep it together.

'You told me you were bullied by the Bradberry kid . . .'

'Jackie. Why do you ask this *now*, exactly?'

'Because when you were venting your spleen out there on the highway, free-associating and motherfucking and damning everyone to hell and beyond, Jackie Bradberry was one of the prominent names on your shit list. Along with his brothers, Eric and, and . . .'

'Brian. OK. Go on. So back then.'

'So back then you told me you were bullied over a period of six to nine months, first by Jackie, and then, when you stood up to him, by his brothers, who were the threat behind Jackie. That you had to let him kick the shit out of you or they'd more than kick the shit out of you, they'd kick it back into you again. And you were a nervous wreck. And none of your friends would step in 'cause they were all scared shitless of the Bradberry brothers too—'

'Gene Peterson stepped in. Actually. And they broke his arm. So after that . . .'

'Whatever. The fact remains, it was like you had nobody to turn to, and no way out. Your father was a nasty old drunk, or a charming but ineffectual old drunk, or a creepy, sleazy old drunk – anyway, he was a drunk, and no use to a boy in trouble, he had no advice to give you. And you felt like you couldn't take much more. So you decided you had to kill Jackie Bradberry—'

'I decided he had to die. I never . . . it wasn't like there was a masterplan, like it was a hit, and I was an eleven-year-old assasin . . .'

'OK. So you told me about it, that you feel . . . or at least, you *felt*, that you were responsible. A Halloween prank got out of hand, and thirteen people died, and it was your fault.'

Danny takes a long hit of his drink and stares into it, through the cracked ice and the pepper flecks, sees the green of the celery, the crimson of the juice, blood among the leaves, the garden ablaze.

'But it wasn't clear to me why. I mean, there was so much confusion, you were concussed—'

Danny nods impatiently and holds up a hand to cut Jeff off.

'You know she grew up here? I mean, in Rockford, not in this so-called resort,' Danny says.

'Who?'

'Claire. My wife. She was adopted at the age of three, and grew up in Rockford. Her parents, that is to say, her adoptive parents, ran a flower store, more than that, a garden center, seeds and plants and cuttings and so on, attached in some way to the arboretum. Rockford has a small arboretum, it's almost the dump's saving grace. Anyway, when we met, and Claire saw my house, how it was embedded in the UW Arboretum, I think she took it as a sign, that we were meant to be.'

'I'm sorry, Danny. Does that have something to do with the Bradberry fire?'

The Bradberry fire. The central event in his life. It has never gone away, and it never will. Danny looks at the red and green in his glass and again sees blood, sees flames. That's how he remembers it back then, and that's how he sees it now, as if the world is a dark wood, dimly visible through a glistening, pulsing caul of crimson fire. How could he ever escape it? Ralph Cowley had written a book about it, or at least, a manuscript. Seventy or eighty pages of closely spaced typescript, thrust into his hands last week at Danny's garden gate, Ralph in his Death cowl, shaking with excitement and fear. And the thing about it was he had written it all from Danny's point of view.

Danny finishes his drink, which he had thought was keeping him clear-eyed and vivid and fresh, but which he now realizes, stupidly, of course, was making him drunk.

'We never meant it to happen!' he says abruptly, too loud, and again the diners in Ruby Tuesday's turn to gaze at this man, a little too bright and shrill for lunchtime.

'We made sure to keep the gas away from the house, ten or twelve feet away, we made a point of it,' Danny says, quieter now, as if, even at this late stage, what happened could be undone. Jeff nods his reassurance, and holds the back of his hand up to their impromptu audience: *show's over, folks.*

Danny winces at the memory, tries to turn it into a nod of assent, succeeds only in looking like a man trying to shake a bug out of his ear.

'There was one Bradberry child that survived, remember? A little girl, three years old. She had got up in darkness, between the time the last of the family returned home and before the fire started, and had wandered about downstairs, and let herself into the old porch, which is where she liked to play during the daytime, she had a toy farm there, buildings and animals and so on, and after a while she fell asleep. And this porch had the only door and windows that didn't have vinyl frames, and the fire fighters arrived before the flames reached her, and it was still drafty enough that the fumes hadn't overwhelmed her, and she survived.'

Danny pauses as their waitress passes by. Drunk or not, he needs a bump to get through the rest of this.

'How're you guys doin' here?' she says.

'Another of these, and another green tea,' says Danny, flourishing his empty glass. Jeff shakes his head.

'Black coffee. There's only so much green tea a man can drink.'

The waitress departs.

'The little girl survived. Her name was Claire. Her adoptive parents were called Taylor. They lived outside Milwaukee, ran some kind of gardening business, but when Claire was about five, I think there was some stuff in the local paper, some rumor-mongering about who she really was, so the Taylors upped sticks and moved to Rockford. That's pretty much all I know about them. I never met them, they died pretty quickly, one after another, when Claire was in Chicago.'

'Your Claire . . . Claire Taylor . . . was Claire *Bradberry*?' Jeff says, his mouth slack with wonder.

'And I didn't know, I didn't know when I met her first, I found out . . . just after we got back together, I . . . was told.'

'And does she know?'

'For a long time, she didn't. She had no interest in finding out, she said. All she wanted to know was if she had any heredi-tary medical conditions. The Taylors told her there was nothing serious, apparently – and she's never been much of a drinker, so that gene appears to have been skipped.'

'"For a long time she didn't." Do you mean, she does now?'

'Jonathan Glatt told me there were four other investors in his Ponzi scheme known to me: Gene Peterson, who got us in, Dave Ricks and Ralph Cowley, all present at the Bradberry house, Halloween, 1975. And somebody who was there also. Somebody called Claire Bradberry.'

The waitress brings Danny's drink and Jeff's coffee. Jeff looks like he's preparing to speak but can't work out what to say. Danny, relieved to have unburdened himself of his terrible secret, and feeling ever so slightly dreamy and associative and insightful, because he's relieved, and because he's drunk, takes a hefty swig of vodka and spiced tomato juice and looks around the room. The lunch crowd has dwindled; if they're not the last people here, there's no one else Danny can see. Two staff members in chef's duds have emerged from the kitchen and are leaning at the bar, shooting it with the bartenders. Danny likes this time in Brogan's, the slow set in the frenzied rhythm of the restaurant day. There's a sudden, unbuttoned intimacy between the workers, a playful ease. If you want to know who's sleeping with who, or who's about to start, this is when you spot the signs. He tried to explain it to Claire once, and she said it sounded like when the curtain has come down in the theater, and the cast reveal their true faces to each other once more, only there's still a trace, a remnant, a shadow of the part they had played on the stage: they've more than one face, and that doubleness is kind of sexy, the sense of there being something mysterious or elusive about a person. Danny thinks that's right, and wonders if that is why actors' marriages don't seem to last, because they are more afflicted by duality than most, and then decides maybe everyone has a second face, a face you can glimpse but never truly know. And then he thinks, almost laughing, *Jesus, the stuff that slides through your brain when you start drinking at lunchtime.*

'So,' Jeff begins. 'So look, for the purposes of what the fuck do we do now, I'm going to skip the part where I ask you how you feel and doesn't Claire have a right to know and all of that and cut straight to this: were you being, like, blackmailed or something? Because even if you'd lost two hundred grand, the income from Brogan's would have covered it, right? Unless . . .'

Danny nods.

'Unless I was already up against it for other reasons, that's right. I had gotten used to it.'

'How long?'

'Fifteen years. It started just after Claire came back from Chicago and we got married. A couple of weeks later, I got this letter, the way they do it in the movies, all letters from magazines pasted on to a sheet of paper, the address typewritten. It read: *Laugh at me an you are dead.* That was the first note Jackie Bradberry sent me. And then a week later came the second: *You are dead meat. Killer.*

'All the others followed, one a week, calling me out to the death ground, telling me I was dead. Even the spelling was right: *See what a fare fight is like, bitch boy*, with "fair" spelled f-a-r-e. Then nothing for a few weeks. I was reeling at this stage, obviously. And then the coup de grace.

'*Maybe it would be best for you if you let your wife know that you burnt her family to death and took your chances. Do not take for granted the patience and discretion of your so-called friends. They are not the only ones who know Claire Taylor is the Bradberry girl who alone escaped on Halloween 1976.*'

'Oh, man. And did you know?'

'How would I have known?'

'So it came as a bit of a shock.'

'That's about right. And all I wanted was, for it not to be true.'

'And you said, she didn't want to know.'

'That's right. But I *needed* to know. If not after the first letters, certainly when that one came along. The next communication was a little more direct. It had a PO box number I should send a check to every month. At first it wasn't for very much, three hundred bucks. I say not very much, it rose eventually to five grand, still, three hundred felt like a lot back in 'ninety-five, just married and so on. But I paid it.'

'Five grand a *month*? You didn't go to the police?'

'Then I'd've had to explain about the Bradberry fire, what I was doing there. Implicate the guys, hey, maybe end up in jail on manslaughter, even murder charges. Are you kidding me? The blackmailer spelled it out: Claire would be told first, the cops second. Besides. I knew the truth at that stage.'

'You knew the truth?'

'Claire had an envelope with her details in it, adoption forms and so on. The Taylors had given it to her, so any time she felt ready, she could find out who her parents were. She kept it among her things. And one night when she had gone out with Dee St Clair, I found it, didn't even have to steam it open, there was a ribbon like on a notarized document, but no wax seal or anything. So I opened it, and there it was, a copy of her birth certificate, Claire Mary Bradberry, born January eighteenth, 1973, to William and Agnes Bradberry, Schofield Street, Madison, Wisconsin.'

'Oh, *man.*'

'And it was, like, one thing on top of another, you know: I couldn't let Claire know I'd had a hand in the fire that killed her family, I couldn't let Claire find out who her real family was from this malicious asshole, and I couldn't let the cops know about my involvement in the Bradberry fire. Over the years, I thought of hiring, like, a private investigator to look into it, only, I don't know, if I were a PI and I located the guy who started the Bradberry fire, I'd consider that a higher value scalp, I'd turn me in. I didn't trust anyone not to spill the beans.'

'And what about the guys? Surely you figured it must have been one of them?'

'Logically, that's how it looked. But here's the thing: it wasn't Dave Ricks, no way, Dave and me were the tightest. And Ralph is just such a solid guy, not an ounce of bad in him. And Gene, well, Gene, up until the Jonathan Glatt thing, I'd've thought it impossible, the very idea of anonymous letters, of blackmail, if Gene Peterson was going to do anything, he'd come round your house and shout through your window, you know, straight as an arrow, Gene. Or so I would have said. I mentioned it to each of them, obliquely, mind you, not the blackmail, just, if they thought anyone else knew about it. Each of them swore he'd never told a soul. And I didn't want them to know the truth about Claire, so I didn't take it further.'

'And the bank have foreclosed on the house? Jesus, Danny, the family home? Didn't your grandfather build it?'

Tears brim in Danny's eyes, booze the forcing agent but the emotion no less heartfelt for that.

'It's terrible. And hiding it has been worse: it's three months now since the court ordered it. Technically there's one month to go before the auction, one month to turn it around. But maybe . . . maybe I don't want to . . . maybe living there all this time hasn't been a good idea either. Maybe not everything in the garden is what it should be. But it's not as if I had a lot of time to make up my mind, it seemed to happen so fast. The return from the investment with Glatt was servicing the mortgage, and then the money from Glatt was gone, and suddenly I had a mortgage I couldn't pay because I was hemorrhaging five grand a month to this blackmailing motherfucker who was trying to destroy my life and succeeding. And . . . and I both did it, intentionally, and let it happen, unconsciously, because . . . because my wife is not . . . because not everything in the garden is . . .'

'Rosy. Something about Chicago, and faithless wives, and Facebook, and an ex-boyfriend were all parts of your highway rant. And the clearing out of the house and the bolting with the kids is part of that? Along with all the financial shenanigans? To punish Claire? Or to protect her? Or some fucked-up combination of both?'

Danny grimaces, then laughs, a dark, self-loathing laugh.

'Some fucked-up combination of both is about right. But also, to find out who's behind this. When it comes down to it, it can only be Ralph, or Dave, or Gene. And here's the thing. Last Sunday, the night of the barbecue—'

Danny stops talking because Jeff has held up his hand and pointed to the TV screen to their right, one of several dotted around the restaurant. Danny looks up at the screen. The sound is down, but the images tell their own story: helicopter and angle shots of his own backyard on Arboretum Avenue, secured as a crime scene with police tape and a white paper tent and figures in protective clothing pacing about. There are uniformed officers and police cruisers and a shot of the Madison Police Department Western District station house on McKenna Boulevard. There are shots of a body being wheeled past on a gurney and loaded into a Dane County Medical Examiner's vehicle.

There's a photograph of Ralph Cowley taken in high school, or it could be Dave Ricks, those guys had always looked alike, but it's got to be Ralph, since it was Ralph who came to the house. Ralph, the Angel of Death, with his novel, his book of revelations. There's a photograph of Mr Smith, and a photograph of Danny, the one where he was in a tuxedo dancing with Claire in *The Way of the World*. Before Danny can process it all, the question flashes through his mind: why is a murderer on the run nine times out of ten photographed in a tuxedo? Do murderers on the run take care never to be photographed after their prom night?

'Time to go, Dan,' Jeff says.

Jeff throws a couple of fifties on the restaurant table and nods his head in the direction of the parking lot.

'I think we need to hit the road, round up what's left of your old friends and ask them a few questions.'

Marry the Man Today

'There's no way you can just leave the kids behind,' Angelique says, wiping her lips and cheeks with a tissue and reaching for the flask of iced camomile tea she has brought and letting it sluice around inside her mouth before she swallows it. She perches on the car seat beside Charlie T and gives him the perky Angelique smile that brooks no argument and retrieves her gum from the clasp of her purse and, with the aid of a hand mirror, starts to repair the make-up she's smeared.

'I mean, you have to think this through. It stands to you that you won't kill children, or physically harm them. But what about the psychological consequences of leaving them with the body of their dead aunt in the house? Know what I mean?'

Charlie T closes his eyes so she can't see him roll them in despair. How had this happened? They had always had an understanding that his work was not up for discussion. She knew she was the only woman he had ever told about it, and had respected a) the necessary secrecy, and b) the facts of what he actually did. Or so he thought. But as soon as she got wind of the fact that there were kids involved in this job, she was like a dog with a bone. He reaches for his Miraculous Medal – *O Mary conceived without sin, pray for us who have recourse to thee* – then remembers he has lost it. Hopes that's not a bad omen, he's never killed anyone without it.

The Angelique thing was his own fault. First of all, he had brought her along on yet another job. Not that he thought there was going to be any work done today, just a reconnaissance trip to Cambridge, Wisconsin, but then the call had come through and he had to stop off for *this* job. And he'd tried to get her to go on home, *insisted*, but to no avail. He didn't know what it was, this girl, she could always get her way. And fair play, she had dealt with the dog beyond in Madison, so it was hard to argue her down.

In any case, he had talked himself up, the big man who wouldn't take any shit from the boss, the hardened killer with principles, how a man should know where to draw the line and how he drew the line at harming kids.

He should have known better. 'Kids' was like a trigger word for Angelique. Professionally, she may have dealt with geriatrics, and not always in a way that was medically approved, but on her own time, kids were the answer. In whatever context it came up, on TV or whatever, trafficked kids, kids in daycare, gifted kids, kids kids kids: Angelique knew all there was to know. Her hunger for a child was fierce and unabashed, and it sometimes seems as if she believed the more expertise she amassed on the topic the greater the likelihood of her acquiring one of her own would be.

The car was parked in the woods on the Rockford side of the Clock Tower Square Resort, concealed from the scrub road by a stand of shabby old pines by a deserted caravan park. It was the perfect vantage point: he could see all the cars, including the target's red Mustang, and the exits from the Best Western, Ruby Tuesday's and the water resort, although he doubted very much if the mark had popped in for a swim or a ride on the water chute. Charlie T had his Barrett M82A1 along, as he always did. When Mr Wilson had asked him, starting out, what kind of SASR (semi-automatic scoped rifle) he'd feel comfortable with, he didn't have to give it too much thought. He'd never shot anyone in Ireland with the M82, but he'd practiced with it many's the time: it was the IRA sniper's rifle of choice, and as such, it would do Charlie T nicely. He'd assembled it and chambered the .50 mm Browning MG cartridge, and was watching and waiting and wishing a) he hadn't brought Angelique along, and b) that, at least occasionally, she would stop talking, or rather, telling him what to do.

When b) finally occurred, he nearly wished it hadn't, because he needed to keep his wits about him, but fuck it, he'd be a long time dead, and last time he'd checked, there was nothing said about blow-jobs in heaven, although you'd have to wonder about the meaning of the word 'heaven' if the best things in life weren't available. Quite aside from the fact that, as the entrance requirements were currently constituted, Charlie T wasn't headed heavenwards any time soon, so get it here, and get it now.

Angelique starts in about the kids mere seconds afterwards. His heart rate has barely slowed, and here she goes again.

'I don't think we can inflict that on them, Charlie.'

'Sorry, but where did this "we" come from, exactly? I agreed that you could come on the trip because it was your day off and you wanted to see the craft shops and galleries in Cambridge. I drop you off, I go to work, I pick you up: that was the deal.'

'The *deal*. The deal has already changed, hasn't it, now that we're sitting in a car with a sub-machine gun—'

'It's not a sub-machine gun, it's a semi-automatic—'

'Yeah, whatever. Don't talk to me like *I'm* the child. You brought up the ethical dimension. You told your boss where you draw the line. Don't set yourself up and fail to deliver. *That*,' she says, baring her teeth in a cheerfully lewd grin, 'is not the Charlie T we know and love.'

Charlie grins back in spite of himself, at her flashing green eyes and her red hair in an up-do and her white pancake face – like a real Irish girl, she is, only you never see Irish girls like that in Ireland. You only see them in America, the same way Charlie always feels Irish-Americans are actually more Irish than Irish people are, or at least a lot of the regulars at the Dark Rosaleen are, with their diddley-eye music and their 'did you miss mass?' Although maybe the clientele at an Irish pub in Chicago are a whatdoyoucallit, a self-selecting sample. Anyway, Angelique McCarthy is the one, isn't she? He can't seem to resist her. He'll be up the aisle before he knows it, or on the steps of City Hall at any rate. He buttons his pants and reaches for the M82, just so he knows it's there. Angelique, you're a darling. If only you wouldn't talk quite so much. Say something before she starts up again.

'You know the trip to Cambridge is a recce as much as anything else, we don't even have an address for the woman. And if it happens that we get it, there's scoping out the location, the neighbors and so on, it's extremely unlikely anything will happen today. So the whole thing is a bit hypothetical.'

'But that's exactly when you should be thinking about it, before reality lands in on top of you in the shape of two wailing kids. I mean, what—'

'Jesus Christ Almighty, Angelique, do you think I've never done this before? Had to separate children from adults? Had to engineer a situation where the kids are confined somewhere, safe and secure, while the work is done? It's not always easy, and it's far from ideal, but it's what you do, even if you have to tie them up. I'd rather not let it get to that, upsetting for everyone, but your timeframe is not infinite, and sometimes you've got to. And then, as soon as you're clear, you alert the authorities, and they go in and release the kids.'

Angelique lets a hiss of air out loudly through her teeth.

'Oh, Charlie. That is neither acceptable nor appropriate.'

'Neither what nor what?'

'You need . . . you need me with.'

'I have you with.'

'I mean, to look after the kids.'

Angelique reaches around and takes the photographs from a brown leather satchel Charlie's left on the back seat. She looks at the shot of the girls beneath the apple trees.

'Barbara and Irene. Aw. Aren't they cute? I love those names, real old-style names, aren't they? Barbara and Irene. I had an Aunt Irene. Drank like a fish. Even as a kid, her name seemed like something from another time. Old Bing Crosby movies. *The Bells of St Mary's*. Barbara and Irene. I could look after them for you, Charlie.'

'What do you mean, look after them?'

'Well. This is an operation your boss is getting paid big money for, is that right?'

'I guess.'

'Well, maybe there are angles he hasn't considered. That you could.'

Charlie T looks at Angelique, and wonders if he sees something else in her eyes apart from mischief, and liveliness, and lust, and concern for children, something he has seen before when she spoke about one of her elderly patients who was really annoying the other nurses and the orderlies, a patient who, days later, has ceased to be a live issue. Charlie has done something very Irish with the knowledge he has about Angelique, which is, to pretend he doesn't know what he has maybe known all along.

'Like what?'

'I don't know. Just . . .'

'Just what? We could snatch them? Hold them for ransom? We could harm them? Fuck, Angelique . . .'

'Not *harm* them, Charlie, I would never harm them, never harm a *child*. Just, don't close yourself down to the possibilities. If there's something to be *gained* . . . you could take advantage. Don't miss out on that.'

'For the money?'

'Well, that. And the control. I mean, do you know what's going on?'

'I don't care what's going on. I do my work and I get paid, the end.'

'But how much are you into your boss for? Do you want to owe that the rest of your life? Maybe there's a way out of that, you snatch the kids—'

'Oh, you *are* talking about that? About kidnapping?'

'And a woman living in a lakeside house in fucking Cambridge, Wisconsin. No recession up there, baby, those people are loaded, her brother is her only next of kin, he's gonna inherit, that's gotta be a lot of dough to get his darling daughters back, Charlie, nice for a couple who are just starting out. Clear some debt, maybe acquire some property. And you know me and kids, I'll treat them in an appropriate, holistic, child-centered manner.'

Charlie stares at her now in astonishment. One road trip and the sight of a gun, and his girlfriend the nurse has turned into Bonnie fucking Parker. And she's supposed to be the *normal* one, the refuge, the antidote to the strippers and hostesses and crystal meth queens. She's supposed to be his salvation.

'And maybe then you won't need this guy, Mr Wilson, maybe you can set up in business on your own. Call it a side deal, call it initiative, call it what you like.'

And Angelique looks at the photo of the Brogan girls and smiles a little smile to herself. And before Charlie can say another word, or reflect that having a stable girlfriend is not now the bargain he had hoped it would be, seeing as the price he must pay is to acknowledge that she is completely fucking nuts, Ruby

Tuesday's door swings open and two men appear, one of average height, dark hair in a gray suit, one very tall with a black suede coat and long silver-flecked blond hair and a cowboy look about him, older than Charlie but he likes the style, fair play to him.

Charlie is out of the car now and training the scope of the Barrett M82 on the men as they cross the Clock Tower parking lot, Jesus, they're moving at some clip, he'll only get one chance, can't afford to slip up, steady boy, steady. The gray suit, that's Brogan, he stumbles, and Cowboy catches his arm and keeps him upright. Drinking at lunchtime, that's what Charlie T will be up for when this job is through. He hears a noise from the car, looks down quickly, sees Angelique scooshing over, ready for a quick getaway. Nice work babe. Bonnie and Clyde, how are you! Eyes front, and the scope hovers over the Mustang now as the boys stand outside the drivers' door, what the fuck . . . ah, brilliant, they're having the old drunks' quarrel about who's driving, Brogan is waving the keys and trying to get in and Cowboy won't let him, he holds him by the shoulders and talks at his face, and Brogan stares back, then nods, and grins, and surrenders the keys and goes round the passenger side, and Cowboy walks back around the red Mustang and looks over the Mustang's roof at Brogan, and then lets his eyes drift up in Charlie T's direction as if he can see him, which he can't, too many trees, too far away, and Charlie trains the scope on the Cowboy's face, full frontal, and squeezes gently but firmly, and puts a bullet through the Cowboy's nose.

Just Friends

'I think there's one thing I should probably make clear,' says Paul Casey, waves of anxiety emanating from him like heat haze on a city street. As soon as Claire set eyes on him, in the tan polyester suit with the pens and propelling pencil set in the top pocket and the thick-soled shoes and the rayon tie, she thought there was probably going to be something he would want to make clear all right. That he had worn a cheap suit for a bet, say, because he got such good odds he would be able to front up for lunch. But the longer she looked at him, the more she realized that the suit was right; it was she who had been wrong. Where last week she had seen the sunken cheeks and dark haunted gaze she remembered from twenty years ago, today, in the crush of the Twin Anchors, she sees dry, pasty skin and tired, watery eyes, and that mouth she had thought delicate, but had come to know as weak by the end of their relationship first time round. What had she been *thinking*? Had last week been spent entirely in the dark? Counting the number of bars and restaurants, parties and clubs, the answer was probably yes. And the hotel room, Claire – don't forget that, she was going to say, but that's the problem, isn't it, or one of them: she can't remember exactly what happened in the hotel room.

'Couple of things, in fact,' Paul says, and he does his half-laugh, the one which is supposed to be ironic, all isn't-life-strange, but simply comes across as nervous. 'When I said I was divorced . . .'

Claire, who has been in a hurry to get to her stuff, is almost relieved by the diversion, the simple human relief of knowing that someone is a greater idiot than she is.

'When you said you were divorced, what? You forgot that you weren't?'

'Kind of. Thing of it is—'

Claire can contain herself no longer. 'Paul, what are you *wearing*?'

Blotches of red appear on Paul Casey's cheeks and he looks down into his Diet Coke.

'I'm wearing . . . well, my dad likes to keep things traditional, and he insists everyone wear a collar and tie, all the guys on the floor included. And he has his preferences. "No one wants to buy nails from some dude in a fancy East Coast sissy suit," is how he puts it.'

'Your dad.'

'Sixty-seven and no sign of lying down.'

'Your dad . . . runs a *hardware* store.'

'That's right. On West Montana, remember. You can see the Biograph Theater from—'

'Your dad runs a hardware store.'

'Well. I'm glad we've got that straight.'

'You're working for your father?'

'I'm not ashamed of it.'

'I never said you should be.'

'Your tone said just that.'

'I'm sorry, I didn't mean . . . I just . . . I'm surprised, I guess I thought you were still . . .'

'Flying the flag.'

'But last week . . . I mean, we hung out with all the old crowd, a lot of them are still acting, or directing, they're on the scene one way or another, I thought . . .'

'I see them very seldom, Claire. I . . . the whole scene is pretty insular, obsessed with itself. That's not a criticism, it has to be like that, it's a . . . a parallel world, its own private eco-system: The Theater! I don't really—'

'Weren't you running that acting school on Schiller?'

'For a while. But eventually, it began to feel like a scam, you know, taking money from deluded people without enough talent or determination to make it in the business. It felt like we were exploiting their haplessness. So I quit. School's still going, I might add, and every so often, someone goes on from there to have a career, or at least, to get a part somewhere. So maybe I overreacted. Maybe I just wanted to be done with the theater once and for all. I was gonna say I don't really have what it takes, but I'm not gonna run myself down like that. Truth is, I didn't *want* to be involved, except the way we were. You know, doing it for real. We gave it a shot, and then we—'

'Gave up. I gave up. But still, I teach. Sometimes, I feel like I'm still involved, still doing it. More often it's like I'm taunting myself every day with my own failure.'

Claire holds Paul Casey's gaze now, wanting him to say something, although she doesn't know exactly what. To tell her she didn't fail, and make her believe it? To tell her he wants them to be together, so she can kindly and gently reject him? There's nothing he can say, nothing she wants him to say, really. She looks away. This is how it is, twenty years on: disappointment and regret, and the worst thing is, they don't even hurt that bad.

Their lunches arrive. They've both ordered ribs, because that's what you do in Twin Anchors. The restaurant is not usually open for lunch on weekdays, but they've made an exception because it's Halloween, and judging by the fact that the place is still jumping at three-fifteen, it looks like they made the right call. The nautical theme of the decor is offset by Halloween lanterns and witches on broomsticks, giving the room an eerie, Ship-of-Fools aspect. Voyage of the Damned. Claire looks toward the street, notes the yellow flare of autumn light outside, the last blaze before nightfall. *I should be getting the girls ready for Trick or Treat*, she thinks. *I so should not be here.*

'I'm happy enough not to be involved any more,' Paul says. 'At least, I think I am. Most of the time.'

'I don't understand . . . why didn't I find this out last week? What were we talking about?' Claire says.

'Well . . . about old times. And about, of course, The Theater. How good is Tracy Letts, really, or Tony Kushner, or Martin McDonagh. Who the new voices are, is Broadway fucked, what about London, what about Dublin. You were pretty high most of the time.'

'I was out of my mind.'

'Yeah, but not, like, drunk, or not necessarily. More like, like someone who'd just got out of jail, total adrenaline surge. And you were kind of seeing and hearing what you wanted to see and hear.'

'So what, it was all my fault?'

'No. That's why I said—'

'Because I have this card here, Paul, this card you put in my bag, with some pretty heavy stuff written on it.'

'Which is why I said, I needed to . . . hey, I was pretty high myself. Seeing you . . . all our yesterdays. I took so much time off work I nearly got fired. By my own dad. Had to explain to him, you were in town, first time in fifteen years. He always had a soft spot for you.'

'Does he think you're divorced as well?'

'That's funny.'

'But seriously. Do you remember how divorced you are? A little? A lot?'

Paul Casey frowns, and purses his lips until they disappear. He looks around the room, catches the bartender's eye, fits his hands one above the other to the height of a pint glass.

'Honkers Pale,' he calls, and turns back to Claire.

'I'm separated. Have been separated. But we're trying to get it back on track. Of course, bouncing round the Old Town with your ex-girlfriend probably doesn't help on that score.'

'Probably not. Neither does writing that I was the love of your life on a card, or that no one has ever made you feel the way I did,' Claire says, the words coming out shriller and more recriminatory than she intends.

'Well. It's the truth. But then again, you didn't strike me yourself as a brochure for the joys of married life last week. "Let's not talk about Danny." If you said that once, you said that, uh, more than once. Thank you.'

A pint of pale ale has arrived in front of Paul Casey, and he takes a deep draft of it. The waiter checks on Claire and her empty greyhound glass, but she shakes her head. Jesus, what is she doing here? She wants to retort to Paul's crack, but she has no right to the moral high ground.

'Look, I wrote what I wrote,' Paul says. 'It was kind of a wild night. I . . . well, I didn't know what to make of it. But I certainly didn't expect you to be back here within the – is it even a day? I mean, I only dropped you at O'Hare—'

'*Oh.* Do you think that's why I'm here?'

'Well. If you're not, that's fine. But yes, I kind of assumed, the things you had been saying . . . that you'd left Danny. And here you are. And so . . .'

'And so you thought you'd better make a few things clear.'

Claire puts her head in her hands. Clarity, isn't that what they call it? A moment of clarity? She's having one now, big time. It's as if the hangover from her trip, plus the shock of what happened when she got back, formed an impenetrable, blinding cloud, and she's finally emerged from it, and can breathe, and, more to the point, see.

'What was I saying? What did we *do*? Did we . . .?'

'No. No, we didn't. All right?'

'Because I remember the Tuesday, there was just some fooling around in the room, and then you left. But the Saturday, after shopping at Macy's . . .'

'There were drugs involved on Saturday. There was coke. And E.'

'I can remember . . .' Claire starts, and stops abruptly, her voice too loud, her face flushing now. She would very much like to hide at the bottom of that second drink, but she's done enough of that. She needs to talk herself down and start again.

'I can remember rolling around on the bed,' she says carefully. 'With you. Wearing not very much.'

Claire has a flash of her reflection in the hotel bedroom mirror. Too vain to take her underwear off, too anxious about what age and gravity had wrought. Maybe too reluctant to go the whole way? Paul Casey raises his eyebrows and nods.

'What was it? Did we just not want to?' Claire says, more or less knowing the truth by now but wanting Paul to spell it out.

'I wanted to. Not sure if you were quite so keen. But . . . well, as I said, there were drugs involved, and a lot of booze, and when it came to it, you were maybe not quite one hundred percent consenting. And I'm forty-two years old and it simply wasn't going to happen. We both passed out. And then the next morning, when it might have been actually, physically, feasible, the moment, such as it was, had passed. We both just seemed to know. Or at least, you did.'

'So . . . I have all the guilt, without even the sweet memory of the sin,' Claire says.

'I don't know. I think at the last fence, you pulled up. Mostly, you were full of talk, how you were going to change your life, shake it up, how you were tired of being invisible, how Danny and you weren't equal partners and that was your fault but you were going to change, you weren't going to be frightened or, yes, like Masha in *The Seagull*, you weren't going to be in mourning for your own life any more.'

Claire shuts her eyes tight and makes an anguished, high-pitched sound, as if she has scalded herself. Masha in *The Seagull*, what did she think she was, *fifteen*?

'Coke talk,' she whispers.

'Maybe. Not without a core of something real, though. I think the coke talk was where you and me were going to get back together and reform the theater company and, I don't know, show everyone a thing or two.'

'I'm sorry, Paul. I'm a fucking liability. I—'

'Hey. Why do you think I'm separated? Because I woke up

one morning and decided I was going to die if I didn't have sex with one of my wife's friends, not sure I minded which, just so long as it was the one who would tell her, and they all would have. Why? For the sex? Or just to make something happen? Something happened all right: I had to move back in with my mom and dad and I only see my kids at the weekend.'

'You have kids?'

'I did lie about that. Because . . . I thought you'd be more likely to sleep with me if I didn't have kids. Less complicated. More fantasy. God, I miss them.'

I miss mine too, Claire thinks, jitters of panic rippling through her. *In fact, I need to get back to them as soon as possible. Whatever Danny has done, however we're going to get out of this, or if we can't, the best thing – the only thing – for me is to be with the girls. If I leave now, we'll be in time for Trick or Treat.*

'I need to go, Paul,' Claire says, gathering her purse, finding some money for the check.

'Wait a second. If you're not, you know, Nora leaving the doll's house, what are you doing here? What's up?'

Claire breathes deep and stays sitting. Shouldn't take long. But this is after all why she came.

'Do you remember that night, I think it was during the run of *Aunt Dan and Lemon*, when I went off with that guy . . .'

'One of Danny's old school friends. It was during the run of *Our Country's Good*. Sure I remember. We all nearly ended up in jail.'

'Gene Peterson. He turned up in my backyard this morning, stabbed to death.'

'Get the fuck out of here.'

Claire takes Paul through what's happened in the last twenty-four hours, insofar as she understands it. When she's finished, he is staring at her, half astonished, half warily amused, as if she's suddenly going to mock him for believing such an unlikely tale.

'And you think, what, this has something to do with that night?'

'I don't know. That maybe Danny found out, and killed him?'

'Because you slept with a guy while you were broken up with him? Why hasn't he killed me too?'

'Maybe if you crashed one of his barbecues, he would.'

'Do you really believe Danny killed anyone?'

'No. I don't think so. I don't know any more. Jesus, if he can keep the foreclosure on a mortgage I didn't even know we had secret from me, fuck knows what else he's capable of.'

Hot tears sting Claire's eyes and she blinks and breathes deep to keep the panic at bay. 'I need to be with the girls, Paul. I need to protect them.'

'But not from Danny.'

'No. Of course not.'

'Well then. If the knife is his knife, he's being set up. Someone is fucking with him. And with you, if burying and then digging up the body is anything to go by.'

'And the only people I could think of who might be capable of that were those guys we met that night, remember?'

'The night you took that guy back to your place, and then called me to come and get you because he was freaking you out? I remember that night all right.'

'Not my finest hour.'

'That was Gene Peterson?'

'Yes. That was the guy; he turned up at the barbecue, and now he's been stabbed to death, the cops think with Danny's chef knife. Which Danny had when he went down to see him at the gate.'

'OK. So what I remember is, you ringing, waking me up, "Oh, Paul, I'm so scared," and my having to get dressed and come over and rescue you, and this guy, who's understandably pissed about the situation, and then a whole pantomime about having forgotten this party—'

'That warehouse party in Wicker Park.'

'And we were split up at this time, one of many splits, always instigated by you—'

'I was not a good girlfriend, I concede that.'

'You were a total bitch, and what's worse, I let you away with it. As in this night, where we go to the party, it was that tech guy we hired the lighting rig from who was throwing it, the fat guy with the ponytail and the black T-shirt?'

'All the tech guys were fat, dressed in black and wore ponytails.'

'And your friend Gene was being a total dick. What was the deal with him anyway? Having come to your rescue you refused to explain any more about it, as if somehow your fucking the guy was my fault.'

'I didn't fuck him. I might have, but he . . . had a dose of your trouble. He couldn't get it together.'

'Him as well. Maybe it's not us, it's you.'

'I'm just too much woman for you to handle.'

'Or something. Anyway, what was up with him? Did he hit you?'

'No, he was scary, but not that way. He was obsessed with Danny. He couldn't stop talking about him . . . we'd be, like, fooling around, and then he'd go, "Did Danny like it like that?" Or, "Is that the way Danny did it?" Which started out funny, and then got pretty creepy. And he kept talking about this family in Madison that got burnt in a fire when they were kids, the Burnabys or the Bradfields or something, how it was a mystery and how nobody knew what really happened except him and Danny and the other guys.'

'What was that all about?'

'No idea. And then when we got to the warehouse, he wouldn't leave us alone.'

'He wouldn't leave *me* alone; you escaped to the toilets.'

'Or, the recreational drug use cubicles. Hey, I came back. And Peterson was really creepy, he was . . . he started getting kind of angry . . .'

'Was he drunk?' Paul asks.

'I don't know. I know I wasn't. I had some ecstasy as well, but I was too freaked out to take it, I wanted to keep a clear head. I was just trying to dance and ignore the guy. And then he started in on Danny again . . . I don't really remember what he said, more that it was just . . . very bitter, you know? That Danny was very lucky, everything he ever wanted had been served up to him on a plate, but people would think again if they knew the truth about him. And you know, it wasn't even what he said, more the way he said it, this resentful, bitter tone, this *rage*.'

'And the tech guy—'

'Anthony Vasquez.'

'Anthony, that was him, he came to the rescue.'

'Because I asked him to, I went up to the decks and I yelled in his ear and he said, "Get out on the street and I can arrange that you lose the guy. Walk down the alley toward Division Street." And he got on the radio, he had a two-way radio. So we left, Peterson still tagging along, and we're going down the alley—'

'Which was not a great idea anyway: Bucktown was beginning to gentrify back then but Wicker Park was still a fucking zoo.'

'And Anthony's guys appear, these three no-neck Latino body-builders, and they go, "Which is the guy?"'

'I remember *that*. We both went, *"Him!"*'

'And they started to kick the shit out of him. We ran out on to the street and there's a cop car, cruising, and you flagged it down—'

'With you hissing at me not to.'

'I was afraid we'd get arrested for setting the whole thing up.'

'I was afraid they were gonna kill the fucking guy – they were seriously heavy hombres, jailhouse tats, gang bandanas, the whole bit – and we were going to end up in jail having commissioned a murder 'cause some guy was really annoying?'

'I don't think they say "commission" a murder.'

'Well, whatever they say. How the fuck would I know what they say?'

'Anyway, Peterson didn't die. His attackers took off. And we got back together again. That night.'

'All drama, all the time. Where are you going with this – that these guys in the alley have been harboring it all these years, this resentment that you sent the cops after them, and finally they snapped and decided to kill your dog in Madison? And happily for them, the night they choose, why, Gene Peterson, the guy they only half beat up in Wicker Park all those years ago, is on the scene, so they get the chance to finish the job?'

'You're making fun of me.'

'I don't need to. You're doing fine without my help. Why don't you suggest it to the cops? You could be like one of those old ladies who used to ring Kojak and tell him if he peels an orange and throws the pieces of skin in the air, they'll land and spell out the murderer's name.'

'They came around the theater looking for me, you know.'

'They did not.'

'The cops caught one of them – he had an unlicensed weapon, he got six months or something. The other two made Anthony Vasquez tell them who I was. They beat him up.'

'And what happened, did they catch up to you?'

'One night on my way to the theater. I said I didn't set the cops on them. They wanted money, and I told them what we earned in the theater, and they looked at me like I was a moron, and I privately agreed with them. There was a moment when I thought they were going to try and get paid in kind, but then they just shrugged it off and left. Anthony Vasquez told me I was very lucky, and that I should lie low when their buddy got out. And that was that.'

Paul Casey shakes his head.

'I know,' Claire says. 'It's just, that's all I can think of. That's the sum total of my experience with bad guys. But it's ridiculous, isn't it?'

'It's more likely Gene Peterson came down to kill your dog himself. Seeing as how he disliked Danny anyway, and probably contracted a strong dislike of you after that evening, I know I would have in his shoes.'

And Claire realizes that yes, of course, this is true, and that Danny had been armed with many good reasons for killing Gene Peterson, she had seen him herself, for God's sake, advancing on him armed with the knife that was used in the killing. Her hope that somehow it was her fault was a kind of magical thinking, a prayer that her husband was not a murderer. She still prays, but she's not sure how alive her hope is.

'You've got to go,' Paul says.

'I feel embarrassed.'

'Don't be. That's what the cops do all the time, don't they, check out leads?'

'Not about that. About . . . last week. You must have thought I was nuts. Woman on the verge, type of thing.'

'Well. It wasn't as if I hadn't been warned.'

'What do you mean?'

'I mean . . . I had fair warning of how you were feeling, or how you thought you felt.'

'Paul, I didn't even know you were going to be in the Old Town Ale House until you showed up last Tuesday.'

'Maybe not. But the messages you sent me were pretty to the point.'

'What messages?'

'On Facebook.'

'I didn't send you messages on Facebook. I don't do Facebook.'

'Well, someone does, with your name, and a whole bunch of shots of you, and links to your website.'

'And this person, pretending to be me, sent you messages saying what?'

'Saying . . . that you missed me, and wondered how I was, and if I was lonely, and . . . and then they kind of got riper.'

'Riper?'

'Yeah. Pretty much . . . that if I wanted to sleep with you, you'd be into it, no questions asked, no strings attached.'

'That subtle?'

'Actually, less subtle than that. Totally not suitable for work.'

'On Facebook?'

'Yeah.'

And Claire, who has never even visited her Facebook page, nonetheless must concede that one exists, set up for her by her friend Dee. Could someone have hacked into it? Claire wouldn't know how you did that. But Dee would.

More than You Know

In the parking lot of the Clock Tower Square Resort in Rockford, by the red Ford Mustang, without warning, without a sound, Jeff Torrance suddenly hits the deck.

'Jeff? Jeff, are you OK?' Danny says.

Danny hears a kind of growling sound, hears Jeff's boots kick against the concrete, hears the car keys jangle. He rounds the car and rears back involuntarily, crying out in shock and then rushing to Jeff's kicking, flailing body, to the bloody hole in Jeff's face where his nose was. Jeff's breath comes in gurgling spurts, as if he's drowning in his own blood. Danny reaches his hands in and tears them away, not knowing how to help. What the fuck has happened?

'Been shot,' Jeff manages. 'Get . . . go. *Go.*'

A last sluicing rattle from his throat, and then he's gone, his body still, his eyes staring up at the gray afternoon light.

He's been *shot*? Danny stands and scans the surrounding area, but can see nothing and no one, except a couple of people collecting their cars and a bus turning in off the highway to set down passengers. What the fuck? Someone shot Jeff? Maybe they'll try and shoot *him*.

Go. *Go.*

'Something happen to your friend, mister?'

It's a man in his sixties, plaid shirt, windbreaker, big jeans, Bulls hat.

'I think he's been shot,' Danny says, gesturing with his hands, which he sees are coated with Jeff's blood. He sees the man staring at his hands, and then at his face.

'One minute he was there, the next . . .'

'You see where it came from?' the man says, looking around. Go. *Go.*

'No. I . . . could you call for some help? An ambulance. And I'll . . . stay with the body.'

The man nods. He trusts him. Of course he does. Everyone trusts everyone. It's the Mid-fucking-West for Christ's sake. There he goes, in his big-ass jeans, jogging towards the door of Ruby Tuesday's.

Everyone trusts everyone, except for the guy with the gun. Go. *Go.*

Danny grabs the keys out of Jeff's hand, gets in the Mustang and hits the gas. He doesn't look back. He doesn't wipe the blood off his hands. He drives just below the speed limit. He doesn't rant and rave, he doesn't swear, he doesn't even think. He keeps himself very still, concentrating only on the next mile of highway, and then the mile after that. He needs to be calm, and hold firm. He needs to talk to Dave Ricks and to Gene Peterson. He needs to find out who is trying to destroy his life.

* * *

Detective Fox didn't tell Claire Taylor she was forbidden from leaving Dane County, but she hadn't expected her to bolt. She wasn't a suspect; her alibi checked out – indeed, they had told her that, if anything, *she* could well be in danger. Mostly, they wanted her in plain sight, because if Danny Brogan was going to reappear, it was likely going to be to see his wife. But she had taken off, telling Officer Colby quite truthfully she was going to her friend Dee St Clair's place downtown. Colby had let Fowler know. But Fowler was in the middle of issuing an inter-agency BOLO to the assorted state and county police and highway patrols in Wisconsin and Illinois for Danny Brogan on suspicion of murder, then ensuring TV and media had the photographs and information they needed. Whatever else he had found to do after that – get a cup of coffee or check whether the uniforms had uncovered anything going door-to-door, which of course they hadn't because the nearest doors to the Brogan house on Arboretum Avenue weren't near enough to let anyone see or hear anything of use – turned out to be just long enough to allow Claire to get away.

'She told Colby she needed to have a shower, change her clothes, borrow things from her friend, so on. I thought, first, that figures, and second, well, she'd probably be a while.'

Because women take so long to get ready, you know what they're like, Nora Fox thinks but doesn't bother saying. Which is why she's left Fowler at the station house, where he's happier anyway, running background checks on Danny Brogan and the victim Claire Taylor identified as Gene Peterson and trying to get prints on the murder weapon fast-tracked through the lab. They dusted the photograph and the figurine at the Arboretum Avenue house for Brogan's prints and if they can get a match with the Sabatier, that'd be free drinks at the Old Fashioned tonight. Ken might even stay for a third.

First, Nora swung by Brogan's and quizzed an extremely blonde bar manager by the name of Karen Cassidy, who had been present at the family barbecue the previous Sunday, and who immediately went on the defensive.

'Even if I could remember something, I probably wouldn't tell you, but since I can't remember anything, it means I had too much to drink, so I can't tell you,' said Karen Cassidy. Brogan had been in the bar sporadically for the rest of the week, he hadn't appeared any more distracted than usual, she didn't know of any money troubles – certainly there were none at Brogan's. Nora pressed her further for signs of erratic behavior on Danny's part.

'Look, you're wasting your time,' the diminutive blonde snapped. 'First, there's no conceivable way Danny Brogan would let his kids come to any harm. Second, if he's in any other kind of trouble, I told you, I'd always try and protect him. So would anyone else in here.'

'Karen, what if I told you I thought Danny might be in trouble himself? That this Gene Peterson was some kind of threat to him, that they maybe had a fight, there was an accidental killing, Danny panicked and took off, taking care to keep his kids safe first, as you said. What if the best way of protecting him is to find him?'

Nora was kind of winging it, but only kind of; for whatever reason: Claire Taylor's poise, Danny Brogan's profile, the way the house was left, the fact the wife wasn't murdered, none of these pointed to a serious kids-in-jeopardy situation or the need for an Amber Alert. That was as far as Nora was prepared to go for now.

'In that context, Karen, anything you can give me? We know he didn't take his own vehicle. Would he have traveled with a friend?

Nora was sure Karen Cassidy knew the answer to that one, and there was a moment when it looked like she would tell, but then a dishwasher growled its rinse refrain behind the bar counter and Karen's gaze returned to blank.

'The other scenario, which makes things look even worse for Danny, is that he is being set up to take the fall for this Gene Peterson's murder. The family dog was mutilated and killed, which his wife said Danny could never have done.'

Karen's eyes opened wide on that one, and her mouth formed an O of outrage. Nora pressed home.

'In which case, it's not the Police Department finding him he has to fear, it's whoever committed these violent crimes.'

And Karen bit her lip, exhaled and said, 'If he went with anyone, it was likely Jeff Torrance.'

Nora got a Spring Harbor address from Karen for Jeff and immediately called Ken Fowler and asked him to check it out.

Now she is in Dee St Clair's salon on Dayton. It's quiet on Monday near lunchtime, and four young hairdressers with just-so haircuts are watching raptly as an extremely slender Chinese gentleman with black hair to his ass is doing something asymmetrical to the head of a fifth young hairdresser. Every so often he says something like, 'Always weighing for balance, for fall,' or 'Cut brisk, not rushed,' in a self-caressing little voice, and the hairdressers murmur their approval.

'The Maestro at work,' Dee St Clair says, having introduced herself and led Nora to a low-lit spa room in back with mirrors and basins and couches and scented candles and repetitive electronic music trilling soothingly from concealed speakers. Nora would like to spend a relaxing hour or two being pampered here. Later. On someone else's dime.

'Ms St Clair, you've heard about what happened up at Claire and Danny Brogan's house, I assume,' she says.

'It's so unbelievable,' Dee St Clair says, and makes what Nora can only describe as a face, a kind of fright mask of horror and concern that is presumably genuine but looks so fake it makes Nora want to laugh.

'Were you aware of the gravity of the situation when you assisted Ms Taylor in her flight?'

'I let her borrow my car to drive to Chicago. I don't think that amounts to "assisting her in her flight". She wanted to go, and figured it would be too complicated to take one of her own on account of her backyard being a crime scene. Anyway, Claire has nothing to do with what happened, does she?'

'I don't know. You tell me. You are her oldest friend, is that right?'

'I've known her a long time, yes.'

'Since she was at UW Madison. And that would have been the early nineties?'

'I opened the salon here in 'ninety-three.'

'So do you have any idea what made her take off so rapidly, or who she would have gone to see in Chicago?'

'I don't know. She said she had a plan. I . . . look, I don't know if this is relevant or not, but I think she might have hooked up with an old boyfriend when she was in Chicago last week. Guy called Paul Casey, she used to work in the theater down there with him.'

'So what, was she planning to leave her husband?'

'God, no. At least, I don't think so. Did she tell you she was? She didn't tell me. God, how amazing if she was. I don't mean, amazing good, just . . . amazing. I did ask her, you know, if anything happened. Not a glimmer.'

'If something had happened, could Danny Brogan have found out?'

'I have no idea. She's very cagey about stuff, Claire, not like me, I'll tell you whatever you need to know, and a lot you don't; Claire, she'd've worked well in the CIA, I think. Or like an undercover cop. Keeps stuff from me, I'd say she could keep it from him too.'

'Any other stresses on the marriage recently?'

Dee does a funny-you-should-ask thing with her eyebrow that makes Nora think fleetingly of a drag queen.

'Well – they did lose some money with Jonathan Glatt.'

'She told us that.'

Dee almost pouts, like a teen sulking because her news is no longer news. Nora hands Dee a copy of the photo of the victim Claire found among her possessions.

'Your friend Claire Taylor identified the body as being that of Gene Peterson. Did you know this man? If not Peterson, we certainly think it was one of Danny Brogan's old friends. This is what he looked like in high school.'

A frown creases Dee St Clair's forehead, as if she is trying to stop herself from expressing the emotion she naturally feels. In the normal run of things, Nora Fox would identify this as a fairly straightforward tell, but St Clair's mannerisms are so generally off-kilter it's hard to tell. When she lifts her face, it's devoid of any expression.

'I've never seen him before in my life. But I only came to Madison in my twenties, all Danny's buddies had gone by then.'

'And, Ms St Clair, do you have any idea where the Brogan children might be?'

Dee shakes her head, and makes a face eloquent with pain and distress – the most persuasive and lifelike she's looked, Nora thinks.

'I'm afraid I have no idea.'

'One more thing, Ms St Clair: Danny Brogan. You say you

first met Claire Taylor when she was at UW. She would have
been going out with Danny then, right? But when she left for
Chicago, you stayed here, isn't that right?'

'Salon wouldn't have run itself, Detective,' Dee says. 'And we
were friends, not lovers.'

'Of course not. Did you and Danny see anything of each other?
I don't mean romantically – necessarily – I mean as friends?'

And whatever faces Dee pulls in reaction to this, genuine or
cosmetic – and she seems to run through panic, outrage, fear and
bitterness in short succession – there's no mistaking, in Nora 's
eyes at any rate, a glitter in the eyes, a flush of heat in the brow,
a thickening in the voice when Dee replies.

'Not really. I mean, we bumped into each other from time to
time – hard not to, in a city the size of Madison – but I was –
am – Claire's friend, not Danny's. Not that I'm not Danny's
friend too, but . . . well, you know what I mean.'

'Of course,' Nora says. Of course, she *thinks*, as well. Maybe
nothing happened, but if it didn't, you wanted it to. Maybe
something happened, but then it stopped, and you wanted it to
continue. But what did that amount to? God knows, she has
friends and exes in common. Some you stay friendly with, others
you drift apart from. Might add up to something, might not. The
thousand and one details that together make up police work. Of
which, one might be useful.

That's all she wants from Dee St Clair for now. Nora notes
down the Toyota's plate and asks her to get in touch if she hears
anything more. She can't say for sure, but she thinks Dee looks
kind of shaken by the encounter as she stands in the doorway of
the salon, seeing her off, or just making sure she goes. Maybe
it's just what normal, innocent people feel when they've spoken
to the cops: relief that they don't have to do it every day. Or
maybe it's what every woman her age is prone to (because
Nora's roughly of an age with Dee St Clair): in one light, you're
the essential you, you're who you always were; in another, or
in the morning, or without warning, you look tired, and lonely,
and scared.

In the car on the way past Camp Randall Stadium, headed for
Monroe High, Nora is still thinking about Dee St Clair. Maybe
anyone is vulnerable to the badly timed question. God knows,

there was one guy in her twenties, if he walked in front of the car now, she doesn't know what she'd do. Run him over, perhaps. She doesn't like to talk about him, gets all hot and bothered, or unconvincingly nonchalant, if anyone brings him up. He's married now, with kids, and she still feels . . . what? She still is not prepared even to analyze how she feels. It's why all those websites are just *wrong*, Friends Reunited and Facebook and so on. Because it would be one thing if she ran into . . . *Gary* . . . she feels a frisson mouthing the word, like a schoolgirl writing her crush's name on her pencil case, *Gary*, God, she is *ridiculous*. It would be one thing if she ran into Gary again in a bar, say, or . . . well, in a bar is the way she's decided it would happen, a hotel bar actually, for reasons, yes, pretty obvious reasons. And whatever happened, would happen. It would be chance. It would be fate. And we're all at the mercy of that.

It's another thing trawling through your past for everyone you ever kissed and getting in touch with them all and putting yourself in the way of them, like you could rewind your life and start afresh. Last time Nora checked, that was called soliciting. And it never works out, because you can't go back. Dance in one direction only. She knows that if she did bump into Gary (in New York, where nobody knows her, she doesn't care which hotel), within minutes of the second drink, she'd probably remember all the things about him (because he'd remind her of them) that used to get on her nerves, and eventually caused her to dump him in the first place. That's right, she dumped him. And that's that. No second chances. Is that what Claire Taylor wanted in Chicago, a second chance? And what did Danny Brogan want? And did he want it enough to kill?

First things first, Nora thinks as she gets out of the car and climbs the steps of Monroe High. *Let's establish exactly who got killed here.*

Love Letters

On the walk from Twin Anchors to her car, Claire tries to bring her thoughts to order. She needs to get back and be with Barbara and Irene, but they are safe with Donna, so there's that. In the meantime, she needs to find out what the hell has been going on. If Paul Casey thinks she was flirting with him online, what else has she been doing? And who has been pretending to be her? She has already called Dee to ask for – well, technical support, she supposes you'd call it, since Dee is the only person she knows who is really knowledgable about all of that stuff, but Dee's cell went straight to voicemail. Crossing West Menomonee, she sees the Caprice Internet Cafe half a block up the street, and on impulse decides to see if she can figure it out herself.

Five minutes later, having parted with three bucks for a computer screen with Internet access, and a further three for a cafe latte, she is ready to go.

First step, Facebook. She types the address, and arrives at the page: Welcome to Facebook – Log in, Sign Up or Learn More.

At the top, there's space for her email and password. Her email she knows, but her password? Maybe it's Barbara1 – isn't that what Dee said her email password was? She fills both boxes and clicks the log-in button. Within seconds, a screen pops up, asking her to update her security information. She clicks through email address, her cell phone number, and a security question (what's your youngest child's name?) and finally lands on a page with News Feed at the top, and on the left-hand side, a small photograph of herself. She stares at the information on the News Feed. There are posts from a handful of moms at the girls' school, and from some of the theater people she knows in Madison. The theater people are advertising shows that are coming up, or linking to press articles about productions that have just opened, or, in

her friend Simon's case, a bitchy blog, written anonymously
under the pseudonym Addison DeWitt, savaging shows across
the land. The moms have posted assorted pumpkin recipes: pie,
soup and so on. There's also a mom, Diane Crosbie, who has
posted her own review of a novel her book club has just discussed,
Lorrie Moore's *A Gate at the Stairs*. The review, which Claire
clicks to without even thinking, seems more concerned with
spotting the similarities between Lorrie Moore's fictional town
of Troy and the real Madison, upon which it is apparently based,
than in discussing the novel's plot or characters. Claire shakes
her head with irritation, not just at the review, but at the fact that
she has clicked through to it, that she has started to read it at
all. This is exactly why she doesn't like going online: it's not
just that she ends up getting distracted, it's that distraction seems
the entire point of the exercise. Mind you, the spicy pumpkin
soup recipe Ragna Glenny has up looks kind of tasty.

She's back at the News Feed page. Along the top right-hand
corner, she sees three options, Home, Profile and Account.
Clicking home simply refreshes the screen she already has.
Account brings her a pop-down menu of settings. Profile brings
her to a page with her name at the top. This is what she needs.
There's her date of birth (but not the year – thanks, Dee). But
the date of birth is wrong. It says November 12, but Claire's date
of birth is November 24, or at least that's what the Taylors always
told her. Well, she's not going to get bent about two weeks.
What's more alarming is the information that she's single, and
that she's interested in men. Jesus, Dee. That's just not funny.
There are four photographs of her along the top taken relatively
recently, by Dee, she assumes; she can't remember, but Dee is
always snapping things on her phone.

On the left in a sidebar comes the news that she has forty-
seven friends – of the ten they show, Claire would classify four
as acquaintances, and the other six as not even that: people she
might just about wave to in the street. Above that, there's a menu,
one of whose items is Photographs (7). That's three more than
are visible on this screen. She clicks through to a page marked
Claire Taylor – Photos, and the pit of her stomach lurches. The
four she's already seen are there. The other three are of her and
Paul Casey, from their theater days: young, and high on love

and art. They were all taken the same night. The photos are in a box in her hide-out in the house on Arboretum. She has never shown them to anyone, not Danny, not Dee, no one. She doesn't look at them herself, either. They are . . . memories. Her memories. Someone has taken her memories and shared them with the world. But who would want to do that? The same person who said she is single and interested in men? Dee may have set up the page, she might even have depicted her as a lonely heart, but she'd never go through her personal stuff and put it out there. That crosses the border from mischief to malice. No, this must be courtesy of the same people who killed Mr Smith, who killed Gene Peterson. She's read about websites being brought down by geeks with a grievance. If they can hack into Visa and Mastercard, they can hack into Claire's Facebook page.

She clicks back to the News Feed page and scrolls down. Paul said there were messages she had sent him, and his replies. But she wouldn't have done it in full view, would she? She looks left and finds the sidebar with her name and photo. Below, highlighted, is News Feed, below that, Messages, which she selects.

There is a photo of Paul Casey, and the first line of a message. She clicks it, and sees a five-message exchange entitled 'Between *You* and *Paul Casey*', and her stomach lurches again. The messages are all dated during the ten days or so before she went to Chicago.

Claire Taylor *October 16*
Hey Paul, it's your past catching up to you. I'm going to be back in town for the first time in, well, an age, and would LOVE to see you. There's so much that has happened . . . and so much I wish hadn't happened . . . and so much I'd LOVE to happen. Looking pretty steaming in your mugshot, by the way. I arrive October 23. Claire xxx

Paul Casey *October 18* **Report**
Hey there stranger, accepted the friend request and thought it best if you made the next move. Leave it to Claire, it's a spectacular. Well, I will be in town that week, and I would LOVE (we are all upper case now) to see you, and am INTRIGUED by what you might consider a 'happening' . . . speaking of mugshots, you must have locked yours in

a lead box in the attic. You look AWESOME and younger than you did when we were dating (although that could be cause you're relieved of the stress of a) Theater and b) me). Can't wait to see you, Claire. Paul xxxxx

Claire Taylor *October 18*

Hey you, am sitting up late with third enormous glass of sauv blanc, thinking of something else that's pretty enormous and wondering if I'm going to get to see it at close quarters in Chi-car-go there that's my attempts at subtlety pretty much blown I could go back and erase it and say something all coy and when I got there you would be guessing and drumming your fingers on the bar top and tapping your feet the nervous way you used to have and I hope still do my gorgeous boy but there will be no need i xxx you very very much indeed and have often thought about what we used to do and wished that we could do all of it some more lots more and don't worry if you married or 'in a relationship' don't want to steal you away or boil your bunny just want your xxx must stop before i make even bigger fool than have already made hope not scaring you away drunkgirl xxx

Paul Casey *October 20* **Report**

Wow, Claire. I mean, WOW! Had a few cold ones myself to try and do my reply justice, but not sure I can compete with yours. Which is not to say I'm not up for it, totally, the thought of you still makes me hot on a cold Chicago night. Tell me when and where, with a little advance notice, and I'm all yours. Pxxx

Claire Taylor *October 22*

Don't take anything back but a bit embarrassed by my ravings above. PLEASE do not allude to this exchange when we meet, or I will probably come apart at the seams (drink is evil). That does not mean I didn't mean every word, just don't want to be reminded of them (this is a strict condition; I know, I am nuts, but then, I always was!) Will be in Old Town Ale House Tuesday night see you then c xx

The worst thing, Claire thinks, after she's taken five minutes to stop shaking, and blushing, and practically hyper-ventilating, and get herself a cup of peppermint tea (her heart is already beating so fast, another cup of coffee and she'd explode), the worst thing is she *could* have written those messages. She has thought that way over the years. Not every day, or every month, but from time to time, she has had her regrets, and her wishes, her dreams that maybe Paul was the one. She has sat up late in her nook, hiding from Danny and the kids and drinking too much white wine and thinking X-rated thoughts about Paul, running selected scenes through her private screening room. That is how she sounds and how she gets when she is drunk: whatever polish and sophistication and self-control she thinks she possesses simply evaporate on a cloud of booze. And she does then go firmly into denial, embarrassed, and ashamed even, about what a sewer her mind can be, while knowing perfectly well that if she had bumped into Paul Casey in Madison, she might well have flung herself at him. She pretty much did, when she got the chance in Chicago.

What a lot of time and energy wasted. Because when it came to it, nothing happened. Or rather, a lot of things might have happened, and nearly happened, and she certainly did not resist temptation, but . . . with a little luck, she thinks, a little *grace*, even though she didn't deserve any, she didn't do anything that can't be undone. And she misses Danny now, right now, as much as she ever did. She knows some people would say, if you have thoughts about other lovers, and then *act* on those thoughts, then you're not entitled to a second chance – you should walk out, you should break free, you should be true to your discontented heart. But Claire thinks that is as rigid, as fanatical, as saying you shouldn't allow yourself to have the thoughts in the first place, that they are in themselves wrong. Maybe sitting up in her sanctuary steaming it up on white wine and thinking of how things used to be is *unwise*, but no situation is completely satisfying. No life ticks all the boxes. And she knows from lunch today in Twin Anchors, what she was looking for wasn't Paul, but some dream of Paul, Paul-when-she-was-single-and-free, some passport to a fantasy version of her own past that wouldn't include the mess they had together, the fights and the career disappointments, all the reasons they split. What she was looking for was an escape she knows now is an illusion.

What she wants now is her life back.

Who the fuck has done this to her? Someone who knows about her and Paul, her and Danny, someone who knew she was going to Chicago.

It's a short list: Danny and Dee.

Neither of them are going to do this. Who else is there?

Could it have been Gene Peterson?

Without thinking further, Claire types Google into the address line, and when the window opens up, inserts Gene Peterson's name and waits for the results. The first ten results are devoted to Gene Peterson the Australian jazz drummer. She adds Chicago to the search terms and tries again. This time there's a doctor, a choir director and a sportswear manufacturer. Sportswear. She's pretty sure Danny said that was his line. She clicks on Peterson Sportswear, and a page with brightly colored sports tops, track pants and rucksacks appears. At the top, there's a headshot of a square-jawed guy of about fifty with sandy hair and a dimple in his chin. Wrong Gene Peterson.

Start again. Gene was one of Danny's childhood friends. They went to school together. Name of the high school? Monroe High.

Try Gene Peterson Madison WI Monroe High.

First item is a news feature on Madison.com. She clicks the link.

Madison Man Adds Bulls to Badgers, reads the headline, which goes on to explain that Gene Peterson, who played high-school basketball for Monroe High in the 1970s, has become the official supplier of uniforms to the Chicago Bulls as well as the Wisconsin Badgers. Basketball for Monroe High in the seventies. That's the right time frame. Were there two of them?

She clicks back, and finds that Gene Peterson has a Wikipedia page. Nothing fancy, but to the point:

Gene Peterson is the founder and CEO of Peterson Sportswear, Chicago. Peterson is a native of Madison, Wisconsin, and attended Jefferson Junior High and Monroe High schools. He went to DePaul on a basketball scholarship, but a severe anterior cruciate ligament injury brought a premature end to a promising career. He founded Peterson upon graduation in 1986, and has built it to the major national brand it is today. Among the NBA franchises Peterson supplies exclusively to are . . .

Claire's eyes shift down the page. Sure enough, there's a photo of Mr Square Jaw again. That has to be Gene Peterson, the Gene Peterson Danny was at school with. But if it is, who was the weird guy she nearly slept with in Chicago? Who is the dead guy in her backyard?

She gave the cops the picture, the only picture she had of any of Danny's high-school buddies. Danny didn't even know she had it; she had found it tidying a closet one day. There were no names attached to it, it was just a picture of Danny and another guy – the guy in Chicago, the guy who was dead in their yard. Although the guy in their yard had been through the mill, he looked like he'd been having beer for breakfast for quite some time. But she was pretty certain it was the same guy. Why had he lied and told her he was Gene Peterson? Who were Danny's other friends? She knew there were four of them, he had told her that much, back in UW, when he used to talk about the past. It was after they got married, or told the world they had got married – that was when he began to clam up. That was when the past became enemy territory.

What was it he used to call the guys, back in UW? God, it was such a long time ago. The Four Somethings. Seasons. Winds. Tops.

Steady, Claire.

The Four Horsemen. That was it.

The Four Horsemen.

Danny, Gene . . . Dave, Danny and Dave. Dave, Danny, Gene . . . plus one.

Don't they have high-school reunion websites?

Monroe High, 1982/83.

Let's go.

Lonesome Road

The first thing that occurs to Danny as he hits the I-90 is that he's being followed, or at least, that he was traced to Rockford. So he can get over his paranoia about using his cell phone. He turns it on and calls Dave Ricks and tells him he's in trouble and needs to see him urgently, and Dave hears him out and talks him down and gives him directions to his studio and Danny turns his cell off again, just in case – and without checking his voicemail messages – and drives.

He doesn't feel he can afford to stop until he hits Chicago, in case there is anyone in pursuit, but his hands and face are smeared with blood and while he could live with it, not a bad visual representation of how he feels, he doesn't want some other driver reporting him to the highway patrol as if he's some kind of runaway axe murderer. Or indeed, as if he's Danny Brogan. He finds a box of tissues in the glove compartment, folds them into wads, dabs them with one of the bottles of mineral water that roll around the floor of the Mustang and cleans himself up as best he can. Catching sight of himself in the rear-view mirror, he can't quite believe what has happened. Jeff is dead. Somebody shot Jeff, a sniper, a hit man. A *hit man*? What kind of world is he living in?

Danny stalls on that for a while. Someone shot Jeff, Jeff is dead, and that segues into the TV report as they left the restaurant: *Ralph* is dead, Ralph Cowley, and the photograph of Danny, they must think Danny did it, well of course they do, there's a dead body in his backyard and he's taken it on the lam, what are they supposed to think? Then there was a shot of Mr Smith. What's up with that? Mr Smith might nip a child's ankles, but that's the height of it. Unless . . . but the idea something bad has happened to his dog is just too much to bear. Jeff, Ralph, Mr Smith, round and round they go, Danny shivering and muttering and crying a bit, and he is on the industrial outskirts of Chicago before whatever life-preserving adrenaline he has – or whatever he has left over from when he floored the car away from Rockford and placed the call to Dave Ricks – floods his system and enables his brain to function.

First thing, did whoever shoot Jeff aim for Jeff, or were they trying to hit Danny? There wasn't a second shot, and Danny was in full view, so chances are it was Jeff. In which case, they – whoever 'they' are – were trying to scare him. Good job, guys, you've scored a hundred percent on that front.

Second, it's looking increasingly like Gene Peterson is behind all this. Peterson had got him into Jonathan Glatt in the first place. He thinks of it now, in that Irish pub near City Hall, what was it called? The Dark Rosaleen? After a dinner at Everest on South LaSalle that must have cost four hundred dollars, Gene picking up the check, flush with his sportswear business. How everyone did well in Glatt's fund, the trick of it being, to receive the invitation in the first place. How the annual return was between ten and twelve percent, and had been for the three years he'd been involved. All the guys were in, Gene said, him, Dave and Ralph. It was almost impossible to get in, had been for a long time, but Glatt made an exception for Gene because he'd been able to point some high-worth individuals in Glatt's direction, guys with serious money. Danny had enjoyed the night, and felt flattered to be asked, and emboldened by Gene's success, as if it was his success too, or soon would be. Why limit it to the fifty grand they had in savings? Why not think big? He rang the bank the next day and had his two hundred grand in a matter of weeks, making sure the house was valued when Claire wasn't around. The bank would have lent him more, lent him twice as much. 'It's a no-brainer,' the guy kept saying, nodding his approval at Danny's financial acumen, his sudden and mysteriously acquired market perspicacity.

And now he knew the truth about that: all the other guys were in, and then all the other guys were out, and he was left to pay the price. Everyone got away with it except Danny. The same way everyone seemed to get away with the Bradberry fire except Danny. Danny was to blame for it happening in the first place, it had all been set up so that he could get his revenge on Jackie

Bradberry. Danny threw the fatal missile that set the house alight. And to top it all, Danny would in time marry the only child to walk away from the disaster.

And what about the fifth investor? On top of Gene, and Ralph, and Dave, and Danny? Claire Bradberry? There was no way that could be Claire herself. What could it have been though? Some kind of cruel private joke? Whoever invested under that name must have known the truth about Danny and Claire. It all pointed to Gene.

And then there was the thing Dee St Clair had told him, back when they had their . . . what would you call it, less than an affair, little more than a fling. That was what *he* called it, he knew Dee had felt differently, but that was just the way it went sometimes between two people. Would he have taken it further if Claire hadn't called from Chicago and asked him to take her back? It's not a question he can answer, or even contemplate. He simply can't imagine not spending his life with Claire. It had always been a bit awkward between Danny and Dee after that, but Dee had never said anything to Claire, and neither had he.

On the other hand, Claire had never said anything about her time with that guy Casey, that fucking guy, Jesus, how long has it been back on between them? Was it just a fling, a one-time thing, or has she been missing him, *loving* him, all this time? He knows the marriage had been light on thrills for a while, but it had never collapsed into coldness, let alone hostility. Just a certain distance now and then, the silences longer than they used to be, the flame guttering maybe, but never doused completely. Passion was still there. They'd had sex the night before the barbecue, for fuck's sake, and not just dutiful let's-get-it-done-because-we're-married sex; they had fucked like horny teenagers – better than that, horny teenagers who knew what they were doing.

Claire's trip to Chicago. He knew it was a crucial week for her. He had encouraged her to go since way back. She had avoided the site of her so-called failure for fifteen years until it loomed so large it had become an obsession; any time the city was mentioned on TV or the radio, he'd steal a look at her to gauge how she was taking it. He'd think twice even of renting a DVD or buying her a novel set there, in case it sent her into days of dreaminess and melancholy. It got so he would lose his patience with it all; what kind of narcissist thinks an entire city exists just to hold a personal meaning for her? Unless of course what she had been mourning (for that is what it seemed like to him, a deeply held, impenetrable grief he could neither pierce nor alleviate) was not so much the collapse of her theatrical career as the break-up of her relationship with Paul Casey. That, coupled with the integrity of a woman who would never dream of cheating on her husband, for Claire was straight about those things, for all her drama. She had not gone back because she didn't want to be tempted, and was realistic enough to suspect she would be. *Lead us not into temptation.* What had Jonathan Glatt said? They didn't make that prayer up without a reason. And – savor the irony – Danny had, not just persuaded her, he had practically goaded her into making the trip. He had led her into temptation. Had she fallen?

He had missed her desperately. He hadn't wanted to discuss Ralph's visit the night of the barbecue because Claire was so hyped about her trip, told her it was just some Halloween drunk who'd got lost in the Arboretum. But that night, after she left, and the next morning, hungover and lonely, the fear began to kick in. And then someone sent him an email with a link to a Facebook page. Claire's Facebook page. Even though she claimed to despise Facebook. There was nothing incriminating on the page itself. She was 'friends' with Paul Casey, but she was friends with a whole bunch of people. Although not Brogan's, he noticed: the bar had what he considered a deeply tedious Facebook page full of chirpy announcements about specials and cocktail recipes and so forth, Danny couldn't see the need for it, business hadn't been dwindling. But it seemed to keep the younger staff amused, and committed. Shouldn't Claire have been friends with the business that put food on her table and clothes on her back? The shrill petulance of the thought had embarrassed him then, and embarrassed him still.

Then a second email arrived. Attached was a screenshot of explicit Facebook messages between Claire and Paul Casey, messages that left little to the imagination. He tried hard to see them as flirtation, but the fact was, she had been making all the running. She was offering herself to him. It was hard to see it any other way.

That's what drove him to Chicago on her trail.

He had rung her room, had got the room number by insisting the room was, he can't remember now, maybe 790, repeating her address; he had tried this twice or three times with different receptionists until one of them had said, 'No, Miss Taylor is in Room 435'. He remembers the thrill he felt when he got the room number, like he was a private detective on a case, and then the foolishness that followed: what the hell did he think he was doing?

The Allegro was a mid-price tourist place that catered to weekend visitors and groups in town for theater and shopping trips. He rode the elevator to the fourth floor and walked down the corridor past Room 435. It was six-thirty in the evening. Maybe she would be there, changing before going out for the evening. He thought about knocking on the door, but he couldn't bring himself to do so, in case she was in there doing something else. Back by the elevators, there was a kind of lounge area in a recess by a window with a yucca tree and a couch and some magazines. As he sat there pretending to read the *Tribune* and surveying in what he hoped was a casual way everyone who entered or exited the elevator, his feeling of foolishness intensified.

He had never been jealous before, had always considered it an absurd, undignified, *unmanly* emotion. If your lover loved someone else, let her go, he reasoned, and had said as much to the countless lovelorn bar staff in Brogan's over the years. All of which amounted to this: he had never *felt* jealousy before, and was imaginatively incapable of understanding it. For when jealousy came, its venom was fast-acting and mind-altering, and the fear attendant on it (jealousy being fear plugged into the mains) – the fear of rejection, of betrayal, of humiliation – those fears cut deep and reach way back, back to childhood, to every moment he felt unloved, passed over, excluded. Danny couldn't bear to feel this way, like a neglected child, and yet he seemed powerless to do anything about it.

After an hour, he rode down to the lobby. It was Tuesday night, and his plan was to position himself at a table in full view of the door – Claire might have brought her key with her, and so watching reception wouldn't be enough. The problem was, the entrance was a floor below reception, which was where the bar was situated. He began to feel like he was being watched after spending ten minutes assessing various tables for their views, so he left the hotel and decamped to the bar across the street. He found a stool by the window. You could see the door clearly, although taxis and buses sometimes obscured it. This was probably as good as it was going to get. He sat there from about seven forty-five, first drinking coffe, then eating a burger and fries, not as good as Brogan's but not bad at all. The food revived his spirits; the coffee gave him the jitters. Around ten, he cracked and ordered a double Woodford, water back with a Honkers Pale to chase. The Honkers was a mistake, or at least, the second was, as it meant he needed a trip to the bathroom. He held out as long as he could. When he got back to his perch, it was twelve-forty, and three taxis were pulling away across the street, and he saw a flash of auburn hair in the revolving door of the Allegro Hotel, arm in arm with a dark-haired guy. He wasn't certain it was Claire, she moved so quickly, but he wasn't certain it was not. And if it turned out to be a false alarm, he would take it as a sign and call it a night.

He took the same route as before, wondering if he could smell Claire's scent – Cristalle by Chanel – in the elevator, praying she was alone, persuading himself there's nothing to worry about. He slowed down as he approached Room 435. Should he knock on the door? He could hear a TV, sounded like an old movie. The hotel walls were like cardboard. The TV was coming from 435, Joan Crawford, it sounded like, one of the old Warner Brothers ones, *Possessed*, or *The Damned Don't Cry*, that's totally what Claire would be watching, they're both addicted to old black-and-white movies. Better living through TMC. Except now, it was as if they were trapped in the middle of one. He was right outside the door, a big blast of Franz Waxman strings shrieking, his hand poised to knock.

But something clicked inside his head, and he didn't knock. He breathed deep, and bit his lip, and turned and walked away. He rode the elevator down to the lobby, crossed the street and ordered a Woodfords in the bar he had spent the evening in. He gazed across the gantry at the range of bottles and taps and drank his whiskey and knew he'd had a narrow escape.

Because what were the alternatives? If she was with somebody, with Casey, what could he have achieved by walking in on them? If she wasn't, what kind of creepy, stalking, controlling mother-fucker would he have been? He didn't knock because he wanted to trust his wife. And because all he got to be in charge of were his own actions. If she felt she needed something else, something she'd had before, well maybe that was up to her. Maybe she had a right to cheat. Maybe the marriage had never had a chance in the first place; maybe it was doomed from the day of the fire, doomed because of what he had done. Why couldn't he just tell her the truth? And then it would be over, one way or the other. She could leave him – she *would* leave him, of course she would, or . . . he's dared hope a hundred, a thousand times, that she could, in time, forgive him, he was just a boy, a child, the same age Barbara is now. But how long would it take to fathom: the depth of it, the scale of it, that her entire family was destroyed, and that it was his fault: months? Years?

Why can't he just confess? God knows at a certain level it would bring him nothing but relief. Because . . . because he has no right to tell her who her parents were if she doesn't want to know. Is that true? Round and round it goes, has always gone, the spectre at every feast, the four a.m. wake-up call he's lived with every day of their marriage.

Getting Some Fun Out of Life

'Is Halloween second after Christmas of the holidays?' Irene says.

'I don't know. I sometimes think Halloween is actually *better* than Christmas,' Barbara says.

'They're totally the top two. And Easter,' Irene says.

'But you don't have to go to church on Halloween,' Barbara says, making a face at her sister.

'Oh,' Irene says. 'Right. I forgot that. Well then. Halloween is *definitely* the best.'

They are sitting on the floor by the fire. Barbara is wearing her vampire costume and writing a story about a werewolf in high school. Irene is wearing her kitty-kat costume and drawing a picture of a spaniel puppy with devil ears taking a ballet lesson. Donna is finishing a quilt with a Halloween pumpkin motif, and trying neither to giggle at nor succumb to the girls' campaign to persuade her to bring them trick-or-treating.

'Because,' says Barbara, suddenly full of high moral purpose, 'on Christmas, you can get pretty *greedy* about all the *stuff* you want, and the stuff you get and don't get, and I think it's *wrong* to be so *selfish* in that way. Whereas on Hallo*ween . . .*' she says, and then lapses into silence. Presumably, Donna thinks, because the purpose of Hallo*ween*, as far as Barbara is concerned, is accumulating a major haul of *stuff* in the form of candy and then scarfing as much of it as her stomach will allow.

'On Halloween, we remember the dead,' Irene says solemnly.

Donna makes a noise.

'Bless you,' Barbara says. Donna is unable to answer.

'That's true, Irene. On Halloween, we do remember the dead, the . . . souls of the dead,' Barbara says.

'Day after,' Donna barks.

'What's that, Aunt Donna?'

'Day after. In fact, day after that. All Souls Day. November second.'

'I know this,' Barbara says, loftily. 'All Saints Day, November first. I did a project on Halloween last year. The ancient . . . ways of it. It's like mythology.'

'Barbara's a Halloween expert, actually,' Irene says.

Donna makes a longer, more complicated noise.

'Bless you,' Irene says.

'And as well as All Saints and All Souls, Halloween is about the dead too. Doing battle with evil spirits,' Barbara says.

'Like the death-eaters,' Irene says.

'No, not like the death-eaters, stupid,' Barbara says.

'Is too.'

'Is not. And how would you know anyway, you've only seen the movies, you gave the books up halfway through *Sorcerer's Stone*. Anyway, you were right before,' Barbara says, modifying her tone from sharpness to sanctimony. 'At Halloween, and for two days afterwards, we dress up, and light fires, and remember the dead. So that the harvest . . . to give thanks . . . for the harvest, and the coming of winter.'

'Why do we want to give thanks for the coming of winter?' says Irene.

'We light fires, and give thanks . . . and in the night, *on* the night, the . . . the border between the . . . there are spirits in the air. Spirits *abroad* in the air.'

'That's good, Barbara,' Donna says. 'Spirits abroad in the air. I like that.'

'And the border, the *veil* between the . . . the living and the dead becomes—'

'See-through,' Irene says.

'Transparent. That means—'

'See-through,' Irene says.

'Stop inter*rupting*, Irene. That means we feel very close to those who have gone before. And just because we're – even *though* we're – *afraid*, we . . . we just say, no. That's why we dress up as ghosts and demons and vampires and everything, to . . .'

'Confuse them,' Irene says.

'To conquer our fears. Or something like that.'

'You got an A-plus, I hope,' Donna says.

'I got an A-minus. Because the layout wasn't right. And my handwriting—'

'You should have typed it,' Irene says.

'I like my handwriting. Anyway, Megan and Susie got A-pluses and their moms typed theirs. Their moms *wrote* theirs. Megan's was on Halloween and it was word for word from the Internet, I know, I read those pages too. And Susie's was on Holyween.'

'Excuse me?' Donna says.

'Holyween. Because they're Christians, she said they don't believe in Halloween. So she was allowed do it on Holyween. Which is what Christians have instead. I think.'

'Is that right?' Donna says.

'And it isn't fair that if you do all your own work, you get marked down, but if you let your mom do it all, you get an A-plus.'

'No one said life was gonna be fair,' Donna says.

'That's what Mom always says. And to be fair to Susie and Megan, I did try and get Mom to do it for me, but she said no, that it was better to do my own work, that's the only way I would learn.'

'Good for her.'

'We're Christians too,' Irene says. 'At least, we are at Christmas and Easter. Aren't we?'

'There's a difference between being a Christian and being nuts,' Donna says tartly. 'Holyween. Jesus Christ Almighty.'

'That's exactly what Mom said,' Barbara says. 'Those exact words. "Holyween: Jesus Christ Almighty."'

'I miss *Mommy*,' Irene says tearfully. 'Mommy always has the best costumes, *makes* the best costumes, and she brings us to a Halloween House when it's getting dark, and then to one of the local neighborhoods for Trick or Treat—'

'Last year we went somewhere off Nakoma—'

'Mandan Crescent, my friend Holly lives there. And then we went to Daddy's office and had burgers and fries and blonde Karen sang "Goldfinger" and threw her shoes in the crowd, which wasn't really about Halloween but Mom and Dad thought it was hysterical.'

'All right, all right, all right,' Donna says, unable to stand it any longer. 'There's a subdivision called Ripley Fields, we can walk along the river bank to it, so long as we bring flashlights.'

'And? What do we do when we get there?' Irene says.

'We trick or treat, baby, we trick or treat!'

How Long Has This Been Going On?

J eff Torrance's mother was willing to concede that Jeff had
gone somewhere, and taken his car, but where he'd gone and
who went with him she either didn't know or refused to say,
nor would she give Ken Fowler any details of the vehicle's make
or registration beyond that it's red, so Fowler is running Torrance's
name and address through the DMV to get the make and plates.
Meanwhile, Detective Nora Fox is in the library at Monroe High,
which is on the fifth floor, and commands spectacular views of
Lake Wingra. Having closed the call with Fowler, she looks out
the window in the direction of the Brogan house, but all she can
see is the wind creasing the oak prairies of the UW Arboretum,
the trees flickering in the last of the afternoon light. Maybe it's
the proximity to all these books, maybe it's being back in high
school after all these years, but she remembers a line from a
poem, something about ghosts being driven out like leaves in the
wind: 'Yellow, and black, and pale, and hectic red.' Nora hasn't
retained much poetry by heart – hasn't retained any, truth be
told – but that line sometimes comes back to her in the Fall, and
each time she wonders if all the adjectives apply to the 'red,' and
thinks that they should: yellow-red, black-red, pale-red, hectic-red.
The leaves are like a fire about to expire, she thinks: one last
blaze and then they're blown asunder like embers on the wind.

'Detective Fox?'

Nora turns with a start to Ms Johnson, the librarian ('call me
Doreen, Detective'), aware that her name has been spoken
more than once, and a little embarrassed, as if her thoughts could
be read. A cop quoting poetry, like some English detective in a
book: who does she think she is?

'I sometimes lose myself in the view, too,' Doreen Johnson
says. 'Here's the 1982 Yearbook you asked for.'

'Thank you,' Nora says.

They have the library to themselves, apart from four Chinese students poring over complicated math problems. 'Halloween,' Doreen Johnson had said with a shrug, and Nora had nodded in response: no further explanation necessary. Nora indicates that she's going to sit at a desk and peruse the book; Doreen Johnson looks like she's about to speak, then turns and goes back to her desk by the door.

The first thing Nora establishes is that whoever the dead man is, he wasn't Gene Peterson: the photo Claire Taylor gave her and the photo of Peterson in the yearbook don't resemble each other in the slightest. Peterson at eighteen is fair and square jawed, a jock type. Where does he see himself in five years? 'Achieving one goal, only to set another: the only place success comes before work is in the dictionary.' She rolls her eyes and sighs. Not only in Wisconsin; the jocks in her high school were big on Vince Lombardi quotes too – or at least the ones their coach drummed into them. There were 479 students in Peterson's graduation class, 243 of them boys, and the only other one she can definitely rule out is Danny Brogan. The photograph she's trying to match is one of the dead man as a seventeen- or eighteen-year-old; he has a mullet and an optimistic smear of moustache. At least, Claire Taylor told her it was the dead man. But if she lied about it being Gene Peterson in the first place . . . well, here we go with some of that glamorous police work.

She looks up at the sound of Doreen Johnson seeing the Chinese students out. With the tiny, elegant frame of a dancer, she is wearing a blue floral pinafore over a gray long-sleeve t-shirt and gray leggings, and flat-soled black wing tips on her feet; her unruly, undyed, salt and pepper hair is barely contained in a loose ponytail; her skin is tan; her blue eyes radiate curiosity and intelligence; she wears blue gemstones in her ears and at her throat. Doreen checks her watch, takes a bunch of keys from her pinafore pocket and turns one in the library door, then, smiling, crosses the floor towards her. Aging hippies in Madison aren't always this friendly towards the police.

'Just so you know, Ms Johnson, detaining a police officer in a high-school library in the conduct of her duty is a serious crime.'

'You'll never take me alive, copper. And it's Doreen, please.'

Doreen Johnson pulls a chair around and sits beside Nora Fox, maybe a little closer than personal-space guidelines would warrant.

'I just thought it would be better if we weren't disturbed,' she says.

Reflexively, Nora's eyes flicker towards the librarian's ring finger: no metal, but a white line where a ring once was. Back to her face, where her eyes are dancing with cloak-and-dagger excitement.

'What's on your mind, Ms— Doreen?'

'I taught those guys in middle school. Before I became librarian here, I used to teach at Jefferson. Junior high, as it was back then.'

'You did? What do you mean, "those guys?"'

'They were, not exactly a gang, they weren't tough like that, but they were inseparable. The Four Horsemen. Gene Peterson, Dave Ricks, Danny Brogan and Ralph Cowley. I saw it on the news at lunchtime. It looked like Dave Ricks to me. Is he dead? Did Danny Brogan do it? Of those guys, he'd have been the last one I'd have picked.'

Nora looks at Doreen, makes a calculation based on character arithmetic, and decides to trust her. She shows her the photograph.

'We're having trouble identifying the body. There was no ID. Mrs Brogan appeared to think it was Gene Peterson, but . . .'

'No. It's Dave Ricks. Unless it's . . . no, I'm pretty sure it's Dave Ricks. Danny and Dave, it was like they were joined at the hip.'

Nora turns to Dave Ricks' graduation page and compares the photograph. There's the mullet, but all the kids had them back then. No moustache. Same shape of face, high cheekbones, aquiline nose. The mouth looks mean, the lips thinner. Maybe that's what the moustache was for. The eyes are piercing, intense. In five years time?

If you have nothing within you, you'll have nowhere to go.
Deep.

Nora looks at Doreen, raises an eyebrow.

'What do you think, Doreen?'

'The resemblance is very close.'

'But? You started to say, "Unless it's . . ." Unless it's who?'

'Dave and Ralph looked weirdly alike. Not identical, not up close, anyway, but they were two guys everyone used to get confused. One could fill in for the other. And did sometimes. Take a look at Ralph. Ralph Cowley.'

Nora turns to Ralph Cowley's page, and is immediately startled by the resemblance. It's not like they're twins, more like . . . like when you look at the photo of some rock band for the first time, and the singer and the gutar player seem identical, like constant proximity has rubbed off. The mullet, the cheekbones, the piercing gaze. Ralph has the smeary moustache, but the lips look fuller. And there's something, she's not sure, *softer*, around the eyes and the mouth. Softer, or is it weaker? The boy in the photograph is smiling, as Ralph is; Dave is giving it mean and moody, a rebel with too many causes.

'Oh my,' Doreen says. 'It's impossible to say.'

'We have people who can make a more informed judgment,' Nora says. 'Analyzing the photographs for points of comparison . . .'

'No doubt. It's just personally so frustrating not to be able to tell them apart.'

Doreen Johnson bites her lip, and her eyes seem damp all of a sudden.

'Why would you expect yourself to? You taught them, what, junior high, thirty years ago, more. Why would you expect to remember?'

'I remember those boys. They were the first class I ever had. They stood out; they had something about them. A kind of . . . glamour is overstating it, but they had charisma. They held themselves apart. And of course, there was something so troubled about Danny Brogan in particular. Maybe there was something . . . *off* about all of them. And then the Bradberry fire came, and none of them was ever the same again.'

The Bradberry fire. After a fortnight in Madison, she pulled clippings and microfiche files on the Bradberry fire. Eleven kids and their parents, all wiped out. A Molotov cocktail the likely cause, but much reluctance to call it arson. A Halloween prank that got out of hand, a tragic accident. No one ever found the kids that set it. Everyone mentioned it, no one wanted to talk about it. It was the city's secret shame, the mad first wife in the attic. The Bradberrys had been burnt to death, and everyone was shocked, but no one, Don Burns, her sergeant, had told her, drunk one Friday night, 'Kiddo, no one was really sorry.' The Bradberry kids were too wild, and had bullied too many other kids; the parents were drunk and probably abusive. It was a terrible thing, no doubt, and you wouldn't find anyone saying they were *glad* – or at least, not out loud – but in a lot of families, there was a kid getting up and going to school relieved he wouldn't have to face a Bradberry that day.

'What are you saying? That they had something to do with what happened?' Nora says.

'Well, Danny Brogan was being bullied by Jackie Bradberry, backed up by his brothers. And in a way, it was my fault. I thought . . . stupidly . . . that the problem with Jackie Bradberry could be solved. That you could solve people's problems by intervening. I put Jackie and Danny together. And they simply did not hit it off. The scale of the neglect inflicted on those Bradberry children was so great. It was hard to comprehend their father had been a physician: there were no books in the house, no conversation – it was an indictment of our child protective services that they were kept with their parents. But the attitude at Jefferson was, the Bradberrys are always with us, just got to deal with them. I was a young teacher, full of idealism, I wasn't going to stand for that. I put the boys together. And then Dave Ricks's mother, who was on the school's board of governors, made her own intervention, and got Danny back sitting with Dave. And Danny's relief at being back with his own people dented Jackie Bradberry's feelings. And the bullying began after that. So in a way, my well-meaning, blundering attempt to help caused all the trouble. The road to Hell . . .'

'What do you mean, they were never the same after the fire?'

'I guess, they were relieved. Jackie's brothers broke Gene Peterson's arm, and the other guys knew what was happening to Danny, but they were too frightened to do anything about it. And the school . . . I had already done enough. What else could I do? Tell Jackie to stop? I did, several times. He near as well laughed in my face. It was a different time. To be a snitch was the worst thing. I tried to get Danny to tell, but Danny . . . Danny Brogan had been so browbeaten, and beaten, by his father, he was like a dog who always feared the worst. The other guys, his friends – well, Ralph and Gene anyway, they kind of bullied Danny too. It was like, he always had to amuse them, to entertain them, to smuggle free Cokes out of his dad's bar for them. And maybe that was his impulse, that he didn't deserve love, so he had to work hard for it, he had to work at pleasing other people and that was clearly going to be difficult since he couldn't please his old man. But it soon became a pattern with the guys, an MO. And in a way, when the Bradberry thing began, you could see them thinking, it would be Danny. Not, he had it coming, but . . . he had the mark upon him, you know what I mean? And maybe that's why I chose him too, for my little experiment: because I knew he'd try to please me.

'So they were relieved, but they were guilty about feeling relief after a family of thirteen burns to death. And guilty, too, about how they hadn't stepped in to help their buddy. Their Musketeers, all-for-one-and-one-for-all aura had gone. They were still inseparable, but there was something forced about it, like they'd all had to grow up too fast. Like it wasn't their friendship that bound them together, but their guilt.'

'Gene Peterson stepped in.'

'That's true. Gene was the class hero. I still have dreams in which I say something noble, or help an old person across the road, and Gene is there, and gives me a nod of approval. It's ludicrous, the guy runs a sportswear brand in Chicago, he's not in the desert helping the starving. But you just wanted him to think well of you. Flipside was he withheld that with people, with Danny. A little cruelty there, maybe, or simply pulling rank.'

'And the other guys? Dave?'

'Dave Ricks was a straight-A student, he could draw, he played guitar and piano, he had . . . I guess he had an artistic sensibility. He and Danny were like brothers, they finished each other's sentences, always joking and wisecracking. If anything, Dave was needier than Danny in the friendship. When I moved Danny to sit with Jackie Bradberry, Dave was distraught, he came up and told me, "We've always sat together. We sit together." And then he got his mom to fix things. Dave was . . . kind of vain?

He was much better looking than Ralph, even though they looked so similar. If that makes sense.

'And Ralph was a nice kid, you know, Mr Go-Along-to-Get-Along.'

'I thought that was Danny's role.'

'No, Danny felt he had to sing for his supper. Ralph was just an easy-going guy. Head always stuck in a book, like he was hiding behind it. Did enough to get by, not enough to get noticed. He tucked in behind Gene, like Gene's right-hand man. As long as he was onside with Gene, he was happy.'

'And you followed their progress?'

'Dave became a commercial artist, I think, runs a graphic design studio in Chicago. Far as I know, Ralph teaches high-school English. One of the best ways to hide in plain sight.'

'The consensus seems to be that the Bradberry fire was probably an accident, but that it was caused by a Halloween prank that got out of control. Did it ever occur to you that Danny and his friends were responsible?'

Nora sees Doreen Johnson redden, senses her bridle, keeps going so she can't interrupt.

'Maybe they had good reason, after all they'd taken. And who would begrudge them? It wasn't their fault it got out of control. And you said yourself, in the aftermath of the fire, it wasn't friendship that bound them together, it was guilt.'

Nora stops, waits for Doreen to defend her former charges, her first class. But Doreen is silent. Fireworks crackle and swoosh outside, and she looks towards the window.

'Did it ever occur to me? Two-and-a-half years of middle school to go, and I don't think one of those boys looked me in the eye during all that time. Even if they had just wished for it, they must have wished so hard, they ended up feeling the guilt as if they had set the fire in reality.'

Rockets cascade across the sky, leaving a trail of stars falling past the window.

'What if they did do it, and now one of them is threatening to tell, to confess?' Nora says.

'And that's a motive for Danny Brogan to murder one of his friends?'

'It could be.'

'Detective, do you think Danny Brogan is a murderer?'

'I'm not in a position to judge his character. The evidence, certainly the circumstantial evidence, points in that direction.'

'Well. I'm not in a position to judge his character either. He was fourteen the last time I saw him, and eleven the last time I knew him. But from what I knew back then, he was the last, he and Ralph, the last of those boys who could conceivably have done such a thing.'

Nora sits for a while, listening to the ticking of the library clock and the occasional snap and starburst of Halloween outside. And then something occurs to her. 'Did anyone survive?'

'Excuse me?'

'The Bradberry fire. Thirteen died. But I seem to remember . . . weren't there survivors? A couple of brothers?'

'They had already left home. One was in juvie in Racine, for sexual assault, I think. Don't know what he did when he got out. And the other was some kind of criminal too, loansharking, drug dealing, in Chicago, petty stuff. People felt it was being judgmental to describe them accurately, as the lowlifes they were. So they just didn't mention them at all. The press too.'

'They change their names?'

'Wouldn't you?'

'They must have inherited the house, or the insurance settlement, right?'

'I guess.'

Nora scribbles it all into her notebook.

'And there was one Bradberry who survived the fire.'

'A little girl, right?'

'That's right. No one wanted to talk about her, either, for altogether more exalted reasons: so that she could have a chance in life. So that she could escape her past. Escape her destiny. But maybe she doesn't want to. Maybe she wants to revisit it all. Maybe she wants revenge on the guys she thinks killed her family.'

I Couldn't Sleep a Wink Last Night

Danny is with Dave Ricks in his office at the top of the restored grain warehouse and store on West Wacker Drive that houses Dave's design agency, Dare To Dream. Three of the office walls are glass and look down and out across a large, vaulted room divided into, not cubicles so much as loose corrals, where about thirty people work at screens, desks, easels and whiteboards. None of the workers, men and women in roughly equal number, are dressed for a conventional office, yet, despite their apparently casual clothes, their khakis and jeans, their smocks and scarves and boots, they look simultaneously kitted out for work and adhering to a definite dress code, even if it is one only they fully understand. Danny is pleased by this insight. When Dave started, back in the eighties, he was bunkered in a windowless stone silo in the basement, or dungeon, and he designed posters and handbills for local businesses and rock bands, so at least Danny understood what he was doing. Now the agency has expanded to take over the entire building, and it encompasses everything from website design to corporate branding to 'creative solutions' to multi-platform consultancy to something called 'synergistic spatializing,' Danny is less sure what is actually going on. Of course, it's been a while since he visited, a long while since he even saw Dave Ricks – is it five or six years since Dave was last in Madison?

'Just under five,' Dave says. 'My mom's funeral.'

Having greeted each other with a loose, awkward embrace, as men must these days, they part, and Danny nods, arranging his face in a slow wince so as to convey his apologies for having forgotten Dave's mother's funeral. He has no great recollection of the day, the last time all the guys met together, except that each of them went to great lengths to avoid mention of the Bradberry fire, or at least, that's how Danny saw it, or sees it now. He takes Dave in, the contrast between the Dave he carries around in his head and Dave in real life. In truth, Dave has aged well, hair still dark, forehead relatively unlined, body the same shape, a few pounds under, if anything; Dave and Danny both, well weathered, guys. Not like Ralph, Jesus. Ralph looked like someone had set about him with a foot pump and then a blow torch, so bloated and scalded and frizzed had he become.

Danny and Dave forever, that was how it went from the first time they met, on their first day of school; they sat beside each other for the next fourteen years. And then they didn't really see each other much any more. That was how it had gone with all the guys, but with Dave, it was weird that they hadn't kept up. Or was it? Sometimes Danny reckoned they were more like brothers than friends. Nothing needed to be said; it was understood that they got along. But maybe there was nothing there, deep down. When Dave went off to school in Chicago, that was it, end of story. Sure, Dave had called a bunch of times, they had met once or twice, but it felt like the train had moved on. Not unusual. Just one of those things.

Good to see him, though.

Danny and Dave today.

'Ralph Cowley,' Danny says – blurts, in fact.

Dave's eyes do nothing, and Danny wonders if he heard him, if his words are actually audible. A little nod from Dave suggests they are. 'Ralph Cowley,' Danny repeats, before coming to a stop again, caught between recounting the story of his visit and announcing the fact of his death.

'How is Ralph?' Dave says. 'You know, I hardly ever see the guy?'

Danny lets his gaze sidle out the window to take in the rush-hour traffic streaming below, the dark oily swirl of the Chicago River alongside.

'He came to see me,' Danny says. 'All worked up.'

'That's Ralph,' Dave says. 'Sit down, Danny. It's good to see you. Would you like something to drink?'

Danny runs through the things he'd like to drink: scotch, bourbon, gin. He doubts whether Dare To Dream keep any of them, even for clients. Not that he is a client. He had asked Dave to do a logo for Brogan's once, years back, when everyone thought they needed one, when branding became king. Dave had done something involving Japanese comic book figures, the kind of thing the girls like, manga-style, big eyes, and used the colors of the Irish flag, green white and orange. It looked hideous, garish and vaguely pornographic, the worst of at least two kinds of national kitsch, although, Danny reflects now, the girls would probably adore it. So if business in Brogan's ever gets so bad they need to hustle for the custom of the under-twelves' market, maybe he'll roll it out. As it was, he just pretended the whole thing had never happened, and Dave had never mentioned it again. They'd had scant contact since, in any case.

'Tea,' Danny says. 'English breakfast?'

'Milk or lemon?'

'Milk.'

Dave presses a button on the desk phone and asks someone called Lauren for two English breakfast teas with milk.

'All day breakfast,' he says, and smiles. 'Make you feel at home.'

'We don't do breakfast,' Danny says, smiling himself. 'Breakfast in a bar, it's not an auspicious concept.'

'It's not that you don't want problem drinkers.'

'We'd just prefer them a little later in the day.'

'Let their breakfast problems be someone else's problems.'

'We're not in the breakfast solutions line.'

'You could offer a breakfast solution, but it would come with vermouth.'

'Well. It would have shared a shelf with vermouth.'

'Breakfast: the most important drink of the day.'

'Two olives with mine.'

'Two? Steady. Don't want to soak it up entirely.'

Danny and Dave, the banter boys. They kept themselves amused.

'I don't see any paintings, Dave.'

'I don't do that any more.'

'No? You were good.'

'I put it to work here,' he says, and gestures down out towards the agency floor. 'There's a time when you put away childish dreams. Isn't that right? Take you, Dan. You wanted to be an actor.'

'Not really. My wife was the actor.'

'Oh now. At school, you did a lot of acting. Said you were going to try out, give it a shot, see what happened. But . . . you grew up. You accepted your lot. You knuckled down. So did I. Not like Ralph.'

'What do you mean, not like Ralph?'

Dave gives Danny a keen look, an I-am-taking-a-good-look-at-you look.

'Things didn't really work out for Ralph. Not the way they have for you and me.'

Dave is still smiling. You and me. Danny remembers this side to Dave, all you and me, all I-know-what-you're-thinking-because-I-am-thinking-it-too. Danny feels uncomfortable, like he should know about Ralph, about how things didn't work out. But he doesn't, or at least, hadn't until last Sunday, doesn't know anything about any of the guys, or rather, he just assumes, or assumed, they were the way they always had been: Dave with his designers, Gene with his sportswear business, Ralph teaching high-school English literature. Lack of curiosity? Perhaps. Equally, Danny wouldn't have relished anyone checking up on Brogan's year by year, given that he is doing essentially the same things he was doing fifteen or twenty-five years ago. Dave would have formed a view though. Dave always formed a view, had been the one to assign the roles: Danny, the pleaser; Gene, the captain; Ralph, Gene's right-hand man; Dave . . . what had Dave been? The jester? The artist? The class cut-up?

'What happened to Ralph?

'Ralph had a lot to put up with, Danny. Teaching school wasn't what he had hoped for. He had a novel he was writing, I don't know if it was the same one all along, or a succession of different ones. The cliché, you know, the teacher with a novel, "I have a suburban dream". And I don't know what was worse for us, for all of his friends, his continually referring to it over the years, when the novel is finished, when the novel is published, so on, because even if it had grown embarrassing, everyone pretending to believe in this novel and its fate, even Ralph pretending, the strain of all that was somehow preferable to how he was when he finally gave up believing in it. I heard a shrink say once, to preserve mental health, it's vital to believe in something, not necessarily God, maybe anything, as long as it keeps you on the road. And when Ralph stopped believing in his novel, he had nothing left. It was like someone had taken his engine out, and all he could do was coast along, freewheeling, hoping for a steady downward incline to see him home.'

'He's home now,' Danny says. 'He's dead, Dave. Ralph was murdered. They found his body in my backyard.'

Lauren, brown curly hair and a trace of freckles, in blue jeans and rope wedges and a floral print wraparound top, exuding a Zen mixture of artiness and efficiency, comes into the office with the tea, and there is much politeness and business with cups and milk and so forth. When she goes, Dave abandons his drink and moves to the window, staring down toward the river. His cell phone rings, and he looks at it and frowns and presses a key. After another moment or two, he looks up, frowning.

'What the fuck?' he says. 'Ralph, murdered? What kind of . . . what happened? You said he came to you . . . what was the deal?'

'A week ago,' Danny says. 'He was, as I said, all worked up . . . about the past. About the Bradberry fire, specifically.'

Dave nods, his face seemingly held steady by an act of will. *He looks like he's afraid I'm going to ask him for money*, Danny thinks. Maybe that's how we'd all look. Don't talk about it, don't mention it, don't remember it.

'That's all ancient history at this stage, surely?' Dave says.

'Well. In one way, of course.'

'I mean . . . Christ, it just goes to show what kind of state Ralph was in, that he should be brooding about the past like that.'

Danny shrugs. 'I don't know. Age we're at, I find the past more and more rears its ugly head.'

'Don't look into its eyes, is the trick, Dan. Or it'll look back at you. And then you'll be lost.'

'That's some kind of quote, isn't it?'

He thinks of Claire, the quote-mistress; more than a thought, a pang, an ache. No matter what, he misses her.

'It's a paraphrase of a quote. What did Ralph say?'

'Well. He said . . . he said that he couldn't stop thinking about it all. The fire, the dead children. How he had tried to deal with it in a creative way . . . I didn't understand what he meant by that, but I got the impression that the novel he was writing, or failing to write, he told me about it too, was maybe about the fire.'

Dave rolls his eyes. 'Jesus.'

'He said he felt guilty that he'd allowed us all to think one way about the fire. When there wasn't just one way to think.'

'I haven't thought one way about it,' Dave says. 'I haven't thought about it at all.'

Dave's face settles into a skeptical half-smile, as if all this tragedy and melodrama are a bit *much*, and looking out through the glass walls at the room full of workers, the creativity, the industry, the *normality*, Danny can't help agreeing, can't help feeling just a little absurd, as if the whole thing is too febrile, and somehow unmanly. He is reminded of his childhood, of trying to keep in with the guys, the effort it took, all the unspoken rules: don't show any emotion, don't obsess about things, don't over-explain, or over-think, don't go off on one. Moderation in all things, and while you're at it, shut the fuck up. Danny learned it all well, too well, had become almost incarcerated within it. But not now. He thinks of Ralph, and Jeff, of the money he's lost and the house he stands to lose, of his family life in danger of falling apart. It may feel like melodrama, but for Danny, it's the new normal, and he's living it.

'Maybe not, but that doesn't mean there wasn't an agreed version of what happened. A version in which I was the . . . the guilty party, I suppose you'd say. I was the one who lost his head, who got carried away, and not content with scaring the Bradberrys half to death, I suddenly decided to go the whole hog, to fling a fire bottle at the back door and burn the whole house down. That's . . . later that night, back in your place, that was what had happened, that's what became the Authorized Version, right?'

Dave grimaces, as if it's childish and silly to be raking over these dead leaves.

'The only reason we even talked about it was because you hit your head, you knocked yourself out. So you were all, "how the fuck did that happen, guys?" I mean . . . should we have not told you? Maybe it would have been better if . . . because honestly, we brought the fire bottles along, what were we, not gonna use them?'

'We had agreed not to throw them at the house. We had ruled that out. The deal was we would use them if there were trees, we could set some trees ablaze. They were the conditions we set. That they wouldn't get anywhere near the house. We took care to set the fires on the lawn some way back from the perimeter for the same reason. I mean, we talked all that through, Dave, absolutely we did.'

Dave flushes, as if he had forgotten, or, more likely, Danny thinks, because he is embarrassed by Danny's vehemence, by the freshness of his recall, by how raw it clearly still is for him.

'So Ralph said that's not the way he remembers it now. That he wasn't sure what he had seen in any case. But that the guys were so sure that it had been me, he took it for granted.'

Dave is shaking his head, pacing about the room, holding his hands up as if he is about to speak and then stopping and sighing and pacing about some more. He reminds Danny of an actor who's been allowed too much freedom on stage, and as a result looks like a less than convincing version of himself.

'Ralph is dead? Fuck, man, what happened?'

'I'll get to that,' Danny says. 'First, I want to talk about what he told me, all right?'

Dave doesn't quite flinch, but he looks unprepared for Danny to be quite so firm, and something flashes in his eyes: resistance, it looks like. *Welcome to the physics of my world, baby.*

'You mentioned the novel he was writing, I think that's the way to understand what Ralph meant. He kept saying things like, that was the original version, how he couldn't get beyond that, but then he tried to see it from the angle of the other characters – meaning us – and that was when he began to revise it, to see that it was more complicated than it originally appeared.'

'Go on,' Dave says, head down, voice muffled.

'OK, well, he said that, once we had the yard blazing, and we were kind of running around through the flames—'

'We were *dancing* around, like little savages—'

'We were dancing around. We had done it. And the two little kids' faces at the window, staring out the window, Ralph remembered that, how frightened those kids looked. But that wasn't enough for the little savages. We were going to scare them even more. We had the fire bottles, each of us had one, and Ralph said we were picking out trees to pitch them at, and, and . . .'

'And you lit yours, I remember this, actually, you fired yours up and you ran at the tree, the big sycamore in the corner by the fence we piled over, you ran headlong at it as if you were going to fling yourself into it, but there was a blaze in your way, a skull or something, the flames kicking high, and you just looked like you thought you could run through it.'

Dave is nodding his head now, almost smiling, as if relieved he too can see it plain, as if the smoke has cleared.

'You swerved to avoid the fire, and whichever way you did it, arms flung out to keep your balance, the fire bottle left your hand and hit the house, and you blundered headlong into the tree and knocked yourself out.'

Danny is shaking his head. 'That's not the way Ralph saw it.'

'That's the way I remember it, Dan. And that way, it clears you of any . . . not that anyone "blamed" you, we were all—'

'I blamed myself. All these years.'

'It was an *accident*. You ran, you slipped, it left your hand the wrong way, I can see it clearly. If we had, because what you call the official version—'

'The Authorized Version—'

'OK, like the Bible, very good, and we all authorized it, but after all this time, if we had only talked about it, if you had called me up, said, let's meet, let's try and piece together what happened. Instead of, because we were scared, panicking, frightened kids, and we were angry too, I guess—'

'Angry at me. Gene was angry. Gene was furious.'

'Gene was the one,' Dave says, and nods, and Danny feels like high-fiving him. 'Because I, I was never sure . . .'

'We all agreed, but Gene was the one that led the charge.'

'Man, he was righteous . . . because he was like, Sheriff in the White Hat, Dudley Do-right, Gene made a call and it was like, the tablets coming down from the mountain, it was written in stone.'

'That's totally . . . yes, that's right. That's right.'

Danny is breathing deeply, almost moved; there are tears in Dave's eyes too, he thinks, although he's not going to draw attention to them. He's not done yet.

'If only we had talked about it before,' Dave says, as if now it's too late.

'Gene was the one who wanted me to take the blame,' Danny says carefully, 'but that's not the whole story. At least, not the way Ralph saw it.'

Dave nods again, and then exhales, his head to one side, and makes the face again, the raised eyebrows, the grown-up skepticism, the manly assessment: the shit we've seen, after all this time, what are you gonna do?

'I guess it's like that Japanese film, everyone remembers a slightly different version of what happened. The reality doesn't change, though,' Dave says.

Which is to totally misunderstand that Japanese film, Danny thinks. Not to mention the fact that either you threw a fire bottle or you didn't. But it didn't matter, Dave was on his side, and Ralph had told him what *he* saw, and that led straight to Gene. He didn't need to have a debrief with Dave, didn't need to compare notes or seek closure.

'If only we could have talked about it,' Dave says again, and looks him in the eye, and there's something about the intensity of his gaze that takes Danny aback. As if it's too late now. What does that mean? Danny talks briskly about Jonathan Glatt, and Dave laughs and says phew, missed a bullet there, Gene got them out in time, and Danny says Gene didn't get him out in time, and Dave just stares at him.

'How much did you lose?' he says.

Danny shakes his head, gives him the you-don't-wanna-know look.

'So it's Gene? You think it all points to Gene?'

'What Ralph told me would confirm that, all right.'

'And what, do you think Gene killed Ralph? Had him followed to your house or something? Man, this is pretty wild stuff, Dan.'

'I don't know . . . I can't think of any other way it happened.'

He doesn't want to talk about the blackmail. Even now, he feels ashamed of himself, that he let it go this far. He has to get out of here, has to confront Gene Peterson, has to finish this once and for all. Dave's cell phone rings again; again, Dave stops the call. Danny gestures to the phone, indicating that he understands

Dave is a busy man and he's taken up enough of his time. But before he can move, Dave stops him in his tracks.

'There's something . . . I never thought it was anything, really, I mean, these things happen, and you and . . . Claire, isn't it, that you're married to? Measure of how far we've drifted apart, that I have to reach for your wife's name. I'm divorced, no children, for the record.'

'I know that,' Danny says, and it is something he remembers, although please don't ask him anything about Dave's ex-wife, he's almost certain he never met her.

'Well, I think it was when you and Claire were broken up, you met at UW and then split up and then got back together, I seem to remember.'

'That's right.'

'Well. I always thought it was kind of an uncool thing to have done, and maybe it's the reason none of us were invited to the wedding . . .'

'We didn't have a wedding. We're not . . . I mean, not officially, but we declared ourselves to be . . . we're not legally married.'

'How come? Or are you just Madison through and through, Dan?'

'Claire didn't want to. She's . . . she was adopted as a young child. And she didn't want to know about her birth parents, who they were, she didn't want to delve into any of that. She loved the Taylors, they were her adoptive family, and she didn't see why she had to complicate things. She said . . . she didn't need a piece of paper to tell her who she was, or what she was.'

Dave smiles. Is there something cynical, or satirical, bordering on cruel, about the way he smiles? Right at that moment, Danny doesn't know. And because of what Dave Ricks says next, the smile disappears from his mind as if he had never seen it in the first place. But in time, it will come back to him, and stay with him. It is a smile Danny will remember for the rest of his life.

'"We don't need no piece of paper from the City Hall,"' Dave says, as if it's a quote from something. Claire would know, Danny thinks. 'But look, and maybe this gives Gene another reason to have it in for you. Back then, when you guys were split up, Gene bumped into Claire in the city. And they spent the night together.'

(Love Is) The Tender Trap

C harlie T and Angelique have strolled up and down Cambridge's main street for what must be half a dozen times as the afternoon light dimmed. They bought a glazed salad bowl at Pat's Pottery; they looked at an exhibition of paintings by 'emerging artists' at the Jordan Gallery, and at nineteenth-century creamery equipment in the Dairy Museum, where Charlie T bought Angelique some frozen ice cream and they sat on a bench on the sidewalk so she could eat it. Every second spoon she gave to Charlie, and she rubbed his arm with her hand and nestled her head against his shoulder from time to time. After that, they stopped by the realtor's and picked up a bunch of brochures, and looked at old clocks and mirrors and chairs in two antique stores. In Janine's Quilts, Angelique found a *Goodnight Moon*-inspired quilt and place mats, and in The Gingerbread House, they bought German Lebkuchen cookies. In The Great Outdoors, Angelique made Charlie T get a red plaid coat with a fleece lining and a Wisconsin Badgers baseball hat. Now they are in Cindy's Country Bake, drinking milky coffee and eating cinnamon scones and smiling into each other's eyes.

It's an act, but it isn't all an act. This is what normal people do, Charlie T kept thinking – at least, normal people who wear sweaters and have weekend places and drive European cars. Rich normal people. Normally Charlie T would hang out in the nearest dive bar, or the strip club his girlfriend would be working in later that night, or already, depending on the town. But Cambridge didn't have a strip club, and his girlfriend wasn't a stripper, she was a nurse. Scratch that – his fiancée.

He had asked her on the trip up to Madison, and when they turned east on to the 12-18 headed for Cambridge, she said yes. He didn't know for sure if it was exactly what he wanted, and he knew for damn certain that he hadn't had his fill of other women yet, but there was something about Angelique, how, after he'd taken the Cowboy out, she'd stroked his thigh as he drove, not as a sex thing, more, she was proud of him. She spoke quietly of her plans, what she could expect as a nurse, what he could expect of her. Maybe she'd been fishing. Maybe she had manipulated him. The thing of it was, even if she had, he didn't mind. Even if she had, he *liked* it. He liked the idea they might be together. He hadn't realized he was lonely until she showed him there was an alternative to chasing after skanks.

Maybe she had set him up. And then, true to female form, made him wait: he proposes on the I-90, she accepts on the 12-18, an hour later. Silence in between. The longest consecutive silence he's ever witnessed from her. He found a radio station – he thought this was class, actually, a radio station that played all those old songs out of musicals and that, Ella Fitzgerald and Frank Sinatra and the like singing them, the songs his grandparents danced to. And of course, wasn't every single one a love song? 'The Tender Trap'. 'I'll Be Seeing You'. 'All The Things You Are'. He thought he heard her suppress a sob once, thought he caught a sidelong glimpse of her wiping a tear away. Didn't look around. Didn't say a word. Kept his eyes on the road. 'Let's Face the Music and Dance.' He thought of his grandparents, of his ma, of his sister and her kids. Angelique always mentioning her mother, her aunts, her sisters. Family. That's what it was all about. The future. Nearly shed a tear or two himself, so he did.

Mr Wilson still hadn't delivered an address when they were on the outskirts, so they rolled into town and spent their romantic afternoon. Charlie isn't a hundred percent convinced antique stores and art galleries are where he'd like to spend all of his afternoons; maybe he'd be more the champagne-on-a-yacht type of rich guy. But it's not all romance. Angelique's idea, that they should look like they're thinking of moving here. It's a game couples play all the time, she says, visit a place and imagine you lived there. And people talk to you. And maybe you don't need the address.

'Because,' she said, spooning ice cream into his mouth, 'where do you think they're gonna be at five-thirty, six, once it gets dark?'

'I don't know. At home?'

'On Halloween?'

'They know to stay out of the spotlight.'

'They're already out of the spotlight, they live in a twinky little burgh like this. You think – what age are the girls, eleven and nine – you think they're not gonna want to go trick or treat?'

'They're not?'

'Only if they've got no self respect. Now put your coat on, and tuck your hair under your cheesehead hat, and try to look like you're not so goddamn gorgeous.'

So now they're in Cindy's, and Angelique is oohing and ahhing over the lakeshore cabins and the hillside villas in the realty brochures, and Charlie T is nodding away. Soon enough, Cindy sits down with them: Cindy, who has frizzy curls dyed the shade of an ear of corn and tied up in a batik scarf and gypsy hoop earrings and a figure and complexion that look like, once she's closed up Cindy's Country Bake, first she eats whatever country bake is left over, then she rolls across the street and orders the first of several at Andrew's Bar.

'You folks like the area?' Cindy says, and laughs, as if she has said something funny.

'Who wouldn't?' Angelique coos. 'Such a great place to bring up children,' she says, and ever so subtly brushes her belly with the palm of her hand.

'Oh, well, that's just what we need. Prices went so high, it got that young families couldn't afford to move here,' Cindy says, and laughs again.

Angelique simpers a little in Charlie T's direction.

'Well, I'm just a beauty therapist, but my fiancé is in risk management, I know, don't ask me either, he's explained a hundred times but I can't seem to keep it in my head. Just, whatever it is, it's in great demand these days. This must be our first day off for months, isn't it, sweetheart?'

Charlie T nods and smiles. He'd rather not speak, because then he'll get into a whole 'Oh, I love your accent, are you from Ireland, I'm Irish!' sequence and the next time an American with a broad American accent tells him she's Irish because of her grandfather or she was on vacation there or she loves Colin Farrell he's going to say, *No you're fucking not*, which might not be much of a help with Cindy. In any case, in his experience a woman would much rather have you listen to her than have to listen to you.

Cindy is asking Angelique about the beauty business, and if she'd keep it up when they move, and Angelique says she was thinking about a spa, a wellness center, and Cindy says they have a couple already but that's an area that's growing, and Angelique says, alternatively, something in the childcare area.

'And on that theme, my fiancé here said the town looks a bit like *Chitty Chitty Bang Bang* this afternoon.' (Charlie had said no such thing.) 'It's Halloween, but where are all the children?'

'Well,' says Cindy, 'my children are long gone now,' and she laughs an incredulous laugh, as if the notion she might have grown-up children is so unlikely. 'And we raised them above the store, and as you say, there isn't a lot of opportunity to trick or treat on Main Street. But we used to take 'em round a couple neighborhoods. Sycamore Heights was one, but prices there went up and the kids left home and no new ones arrived, that's an example of exactly what we were talking about. The other one . . .' and at this point, she turns around to a younger woman with a ponytail and a bored expression who's working away on an iPhone. 'April, where do the kids go at Halloween these days?'

April, sighing elaborately, raises her head slowly, but it's as if her eyes are a ton weight and don't want to follow.

'Older kids, they go to Cedar Point on the north lake shore, or over to Billy's Roadhouse. Trick or Treat, the best is still Ripley Fields,' she drawls.

And April's eyes drag her head down towards her iPhone again.

Cindy laughs and nods her head.

'Some things just don't change. If you want to see where we're hiding the kids of Cambridge, head on out to Ripley Fields.'

PART THREE
Halloween Night

Sisters

Barbara doesn't want Donna to come around the houses with them when she and Irene are trick or treating. In fact, she'd prefer Donna to wait at the bottom of the road, as if she wasn't there at all and the girls were flying solo, like the teens Barbara thinks they are. But Barbara is still only eleven ('I'll be twelve in March, actually') and in any case, there's Irene to consider. Irene, who competes pretty much at the same level as her elder sister for most of the day (if not remotely interested in boys or babies or the great wide world of sex which Barbara set herself the task of exploring and charting from the precocious age of about six). Irene, who you'd only know was the younger around half nine at night (while Barbara is campaigning to stay up as late as possible, Irene quietly finds her pajamas and curls up in bed, happy another day is done). Irene, who sometimes appears at Donna's side at five or six in the morning and snuggles in like a toddler with bad dreams, thumb hovering within reach of her mouth, still anxious, still the little pet. Irene would like Donna to come up to the doorsteps with them, just in case.

So the compromise is reached: Donna will wait on the sidewalk or in the driveway of each house, as long as she is in full view.

'It's either that or we go home, Barbara,' Donna says, and after a spasm of eye-rolling, Barbara concedes.

'All right, *fine.*'

There has already been sulking because the walk along the lakeside splashed mud all over the girls' Ugg boots, and while Irene didn't seem to mind, Barbara was outraged, as if muddy boots were yet another infernal adult scheme to thwart her. Donna is amused to note that they are both now armed with heavy sticks which they found on the walk and refuse to relinquish:

Irene: They'd be good for beating away werewolves, or zombies.

Barbara: Or boys.

The houses in Ripley Fields are mostly basic ranches and split-levels, peppered with a scattering of larger dwellings: Neo-Tudor, Neo-Colonial, Neo-Victorian. 'A great place to raise the kids' is what everyone says, and Donna has to agree: tonight, the wide tree-lined streets of the estate are swarming with pint-sized witches and wizards, goblins and ghosts and ghouls, some bustling around like Barbara, some hanging back like Irene, their parents either shadowing them like a security detail or hanging back to give them a taste of freedom. There are only about a thousand people in the entire village, so as aloof as Donna has always tried to hold herself, she is inevitably waylaid by this gallery owner or that hairdresser, keen to know who the vampire and the kitty-kat are.

'My nieces,' Donna says, dodging the invitation to explain any further, the girls an excuse to smile and nod and move on. She is spooked a little, by the wolf sighting earlier, by the crackle of fireworks and the piercing squeals of so many jubilant children, high on the prospect of gorging themselves on unfeasible portions of candy. Mostly though, she's spooked by the news item she saw before they left the house, while the girls pulled their costumes on and jabbered about Halloween, the news item featuring the dead man in Danny and Claire's backyard, the dead *dog*, the Be On The Lookout Alert for Danny, the mention of the girls. Donna called Danny's number immediately and shouted at his voicemail, tried Claire but couldn't reach her, then had to make a quick decision on whether to rescind trick or treating on security grounds, and found she simply couldn't.

But she is walking slow and watchful, and if Irene hadn't insisted, she'd be on the girls anyway, like a whatdoyoucallit, helicopter mom. On the plus side, it's Cambridge, where the local paper is full of school sports reports and chamber of commerce press releases and sponsored columns from the local dentist and veterinary surgeon and the murder of that real estate agent a few years back was a total one-off. *It's a great place to raise your kids*, Donna actually mouths to herself. On the minus side, so is fucking Madison, so what the hell is a dead body doing in the backyard on Arboretum Avenue? *Oh my God, little brother, what have you got yourself into?*

Yes, Donna is walking slow and watchful, her hands in the pockets of her Patagonia fleece, her glossy red clutch with her glossy black Glock within reach of her left hand, and she clocks each parent with interest: one of the barmen at Andrew's Bar, the guy from the motor shop, Patricia and Pam from The Gingerbread House. There are some she doesn't recognize, the bunch of teenage guys who look like they're looking for trouble but wouldn't know what to do with it if they found it, or the sexy redhead with the guy in the Badgers hat, who are probably on their way home from work and could care less if it's Halloween or not. Not everyone has kids, after all.

Donna's favorite moment of the evening so far:

A huge, gloomy Neo-Tudor other kids have avoided. Barbara, either oblivious, or reckless, possibly (usually) both, forges ahead, Irene, glancing over her shoulder at Donna, follows. The big old door opens, and a grumpy old guy (there's always one) appears.

'What are you supposed to be?' he barks at Barbara.

'Vampire,' she says in a low voice, poor Babs knocked off course, suddenly deflated, cowed by the old buzzard, Donna wants to march up and smash his mean old face in.

'What's that? Can't hear ya.'

'*Vampire!*' Barbara yells, irritation conquering her fears. *Good girl yourself, a Brogan through and through*, Donna grins.

'All right then,' the grumpy old guy (GOG) grunts, and tips a bunch of candy into Barbara's skull and crossbones tote bag. He turns to Irene, and immediately starts to shake his head.

'Oh no,' he says. 'No, you're not even wearing a Halloween costume.'

'Yes, I am,' says Irene firmly, who is reluctant to get involved, but committed once she is.

'You're wearing cat's ears and a little mask and a fur suit and a tail,' the GOG snarls.

'That's 'cause I'm a kitty-kat,' trills Irene.

The GOG, who Donna is beginning to find kind of funny in a weird way, folds his arms above his huge belly and shakes his bearded head.

'Kitty-kats are not Halloween critters,' he says, like it's the verdict in a trial, and Donna nearly giggles.

'Hey!' says Barbara, outraged on her sister's behalf.

'It's OK,' Irene says. 'Kitty-kats are too. In ancient Egypt, a Roman soldier killed a cat, and the people of the Nile were furious and killed him, because they saw in the cat the Goddess Bast, who is goddess of the moon. And the goddess of the moon is also the goddess of Halloween. And that's why I'm a kitty-kat.'

The GOG is momentarily silenced by this.

'So? Trick or Treat? Where's her *stuff*?' Barbara says, and the GOG shrugs and tips candy into Irene's tote.

'Hey,' he says, as the girls are turning to go. 'Was any of that true?'

'Some of it,' Irene says.

'Which bits?'

'You wouldn't understand,' Barbara says.

'It's stuff only we know about,' Irene says.

'You? Who are you?' the GOG says.

Barbara has almost caught up to Donna now. She waits for Irene and then turns back to the GOG, framed in the gloom of his doorway.

'Who are we?' Barbara says, as a rocket whooshes through the sky overhead, red sparks trailing in its wake, and Irene turns to her sister, on point.

'Who are we? We're the Brogan sisters.'

Willow Weep for Me

At the Brogan house on Arboretum Avenue, no one is sure what to do about the dead dog, and it falls to Detective Nora Fox to make a decision. It is the last thing to be settled before the crime scene is released. The body still lacks formal identification, but by a process of elimination, it is almost certainly that of Ralph Cowley – Ken Fowler didn't get to talk to him, but there is a Dave Ricks Graphic Design consultancy on West Wacker in Chicago, and the receptionist told him Mr Ricks was unavailable because he was in a meeting, not because he was dead. The medical examiner has done his work, and the body has been removed, and the police photographers and technical specialists have taken their shots and collected their samples. Fragments of police tape litter the trampled lawn as Officer Colby and Nora Fox stand in the dark above the exhumed body of the grotesquely mutilated dog.

'We can't just leave it here,' Colby says.

'Him,' Nora says. 'Mr Smith was his name.'

Her tone is harsher than she intends, anger at the savage who did this seeping into it, and Colby winces slightly, as if he has been rebuked.

'We're not going to bury him again either,' she says. 'If there's . . . it's for the family to decide. If there's anything in the garage . . . canvas tarpaulin, or a tent or something? And then they can bury him, as a family, when the whole thing . . .'

Nora lets her voice trail off. It's understood that the whole thing could end in a number of ways, most of them excluding a scenario in which the reunited Brogan family congregate together in the backyard for the burial of their pet. Colby nods quietly and immediately heads for the garage.

Nora looks back to the turreted Queen Anne cottage in the woods that is the Brogan house, and wonders if they were tempting fate, living out here like this, then briskly dismisses the superstitious nature of the thought, and sets her mind to run over what has happened since she left Monroe High School library.

Firstly, Danny Brogan's traveling companion, Jeff Torrance, was shot dead earlier in the afternoon outside a Ruby Tuesday's chain restaurant in Rockford, Illinois. Ken Fowler had already got plates from the DMV for a red 1976 Ford Mustang registered to Jefferson Torrance, Spring Harbor, Madison WI, and added it to the BOLO alert when it emerged that Danny Brogan had taken off in it. An eye witness saw Danny hovering over the body, hands and face covered in blood. Initially the Rockford Police assumed that Brogan had shot Torrance, but once the forensic pathologist from the University of Illinois showed up, his preliminary findings made it clear that, from the nature of the impact wound and the angle of entry, the shot had been fired from some considerable distance. Nonetheless, Brogan was still being pursued, and now the highway patrol had a vehicle to watch out for.

Secondly, Nora has called Cass Epstein at the Wisconsin Department of Children and Families. Nora and Cass are members of the same book group, and when the book of the month was *Conspiracy of Silence* by Martha Powers, with its themes of adoption, the discussion had quickly moved, as book group discussions will, from the book to the issues themselves: what rights do the birth parents, the foster parents and the adopted children have, and who takes precedence? Nora knows she can get access to information based on a warrant or if she can demonstrate it's a vital part of her investigation. She doesn't have the former, and doesn't know yet if the latter applies. But it's Halloween tonight, the Bradberry fire was on Halloween thirty-five years ago, and Nora doesn't think much of detectives who think having a bad feeling means anything, but . . . she has a bad feeling. So she calls Cass and asks her if she can identify the surviving Bradberry child, the three-year-old girl who got away. She tells Cass it may form the background to an investigation she's conducting, and it might be very helpful, and two people are dead already, so time is a factor. She oscillates between calm, because Cass is highly resistant to bullying, and a bit of, well, bullying. And Cass says the office is nearly closed, and she will have to weigh Nora's application on its merits, and she may not hear back from her until tomorrow, and Happy Halloween! So much for the book club network.

Officer Colby returns with an old plaid suitcase that doesn't lock properly and is covered with mold.

'It's so cold in that garage, the body's not likely to decompose,' he says, and Nora nods, and Colby gingerly scoops up Mr Smith's body and drops it in the case, and folds the lid over and carries it across to the garage. When he comes back, Nora tells him he can leave. She stays, staring at the house, and pacing the backyard, opening the rear gate that gives out to the Arboretum and walking the earth that has been turned, a Maglite the size of a ballpoint pen guiding her eye. She always does this, like a criminal herself, returning to the scene of the crime just to see if there's anything they've missed. And there is always something. It takes her half an hour, rustling leaves with her feet like a dog, or a child, crunching dead apples into mulch, until she spots something glittering in the forest scurf. She takes tweezers from her bag and picks it up and inspects it. It's a small oval medal, silver in shade but not silver, probably nickel, with a cross and an M on one side and an engraving of the Blessed Virgin Mary on the other, and the words around the engraving, in tiny print: *O Mary conceived without sin, pray for us who have recourse to thee.*

A Miraculous Medal, she recognizes it immediately: Gary was Catholic and used to wear one, got a kind of illicit thrill from wearing it when they had sex that Nora eventually began to find creepy. But then, Nora never believed in God. Her parents were all, 'We don't want to impose anything on you. When you're old enough, you can figure it out for yourself.' Nora often wonders if this was the right approach, or if faith is only something you have if you contract it as a child. Not that she necessarily misses it, or at least, not day to day, but she does sometimes envy people who believe, even when it lapses. There's something there they can go back to, and often, when the going gets tough, they do. And she doesn't actually think her parents, who were self-absorbed flakes who divorced when she was ten so they could make two other self-absorbed flakes' lives a misery, had any real intellectual rigor to their non-faith-based method of parenting. She reckons they were just too lazy to get out of bed on a Sunday morning.

She stares at the medal. Maybe there are prints on it, she thinks, popping it into one of the self-sealing evidence bags she's never without. Maybe it just narrows the suspect range down to Catholics. Or maybe it was Ralph Cowley's.

O Mary conceived without sin, pray for us who have recourse to thee.

Her phone vibrates. She has a new text message.

Info on your desk dropped it in as I was passing hope it helps Cass x

Ralph's Book

1976

What happened was Danny was Fire, Dave was Famine, Ralph was Pestilence and Gene was Plague. The lawn was ablaze, and the boys could not be contained; their prank had worked to spectacular effect. They were whooping and roaring with glee now, dancing, literally dancing, between the skulls and the spiders, daring each other to run *through* the flames. Their faces were hidden by their masks, but they caught each other's eyes, and their eyes too were aflame, with mischief, with malice. Each of them noticed the two Bradberry kids in the window, staring out, their faces wide-eyed with fear. Each of them pretended he couldn't see them. 'Get the fire bottles,' someone said, and though they had all agreed that they probably wouldn't need to use them, in the moment, everyone wanted to add to the blaze.

They had all agreed that they would throw them nowhere near the house, that had been established in the ground rules. Danny – because it was his operation, after all, his revenge – had been very particular about this. And because it is his spectacular, he gets the first throw, and he lines himself up to pitch it at this enormous old sycamore in the far corner of the garden, diagonally opposite the house, right by the fence the boys had all piled over. The flames are beating hard and loud now, and the heat is building, and a couple of voices agree with Dan that the sycamore tree is the best, indeed, scanning round the yard, the only tree sufficiently far away from the house to be safe.

Afterwards, they decide that Danny broke the rules: he panicked, or freaked out, or slipped and, in trying to keep his balance, lobbed the fire bottle at the house. Whether by accident or design, it was Danny who did it, and the result was the same.

But that's not the way it actually happened.

What happened was they all lined up, Danny first, and as he ran, the others followed, and Ralph skidded and pushed Danny in the back and they both went tumbling through a blazing skull. Ralph landed on top of Danny in the flames – he scooped him up and hurled him away and Danny went flying into the tree and knocked himself out. Meanwhile, the two remaining were lined up, ready to throw. They couldn't throw at the tree, because Danny was there and they would have risked setting him alight. One of them – F – threw his bottle at the fence the other side of the tree, on the boundary with the next yard over. And then P – Ralph was watching, and he *saw* – P, careering through the blaze in Danny's direction, flung the fire bottle over his head and back in the direction of the house. Nobody could find Danny's fire bottle, so it was clear he had thrown his too. And when they saw the house in flames, they panicked, and hauled Danny out of there, and ran.

Afterwards, out of their costumes, it was all decided: Danny had thrown the bottle that set the house on fire.

But years later, Ralph read the report of the investigation into the fire, and found that a fire bottle had been found intact, with the cloth fuse unlit, lodged between the sycamore and the fence on the other side of the boys' exit route. Danny's fire bottle. So it hadn't been him. And it hadn't been Ralph. And Ralph was Pestilence, he'd picked P because Gene had picked Plague, and Ralph did whatever Gene did. Gene was P and P threw the bottle that hit the house.

It wasn't Danny after all.

It was Gene.

Danny had spent all this time thinking it had been his fault, had been *told* it was all his fault. But it wasn't. What's more, it hadn't been all along. It had been a lie, insisted upon by Gene Peterson, and the others had gone along because it had all happened so fast; the heat had been so intense and the flames so bright and so high. They had been scared and uncertain, and Gene had been calm and sure, and that was what they had looked to Gene for all along, and so they believed him.

But they were wrong.

Extract from
Trick or Treat
Unpublished manuscript by Ralph Cowley

I Can Read Between the Lines

Peterson Sportswear's head office is in a building that would look magnificently ornate in any other context, but appears almost self-effacing when set a hundred yards up North Michigan Avenue from the white terracotta facade and French Renaissance ornamentation of the Wrigley Building. With the Tribune Tower glittering like a Gothic cathedral across the street, it's hard for a visitor not to stop and stare in awe at the architectural riches of the Magnificent Mile. Unless he's Danny Brogan, in which case he just pays the cab driver and walks into the lobby of the Ainslie Building and tells the guard at the desk he has an appointment with Gene Peterson. He has to show ID, and sign in, and he gets a clip-on badge to wear, and he walks through a metal-detector gate and takes the glass elevator to the thirty-seventh floor, soaring above the Chicago River. He has already called ahead, of course. He refused to be deflected by his lack of an appointment. 'Just tell Gene it's Danny Brogan. It's about Jackie Bradberry. He'll agree to see me,' he said, and of course, Gene did. And here he is, standing inside double doors by the Peterson Sportswear reception desk as Danny comes out of the elevator, arms extended, face all smiles. Danny takes the embrace and returns it. Even now, with all he knows, with all he has to say, he can't go on the attack straight away. It's not how he rolls, and it seems like it never will be. After all, Gene is the man who blackmailed him, who helped to ruin him, who lied to him all these years, and still he stands, smiling like a fool. Danny Brogan: if not now, when?

'How are you, Danny? Good to see you, man,' Gene says, beaming, no flicker of unease in his expression, and stands back, hands raised in Danny's direction like a fond uncle, gesturing expansively, including the girls at reception in the fun.

'Sharp as ever, I gotta say. Peterson Sportswear will never make a dime out of this man; probably wears a neck tie to the gym. No one rocks a three-piece suit like my friend Danny Brogan. It's Cary Grant here – ask your mother, girls.'

And it's true. Before Danny went to see Dave over on West Wacker, he changed in the underground parking lot from dove- to charcoal-gray wool, fresh white shirt, black knit silk tie. It doesn't come without effort, but it's not affectation, it's . . . for better or worse, it's at the core of who he is. Women understood this better than men, although not Claire, who doesn't seem to care what she wears, maybe because she has the gift of looking good in anything.

Danny follows Gene down a carpet-tiled, fluorescent-lit corridor. Along the partition wall is a succession of functional modular offices with glass panels in the doors and along the tops of the walls. At the end, a similar door gives on to a slightly larger, strictly non-luxurious room, into which Danny follows Gene. There's a desk and a few chairs, a glass and to one side, a costume rail with all manner of brightly colored sportswear. It could be a mobile trailer on a construction site.

'The days of the palatial office are done,' Gene says as they sit, Danny in front of the desk, Gene to one side of it, perched on the edge. 'Don't mistake it for your living room. Not with this employer at any rate. Do your job and go home, that's what everyone wants. Certainly what I want.'

Gene looks at Danny and smiles a not entirely convincing smile.

'What can I do for you, Dan? Jackie Bradberry? Jesus. Haven't thought about that in a long time.'

'No? I think about it a lot, Gene. As you know.'

'As I know? I don't know. Jesus, first Ralph, then you. What is this all about? The past is the past. Over. You've got kids, right, two girls, Barbara and, and, Irene, am I right? And so do I. And the duty we owe them is, not to turn into sad old men, drinking to days gone by, thinking the past outshines the present. We've got to live in the future, Dan.'

'Easy for you to say,' Danny says, his tone sour.

'Easy for you to say, too, and that's what you did say, last time we met. Brogan's Bar and Grill survives and thrives, two beautiful daughters, lovely wife, no doubt in the marriage there's this and that, what marriage doesn't have its interesting moments, its phases, its sequences, but hey. Compared to a lot of people . . . compared to *Ralph*, you're a lucky man. Am I wrong?'

'Yes, you are wrong. I am lucky, compared to Ralph, but then again, so is everyone. But otherwise, I am not lucky.'

'Why not?'

'Because I lost two hundred and fifty-five thousand dollars. Because I am days, weeks away from ruin. Because someone is trying to destroy my life. And that someone, Gene Peterson, my old friend, that someone is you.'

Gene, with his square jaw, his sandy cowlick hair gelled into a helmet of submission, with his khakis and deck shoes and navy blue blazer, Gene with his golf-club ease and his self-made drive, says: 'Are you fucking kidding me? Last thing I remember, I got you into Jonathan Glatt, you know how hard it was to get into that fund?'

'And see what happened?'

'Didn't happen to us,' Gene says, shrugging.

'It happened to me. You didn't tell me I needed to get out.'

'Of course I did.'

'No, you didn't. You told Ralph, and Dave, but not me.'

'Yes I did, I sent you an email.'

'I never got an email.'

'I sent you an email. And you replied.'

'No,' Danny says. 'No, that didn't happen.'

Gene looks at Danny a second, hard, then stands and beckons him over to his desk, where there is a metallic desktop iMac and a MacBook Pro. Gene flips the MacBook open, double clicks the Mail icon in the dock and, when the mail window appears, types Danny's name in the search field. There are more than twenty results, stretching back months. Gene clicks on the second from the top, message from Gene Peterson. Subject: Jonathan Glatt. Priority: Urgent. It reads:

> *Danny, get your money out of Jonathan Glatt's fund, things are not looking good there, cannot expand but trust me, we had a good run, but now it's all going to hell. You have about forty-eight hours. Otherwise, you can wave goodbye to the cash. Please acknowledge this email – and act on it now!*
>
> *All best,*
> *Gene*

Danny is shaking his head.

'I never saw that before,' he says.

'Well,' says Gene, and clicks the top email in the list, message from Danny Brogan. Subject: Re: Jonathan Glatt. The text reads:

Gene – received and understood – I will take steps to get the money out today. Thanks for the warning, you're a lifesaver.
All best,
Danny

'I didn't send that,' Danny says.

'You didn't send it?'

'I never saw the email you sent me; never sent the reply.'

'Can you think of anyone who might have? Because someone evidently did.'

Danny considers this, doesn't want to think about it. It's Gene. It's Gene.

'What about Claire Bradberry?'

'What about her?'

'I went to see Jonathan Glatt. And he told me that everyone got out of the fund early, except me. And that there was one other person, on top of the four of us. Claire Bradberry.'

'Yeah. You keep saying that name, Dan, as if, I don't know, music is gonna start playing, and I'm suddenly gonna know what it means.'

'Bradberry.'

'Oh. You mean, like Jackie. It's a common enough name, Danny.'

'But there was just the four of us. I mean, the four of us and her, Claire Bradberry. Did that not make connections in your mind?'

'Not really.'

'What else in common do we have?' Danny says, his voice a little strained, a little hoarse now. Gene looks at him as if he's volatile material.

'Well. Many things. We were friends for years after. I haven't seen much of Dave. But I saw you over this thing, we had dinner, drinks, four, five hours, you didn't mention the Bradberrys once. And I wasn't waiting for you to.'

'What about Ralph?'

'Well, Ralph . . . Ralph is who I thought of first when the Glatt thing came up. Poor Ralph needed a helping hand, he seemed a bit lost. And I reckoned, make a bit of money, that'll give him a lift. And when I thought of him, I thought of you guys too. How it would be nice to see you again. How for old times' sake, I should spread some good fortune around. God, I'm sorry, Danny, how much did you say, two hundred and fifty K?'

'Two-five-five. Claire Bradberry. Who is she?'

'I don't know.'

'You don't know? Jonathan Glatt said you brought her in.'

'Yeah, but I don't know who she is. Ask Dave. She's a friend of Dave's.'

'A friend of Dave's?'

'That's right. He asked if she could be included. I didn't want to, thought it was a bit cheeky on his part. But I let it go.'

'A friend of *Dave's*,' Danny repeats, wanting to sound ironic, or skeptical, but unable to process this as anything other than news. He's come to a halt. A friend of Dave's? Dave said Gene had slept with Claire in Chicago. Now Gene is saying this Claire Bradberry is a friend of Dave's. Maybe it is a coincidence. But who was blackmailing him? If it wasn't one of the guys, who could it have been? And what about the email? That's pretty irrefutable, Gene definitely sent it. Unless you can fake that kind of thing. But even if you can, is it possible in the ten minutes between Danny calling Gene and his arrival at his office?

'Sorry, a work thing,' Gene says, waving a hand above the laptop whose screen has suddenly absorbed his attention.

Danny had three killer blows, or so he thought. Two have failed to find a target. He still has one left.

'Ralph came to see me.'

'Oh yeah. To talk about his book? No, he abandoned that, didn't he? In the event that it had ever really existed in the first place.'

'He had a, a manuscript – I don't know if you could call it a book. But he certainly did have a story.'

Gene, clicking away at his keyboard, splutters with laughter.

'Well, that was Ralph. A day late and a dollar short. Ralph always had a story. Beats me why they hung on to him in that school for as long as they did.'

'Gene. Can you do that later? Because I want you to look at me now when I'm talking to you.'

Gene looks above his laptop.

'OK, Dan. I do have some breaking stuff here, but . . .'

Gene does something involving the sound of keystrokes, and then gives Danny his undivided attention.

'Shoot.'

'Ralph told me that . . . that he'd figured it out, basically. And you know, because I saw Dave Ricks, and Dave Ricks mentioned Ralph's novel, and I think it wasn't really a novel at all, it was his account of that night, of Halloween night 1976, thirty-five years ago tonight.'

'It was the Bicentennial, wasn't it?' Gene says, a false smile suddenly appearing on his face, his voice a little loud.

'I don't think that mattered to us. Anyway, Ralph would have known immediately what to think of a name like Claire Bradbury. Claire being my wife's name. But then you know that, don't you, Gene?'

Silent now, Gene tries to hold Danny's gaze, breaks it, his eyes flickering to his laptop screen and to whatever else is on his desk.

'Ralph said we'd all agreed it was me who threw the fire bottle at the wall of the house. At your insistence. He said your voice was the loudest, your memory was the clearest, your opinion the surest. You prevailed. And Ralph went along with it for a while. But something just didn't sit right with him. It began to niggle away at him. See, Ralph was behind me when I ran into the tree, he had shoved me, to get me out of the blazing skull. And he never saw me throw the fire bottle.'

'What did Dave say?' Gene snaps.

'He said he saw me throw it, but it was clear it was by accident, it was because I was trying to keep my balance. But Ralph—'

'You know what Dave says, and you know what I say, but the one you want to believe is Ralph, who said, what, let me guess, you didn't throw it?'

'He said he went back a year or so ago and got access to the report of the original investigation. There was one fire bottle found on the site. We didn't bring but four. Ralph said he threw his, after he got me out of the fire. By which time I was unconscious and in no condition to throw anything. He said the other two bottles were thrown then, one by an F and one by a P.'

Gene frowns. 'An F and a P?'

'We were the Four Horsemen of the Apocalypse, remember? Fire, Famine, Pestilence and Plague. I was Fire, Dave was Famine, Ralph was Pestilence, and you were Plague. He remembers yours because as soon as he knew you were a P, that's what he had to be too. Him being your little shadow. And I remember being Fire, so by a process of elimination, Dave was Famine.'

Gene looks at Danny and then towards the window, his mouth opening and closing as if he is having difficulty breathing. He forms his lips into the shape of a word, but Danny doesn't let him speak.

'Ralph said the one who threw the bottle, and it looked quite deliberate, had a P on his shirt. It wasn't him. So it must have been you.'

A phone rings and Gene answers it. 'Yes. Yes. All right. I'll be out now.' He snaps shut his laptop and rises. 'Danny, I'm sorry about this, I have to . . . if you want to wait here, it shouldn't take long.'

'Now?'

'It really can't wait, I'm afraid. But listen to me: Ralph may have got closer to the truth, but it's still not the final version. I hope I can help you, Dan. I really do.'

Gene's phone chimes out again and he puts it to his ear as he leaves the office. There's the sound of voices down the corridor. Danny wanders across to the desk and opens the laptop. Mail, the email program, is the front window on the screen. The message it opens to has the subject line: DANNY BROGAN WANTED, and in the body of the message, a link that has already been clicked. Danny clicks it himself, and arrives at Madison.com, a news source for the city, to find himself today's top story.

BOLO FOR BROGAN, runs the headline. The intro goes:

MADISON BAR OWNER WANTED IN CONNECTION WITH TWO MURDERS.

Oh, Christ. That was what Gene was reading. Where has he

gone, to get the cops? Danny perches on a chair and peers out
through the glass panel at the top of the exterior office wall. He
can't see anything, but he can hear men's voices, and the crackle
and beep sound of what could be police or security two-way
radios. Danny leaps off the chair, flings opens the door and looks
in the other direction. There's a door at the end of the corridor.
He paces out and tries the handle. It opens on to a small room
with a sink and a fridge for making tea and coffee. He hears a
heavy tread coming from reception and retreats back into the
office. The only thing he can think of is the clothes rail. He
stands on the wall side of the heavily laden rail with one end
nudging up towards the door and waits. Either it will work or it
won't, he thinks, along with how the fuck did things come to
this?

The door opens and Danny sees Gene enter at pace, followed
by two uniformed cops. Immediately he rams the clothes rail
against the opposite wall, blocking the doorway, with himself on
the door side and Gene and the cops on the other. Does he have
even ten seconds? He doesn't think, he just runs, along the
corridor, through reception, down a couple of sets of stairs. He's
grabbed some sportswear off the rail and he throws it behind
him as he goes, partly because it reminds him of something he's
seen in a movie and partly because it might catch someone in
the face or under foot. Go. *Go.*

Three floors down, he bolts along the corridor in the opposite
direction from the tea and coffee room side of the building.
He can hear the pounding of heavy cop feet continuing on down
the stairs as he goes. There must be a service elevator somewhere
in the Ainslie building, and there's nowhere else for it to be. He
sees a pair of swing doors at the end of the corridor, and hears
another pair smash open behind him.

'Hold up or I'll shoot!'

He'll shoot? Fuck that. Bluffing. Danny flings a couple baseball
shirts in the air behind him and powers on towards the door. A
shot rings out. Warning. Bluffing. Fuck it. He's not stopping.
A shot? No. It was a door slam, a furniture crash. And he's
through the doors, and there it is, gray doors and a gray metal
meal trolley beside it. He leans on the button, down, down, and
the footsteps are getting closer, and the elevator is coming,

thirty-two, thirty-three, thirty-four. As it pings and the doors open, he swings the metal meal trolley across and jams it beneath the handles of the swing doors and makes the service elevator door just as it's closing and hits the lower-ground-floor button.

As he's going down, his phone rings. He must have left it on after he called Gene to set up the meet. Well, no sense in turning it off again; he's been well and truly traced by now. He looks at the screen, and answers. 'Mrs Brogan?'

'You remembered. Well done. Mr Brogan.'

'Did you remember?'

'All the time.'

'I was there, Claire. The Allegro Hotel. Room four-three-five?'

'You were in Chicago?'

'Just . . . passing through.'

'Passing through? What does that mean?'

'It means . . . Claire, I know we need to talk, but right now, there are cops after me.'

'You're in Gene Peterson's office, right? I'm in Chicago too, in the Old Town? Can you make it over here? You can get the El, faster than a cab.'

'What station? I'm on North Mich here.'

'You're on North Mich . . . go north one block to Grand Avenue, it runs under so you've got to use the steps, then . . . west two blocks, no, three, Grand and State. It's the red line, ride north to Fullerton.'

'Thank you. I've done nothing wrong, Claire.'

'Neither have I, Danny. Neither have I.'

Danny closes the call as the elevator hits the lower-ground floor. If no one has done anything wrong, just how have they managed to land in so much shit?

There Will Never Be Another You

Detective Nora Fox is at her desk at the West District station house on McKenna Boulevard. She has passed the Miraculous Medal on for fingerprinting: cross-checking with the alleged murder weapon may tell if there is a third party in the frame, or if the evidence points to Danny Brogan. She has checked in with Ken Fowler, who tells her that Jeff Torrance's red '76 Mustang was spotted parked on North Clark Street in Chicago by a CPD beat officer, and that the vehicle is now under surveillance ready for the suspect's return. Ralph Cowley was unmarried, but he had a sister living in Milwaukee; she's expected tomorrow to identify the body. He ran a preliminary financial check on Danny Brogan's finances, and found them to be in as heinous a condition as you might imagine of someone against whom the bank had initiated foreclosure proceedings, and far worse than his wife had thought. On top of the money borrowed to invest with Jonathan Glatt ($205,000 on top of the $50,000 in savings) there is a further $5,000 monthly cash withdrawal, which raises the question: who needs five grand a month, on top of all other average household spending? Elton John for fresh flowers? No documentary or anecdotal evidence points to Brogan being a degenerate gambler.

Having delivered his report, Nora expects that Ken will, as usual, want to go home, but no, he's happy to stay at his desk. Halloween is not a night to be in the house. Now Nora is back at her desk, examining the file her friend Cass Epstein from the Wisconsin Department of Children and Families has left for her.

There's a birth certificate for Claire Bradberry, DOB 2/9/1973, with the relevant details: her father's name, her mother's maiden name (Howard), their ages, their states of birth (father Wisconsin, mother Illinois).

There's a report from the social worker who handled the case in November 1976, after the fire, detailing the contacts made with Claire's two surviving brothers (the child having been placed in temporary foster care with a family in the Milwaukee suburb of River Hills that had experience of dealing with potentially traumatized infants). Neither brother expressed any wish to stand in *loco parentis* to Claire, or to have any say in her fate. In fact, it's noted, 'subjects expressed zero interest even in meeting the child, whom neither had seen since she was a baby.'

There's the documentation detailing the contacts between the Wisconsin DCF and the Family Future adoption agency on Miflin St, starting with the rationale for choosing Family Future over any other agency (usually there would have been an attempt to match, socially, culturally, ethnically, the background of the child to the adoptive family, but in the case of the Bradberrys, 'other factors may and should be considered.' In other words, and despite the fact that social services had failed to catch the Bradberry family while they were alive, the level of dysfunction present in the house was such that it was thought better to make a clean break of it.

And there are the records of the adoption: the Consent to Adoption form signed on the child's behalf on February 4, 1977, and the Adoption Confirmation form, signed on Claire Bradberry's fourth birthday, February 9, 1977, by Barry and Janet Marshall of Kenosha, Wisconsin. And although, in the light of the DCF's willingness to dispense with any attempt to match the backgrounds of adoptive parents and child, it would be stretching it too far to describe it as an irony, Barry Marshall's profession is noted as that of medical doctor.

In September, 1980, there are a number of reports and minutes of case conferences between Kenosha Department of Human Services, the Family Future Adoption Agency and Wisconsin DCF following the cardiac arrest and sudden death of Barry Marshall. Case workers agree that, while in some respects Janet Marshall is considered eccentric (she has an interest in spiritualism, and one of her neighbors reported seeing her sunbathing in the nude, although upon investigation, it emerged a) that the sunbathing took place while the child, now called Deirdre Marshall, was in school, and b) that in order for this neighbor to have seen Janet Marshall naked, he would have had to climb up on his roof as far as the chimney pot – which, it subsequently emerged, was exactly what he had done), she and the child have formed an extremely strong bond. A testimonial from Janet Marshall, which is littered with flaky-to-the-max references to birth signs and gem stones and reincarnation but is obviously warm and loving and, as importantly, intelligent and otherwise sensible, and an account of an interview conducted with the seven-year-old Deirdre, in which she displays considerable affection towards Janet, whom she calls Mommy, and recurring gratitude (to whom it is unclear, but it appears to be some indeterminate spiritual power or entity) that while Daddy was taken away, Mommy is still here.

Recommendation: That Janet be entrusted to raise Deirdre as a lone parent.

In 1985 there's a further sheaf of case notes and conference reports between the agencies already dealing with the case and the California DCF and Department of Human Services. Janet Marshall intended to marry another doctor, Thomas Adler, with a family practice in Santa Monica, and to move herself and Deirdre out to live in Los Angeles. Background checks were run on Adler (even though he had no stated intention of adopting Deirdre) and testimonials were recorded once more. Janet's is even flakier than the last time, as if the West Coast is already working its counter-cultural magic in her brain; Nora particularly enjoys Janet's analogy between her imminent wedding and the partial eclipse of one planet by another. But the baseline is still that Deirdre will attend an expensive private school, she will go to university, she will make the best of herself. Deirdre, by now a mature twelve, alternately enthuses about the school she will attend and the fact that she's getting out of Hicksville at last, and worries, in a humorous manner, that California might not only turn her mother into even more of a hippie than she is already, it could start to work its dubious spell on herself. Much discussion is devoted to whether drugs play any part in the Marshall household, and if medical reports and even a police investigation are required, but it is decided that there is insufficient evidence to support this approach, and that, while it is clear that Deirdre is increasingly looking on her mother as, if not a liability, certainly an embarrassment, this is not an unusual development in the relationship between adolescent females and their mothers.

There are several further pieces of documentation. In 1994, requests are made when Deirdre is twenty-one through the Wisconsin Adoption Registry for genetic and medical information on her birth family, and for their identities. There follows another raft of paperwork on the rights and wrongs of releasing the names of her birth parents without their having issued consenting affidavits, notwithstanding the fact that the Bradberrys didn't voluntarily surrender their daughter: they died. There is a strong argument made by several of the case workers to the effect that the circumstances of Deirdre's family's death are so distressing and potentially disturbing that it might well prove more beneficial to her if the knowledge is withheld. Countering this is the position that this would in effect be to play God, and that none of the statutory bodies have this right. Psychiatric assessments and psychological profiles are requested. Eventually, it is concluded that, on balance, the identities of the birth parents should be disclosed. A series of further meetings and consultations ensue, and it is considered that, given the circumstances, the subject is bearing up remarkably well. A few further details of Deirdre's life at this time are noted.

That she married when she was nineteen, and moved to Madison, Wisconsin, not knowing it was in fact the town of her birth.

That her husband was killed in a traffic accident when an oil truck jackknifed on the Beltway.

That before he died, he had set his wife up in her own hairdressing business in the city.

That at this stage, Deirdre had become used to the diminutive name everyone had called her for years, and had taken to signing Deirdre as Dee, even on official documents.

That furthermore, she had taken the surname of her husband, Martyn St Clair, upon marriage, and she had retained it after his death, and from that moment on would style herself Dee St Clair.

Why Was I Born?

In her apartment on East Wilson, Dee St Clair is crying. You can tell by her eyes that she has been crying for some time. She's sitting in that living room of hers with the view out across Lake Monona, and you can see the lights of the houses across the shore, and the star trails of fireworks in the darkened city sky, and smell the jasmine and grapefruit candles burning slow around the room, but Dee isn't looking out the window and even if she was, she probably wouldn't notice the lights or the lake or the fireworks or any damn thing at all. Dee isn't aware of the scented candles either; she is barely aware of her own breathing. Dee is responding to emails and texts and calls because she has no option any more. Not all of them. Sometimes the screen of her iPhone flares up and flashes and she winces and looks away until it stops. She wishes it could all stop without anyone else getting hurt, but the way it's going, that's not likely. She wishes it had never started in the first place. But it did, and willingly or not, she is at the heart of it. So she texts, and she emails, and she sometimes pulls herself together to talk without sounding as if she's falling apart, and in between times, she cries. If only she had never met him. If only fate wasn't fate. She cries and she cries and she cries. But when the call comes, the call to move, Dee will do what she's called to do. It's too late now to do anything else.

In a store room in the cellar of the converted grain store on West Wacker, Dave Ricks is making a telephone call. We can't hear what he's saying, or tell if he's angry, or excited, or upset. Well, maybe we could if we came a little closer, but we don't really want to. We know we're going to find out soon enough, and sometimes it's better to wait. Sometimes it's better, and sometimes we're a little uneasy about learning the truth, even when deep down we know it's what we want. There's a riot of emotion in Dave's face, that's for sure. In the meantime, we're looking around the room, and thinking this must be the office Dave started the design consultancy in. From little acorns. But the longer we look the sooner we stop thinking about design consultancies, or business acumen, or Chicago architecture. The longer we look the sooner we stop thinking at all. Soon all we do is look, is stare, is gape.

For the walls of the cellar are covered with paintings, hundreds of paintings, barely a square inch of wall space to be seen. The paintings are of different sizes. Some are framed, and what a variety of frames, gilt, and steel, and plain and painted wood. Some are behind glass, some are bare canvas. The paintings are in different styles, some clear as a photograph, some thick with swirling paint, some naturalistic, some almost abstract. The paintings come in different colors, some bright and garish, some muted and monochrome.

But for all these differences between them, our eyes gradually begin to find what they have in common. And it dawns on us that every single painting depicts the same scene. The scene is a window, which is dark, but which either reflects, or is surrounded by, not just bright light, but fire light. Sometimes it is the merest flicker, sometimes it is in full blaze. And in the window there are two children. Sometimes you can make out their little faces; sometimes they are abstracted until they are mere shapes; sometimes they are death's heads, skulls or ghouls. But in every picture, it is the same: two children, gazing out in fear, at the flames that will devour them.

I Guess I'll Have to Change My Plan

Charlie T is actually quite relaxed about the whole reconnaissance thing in Ripley Fields. For a start, there's no problem spotting the aunt and the two girls, and since there's a predictable route they're taking, house by house, he and

Angelique can keep their distance. And unless they live here, or close by, it's most likely they've driven. There's a bunch of cars parked down near the entrance to the estate. If that's the way they've come, well, it would be hard to give chase without drawing too much attention to themselves. He could wait in the car, but that doesn't allow for the possibility that the targets are residents here. So there's a limit to how bad things can get.

And that's what concerns Charlie T the most: that he's going to get embroiled in a course of action with Angelique alongside, and end up endangering her, and as a result, himself, the kids, the entire fucking enterprise. Not to mention wanting nothing to do with her harebrained fucking scheme to kidnap the kids and try and extort money out of their father. This is of course also in the context of trying to stop beating himself up over Angelique being here at all, and what a walkover he seems when she wants her way. What Charlie is hoping, basically, is for nothing whatsoever to happen, him and Angelique to drive their car load of yuppie trinkets back to Chicago, hit the bars for a few, decant themselves up to her apartment, pop open the vial of amyl nitrate she filched from the hospital and ride each other into merry, raw oblivion. The idea that Angelique can be both the ultimate porny girl *and* a, well, the, possible mother of his children . . . this happy dream fills Charlie T with a warm, horny glow. This would be everything he could possibly ask for. The only problem is what kind of life can the two of them have together if he does the work he does? Against that, what other kind of work can he do? Tending bar is not going to keep him remotely satisfied, let alone Angelique.

As if in answer to his prayers, if they can be called prayers, his phone throbs with a text message. It's from Mr Wilson: *Client says it must all go down tonight.*

Charlie T fires back: *Does client have an address for mark?*

And by return: *You're in the field, Charles – improvise. Client says it'll be worth double.*

Double? That's not bad. Not enough to clear his debt, but a start. All right. Let's make the conditions a wee bit more secure. The targets reach the house on the far corner and start working their way back towards them. He draws her into a copse of trees between two big neo-Colonials and lays it out for her quietly.

'Angelique, pet, something's come up, I need you to wait in the car. OK?'

'What's come up?'

'Instructions.'

'What instructions?'

'I can't really go into that.'

Angelique gives him that look, the disappointed-in-him look, makes him feel about five years old.

'Charlie. Instructions are for kids. Remember where we're going with this. Whoever that guy is, Mr Weirdo—'

'Mr Wilson.'

'Whatever. The point is, you need to be the sole trader here, not an employee. You're the one who does the work—'

'The intelligence is part of the work – a crucial part.'

'My point exactly. And where is the intel on this job? You don't have a name, an address, you're left to improvise. With my assistance, I surely don't have to point out. So if this Wilson guy is not upholding his end of the bargain, well, you've got to stand up for yourself. A deal is a deal, am I wrong?'

She's not wrong. She's not wrong. And man, she looks hot being not wrong, the streetlights glistening in her hair, her sticky lips red and full, her cheeks hot with passion, with fire. As if she can read his thoughts, she pulls him close and kisses him, rubs a thigh against his hardening cock.

'And the best thing is,' she whispers in his ear, grinding herself against him, 'I think I know how they got here.'

'How?' he says.

'You notice they've all got mud on their boots? The girls are wearing Uggs and there's mud stains halfway up them? And she's got hiking boots caked in mud as well?'

'I hadn't noticed, but I'll take your word for it.'

'Well. It's dry tonight. It hasn't rained in over a week. The ground is hard. Where did they get the mud from?'

'You tell me.'

'Ripley Fields. Lake Ripley. There's a lane way between houses over that side, we passed it our first time around; I don't know for sure, but I've a pretty good idea it leads down to the lake. Maybe there's some kind of walkway down there, a lakeside path or something. I'm ready to guess that's the

way they came, that their house is accessible from the path.
And if that's so . . .'

Charlie T jumps in and has to reduce the volume immediately,
so excited has he become.

'If there's adequate forest down there – and it's wild enough
up here, so there's no reason to expect it isn't – it could be
perfect. Out of sight, easy to separate the kids, to spook them
. . . that's really smart, Angelique.'

'Don't you mean "partner"?'

Charlie thinks a bit, and grins. 'I do.'

My Kind of Town

D anny still has some of the sportswear he pulled off the
rail in Gene Peterson's office: basketball tops and shorts,
shiny man-made fibers unpleasant to the touch, and when
the elevator doors open he flings them in front of him, head
height, before he can see who it is he's flinging them at, and
follows, head down, right shoulder exposed. Hit them low in the
tackle, that's about as much football coaching as he can remember,
let's hope it's a cop or a security guard and not somebody's
grandmother or a pregnant lady, no, it's one of Chicago's finest
and he's on his back, grabbing at Danny's feet, but Danny is
driving his heels and steps off the cop's shoulder.

He can hear him scream as he runs up the incline towards the
exit, up past pallets of crated supplies for the different offices in
the Ainslie Building, hears the cop on his radio now, crackle and
spit, flutter and wow, up past parked cars and a hugely fat security
guy by a barrier who's coming out of his cabin.

Fuck this. Danny heads for the side furthest from the fat guy
and vaults the barrier and runs up the slipway and nearly collides
with a car coming down it and the slipway routes around into
an alley but there's a set of metal steps and Danny piles up them
and there he is, the roar of the street, North Michigan Avenue.

Tribune Tower opposite and what did Claire say? North? That's left, two cops coming out of the entrance to the Ainslie, shit, Danny skids out on to the street and plods around the outside of a CTA bus moving slowly, cars honking, honk back if he could, fuck them, keep your nerve, keep your nerve. He navigates back toward the sidewalk by Nordstrom's looking for the underpass; there are the steps, down and three blocks. Go. *Go.*

There are voices shouting, but he can't be sure if they're cops or people he bumped into or knocked over, or if they're even shouting at him. *Don't look back*, out of the underpass now, cross Rush Street, past the Meridien Hotel, Nordstrom's again, how big is that fucking store? Cross Wabash, Christ, he's out of shape, right side of the street, he can see the red sign on the corner, Grand El Station, past the Hilton Garden Inn and down the steps.

Danny fumbles in his pockets, looks at the vending machine, $2.25, he pulls three dollar bills out and stuffs them in and waits for the machine to whirr and grabs his ticket and walks towards the turnstile.

'Sir?'

Oh, shit.

'Excuse me, sir? You, guy in the gray suit?'

There are people staring at him. His breath is coming hard, hot sweat seeping down his face. He's lost the momentum. He turns around. A thick-set African-American man in navy pants and a yellow and red CTA reflector coat is holding his hand out toward Danny. In it are three quarters.

'You a millionaire today, sir?'

'Far from it,' Danny says.

'Then pick up your change. Maybe you will be someday; stop throwing your money away.'

Danny takes his change. 'Thank you.'

'Best believe I'm not going to be a millionaire, giving it away,' the CTA guy says, and wheels away.

Danny goes through the turnstile and down on to the north platform, still watching for cops, still breathless, still jumpy. But he is smiling too, for the first time in he can't remember how long. It's nice to be nice. Even Chicago's still the Mid-West.

Chicago and Clark underground, up into the light for Clybourn, and then Fullerton. He's stopped panting by now, but he's still sweating like a pig. He gets off the train, and takes the down escalator, and follows the Exit signs and comes out on to West Fullerton Avenue beneath the tracks. There's a jumble of construction work on the street and the sidewalk opposite is closed, concealed behind green mesh fencing. Danny looks this way and that. This way, there's a Dominick's pizza restaurant. That way, there's a parking lot. In front of the parking lot, there's a tall, spindly tree with rust colored leaves. And in front of the tree, there's a woman dressed in black with long auburn hair. He walks toward her, trying to keep his expression steady, and he sees by her face, Christ, her beautiful face, that's she's trying to do the exact same. He looks over his shoulder, and doesn't spot anything, no cops, no one following, but when he looks back at Claire, his eyes flashing, red for danger, red for passion, her eyes flash right back at him, the two of them again, at last, *looking* at each other.

'I've got the car right here,' she says, her voice tight, almost choking, almost laughing with the tension of it all.

'Good,' he says, and he's almost laughing himself, adrenaline lighting him up. 'Good. Let's go.'

PART FOUR
Trick or Treat!

All Alone

Donna wonders whether they take her for some kind of prissy church-mouse school-marm Mid-West mom. Then she reminds herself that that, after all, has been her entire plan, her way of coping with, that is to say, avoiding, life. But it doesn't take long for her reptile self to reengage. First time, the dude with the Badgers hat and the sexy redhead were neighbors, civilians, just a couple on their way home. Second time, they were what the cops would call people of interest. This is the fourth time Donna has spotted them, and she was never even a lookout when she ran with her bikers, she was a diversion, a moving violation in a skirt up to there and a top down to here, *get you an eyeful while my boyfriend raids the till*. Are they amateurs? The guy looks like he knows what he's doing. There's something evasive about him, as if he knows to keep his face out of the light. But the redhead in the kitten-heel boots and the ribbon of skirt, apart from the obvious, what is she for?

Oh, stop it. They could be here for myriad reasons. They could be a young couple out for a leisurely Halloween walk who want to remind themselves of the joys of trick or treating, this being the only neighborhood in which such a thing is possible. Maybe she's pregnant, and they're here to envision the future. Maybe they're pedophiles, sizing up prey. There's an innocent explanation for everything.

'I think we're done, girls,' Donna says, tamping her voice down a panic tone or two.

'There's a few more houses over there,' Irene says hopefully, looking towards a section of the estate they've not been through.

Donna glances at their bulging tote bags. 'Yeah, but where would you put the stuff they give you? No more room in those sacks.'

'You could put it in your pockets,' Barbara says. 'Since you're not doing anything else.'

'I'll put you in my pockets. Pumpkin time, princesses.'
'Are we taking the scenic route again?' Barbara says.
'Mud is the new sand.'
'It's kind of dark down there,' Irene says.
'Well,' Donna says, 'that's what you've got those bats for.'

Donna looks behind her several times as they cut down the lane
between two houses and down the wooden steps and set out along
the path, but she sees no one – no sexy redhead, no guy in a
Badgers hat, no zombies, no werewolves. In truth, the walk is
quite well illuminated from the houses perched forty or fifty feet
above it and from the faint but resilient moon. It is muddy, though:
the water level has been high and has seeped through into the
path; the trees resound to the mulch and slap of their duck paddle
steps and Donna feels the splashes on her cheeks and brow. If
only she had a mask herself, she thinks, and not for the first time.
    One side is banked high and steep with mud and scrub.
Lakeside there are stands of trees and occasional clearings with
picnic tables and moorings for small boats. After about half a
mile, the path follows the lake away from Ripley Fields and the
slope gets a little less precipitous and more trees appear to their
right. It's darker now, without the houses, but they are only
minutes from Donna's house. The girls aren't minding the dark
so much. They are excited and full of plans.
    'If we get two tubs. Do you have two tubs, Aunt Donna?'
Irene says.
    'Tubs. What do you mean, *tubs?* Like, bowls?' Barbara says.
    'They'd have to be big bowls, for all this. No, tubs, like you'd
put plants in.'
    'They'd be covered in mud. We don't want tubs.'
    'Basins. I have a couple plastic basins.'
    'That's what we need. And we can put our stuff in them,
separately. And see what we've got.'
    Barbara always lags behind, and Irene always skips ahead,
and that's how Donna sees Irene stopped, thirty feet in front, a
figure approaching her: the redhead from Ripley Fields.
    'Irene,' she yells, scanning the trees on her right for the guy
in the Badgers hat. She spins around to see Barbara halted,
staring, then spins back.

The redhead reaches for Irene and it looks like she's got some kind of cloth in one hand to muffle or gag or subdue her, and the Glock, which has been out of the clutch since they started down the walk anyway, is in Donna's hand and her hand is pointing at the redhead.

'Leave her alone,' Donna says.

And as she speaks, she catches the guy on her right, the guy in the Badgers hat, moving slowly through the trees, heading past her towards Barbara. She sways, trying to cover him too.

'Get away from her,' she says, and she can see something glint out of the corner of her right eye, but this motherfucking redheaded bitch has some kind of rag or gag over Irene's face, trying to chloroform her? She should shoot the guy she thinks has the gun, but she gets things in the wrong order because she is so incensed and shoots the redhead instead, in the middle of her face, and then she nearly has enough time to shoot the guy as well; she wheels around and he is staring at the redhead where she dropped like he can't believe what just happened, and Irene is screaming, she's kind of being dragged down by the weight of the dead woman. Donna pivots and brings the Glock up and squeezes the trigger and feels like she's running in a dream and thinks *if I don't hit this guy God knows what will happen to the girls* and sees a firework's trail across the sky illuminate the leaves on the surrounding trees and these are the last things she will ever feel and think and see.

It's a Sin to Tell a Lie

The salon is closed, and Detective Nora Fox can't get Dee St Clair on the phone, so she goes to the apartment building on East Wilson and raises the building superintendent, whose name is Steve and who, with long dark hair and a goatee, is kind of cute, and actually looks a bit like Dave Grohl from Foo Fighters and is also younger than she expected, which is a change from the police officers looking younger every year, she supposes, although maybe not a welcome change. Steve, who has somebody blonde with him, is uneasy about giving her Dee's key and Nora talks about a potential missing-persons situation and a double murder case, and Steve still looks doubtful and mentions a warrant and Nora holds her hand up and says:

'Steve, there are children in danger. Tonight!'

Even though she doesn't realize yet that in fact, there *are* children in danger. Steve goes to get the key. She can see that he feels obliged to come with her and she doesn't want that, and neither does he on account of she can smell the blonde's perfume and hear the clink of ice in a glass and if she were him she'd be in there and avid because blondes tend to wilt from lack of attention so she tells him to try Dee on the phone every ten minutes and if he gets through, to let her know.

In the apartment, Nora quickly notes a laptop on the couch by the glass wall overlooking the lake and then comes to rest at a recessed space off the main living room that seems to do dual duty as office and dining area. There's a brown mahogany table here, and its surface is piled high with newspaper cuttings and photocopies of news stories, some loose, some collected in ring binders. Nora checks her time. It's seven-thirty. It's not late. Not yet. She sits at the table and begins to work through the paper.

Danny and Claire are on the I-90 from Chicago, headed for Madison, or for Cambridge, they're not sure which. Danny hasn't been able to talk to Donna, but he's left her messages saying they will come to her and collect the kids, or alternatively if she wants to come to Arboretum Avenue, although that's probably unwise given the house has been cleared out, so in fact, if they manage to get to her place, could they spend the night?

It's not a happy atmosphere in the car. They were genuinely overwhelmed to see each other, and each cried a little, but they barely touched, a squeeze of the hand, a quick brush of the cheek, and what words they did exchange were stuttered and stammered like they had barely met before. They can't seem to bring themselves to talk, maybe because there is so much to talk about, and so few ways they can find to get started, so the journey has been conducted mostly in uncomfortable silence. Claire is driving.

Danny offered to drive, but Claire said no, it was fine, and then wished she had said yes, because she feels she has rebuffed him, whereas she just thought it would be easier if she drove since she had gotten used to the car on the way down. It was a little thing, but it was about so much more than who should drive the fucking car.

It was like they were a couple who had gone on vacation to solve their problems, and instead their problems overwhelmed them, because of course their problem was themselves. Each of them thought separately, in those first few silent miles through the industrial outskirts of Chicago: if this is all that's left of us, then for God's sake, let it die. Each maddened by resentment and rage, and then as quickly exhausted, enervated by it all.

Claire doesn't want to get into the whole thing with Paul Casey in Chicago, because she doesn't know which lie she should tell. She can barely believe Danny came to Chicago in the first place. Where was he? What did he see? What *could* he have seen? He wasn't in the room. And there was nothing to see anyway. Although there was a lot more than she wanted to own up to. And maybe she might have gone much further. Thank God she hadn't. She had been bored and lonely and wanted some attention, and she had had a lucky escape. Tell a white lie or two, and then get down on her knees and apologize.

Also, Claire doesn't really want to tell Danny that, if anyone sinister is behind this, it's more likely to be Dave Ricks than Gene Peterson, because then she'll have to explain that she nearly slept with Dave years ago in Chicago, only he was pretending to be Gene, and obviously she wants to steer clear of the entire Claire-sleeping-with-guys-in-Chicago thing as she feels it's not going to endear her to her husband, and if she knows anything at this stage, it's that she desperately wants to keep her marriage together. Maybe even to the extent of actually getting married. In order to do that, she'll have to go through the whole process of finding out who her birth parents were, and by extension, who she is, or was. She's not sure she wants to, but clearly she's been cast in some kind of mid-life drama, and looking at her birth certificate is probably a more grown-up way to act than fumbling about with old flames in hotel rooms.

Danny doesn't want to talk about the Bradberry fire, because if he does, he's going to get into Claire's parentage and the part he played in that fire, even if it's nothing like what he had thought. In fact, he thinks, maybe he *should* bring it up, confess to her that he has been haunted by a guilt he should never have borne. But it's not up to him, is it? It's not his place to reveal to Claire a truth she'd prefer to live without. Of course, if he doesn't, how is he going to come clean about all the money they've lost? By admitting he was a greedy fool, that's how. The blackmail was one thing, but nobody made him borrow all that extra money to invest with Jonathan Glatt.

He knows that they're going to have to tell each other everything, even if, in the end, it means they're finished. He doesn't want that, despite what happened in Chicago, which might well be nothing, and even if it wasn't, fair enough, everyone's human, there've been a couple of late nights in Brogans where, if he didn't step entirely over the line, he put his foot right on it, and wanted to keep going. But what about Claire's Facebook page, and those messages to Paul Casey? That was a little more than stepping over the line. That was forward planning, calculation, intention.

He thinks suddenly about Gene sending Danny an email telling him to get out of Jonathan Glatt's fund – and somebody had responded, pretending to be Danny.

'Claire, did you have anything happen with your computer?'

'How do you mean?' *Oh please, don't let Danny have read those Facebook messages*

'I don't know. Someone hacking into it, or setting up accounts you didn't know about?'

'I . . . I think something like that did happen. Did you have the same?'

Tell her. Not everything. Never tell a woman everything. But you have to say something.

'The money we lost . . . with Jonathan Glatt? Well, Gene Peterson . . . Gene sent me an email, he sent all the guys an email, warning us to get out, to get our money out. I mean, it was pretty short notice, but everyone else managed it. Because everyone else got the message.'

'And what, you didn't? He didn't send you one?'

'No, I told you, he did. He showed me it today, it's in the Sent folder in his email program.'

'But you never got it? Did he not follow up to make sure?'

'He didn't need to follow up. He got a reply.'

'He got a reply? What do you mean?'

'I mean someone sent an email from my address, claiming to be me, saying that's great and I'd withdraw the cash immediately, thank you very much.'

Claire feels a sudden rush, an excruciating combination of fear and excitement. She can tell Danny something.

'That's so weird. Because you know . . . well, I don't know what you know, and there might have been a bit of stupidity, but it Wasn't. Actually. Anything. You know?'

'Uh huh?'

'In Chicago, I mean. With . . . with Paul Casey?'

'I'm listening . . .'

'How it might have happened was, and I only found this out today, right, I have a Facebook account—'

'You never told me that.'

'No.'

'You were always like, "Oh, Facebook, Twitter, that stuff is for idiots."'

'I know. But Dee signed me up. You know Dee, she won't take no for an answer. When she did that website for me, which I hardly ever go to either, by the way, she said I had to be on Facebook too, and post on both, to increase the traffic. I didn't care, since I wasn't going to use it in the first place. But then I went back to Chicago today, um . . .'

'Yeah, I was wondering, what were you doing there?'

She's going to throw up. 'I had to . . . to ask Paul something.'

'You had to ask Paul something. You gonna tell me what that was?'

'Probably. I'll get to it. It was nothing that affects us.'

'Meaning . . .'

'Meaning stop fucking hounding me, OK? I love you, Danny. I'm trying to talk to you. Stop treating me like a naughty child.'

She's right. He nods, and waits.

'So Paul said, blah blah blah "those messages you sent on Facebook."'

'To him?'

'Yeah. And I said I never sent any messages. And blah blah blah, and then I *went* on Facebook and saw my messages, and it turned out there were three, an entire exchange between me and my ex-boyfriend. Explicit messages, inviting him to be both more and less than my current boyfriend. Messages I never wrote.'

Danny nods. He doesn't want to admit he saw the messages, never wants to think about them again.

'And Chicago?' he says.

'Nothing,' Claire says. 'In fact, better than nothing. If I had some kind of stupid wistful notion that I had unfinished business in that town . . . or in my past . . . well, I don't feel that way any more. And I never will again.'

Danny nods again. He believes her. Maybe not without a certain amount of doubt, but that will pass. And even if it doesn't, well, that's where trust comes in. If there was no doubt, there'd be no trust. And no love.

They flash by the exit for Rockford, and Danny winces, barely able to believe that was only – what, four or five hours ago? Jeff shot in the head by a fucking sniper. Cops chasing him through the streets of Chicago. He puts his head in his hands and breathes in quickly and deeply through his mouth. He doesn't know how long he stays like that, becomes conscious of a steadying hand on his thigh. He feels close to tears, but no tears come. When he lifts his head and turns around, he sees Claire's face crumbling, and it's her turn to cry.

'Danny, they killed Mr Smith,' she says.

'Oh, no,' Danny says.

'They cut his throat. They cut his little body up, they slaughtered him like a pig.'

On 'pig' she turns shrill, and wails, and sobs, and God forgive him, so does he; the dam breaks and all the fears they hold, for their marriage, for their kids, for their future, all collide in grief over the death of their dog.

'How will we tell the girls?' Claire says, when she has recovered somewhat. Danny shakes his head. They drive in silence. And then something occurs to him.

'Claire, how did you know I was in Gene's office?'

'Did I?'

'You called me, and you knew I was there.'

'That's right. Dee told me.'

'Dee told you? How did Dee know?'

'I think she was worried? The cops came and questioned her at the salon, and then she's at home, watching bulletins on TV, she's all worked up about it.'

'But how did she know? I mean, the only one who knew I was coming to see Gene was Dave Ricks.'

'Maybe she guessed. Because of the Jonathan Glatt thing. Does it matter? It meant I was able to get you out of there.'

'This is true. It's just . . . her name is coming up a lot, don't you think? Dee set up your Facebook page. All of a sudden, it has bogus messages on it. And . . . didn't she do, like, tech maintenance for you?'

'She would make sure I downloaded software and . . . yeah, she was always trying to interest me in the latest bells and whistles. I mean, she made me get an iPhone.'

'And what about my laptop? Did she do anything with it?'

Claire shakes her head.

'Not that I remember. No, wait. When something was always crashing on you?'

'Safari.'

'I mentioned it, and she looked at it. It was some conflict between, I don't know, something you'd installed and something else. I told you, she fixed it. And you were, yeah, whatever. What is it with you and Dee? You've never really liked her.'

'You don't see anything suspicious about all of this? Dee sets up your Facebook page, suddenly you're sending Paul Casey sex messages. Dee fixes my computer, I reply to emails I didn't receive. Dee calls you up and tells you I'm in Gene Peterson's office. Dee Dee Dee. Is all I'm saying.'

'My friend. You think my friend is behind this? Killing two of your old friends, slaughtering our dog? Are you kidding me?'

'I don't see who else has it can be. I mean, I thought it was Gene. Who else is there, Dave? Dave was my best friend. Do you think Dave is going to kill Ralph Cowley?'

Claire goes numb, stares ahead. Farmhouses and trees out there, in the great state of Wisconsin. Land stretching away, far away, rich land, good for grazing. The dairy state. Christ, she needs a rest. There's a lay-by up here and she abruptly pulls into it.

'You drive,' she says, and gets out of the car. They swap seats and Danny pulls out and puts his foot down. Claire tries to form a few words, finds she can't, fumbles with the radio, punches past the classic rock and the crazy talk stations until she finds one she likes. Billie Holiday is singing 'No Regrets,' and if that isn't the secret of good comedy, she doesn't know what is.

'When I was in Chicago, when we were broken up, I had a thing, not even a thing, a fumble, with a guy who told me his name was Gene Peterson. Nice enough guy, good looking, told me he was at school with you. Anyway, he got pretty weird, and I had to get out of the situation, and between one thing and another, he ended up getting the shit kicked out of him by this Latino gang.'

'As you do.'

'And when I saw the dead body in our backyard, I thought it was an older, gone to seed version of this guy.'

'Gene Peterson looks nothing like Ralph Cowley, never did.'

'Yes, but the guy I met in Chicago wasn't Gene Peterson. I thought he was, I thought, oh, he hates me because I got him beaten up, which was kind of an accident anyway, and he must hate you because he got us to invest with Jonathan Glatt and we lost all our money. So I came up here to ask Paul Casey about that night, because he was the one who rescued me, and then I looked all this up online. Do you know they have high-school yearbooks online now? Well, there's one of your year. No shots of you, or Gene Peterson, but that wasn't a problem, I know what you look like and Gene Peterson is all over the net on account of his business. But they had shots of Ralph and Dave.'

'And they look a bit alike, so the guy who told you he was Gene, you thought it was Ralph, but in fact it was Dave?'

'Sorry, am I boring you?'

'What are you suggesting, that Dave Ricks is responsible for this? He was my best friend.'

'Was.'

'We never fell out or anything, we just kind of . . . I don't know, drifted apart.'

Danny considers this for a moment. After Dave went to school

in Chicago, he would come home for weekends, hook up with
Danny. At first it was OK, even though Dave had always been
pretty intense, the kind of guy, if you were in his company, he
didn't want to share you, didn't want anyone else around but
the inner circle, the old firm, the Four Horsemen. And then that
side of him got to be, frankly, a pain in the ass. He became like
some possessive girlfriend who rang you up twenty times a day
to check you weren't cheating on her until all you wanted to do
was cheat on her so you could dump her. And Danny had more
or less dumped Dave: not returning his calls, pretending he wasn't
home if he came to the house, switching the places he drank,
avoiding weekend shifts at Brogan's, or alternatively making sure
he was slated to work non-stop Friday through Sunday. And Dave
got the message. It had been a bit cruel, but it was cruel to be
kind: he still liked the guy, he just didn't want to spend his entire
life with him. After that though, he barely saw him, but then that
was the usual pattern if you went to a school too close to your
hometown: initially, instead of making new friends, you retreated
back under the shelter of the old ones. And then, if you had any
gumption, you cut loose and made a fresh start.

Sinatra is singing 'Ill Wind' as Claire begins to speak.

'Oh, I love this song. All *I'm* saying . . . all right, I don't know
the guy, but when I met him, he was kind of, every second thing
he said was about you. Danny . . . likes Frank Sinatra, Danny
knows his cocktails, Danny loves his old black-and-white movies,
like that? He knew we had been together, and that we had broken
up, I mean, did you tell him? I assumed you did.'

'I don't know that I did. We didn't have a lot of contact. But
he could have found out from, I don't know, I might have bumped
into Ralph or someone. Many beers, many late nights, many
years ago.'

'Well, anyway. So, we kind of made out a bit. And in the middle
of it, he would say, does Danny do it like that? Does Danny like it
like that?'

'Fuck me.'

'Well yes. Or, in my case, absolutely do not fuck me. He was
kind of obsessed with you, Dan.'

Danny lets this settle. He has no notion of what to do with it.
He tries to run his mind back though school to examine the

record for any corresponding behavior, but keeps jamming up against the Bradberry fire. Nothing was the same afterwards, but that was because he was like a man whose house is beside the railroad tracks: he spent so long pretending he couldn't hear the noise he began to believe there wasn't any.

Besides, Ralph saw Gene throw the fire bottle.

Danny considers telling Claire about the Bradberry fire. He doesn't have to tell her he knows she is Claire Bradberry (and there's another strike against Dave, bringing someone called Claire Bradberry into the Jonathan Glatt fund, if Gene is telling the truth), but it's a way of edging closer to the truth. Maybe he's on the point of telling her, when his phone rings. He's no longer worried if the cops can trace him. Part of him is hoping they do.

'Danny Brogan.'

'Danny, it's Gene.'

'Hey, Gene. That was exciting.'

'I . . . I guess I owe you an apology.'

'But you don't know for sure. According to what you read in the papers, I'm a dangerous fugitive.'

'I panicked. You looked a little wild, Danny.'

'So much for the Four Horsemen.'

'Yeah. Well, I don't know what you've done, or not done, so we'll see how it comes out in the wash. But something about that Halloween night, big guy. You can talk?'

'I can listen.'

'OK. So you said Ralph was sure I threw the fire bottle, the one that hit the Bradberry house, threw it deliberately. And Ralph knew because he was Pestilence and I was Plague, or the other way round, whichever – I was a P and so was he?'

'That's right.'

'And how he knew was, he made sure if I was P, he was going to be too, seeing as how he was my loyal lieutenant and so forth?'

'Yeah.'

'Yeah. Well, the thing of it is, I noticed, when he was choosing his costume, how he checked to see what I was wearing first. And Dave Ricks noticed too, saw me choosing P and Ralph plumping for it also. And Dave gave me this look, you know, kind of satirical, "Ralph your little nodding dog" type of thing.

I mean, it had already started to get on my nerves anyway, Ralph running around after me all the time, "Yes Gene, no Gene, six bags full Gene." There's loyalty and there's sucking ass. So – very simply – after Ralph had chosen his costume, Dave and I switched.'

'What, and Ralph didn't notice? We were waiting around for hours beforehand.'

'We didn't do it immediately. Remember when you and Ralph went out to trick or treat? It would usually have been you and Dave, Danny and Dave forever, but me and Dave fixed it so it would be you and Ralph. We changed then, and said nothing from then on.'

'Why?'

'I know, pretty childish, huh? Maybe our excuse was, we were kids. I know I just wanted to fuck with Ralph, and the idea he'd be following Dave around like a puppy, thinking it was me, must have amused me. You know how it was; you had the same kind of thing going on with Dave. Anyway, point of the story coming up: when Ralph says the bottle was thrown by a P, well, that wasn't me, man, I had become an F. Ralph was a P himself, and the other one was Dave. Does that make things any clearer?'

'And why was everyone so insistent that it was me?'

'Dave said he saw you. I knew it wasn't me. Ralph, well, Ralph just went along with it.'

Danny is silent, trying to fathom it. Dave. It had to be Dave. Dave had made Danny take the blame, when all these years it had been his fault.

Bing Crosby sings 'Out of Nowhere' on the radio, the sound all crackly, as if the wavelength has been disturbed.

You had the same kind of thing going on with Dave. Had he? He couldn't remember Dave following him around. Certainly not after the fire. If anything, there had been a look in Dave's eye every now and again, a look that said: *I know what you did. It'll be our secret.* None of the others had looked at him like that.

I know what you did.

I know who you are.

Dave.

'Gotta go, Dan. Back to the twenty-first century.'

'Just one thing. When I spoke to Dave earlier today, he said something about a wife, an ex-wife. I never met her. Did you?'

'You know, I think I did. It was a while ago, twenty-odd years. Yes, I did, we had them out to dinner. She was nice, funny, mouthy. She was a . . . what my old man would have called a pistol, know what I mean, like she was one of the boys? I don't know that Dave liked that much. But I guess she couldn't have liked Dave much either, since it didn't last any length of time, the marriage.'

'Any chance you can remember her name?'

There's a pause, filled by Crosby crooning Johnny Green's haunting, off kilter song.

'It was one word. Wasn't Kay, but something like Kay. Bee. Jo. Doh. Dee. Dee, I think that was it.'

Danny finds himself short of breath again. Calm. Calm. 'You sure?'

'Yeah, because she had that Irish name, Deidre, or Deirdre, however you pronounce it, and that's just what she said – growing up she had a pain in her ass listening to people mangle it, so she decided she'd use a name no one could mess up. And that was what she settled on. Dee.'

Lost in the Stars

Charlie T thought, or thought he thought, that he would be devastated by Angelique's death, but he's almost horrified, certainly fascinated, to discover that he's actually relieved. Maybe it was the way she had come out of the trees and pounced on the wee one, rubbing the chloroform rag in her face all crooked backed, like a witch in a fairy tale. Maybe it was the fact that she was too fucking full of herself all of a sudden, bossing him this way and that, not that he didn't like it a bit, but he couldn't have liked it a lot, otherwise he would have been a lot more upset than he is, which is, not really at all for

her, but a lot on account of how the fuck is he going to manage
the kids?

He has a compact Steyr S9 tonight, fifteen in the magazine,
twelve left, one in the chamber. He doesn't want to have to point
a semi-automatic pistol at children, but he will if it's necessary.
The obvious thing is to get to the aunt's house, it can't be too
far, you wouldn't walk kids that size more than a mile at this
hour, or in these conditions. The younger one is wailing, the wee
soul; the older one is over by her aunt's body, touching her face,
trying to will her back to life. She stands then and glowers at
him.

'You are a bad man,' she says. 'Irene, come here.'

Irene goes to the older one and sidles into her, and a protective
arm is placed around her shoulder, like a bird coming under her
mother's wing. He is a bad man, and no mistake. This goes
against every rule in his book.

'We have to move,' he says.

'We're not going anywhere,' the older one says. Irene's wailing
is getting louder. They have to get the fuck out of there now.
Charlie raises the gun and waves it at them, making sure Irene
can see it. Pick on the younger one, there's a brave fella.

'We have to move. Get to the house. And then we can ring
for Mum and Dad, OK?'

Irene nods, her lip out. Barbara frowns, and raises a stick she
has in her hand, but flinches and drops it when he waves the gun
at her. He comes around behind them.

'We'll send back for your aunt.'

'Ring an ambulance.'

Charlie makes a sound that, despite himself, means 'fuck all
point in that.'

'Ring an ambulance or we stay here,' the older one says in a
voice that could curdle butter.

'Barbara!' says Irene.

'I don't care. We don't know if she's dead.'

Fair enough. Charlie T calls Mr Wilson.

'Charlie?'

'Ambulance, please. Yes, I'll hold.'

'Has the target been dispatched?'

'Yes, I'd like to report the body of a woman on the path by

the side of Lake Ripley in Cambridge, Wisconsin. Access from the
steps at the rear of Ripley Fields.'

'The client will meet you at the sister's house, Mr T. And you'll
carry out his instructions from then on, do you understand?'

'No, explain,' Charlie says.

'He has something in mind. Some kind of display. For which
he is willing to pay, more than double. He'll clear your gambling
debt entirely. A fresh start, Charlie. And all you have to do is
carry out his instructions to the letter. Understood?'

Charlie wants to protest, wants to set conditions, wants to
insist that deep down, he's a good man. But he's not, is he? Deep
down, maybe he is, but it's fuck-all use deep down. Up here on
the surface, pointing a gun at two wee girls having just murdered
their aunt, walking past the broken body of his girlfriend and
stopping only to take her purse so that it can't be traced to him,
ready to deliver children into the hands of Satan knows what
kind of fucker. He's already gone through the aunt's pockets, got
her keys and phone. Barbara's right. He's a bad man, by anyone's
definition.

The girls walk in front of him. He trains a small Maglite on
them. He won't ask where the house is, as the teenager in training
there will insist on not telling him, and he doesn't want to have
to bully it out of the wee one, who's still sobbing quietly to
herself, God love her. He'll just watch the way they walk, watch
for tells when they get near. He didn't come down in the last
shower.

He's better off. All that kidnapping crack. Fuck's sake. What
kind of a future would they have, she's smothering old folk in
the hospital, he's a professional assassin. Fantasy land. That's
not the kind of girl you settle down with. Not at all.

Barbara is leaning over and whispering something in Irene's
ear. He can't hear it, but he can hear the squealed reply.

'We can't, Babs, we can't. He'll shoot us, he'll shoot us.'

'What's that, Irene?' Charlie T says.

'Aunt Donna's house is up there,' Irene says, pointing to a
forest pathway leading up the side of a hill.

And Barbara makes a noise, a growl of frustration and rage.

Charlie T takes a coil of nylon rope and, keeping the Steyr in
full view at all times, ties Barbara's right wrist to Irene's left,

then pulls the rope forward and winds it around his right arm and sets off up the hill ahead of them. Too much scope for them to hive off left or right and vanish, or at least, need to be chased down.

'Tell me if I'm going too fast, or pulling the rope too hard,' Charlie T says. Irene is not going to stop crying any time soon. Barbara sets her face in a grimace of hatred and rage. And like that, Charlie T tugs them steadily up the hill toward Donna Brogan's house.

Dancing in the Dark

So it wasn't Danny Brogan who burnt his future wife's family to death after all. They weren't her family to begin with. It was Dave Ricks, and the family belonged to Dee St Clair, or Claire Bradberry, as she had once been called. And here they sit in the front seat of an SUV in the long winding drive of dead Donna Brogan's house in Cambridge, Wisconsin, on Halloween night.

It's impossible to know from the outside what is being said, or even how it is being said. We could make some deductions, based on whose head is bowed (Dee's) and whose face seems the more animated (Dave's). But let's not wait any longer out here in the cold Halloween air. Let's join them inside the car.

'All right,' Dave says, palming his cell phone. 'The target is down; the kids are on their way here.'

Dee looks at him, her lip curling. '"The target is down." Don't you mean, "Donna Brogan is dead"?'

'I don't have any problem spelling it out.'

'It's not too late to stop it, Dave, to stop it all. Just pack up and go, let them get back to their lives. Haven't we done enough?'

'Danny is close to knowing, he was on his way around to Gene Peterson, it's a process of elimination. And the police are sniffing around, or so you say.'

'They've a couple of dead bodies to investigate.'

'And a couple more to be added. So they won't just drop

everything at our say so. You know it *is* too late to turn back.
We can't drop anchor until we bring the ship to harbor.'

'Stop it. "Target down", "ship to harbor". You sound like a
villain in a comic book. It's bad enough, what you've . . . what
we've done, but . . . the *children*.'

'Yes, the children. That's how it all began, isn't it? On our wedding
day that wasn't really a wedding day. Because of my insistence on
telling you everything the night before. Because of Danny Brogan.'

Dee counts to ten, trying not to let her exhaustion and despair
seep into her reply. Tries to keep it neutral, as if it is the first
time she's said it.

'It was a *shock*. To think that you were there, that night. A
shock that I couldn't recover from immediately . . .'

'Our wedding day . . .'

'No one was there. It was a private, almost a secret wedding.
What difference did it make – we had been together a while –
what difference did it make if the day itself was less than perfect?'

'It made a difference. It was the beginning of the end.'

'We could have . . . I've always said this, we could have made
it work.'

'Well. We didn't. And there's no justice in making me the
guilty party. You were just as keen as I was to punish Danny
when he married Claire. It was your idea to plant the notion that
Claire was the missing Bradberry child. You had wormed out the
fact that she was in denial about being adopted, had no interest
in finding out who she really was. You were as motivated, maybe
even more driven than I was.'

'I know, I know—'

'You were a woman scorned, as they would have said in the
olden days. Scorned by Danny Brogan.'

'You were scorned yourself. The first night we met, Danny
was all we talked about. How you had done so much for him,
but he was ungrateful. How he took his good fortune for granted.
How he needed to be taught a lesson.'

'But you contacted me. You made the first move, Dee. You see,
it's important not to rewrite history, not now when everything is
coming to its logical end, not to say, "Oh, it's all Dave's fault, he's
the maniac, he's the monster". Danny planted a seed in your mind—'

'Danny mentioned, or alluded to, some connection with the

Bradberry fire in Madison. And then he clammed up. And you know how good I am at wheedling stuff out of people who think they want to keep secrets. Because no one really does. Everyone wants to confess. And even though he wouldn't say any more about it, he was willing to talk about the guys. The Four Horsemen. Danny, Gene, Ralph and Dave. And you turned out to be the one, Dave.'

'Until you were told the full story of what we did. What *he* did.'

'Even then. Even then. Just the fact you were there. It took me a few days, but . . . I had never had an issue. I never blamed anyone. I had no memory of the night, or the house. My childhood was my adoptive home. Even then, we could have . . .'

'You're going to talk in song titles. Didn't we almost make it? No, we didn't.'

'That was down to you.'

He wouldn't sleep with her afterwards. Hadn't slept with her much beforehand, in truth. She always thought it would develop. But then it stopped, and became something else. She had often wondered whether Dave was gay for Danny, but didn't think so. Dave didn't really need sex, not in the way most people need it. Dave was just too fucked-up.

'It wasn't just that. I could see with you, I was always going to be second best. And you've played your part like a pro, impersonating Claire's best friend.'

'I am her best friend.'

'Yes. How sad is that for her?'

How sad is that for Dee?

'And you may find it in yourself to be forgiving and compassionate, but hey, you still soaked the Brogans dry, money wise.'

'I didn't make him borrow an extra two hundred grand,' Dee says.

'No, but you made sure he missed out on getting it back. Danny got under your skin, didn't he?'

Dave's eyes flash, as they do whenever he talks about Danny. Dee's eyes darken, her face a mask, a Dee face of bitterness and rue, and she thinks back to the few weeks she spent with Danny, twenty years ago. How excited she had felt, and then how humiliated. If there had ever been a 'one' or a notion of what 'the one' might have been like, Danny Brogan gave it body and soul. And then to drop her, to push her away, as if she were nothing. Maybe

Dave is right. Dee is deluding herself if she thinks she's some kind of innocent party. She's stolen from the Brogans for years; she's lied to Claire and set her up to inherit a set of recovered memories that would most likely destroy her.

She doesn't care about Ralph (who showed no interest in her), or Jeff Torrance (who was so vain the one time they fucked, he kept looking at himself in the mirror), or Danny's sister (who was the rudest person she's ever met). She certainly won't miss that horrible, filthy, slobbery dog. It's just the children. Every time she thinks of them, she wants to cry. If there was a way of just stopping short of that, maybe encouraging Dave to have Danny and Claire killed first. Then he might consider it all square. But she doubts at this late stage whether that is feasible. You reap what you sow, and they've sown this all the way along, in their unholy inversion of a love affair. Sometimes it seems as if Dave loves Danny more than hates him. She knows he would have been content to draw this out longer and longer, for years, the pleasure, the power residing in tormenting him, knowing he could strike at any time. But then Ralph materialized, and it was action stations. Maybe that's what has her feeling so deeply, crying so much – because in truth, she doesn't care greatly for Claire's children either, spoilt little brats at the best of times. Maybe the sudden realization that the end is upon them, that the scheming and dreaming is done and the day of reckoning is here. Maybe that's what has her brimming.

Dave rolls down his window and leans out to look across the lawn. The night air is crisp and sharp with the promise of frost.

'Any moment now,' Dave says, and turns to her.

Is it her imagination, or does he smell of gasoline?

'There's something I haven't told you,' he says, his eyes gleaming.

'I probably don't want to hear it,' Dee says, but excited in spite of herself. Any gossip is good gossip.

'The people who are managing this for us.'

'Who are killing everyone,' Dee says.

'That's right. Well, the guy who's running it all, the guy who's in charge.'

'Yeah?'

'Is your brother.'

'My brother?'

Dee feels queasy all of a sudden, and sweat sparks on her brow. Dave passes her a business card.

'I had a PI investigate. There were two Bradberry brothers who had left home. One was a petty criminal in Cicero. He's dead now, murdered. The other had done time for statutory rape in Racine, then became a high-end rent boy, then reinvented himself as this kind of businessman with a lot of serious security and political connections. Wilson, he goes by now. Turns out his business is murder. He runs the hit man who's doing the work for us. He doesn't know why I chose him, but when it's all done, you can tell him.'

Dee opens the passenger door and slips down to the ground and vomits. When she's finished, her hands scrabbled by the gravel in the drive, her throat sore and eyes streaming, she looks up and sees Dave staring at her as if she is a bug on a pin.

'That's exactly what you did when I told you Danny burnt your family to death,' he says.

There is a footfall from the side of the house, and then a man in a red coat and a Wisconsin Badgers hat appears, with Barbara and Irene Brogan tethered to him.

'Ready?' Dave says.

Dee breathes in deeply. There is no way back now. And she is not someone else: this is who she is. Her brother. Her blood. She had all the clippings out again today, just like every Halloween. Even if she says she has no memory, no trauma, there is something there, some reptile stirring deep within her. Is it rage? Colder than that. The sense that she is entitled to revenge – not blood revenge, not heated and delirious, but a revenge that is her due. Maybe not revenge so much as logic, a necessary end to it all. She knows when it comes to it, she won't feel a thing. She never really does. She has spent so long pretending to feel emotions she has never experienced. She is a better actress than Claire, of that there is no doubt. She has been acting all her life. She lets Dave extend his arm and help her rise. She looks him in the eye, holds his hands in hers.

'Why are you doing this, Dave?' she says.

'Because . . .' he begins, and turns away, turns away and looks at his reflection in the glass of his side window.

Because.

Because Dave thought Danny would be grateful that he'd thrown the fire bottle, grateful that he'd burnt the Bradberry house down, grateful that he'd relieved him of his tormentor. Dave thought the guys would be on his side, and Danny would be grateful: grateful then, grateful forever. For the briefest of moments, after the house had gone up in flames, and they had revived Danny and ran, ran through the Halloween streets, for one brief, glorious, exhilarating moment, Dave had felt like a hero, like a star. And then, as the guys' fear and panic filtered through, he understood that he had got it wrong, that they were appalled at what had happened. And a screen memory returned to him, a memory that would stay with him, the fleeting glimpse as he turned from the blazing house of the two young Bradberry children in the upstairs window. And even he knew that wasn't right. And without sharing in the panic or the fear, he quickly saw what he had to do. It was simple: he and Gene had swapped costumes, so he was wearing the same letter as Danny. And who had more incentive to take the ultimate revenge on Jackie Bradberry? And since Danny had knocked himself out, there would be a moment he couldn't account for.

Ralph never put that in his fucking book, did he?

'Jesus, Danny, why'd you do it?' was all Dave had to say.

Because it was Danny's fault, wasn't it? Danny's fault Dave had felt the need to protect him, to help him, even though Danny had never asked him, had never trusted him to step in with Jackie Bradberry the way he had with Gene. Danny's fault they had been there at all.

Things were never the same between them afterwards. There were many times Dave had wanted to tell him, to explain. But what would he have said? That he had done it, then blamed Danny? No, he had to keep it hidden, even as Danny drifted away.

And Dave has had to live with it all these years, until fate brought Claire Bradberry his way, brought her his way and then took her away again. Fate in the form of Danny Brogan.

'Because Danny Brogan made your life a misery,' he says, tears in his eyes suddenly, brimming himself, hands shaking. 'And destroyed the happiness we should have had. And now he is going to pay.'

Dee looks at Dave, and nods, and kisses him quickly, a brush on the cheek really. She is in it with him, and she will see it through. And then, at last, she will be free of him. Free of it all. Dee opens the car door and makes her excited-to-see-you face and runs across the lawn toward the children as if she is their friend, sent to rescue them from harm.

I'm Beginning to See the Light

Detective Nora Fox has worked her way through the cuttings on Dee St Clair's table, which document the Bradberry fire of thirty-five years ago, and include references to the girl that got away, the three-year-old daughter who alone survived the inferno. She has found paper photocopies of a number of paintings in different styles, but all with the same image: two small children, their faces rigid with fear, in the window of a house, flames encroaching upon them.

Turning to Dee's laptop, she has found within her email program folders that seem to be set up for Danny Brogan and Claire Taylor; indeed, while she is inspecting them, an email arrives for Claire, asking if her drama class on Wednesday is definitely on, only Jenna has extra French and may have to skip the last half-hour. Nora doesn't know how you do this – she has a notion there's something called a Trojan, a rogue program that infiltrates another computer and relays the data so a third party can spy on it, and if necessary, manipulate it. The Forensic Services Unit have enough technical expertise to figure it out. But however you do it, it's been done, and it's on Dee's computer.

Nora runs through it in her head. The Four Horsemen – Danny Brogan, Dave Ricks, Gene Peterson and Ralph Cowley – may have had some involvement with the Bradberry fire. From the information she got from Cass Epstein at the Department of Children and Families, it seems certain that Dee St Clair is Claire Bradberry, the surviving child. Judging by the news clippings, she has not forgotten what happened to her birth family.

Nora studies the pictures of the children with the flames flicker-ing around the window. There's a tiny signature in the bottom right corner of each, not even a signature, just initial letters. The second letter is R, the first . . . could be an O, could be a closed C . . . could be a D. D-R . . . Dave Ricks.

She goes back to the computer and enters Dave Ricks in the Search box and reads the three most recent emails. Halfway through the third, she is on the phone.

'Fowler?'

'Ken, you're still there.'

'I was on my way home. But everyone's on the streets for Freakfest, I'm like a one-man band here.'

'Don around? I can't raise him.'

'He's still here somewhere.'

'OK, well, grab him and sit on him, I'll be back in fifteen. I think the Brogan case is breaking, and it's gonna be tonight. And Ken, tell Don we could be talking emergency response here.'

'I'll tell him.'

Nora looks again at the final email Dave Ricks sent Dee St Clair. The last lines read:

> *We'll keep it loose, improvising from scene to scene –*
> *because they're human, and we don't know how they're going*
> *to act – but if we can get everyone there at once, well, what*
> *a grand finale there will be! What a fitting anniversary,*
> *what a Halloween spectacular!*

Me, Myself and I

'**D**onna's just texted,' Claire says, voice thick and teary with relief. They're on the 12-18, about five miles out from Cambridge. 'She says the girls are fine, to come on over.'

'Well then,' Danny says. 'That's what we'll do. And let's hope the Madison police are nowhere near.'

'They don't know about Donna, do they?'

'I don't think anyone knows about Donna. Donna flies under the radar. I'm not even sure what name she calls herself these days.'

'She went back to Brogan,' Claire says.

'Did she? How do you know?'

'I saw some mail in her house when I dropped the kids off, a few months back. Funny thing was, she saw me notice it, and she kind of shrugged, and she said something pretty cool, or at least, I think it's pretty cool now, at the time I don't think I really got it.'

'What did she say?'

'She said, at a certain stage, you stop trying to be someone else. You're who you are. You're yourself, the sum total of all you've done and been all your life. And what you've got to do is, accept it. And you know something, Dan, that's what I feel now. And one of the things I'm going to do, at last, maybe I've been running away from it, in denial or whatever they say, I'm going to look at my adoption papers. I'm going to find out who my birth parents were. Not saying I want to meet up with them or anything, that might be a whole other trip. But . . . just so I know. Because I am who I am. And it's going to be all right.'

It's never going to be all right, Danny thinks. He hasn't told Claire any of it yet. The fact that Dave Ricks threw the fire bottle, not Danny. The fact that Dee is connected to Dave, used to be married to him. They have to be behind it all, the blackmail, the murder. They have to be behind it. But whatever they're behind, they can't change the facts. And the facts are, Claire's birth certificate proves she was born Claire Bradberry. He has to tell her. He has to tell her now.

'Claire, there's something I need to say to you. About . . . about the Bradberry fire.'

'The Bradberry fire? Wow. Which one was that again, where all the kids got killed?'

Which one was that again? He looks around at his wife, her innocent eyes shining now, this wife of his that he's not even married to, and drinks in every detail. This may be the last time she ever smiles at him.

And then his phone rings. Does he answer it? Of course he does.

'We know you didn't kill anyone, Danny.'

'I'm sorry? Who is this?'

'Detective Nora Fox, Madison PD.'

'Why didn't you say so?'

'I didn't want you to hang up on me. When I say we know, I mean we have compelling evidence that the murders were carried out on behalf of Dave Ricks and Dee St Clair.'

'That's what I figured, except without much in the way of evidence.'

'There's an immediate danger to your own safety, and to that of your family, sir. There's reason to suspect some attempt may be made to intercept you, or in some way harm you. You're not considering a return to the house on Arboretum Avenue, are you? If you can let us know where you're at, we can arrange officer escorts.'

'That sounds serious.'

'I believe it is serious.'

Danny considers, but still doesn't fully trust the cops.

'We're fine, Detective. We're all meeting up at my . . . the whole family's meeting up.'

'I want to urge particular caution in relation to fire, sir.'

'Fire?'

'Yes. You know of course that it's the anniversary of the Bradberry fire tonight. We know that you, and Dave Ricks, and your other friends, including one of the deceased, Ralph Cowley, may have had some involvement with that incident.'

'No comment.'

'It's not a reinvestigation of the Bradberry fire, sir. It's, in the communications between Dave Ricks and Dee St Clair, several references are made to a blaze, to, if all the arrangements are correctly in place, a spectacular.'

A spectacular. The word sends a chill down Danny's spine. That's exactly what they called the Bradberry fire when they were planning it, back when it was a prank, before it became a catastrophe.

'And there may be an element of revenge involved, sir. You see, there was one Bradberry child who escaped the inferno on that night in 1976. And we have conclusive proof that Dee St Clair was that child. Dee St Clair was born Claire Bradberry.'

'No,' Danny says. 'No, that's not true, I know that's not true.'

'It is true, sir.'

Danny is aware that Claire is watching him closely. He can't stop now.

'I've seen . . . documents . . . belonging to someone else. Stating that . . . someone else . . . is that person.'

'Sir, Dee St Clair has been spying on you and your wife for many years now. She intercepts all of your emails, sometimes replying to them. It appears, as well as murder, she and Mr Ricks have been extorting money from you. It doesn't seem beyond her to have forged a birth certificate or two, does it?'

Detective Nora Fox is asking again where Danny is headed as he closes the call, palms his phone and stares at the screen, smiling like a man who has forgotten how it's done.

'Who was that?' Claire says.

'Nobody,' Danny says.

'I see. And what did nobody want?'

'Nothing.'

Danny reaches for Claire's hand. She takes his and squeezes it. *Nobody wanted nothing. After all these years.*

And in spite of all that's happened and all that looms ahead, in spite of the danger and uncertainty, the heartache and the shame, Danny Brogan thinks that everything is going to be all right.

When No One Cares

Dee has found the girls' Nintendo DS players and hugged Irene and tried to talk to Barbara and persuaded them that their parents are on their way back to the family home, the 'forever house,' as Irene calls it. By ensuring that both Dave and Charlie, the scrawny Irish guy who clearly thinks the world of himself but looks to Dee like a weasel with bad teeth, keep completely out of sight, she manages to persuade the girls into the back of Dave's SUV. Then, having texted Claire on Donna's phone to let her know Barbara and Irene are waiting to be collected at Donna's house, she takes off for Madison.

Charlie T is stationed up at the gates of Donna's house, ready and waiting in a Halloween mask, a red El Diablo with horns. The only car visible in the drive is Donna's.

Ten minutes, fifteen, twenty, and then a blue Toyota Corolla comes rolling in through the gates and crunching down the gravel to park behind Donna's vehicle. Charlie T has the gate swung shut in seconds, and keeps Danny Brogan and Claire Taylor in his sights as they rush toward the house, Claire forgetting even to close the passenger door. They are in the porch now, ringing the doorbell. Charlie T is closing in on them from behind. The door opens on Dave Ricks in a full face werewolf mask, his arms outstretched.

'Trick or Treat!' he says.

Claire screams, and Danny flies at the werewolf, two hands around his neck, wrestling him to the floor, slapping his head on the tiled porch. Charlie T fires a shot in the air, doesn't like doing it in case there are any pain-in-the-ass good citizens mooching about, but even if there are, it's Halloween, who can tell a gunshot from a firecracker? The second shot does the job.

'Get off him, now!' Charlie T shouts.

As he closes in on Claire Taylor with the Steyr, Danny Brogan releases Dave Ricks, who scrambles to his feet. And here they all are, in the porch together.

Trick or Treat!

'Where are the girls?' Claire says. 'Where are Barbara and Irene?'

'Who is it in there?' Brogan says, pointing at Dave's mask. 'Is it Dave? Dave? What the fuck are you doing? Have you lost your fucking mind?'

Charlie T has given Dave the chloroform rags and is waiting for him to use one on Brogan, but Dave seems shaken, he's just standing there, swaying. Amateur hour. Brogan's swearing and shouting, throwing all kinds of shapes, and Charlie T sees it'll take the pair of them to subdue the fucker and then the missus might get away. Only thing he can do is smack Brogan between the eyes with the butt of the Steyr, then again on the back of the head. Down he goes, that's the way to do it. Claire starts up again with the screaming, but Charlie T moves in quickly behind her and restrains her hands with one arm. He extends the other hand to Dave Ricks, and Ricks passes him a cloth, and Charlie T presses it over Claire's nose and mouth and holds, as she squirms against his hand and wrestles with his arm and kicks back at his shins, hold on, hold on. One hundred, two hundred, three hundred. Fourteen hundred and she goes limp in his arms.

The House I Live In

Making her way slowly and circuitously across town, traffic re-routed as State Street is closed for Freakfest, the city's annual Halloween party, Detective Nora Fox pulls up in the street outside Brogan's and goes in, and of course the place is jammed. Even so, at the door she catches the Dolly Parton lookalike, what's her name, Karen Cassidy, catches her eye straight off where she stands at the bar, and Nora gives her the chin uplift, meaning *hello, we need to talk*, and the pint-size bottle blonde not alone does not acknowledge, she turns her *back* on Nora, and is very, very busy mixing some drinks. Nora, for want of a more felicitous expression, has had enough of this shit, and powers her way through the partying hordes like a football tackle in a bad mood. By the time she gets to the bar, she is in a bad mood herself, so when Karen Cassidy emerges from behind it with two exotic looking drinks, a sparkler fizzing in each one, and says, 'I told you before, lady, I've got nothing to say to you,' it's nothing more than reflex for Nora to pluck the sparklers out of their glasses and douse the fizzing ends in the drinks.

'The name is Detective, Dolly,' Nora says.

A little crowd is gathering around them now.

When Karen looks like she's going to do something very stupid indeed, like toss one of the drinks in Nora's face, Nora grabs her by the wrists and pulls her face close.

'Listen to me. They're going to burn your boss to the ground, him and his wife and his kids, and they're going to do it tonight, do it *now*, and you won't raise a finger to stop them, all because of some misplaced bullshit sense of loyalty and protectiveness. I know there's someone he stays with, another family member, someone who minds the kids for him. Tell me who it is.'

'Who is "they"?' Karen says.

'People from his past. People who've already murdered two men. People who don't care what they do, to Danny, to Claire, to those kids.'

And Karen bites her lip and squints through her false eyelashes and says, 'Donna, his sister. In Cambridge. I'll get you the address.'

Once everyone is in through the gates of the Brogan property on Arboretum Avenue, Dee leads Barbara and Irene into the house, telling them they're going to find their parents. Then Dave Ricks and Charlie T secure the gates with chains and rocks. There's a picnic table with benches attached in the garage. Dave and Charlie T haul it out and set it up in the middle of the backyard. Then they carry Claire and Danny out of Donna's car. They are both still unconscious, although Danny is showing signs of life. Dave and Charlie T sit the Brogans up at the table, facing the back of the house, so they have a clear view of the tower where Claire has her den, and they tie their hands and feet to the bench and the metal struts that affix the seat to the table. Then Dave gets a can of gasoline from the trunk of his car and starts to anoint the backyard with it.

Meanwhile, Dee is ushering the girls toward the tower, which is the only room that has any furniture left, although of course that's not why she wants them up there.

'Where's Mommy?' Irene says.

'Where's all our stuff?' Barbara says.

'This way,' Dee says, sending them ahead of her up the spiral staircase, and sure enough, they go because they think they will find their stuff, and their mommy, and their daddy, and once they're up, Dee shuts the trap door on them and runs the bolt on it. The sound of Irene can be heard almost immediately, wailing and howling from above.

It's difficult to discern what emotion flickers across Dee's face as she descends the stairs, what new Dee face this might be. Grim Resignation, perhaps. It is as if she has been playing a part her entire life, and this is the final performance. When she emerges from the house, Dave Ricks hands her a full-face witch's mask with pointed hat, and Dee pulls it over her head quickly, as if it is a relief to be able to hide inside it.

As she does so, Dave lights a fire cracker and sets the lawn ablaze, the flames in spider and skull and snake patterns, just like long ago.

Detective Nora Fox has discussed the case with her sergeant, Don Burns, and he has referred it to Les Christopher, the West District Captain, who hums and haws about getting Cambridge PD involved. Nora says what they need is the Emergency Response Team and the captain says deployment of a SWAT team is going to need more than what they've got, which, all due respect, is hunches and guesswork, and Nora says in the time it's taking they could be there and Christopher says, well then, go. *Go.* Nora Fox and Ken Fowler ride together, and they cover twenty miles in fifteen, just under twenty minutes, and when they get to Donna Brogan's house overlooking Lake Ripley, the Halloween lights are on and there's nobody home.

'Colby,' Fowler says quickly, neither of them wanting to confess their blunder to Don Burns or Les Christopher, and as they turn the car around and head back toward Madison, Nora calls Officer Colby, who is in State Street on Freakfest duty, and she authorizes clearance from his sergeant to release him so he can go check out the Brogan house on Arboretum Avenue.

Oh, it is a spectacular now. The backyard is ablaze, and Dave with his werewolf head moves between skull and spider and snake, light on his feet; you would be forgiven for thinking he was dancing. Danny has come to, his face a mess, his nose swollen, maybe broken, matted blood on the back of his head. At first, when he sees the flames in front of him, he thinks he is having a nightmare. And this feeling does not change when he understands that it's all too real, when he looks up to the tower window and sees his daughters framed within it, their faces contorted with panic and fear. He rocks the bench, straining against the ropes that bind him tight, and his movements bring his wife to her senses. When Claire sees where they are, and where the girls are, she begins to scream.

Officer Colby can tell before he gets out of his cruiser that there's a fire. The big wrought-iron gates are barricaded and he can't get in, but there's nothing stopping him dialing 911, which he does, and specifying that he's a police officer (because the number of crank and panic and otherwise unnecessary calls on Halloween always puts the switchboard operators on their guard) and requesting an immediate call out, with danger of a forest fire in the Arboretum.

Then Colby goes to the trunk of his vehicle and gets an axe and lays into the centre of the gates, working to remove whatever obstructions are blocking entry. When brute force doesn't work, he finds footholds in the brickwork to the side of the gates and scales up and on to the wall, and it is there that a masked Charlie T, who has heard the policeman trying to breach the gates, shoots him dead. Colby's body drops on the inside of the wall, and Charlie nods his El Diablo head.

Dave takes Claire's screams as his second cue, and produces two fire bottles from his SUV and lights one and offers it to Dee, but she shakes her head, her latex witch's head. Dave, in his werewolf mask, shrugs and flings the lighted bottle at the house and the flames shoot up the ground-floor wall and catch on the patio doors and the house is on fire.

Claire has stopped screaming, is sobbing, unable to let her head fall because she is trying to maintain eye contact with her children in the tower. Danny is shouting something at Dee, it's hard to make out what, hard to hear above the roar of flames.

Dave, with his werewolf head, stands amid the flames like the conductor of an orchestra, like an ancient fire starter, swaying in the haze of heat and light and smoke. Danny is still shouting, and Dee, with her witch's head, comes closer. Danny is gesturing with his head, shaking it in the negative and then pointing it toward Dave, and Dee turns to Dave, and then back to Danny and shakes *her* head, and Danny goes through the same routine again, his head bobbing faster and more vigorously, and we can almost hear what he's saying but not quite, something about Dave throwing the fire bottle and not him, and this time Dee stays with Danny for longer, a witch staring at a man with a bloodied, battered face, and all the while Claire is breathing fast and deep, trying not to cry so Danny can be heard.

Barbara and Irene, at the window, as the smoke raises and the flames approach the sill. Their little faces.

Now Dave, with his werewolf head, lights a second fire bottle and walks toward the picnic table and offers it to Dee. Claire screams at the sight of it. Dee takes the flaming bottle and turns to Dave and says something to him. He raises his hands in the air, as if to dismiss her. She catches his arm, and there is an exchange between them, her voice harsh with passion, his hoarse with jubilant disdain, the yard aflame behind them, the witch and the werewolf center stage in a Halloween inferno. He shakes her hand away and puts some steps between them, and gestures toward the window in the tower, and then at Danny and Claire, and then opens his arms wide to span the entire scene, as if this should be answer enough for her. Dee's head is bowed and she turns away, as if conceding the point, and then she swings right around and hits Dave full in his werewolf face with the bottle, and the glass smashes and the flaming gasoline envelops his mask and his head so quickly you can barely hear him scream. Dee wheels off, one of her own hands on fire, and runs toward the garage, flapping her arm to try and extinguish the flames.

Charlie T, still in his horned devil's head, is standing, gaping. The burning gas spreads in an instant, until Dave's body blazes. He staggers around the yard, a wolf on fire, crazed with pain, limbs flailing. Charlie T lifts his gun and shoots him twice.

Dee is nowhere to be seen. The sound of sirens can be heard in the distance. Charlie T takes a knife from his coat and cuts the cords binding Claire and Danny. Claire runs immediately toward the blazing house. As soon as Danny has his hands free, he lurches at El Diablo, who counters with the Steyr, swinging it in front of Danny's face and then holding it on him. Danny stands a moment longer, then turns and follows Claire into the flames. Charlie looks around the yard, then in the direction of the back gate through to the Arboretum, and moves briskly out that way, and so, away.

The fire has not really caught at the front of the house. Claire shoots up the spiral stairway and pops the trapdoor, and the children come tumbling, and Claire lifts them down and passes them to Danny, trying to make them stop hugging her and clinging to her so she can let them down, trying to stop herself hugging them and clinging to them so she can stop feeling so very, very afraid.

They come out on to the lawn, the Brogan family, kissing and crying and coughing and not wanting to let each other go. There's a fire truck at the gates, and the cops are there too, and no one can get in; they're honking their horns and shouting out the Brogans' names. Danny loosens his hold on the others and walks across to the gates, and starts to unwind the chains and remove the rocks, and then he hears Claire cry out, telling him to stop. He turns back and goes to her. She's holding the girls close, her cheeks blackened and tear-stained.

'Let it burn, Danny,' she says, shaking her head. 'Let it burn.'

'Your stuff,' Danny says. 'All your memories. And the letter from your folks. To tell you who you really are.'

'Who I was,' Claire says. 'I know who I am. Let it all burn.'

I'll Never Be the Same

M r Wilson is standing in his apartment looking out at the city. Things have not worked out the way he planned. Their client is dead, and all over the papers, and was evidently insane, and while negotiations between them were conducted on disposable cell phones, Mr Wilson is not such a technical expert that he can be entirely sure his security was not breached. And there was a lot of money to come, although the advance he demanded was substantial, certainly in excess of any sum Charlie T might have imagined. Not that Charlie T's imagination is a problem he will have to deal with for much longer. Charlie Toland's career of violence is coming to an end today. He is due at the apartment in – Mr Wilson checks the clock – twenty minutes, by arrangement, to collect the balance owed to him, and to discuss their future relationship.

Mr Wilson pats the left side pocket of his navy gabardine blazer, feels the reassuring lightweight heft of the Ruger Compact .38 revolver Carl Brenner acquired for him. He has never shot anyone before, but doesn't feel it's going to be too arduous a task. Carl kindly provided a former Navy Seal to give him some elementary training in the use of firearms. All he has to do is present Charlie with the money, which the Irishman always insists on counting, and that will give Mr Wilson enough time to draw his weapon. And that will be that.

From his right side pocket, he takes the letter he received this morning. It's from a woman who claims she's his sister, Claire Bradberry, the only child to have survived the fire in his family home in Madison all those years ago. She alludes to having known Mr Wilson's most recent client, and is insistent that they should meet. She seems to believe that the coincidence of their common blood has some importance, and merits further elaboration.

Mr Wilson shakes his head, and screws the paper into a ball and clenches it in his fist. What kind of country does she think she's living in? A country where the accident of one's birth has any significance? It has taken him all the momentum and will he was capable of summoning to become the man he is now. Why would he want to jeopardize that now with even a backward glance?

Mr Wilson has nothing to do with who he was. He is all about who he is about to become. He knows that's the only person worth being. It's what the country was founded upon, for God's sake.

He puts the 'Prelude' to Wagner's *Parsifal* on the Bose CD player, turns up the volume, sits back, and waits for Charlie T to arrive.

The Way of the World

Millamant: And d'ye hear, I won't be called names after I'm married; positively I won't be called names.

Mirabell: Names?

Millamant: Ay, as wife, spouse, my dear, joy, jewel, love, sweetheart, and the rest of that nauseous cant, in which men and their wives are so fulsomely familiar – I shall never bear that. Good Mirabell, don't let us be familiar or fond, nor kiss before folks, like my Lady Fadler and Sir Francis; nor go to Hyde Park together the first Sunday in a new chariot, to provoke eyes and whispers, and then never be seen there together again, as if we were proud of one another the first week, and ashamed of one another ever after. Let us never visit together, nor go to a play together, but let us be very strange and well-bred. Let us be as strange as if we had been married a great while, and as well-bred as if we were not married at all.

William Congreve – The Way of the World

All the Things You Are

Christmas Eve

The cold days and weeks trudged by until they were deep into the bleak Madison midwinter. The Brogan children were shaken by their ordeal, and each dealt with it differently: Irene explicitly, with a lot of crying and talking and clinging; Barbara internally, her already-evident mood swings swelling and darkening. Some days, she'd still seem her ingenuous, sweet-natured, bubbly self; others, it was as if she'd become possessed by a nineteen-year-old runaway who'd seen too much too soon, and had lost her faith in human nature, in the future, in life itself. They were both attending counselors and psychologists, and were thought to be progressing as well as could be expected. And of course, everyone spoiled them within an inch of their lives, until Danny and Claire worried alternately that they would emerge permanently scarred by their ordeal, and that they'd morph into some unholy simulacrum of the Kardashian sisters.

There were the funerals to get through: Ralph Cowley's, and Jeff Torrance's, and Officer Colby's, and of course, Donna Brogan's, the only one the girls attended. Apart, that is, from Mr Smith's. Mr Smith was buried in the backyard of the burnt ruin on Arboretum Avenue that was no longer theirs, the afternoon before the first heavy snowfall, and there was a week or two afterward when no one in the Brogan family could be guaranteed to get through the day without breaking down in tears, as if the trauma of everything that had been done to them rested in one small dog's carcass. They would get a new dog in the spring, and at least that was something everyone could look forward to.

The insurance company came to a settlement over the house on Arboretum Avenue. This just about enabled Danny to pay off

the mortgage he had taken out when he thought he deserved to
be rich. For now, they're all living above the store, in the few
cramped rooms over Brogan's Bar and Grill. They're starting
again. It's not easy, but it's never dull.

The police investigations were complicated. Nora Fox worked
patiently with Barbara and Irene to create a photofit picture of
the man who murdered Donna Brogan, while Danny and Claire
were able to identify his accent as Irish. It was only a matter of
time before the FBI got involved, and they soon had a new addi-
tion to their Top Ten Most Wanted: Charles Toland, an undocu-
mented alien from Belfast in Ireland, understood to be a former
member of the Provisional IRA. DNA smears on the girls' wrists,
swabbed the night of the fire, matched with skin particles found
on the Sabatier knife used to kill Ralph Cowley, and with a hair
coiled around the Miraculous Medal Nora Fox found at the
scene. When this DNA profile was added to the Bureau's CODIS
database, it matched material discovered at a crime scene in a
riverside apartment in Chicago. The body of a man in his fifties
by the name of Wilson had been found after an anonymous
tip-off, having apparently shot himself in the head with a
Ruger .38. CPD forensic investigators quickly became suspicious
of the quantity and nature of liquid discharge on the corpse's
face. It soon emerged that a third party's saliva was present. This
saliva was Charles Toland's, and was consistent with his having
murdered Mr Wilson and spat in his face.

For a while, it looked like the Madison captain of police wanted
to re-open the Bradberry fire inquiry and press charges against
Danny and Gene for conspiracy, but the district attorney's office
decided there wasn't enough there to make a case – too much time
had elapsed, for one thing. And given Dave's evident psychosis,
it would be fruitless attempting to link him with such blameless
and productive citizens as Gene Peterson and Danny Brogan. Gene
and Danny were voluble in their regret for having been involved
in a Halloween prank that had gone so tragically wrong, but it was
felt that any kind of prosecution would not only be impractical
but unjust and would probably open more wounds than it would
heal. And who wants to persecute someone for something they
did when they were eleven? That might fly in Texas, but it's not
how it works in Madison.

And of course, the press (and with its macabre Halloween theme, it was a story that went national, and international, went *viral*) very quickly settled on a narrative that dovetailed with the decisions of the police and DA's departments: Dave Ricks, the artistic psycho; Ralph Cowley, the mild mannered failure whose unpublished novel revealed at least the partial truth; Danny Brogan and Gene Peterson, the blameless survivors of bullying and blackmail.

There were retrospective photo spreads of the Bradberry funerals, and the briefest of accounts of the two brothers, amounting to a factual assertion that they had existed. There was much focus on Dee St Clair, formerly Claire Bradberry: one strand of opinion branded her a femme fatale and a woman scorned; another defended her as a victim-survivor. She has joined Charles Toland on the FBI's Most Wanted Fugitives list. Although no relationship existed between them, they are invariably discussed as a couple, a latter-day Bonnie and Clyde. The FBI receives multiple daily sightings of the pair together, from every state in the union. A rap song and three heavy metal tracks have been written about them. They are the most Googled people in the United States.

The scores of paintings Dave Ricks had made over the years of the Bradberry children trapped in their burning house were subjected to endless analysis by forensic psychiatrists, university fine-art professors and that brand of pop psychologist known as the newspaper columnist.

Yet Dave's motives remain opaque. Danny worked it over and over in his mind, what he had done and what he had failed to do to be the object of Dave's obsession. In the end he couldn't get much further than Gene Peterson's verdict, delivered in Gene's blunt, square-jawed, Mid-Western manner: 'You know what, Dan? There was just something wrong with that guy.'

There's a guilt that Danny should never have had to feel, but the truth remains: it had been his idea to prank the Bradberry house, his idea to set the fires. Even if the press and the justice system think otherwise, he knows he bears a share of the responsibility for those deaths. He still wakes up in the middle of the night with the vision of Barbara and Irene in the window, a vision that telescopes back through time to the Bradberry house. He knows the paintings Dave made speak to his guilt, but that wasn't the whole story. Dave had caused the fire, but that didn't absolve Danny of blame, and it never would: he will carry it to his grave.

Danny and Claire remain haunted by Dee St Clair: Claire, by the friend who wasn't really a friend, but who she misses as if she had been; Danny, because who knows how little Claire Bradberry might have turned out if it hadn't been for him? They are exhausted with themselves and with each other; quick to tears and to anger and to recrimination; often unable to decide, or even to remember, what had happened for real and what was invented, concocted to lay them low. Claire sometimes feels as if she *is* Claire Bradberry, so insidious was the deception, and that Danny had betrayed her all along.

And then gradually, as the saying goes, gradually, as the days wear on, and then suddenly, as hand brushes hand and eye catches eye, and at last, a kiss becomes something more than just a kiss, and Danny and Claire start to remember who they are, and what they saw in each other, and in the future, and in love.

(It's not perfect, of course. She still feels as if he is hiding something; he still thinks she is making do with him. Sometimes he just won't look her in the eye, and she feels desolate; sometimes she can't look him in the eye, and he fears the worst. It's not perfect. It never is.)

And here they are, these two people, on Christmas Eve in Brogan's Bar and Grill. Just the two of them, because Danny has closed the bar until five o'clock today, so the staff can go Christmas shopping, he said, but in truth, it's so he can sit here with his girl like he used to do when the world was young, and fix her a drink, and spin her a line, and see how it goes. He's in a suit, but then he always is, because you don't know what might happen if you start to let things go, the charcoal-gray wool, no vest, and she's wearing a dark red and racing green plaid, her Christmas dress, she says, and he says he's never seen it before, and she says that's because it hasn't been Christmas before.

She sits, and he makes them a drink, a martini, and he's playing the music, *Tone Poems of Color,* the music that was playing when they met, and it's all very shaky. Look at them, they're so nervous, it's as if they barely know each other. But Danny has a plan. He usually does. And Claire sort of expects it, and sort of dreads it.

Danny takes some pages from his pocket and hands them to Claire.

'It's the scene from *The Way of the World*,' he says. 'Where they exchange their informal wedding vows. I thought we could read it together.'

And Claire can see he thinks it's an idea she would like, and even though she can't imagine anything more laborious and clunky, she can't say that.

'Does that mean you want to marry me?' she says.

'It certainly does,' he says.

'Well. Ask me then.'

'Really?'

'Of course.'

Danny gets ready to go down on one knee, and Claire stops him.

'Music's too film noiry. What's the one we like again?'

'I know that one,' Danny says, and goes behind the bar and switches the music. '"Black" by Victor Young.'

'And you don't need to go down on one knee.'

'Well. You don't need to be so bossy.'

'And you don't need to be my dad, always being noble and looking after me like I'm a wayward child.'

'Then stop being such a princess, sighing as if things haven't gone your way and it must be my fault.'

They're both hot, cheeks smarting, as if they'd been slapped, but excited with it. It's as if they've been tiptoeing around each other for weeks, always with a chaperone, and now at last they get to be alone.

'You're a cocky bastard now you know you didn't burn my family to death.'

'You're a sexy bitch now you're not saving it up for some guy in Chicago who wasn't all that much in the first place.'

'Not as much as you,' Claire says.

'No one's as much as me. Except you.'

'Lucky I'm here then.'

'Will you marry me?'

'You'll have to kiss me first.'

'Modern girls. No values.'

And they kiss for a long time, as if they've just fallen in love again. Which in a way, they have. The music plays: old-fashioned, string-drenched, absurdly dramatic music. It helps them feel they are the leading characters in their own story. They haven't felt like that in a long, long time. The shadows in the room are breached by low winter sun through shutters partly open, red and green and gold shafts off stained glass, the glitter of white Christmas balls. The light, the way it catches Claire's auburn hair, Danny's silvering brown locks. The smell of gin, and olives, and Chanel Cristalle, and a cinnamon and clove scent that clings to Claire from three days of baking. *Tone Poems of Color.*

All the sounds and sights, the scents and spices that blend together to make a marriage the living, breathing thing it is. Even if they aren't married yet.

All the things they are.

Or almost all.

What's missing?

Watch closely now.

There's a sound on the street, at the door.

'Where are the kids?' Danny says.

'Avol's. I gave them money to buy us books as Christmas presents.'

The voices of two girls outside, of Barbara and Irene.

'That's them. You going to let them in?'

'The door's on the latch. Are we raising stupids, Mrs Brogan?'

'No, Mr Brogan, we're not.'

The door creaks open, and December afternoon light spreads slowly across the darkness of the still old room.

Here they come. The sound of their voices, the canter of their feet.

Here they come. Without them, what?

Here come the children.